GARLIC
& the
WITCH

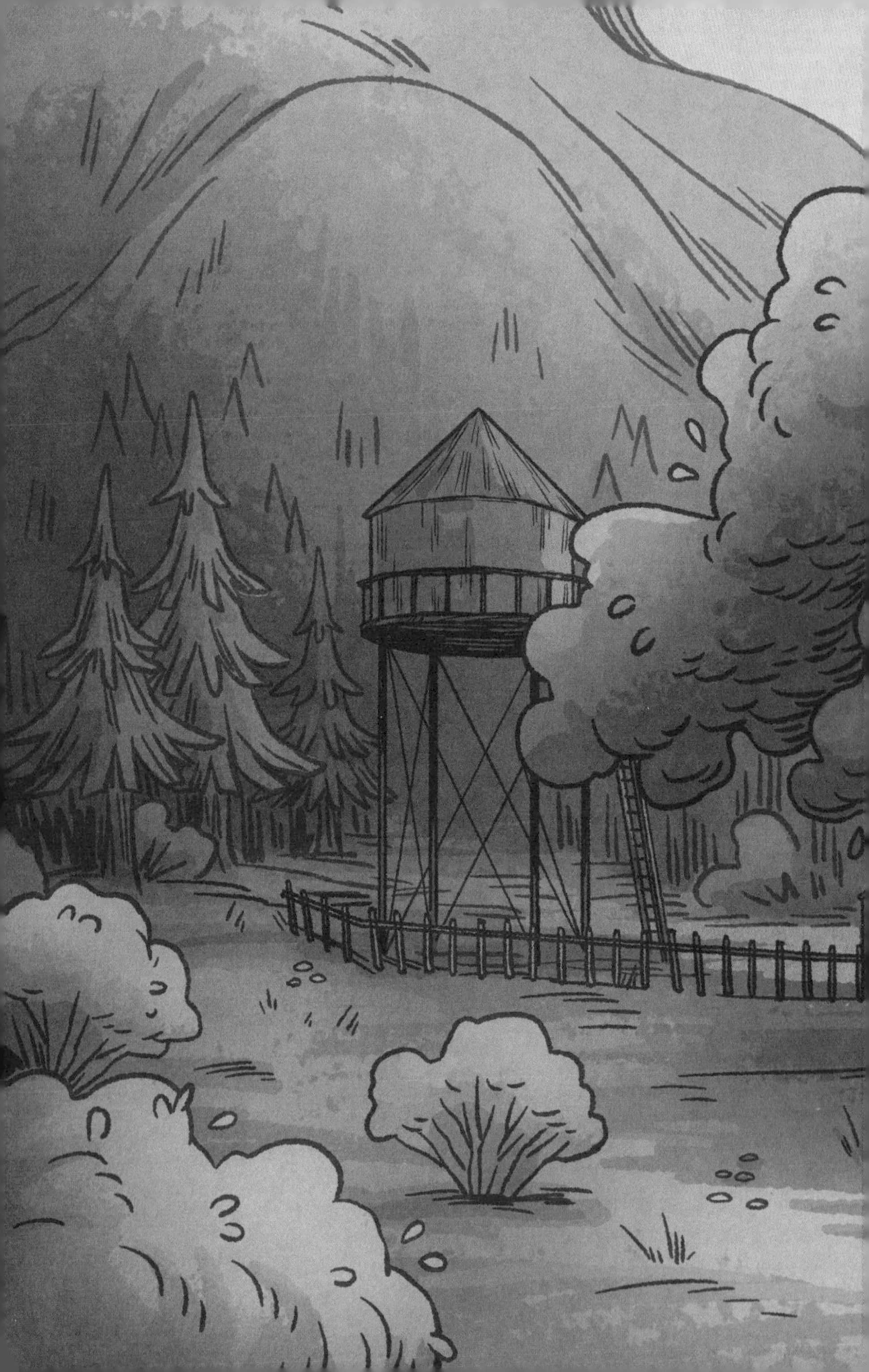

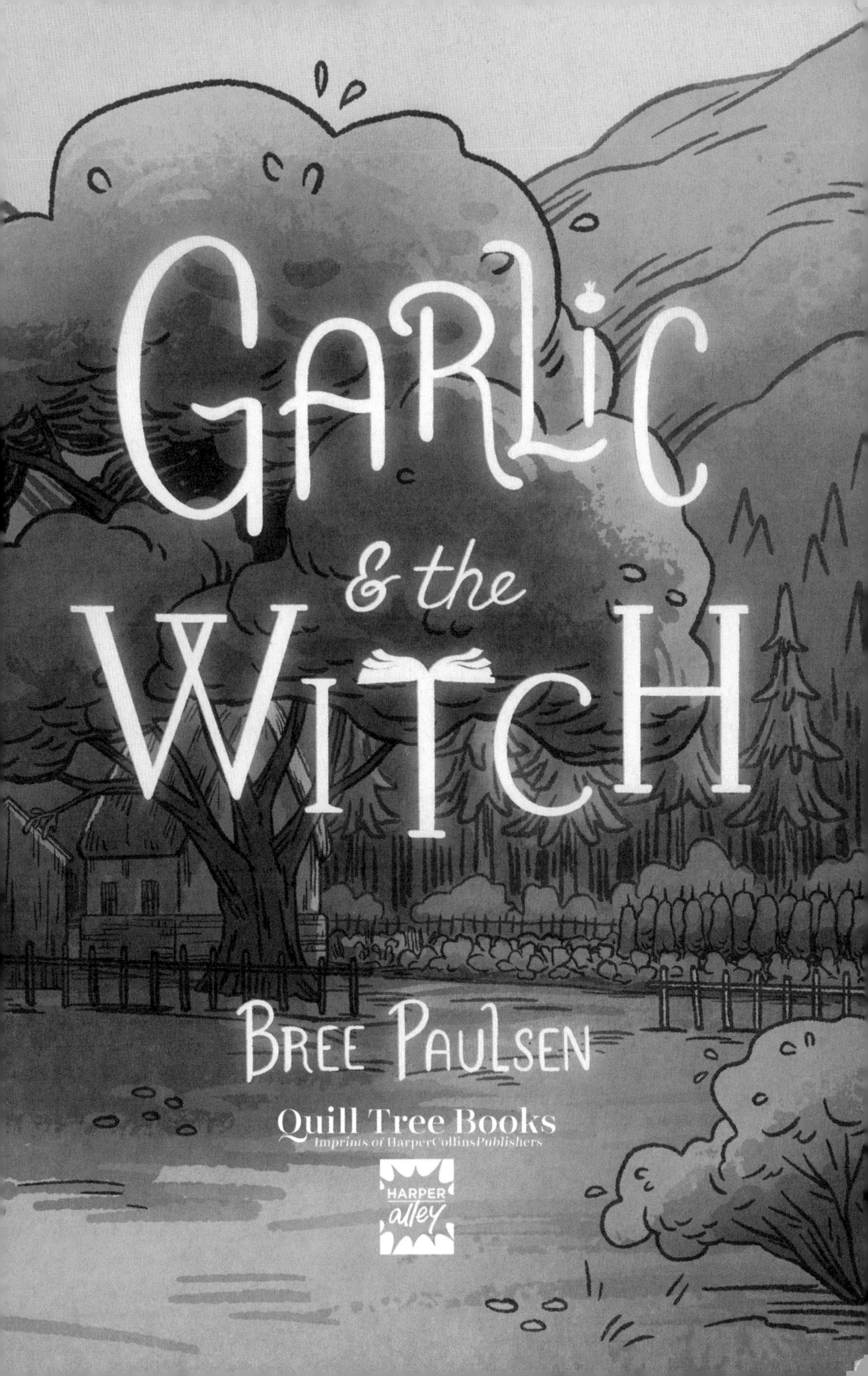

Garlic & the Witch

Bree Paulsen

Quill Tree Books
Imprints of HarperCollinsPublishers
HARPER alley

QUILL TREE BOOKS IS AN IMPRINT OF HARPERCOLLINS PUBLISHERS.

HARPERALLEY IS AN IMPRINT OF HARPERCOLLINS PUBLISHERS.

GARLIC AND THE WITCH

WWW.HARPERALLEY.COM

ISBN 978-0-06-299512-4 (TRADE BDG.)
ISBN 978-0-06-299511-7 (PBK.)

THE ARTIST USED ADOBE PHOTOSHOP AND PROCREATE TO CREATE THE DIGITAL ILLUSTRATIONS FOR THIS BOOK.
TYPOGRAPHY BY DAVID CURTIS
22 23 24 25 26   RTLO   10 9 8 7 6 5 4 3 2 1
❖
FIRST EDITION

TO ALL THE SPROUTS
FACING BIG CHANGES AND UNCERTAINTY

chapter one

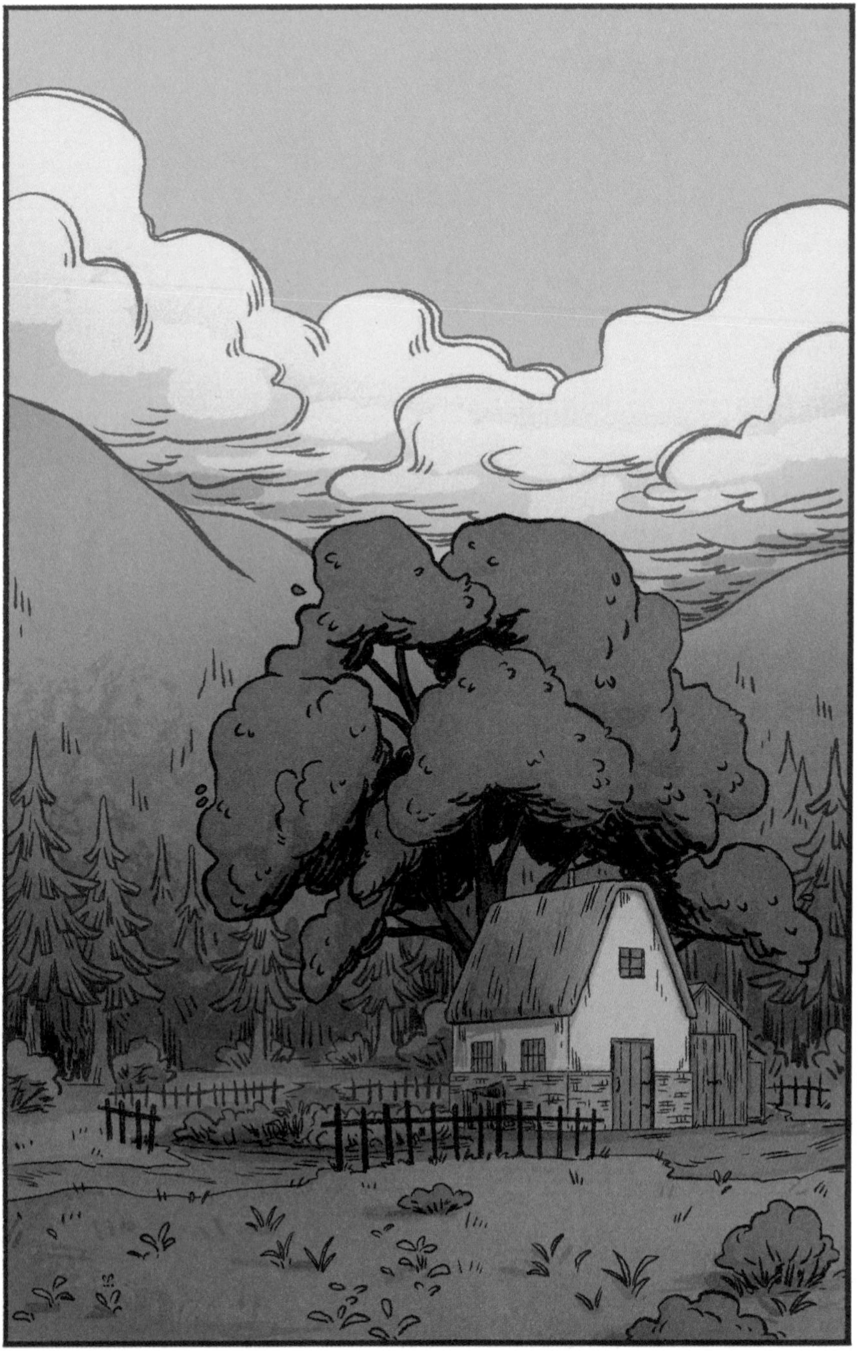

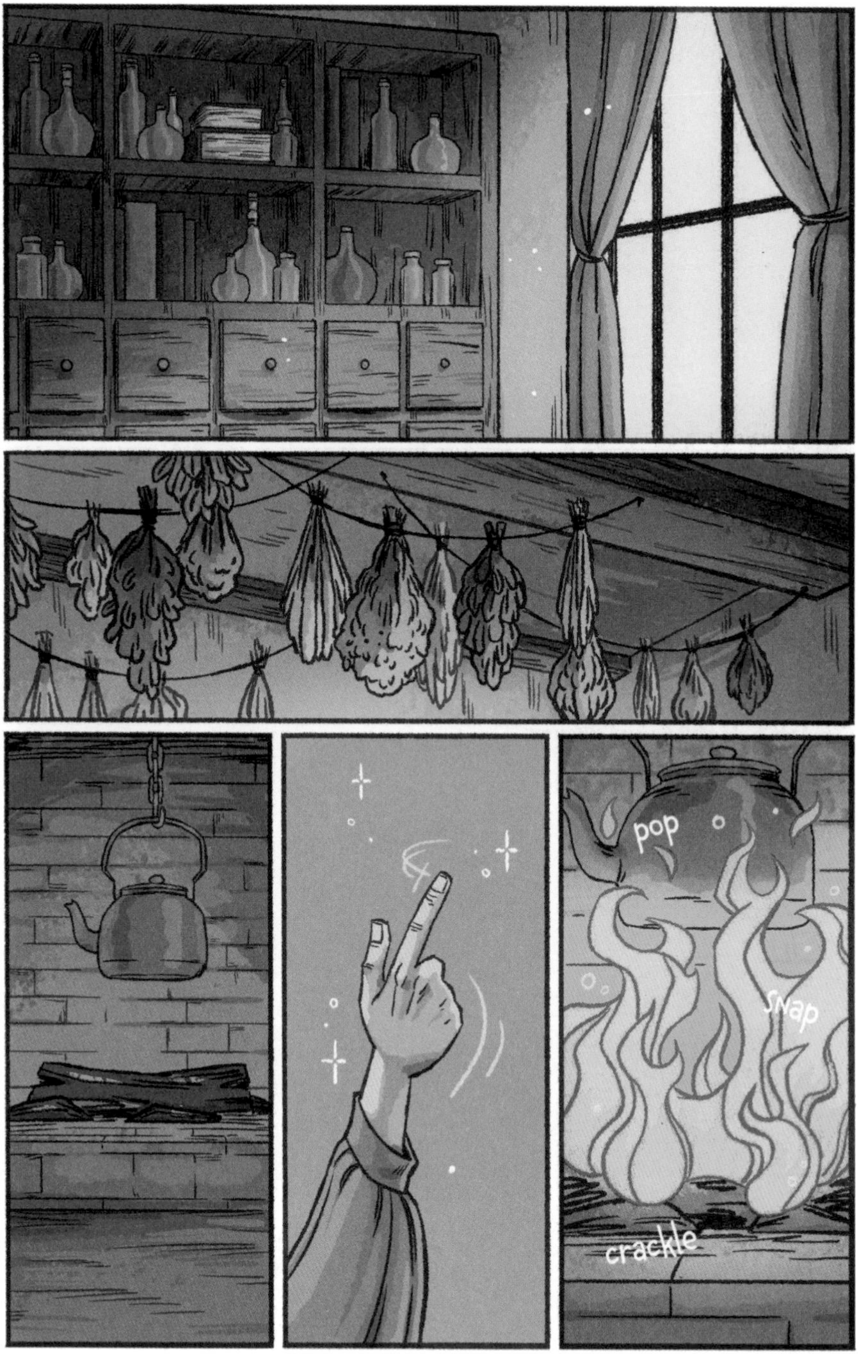
pop
snap
crackle

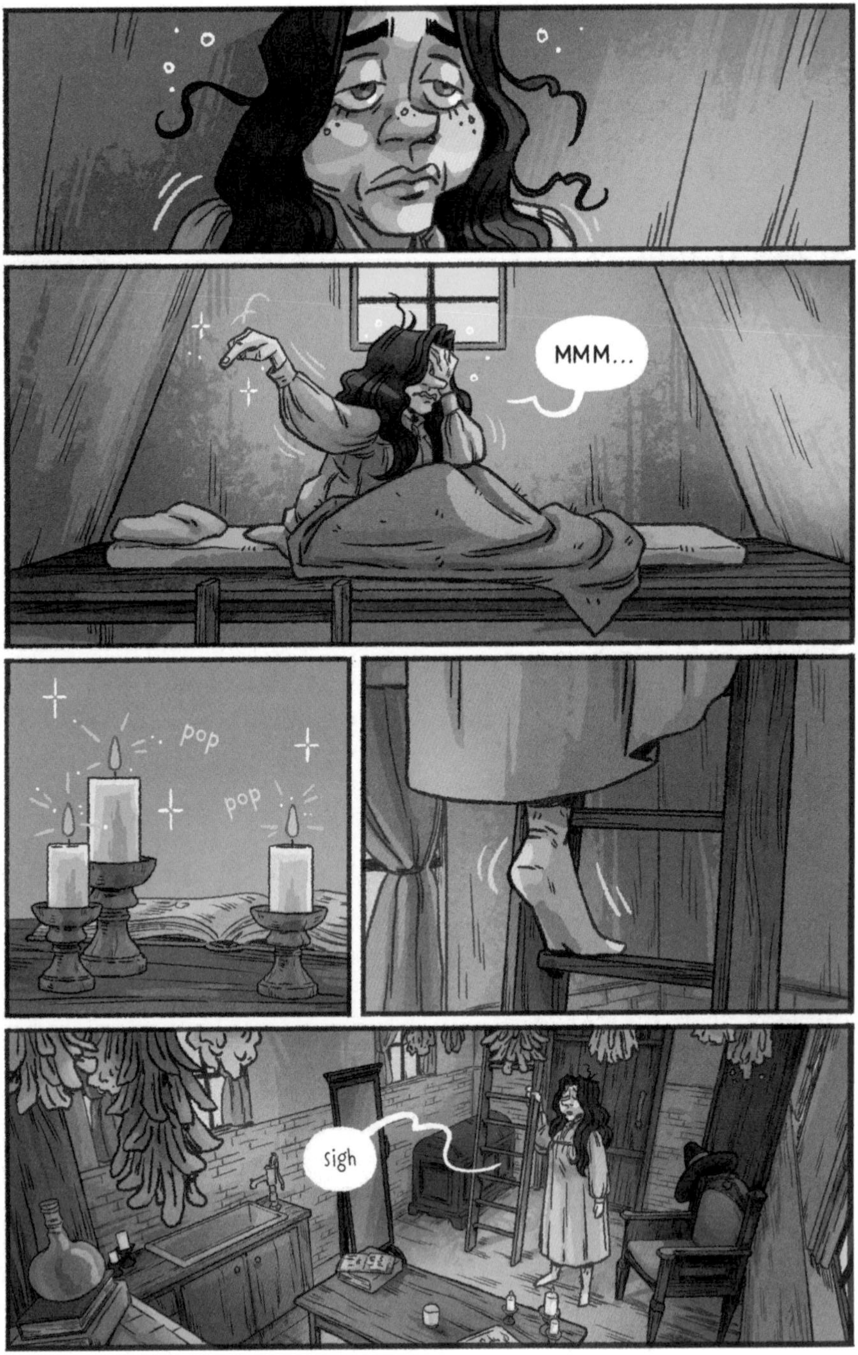
MMM...
pop
pop
sigh

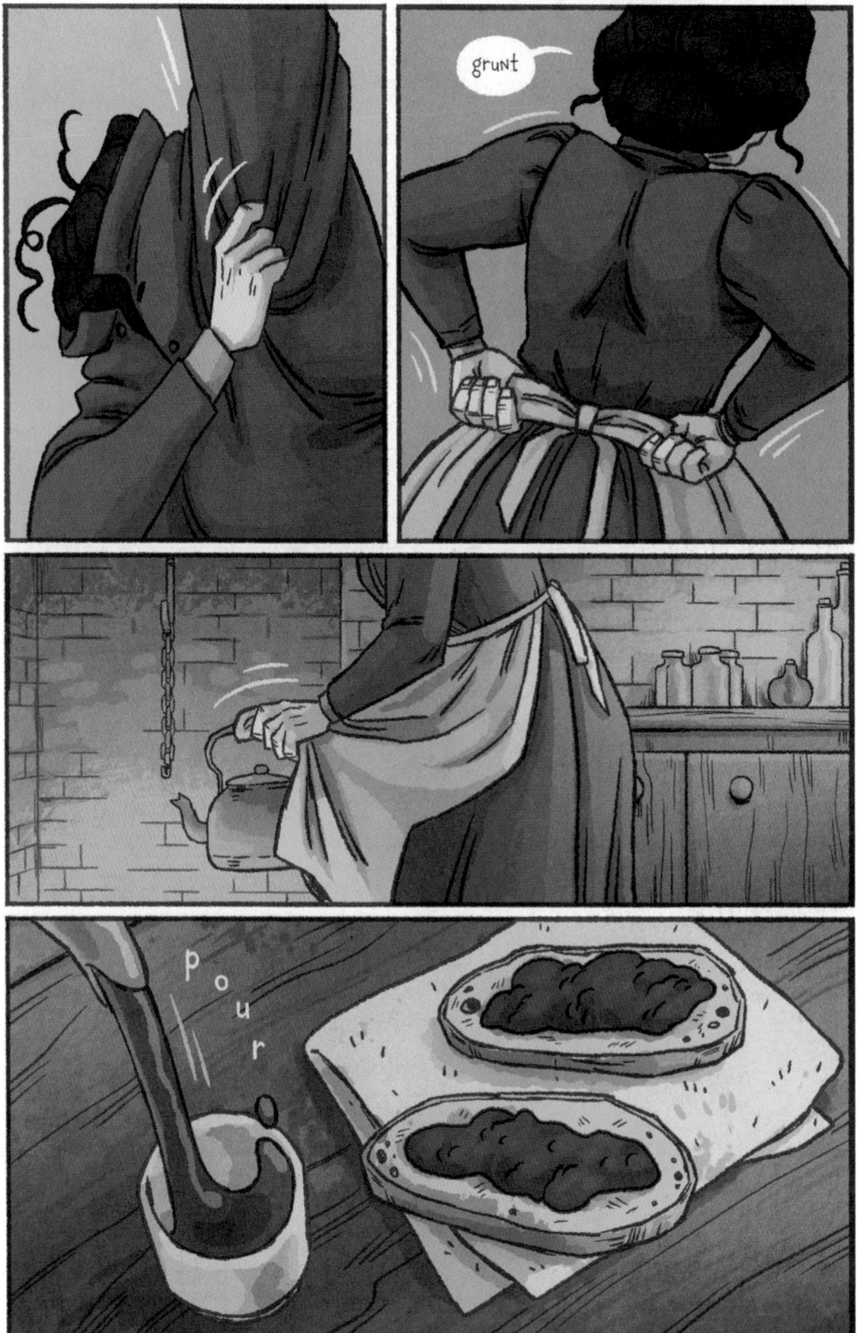
grunt
pour

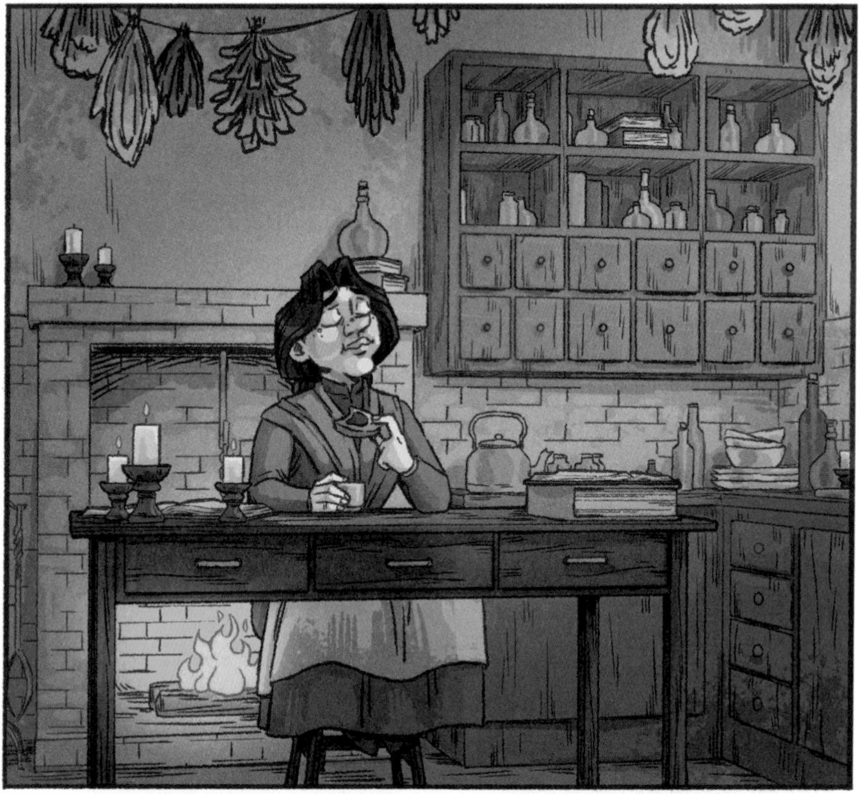

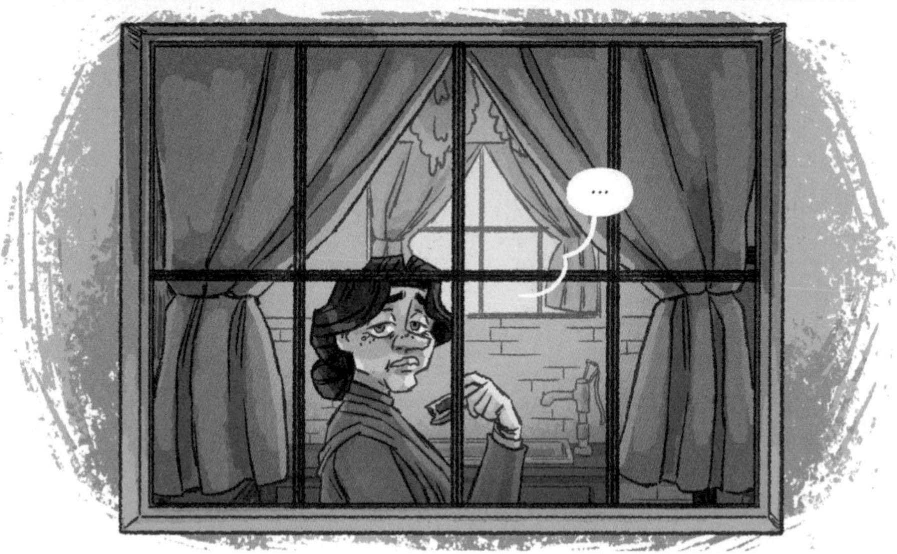
...

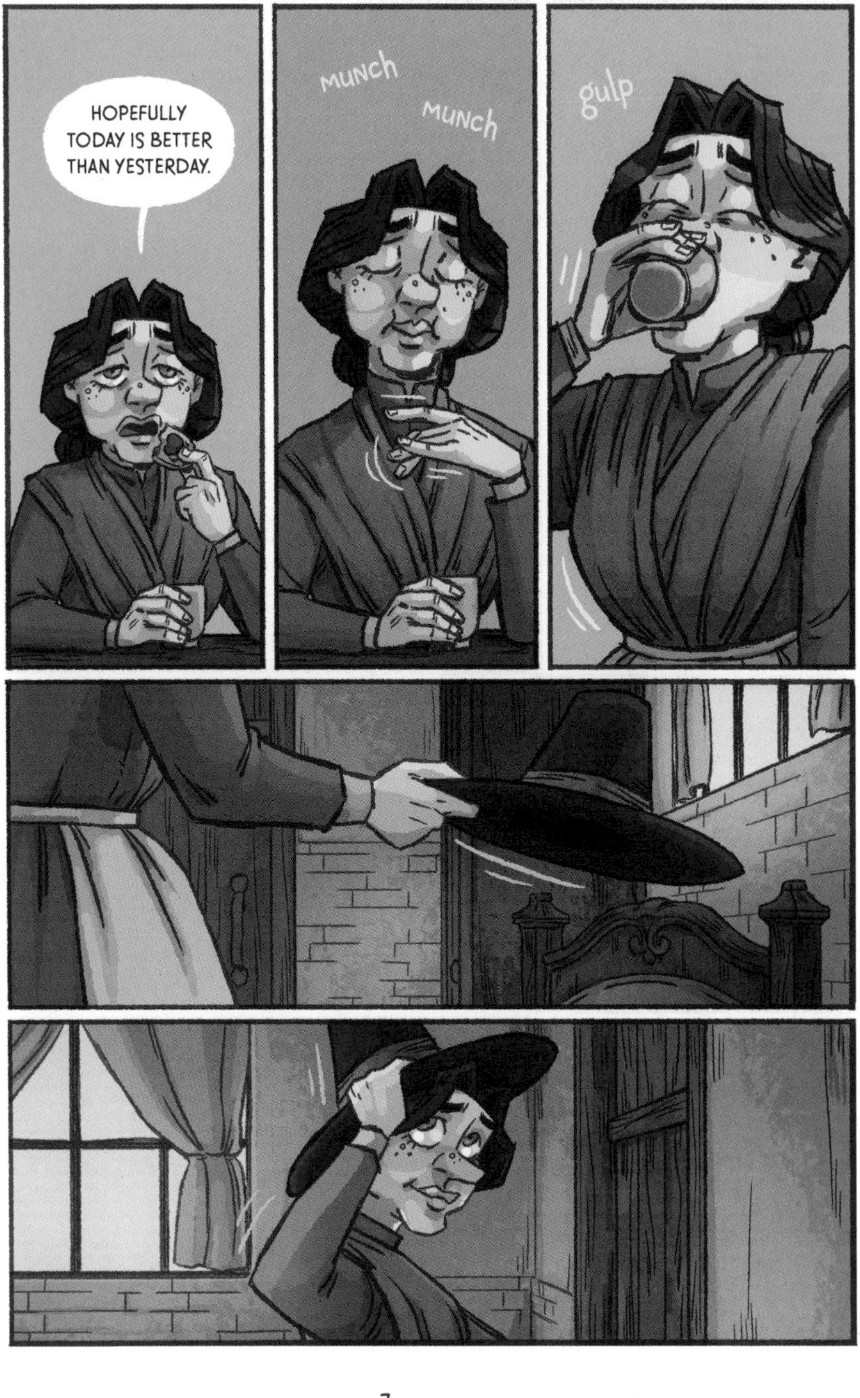

HOPEFULLY TODAY IS BETTER THAN YESTERDAY.
MUNCH
MUNCH
gulp

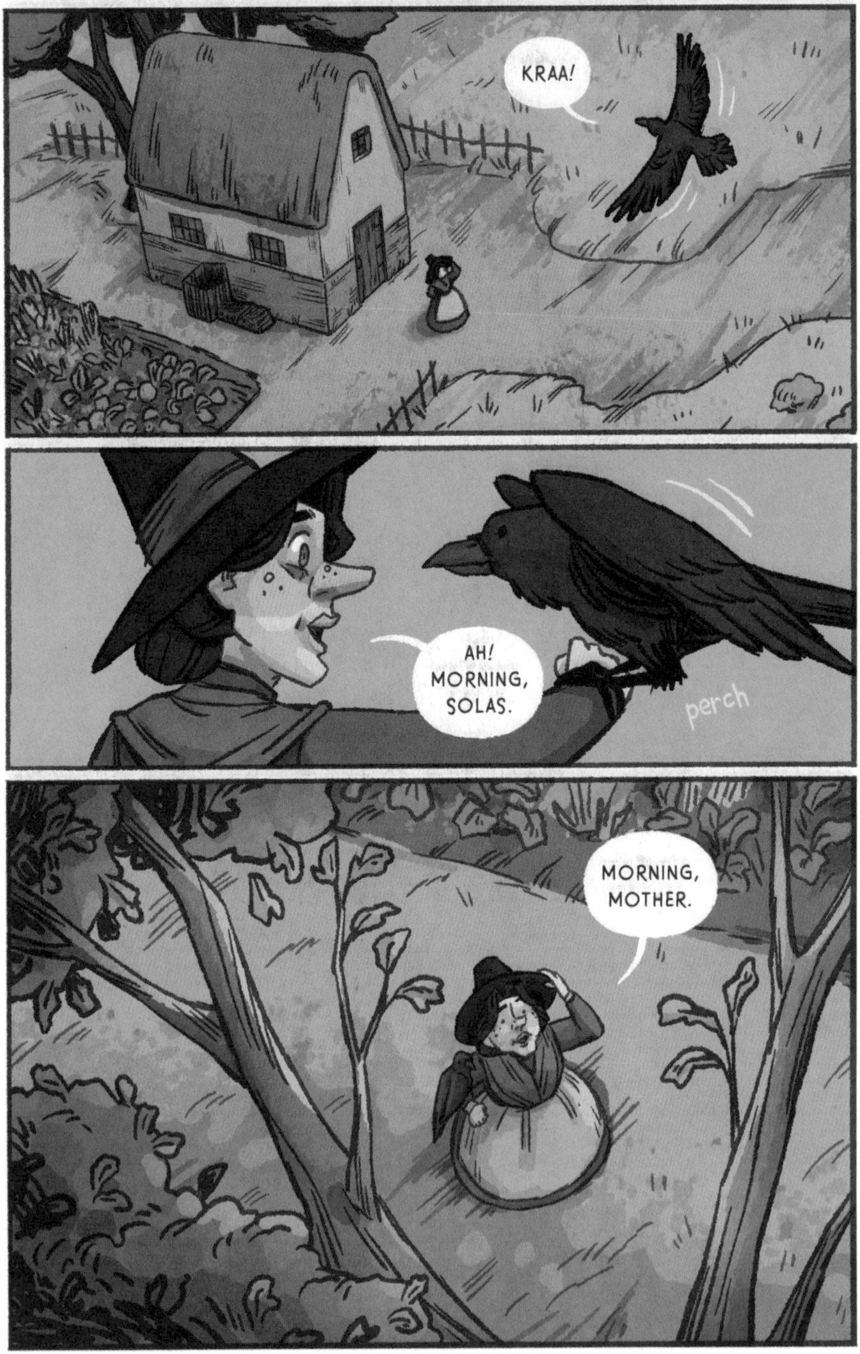
KRAA!
AH! MORNING, SOLAS.
perch
MORNING, MOTHER.

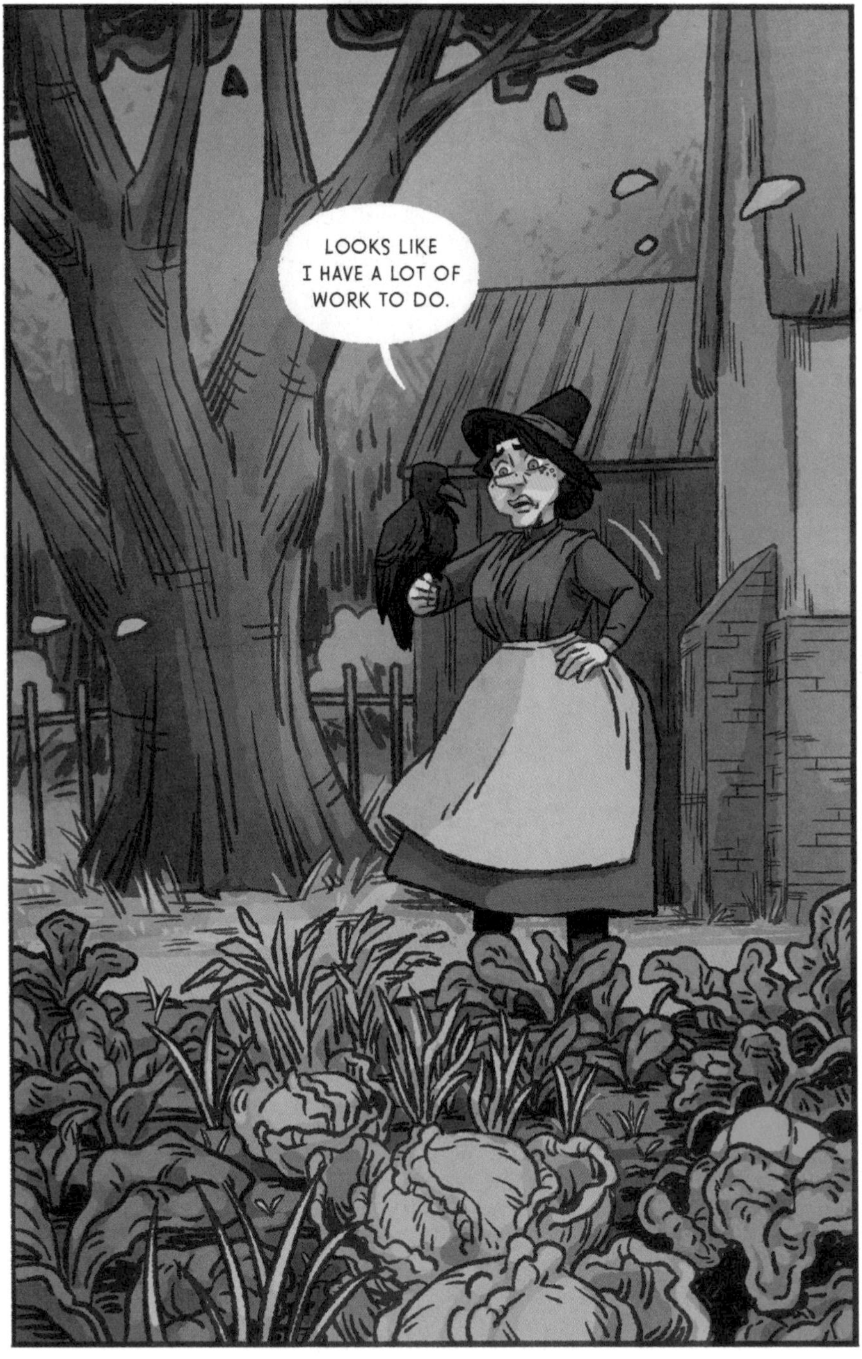
LOOKS LIKE I HAVE A LOT OF WORK TO DO.

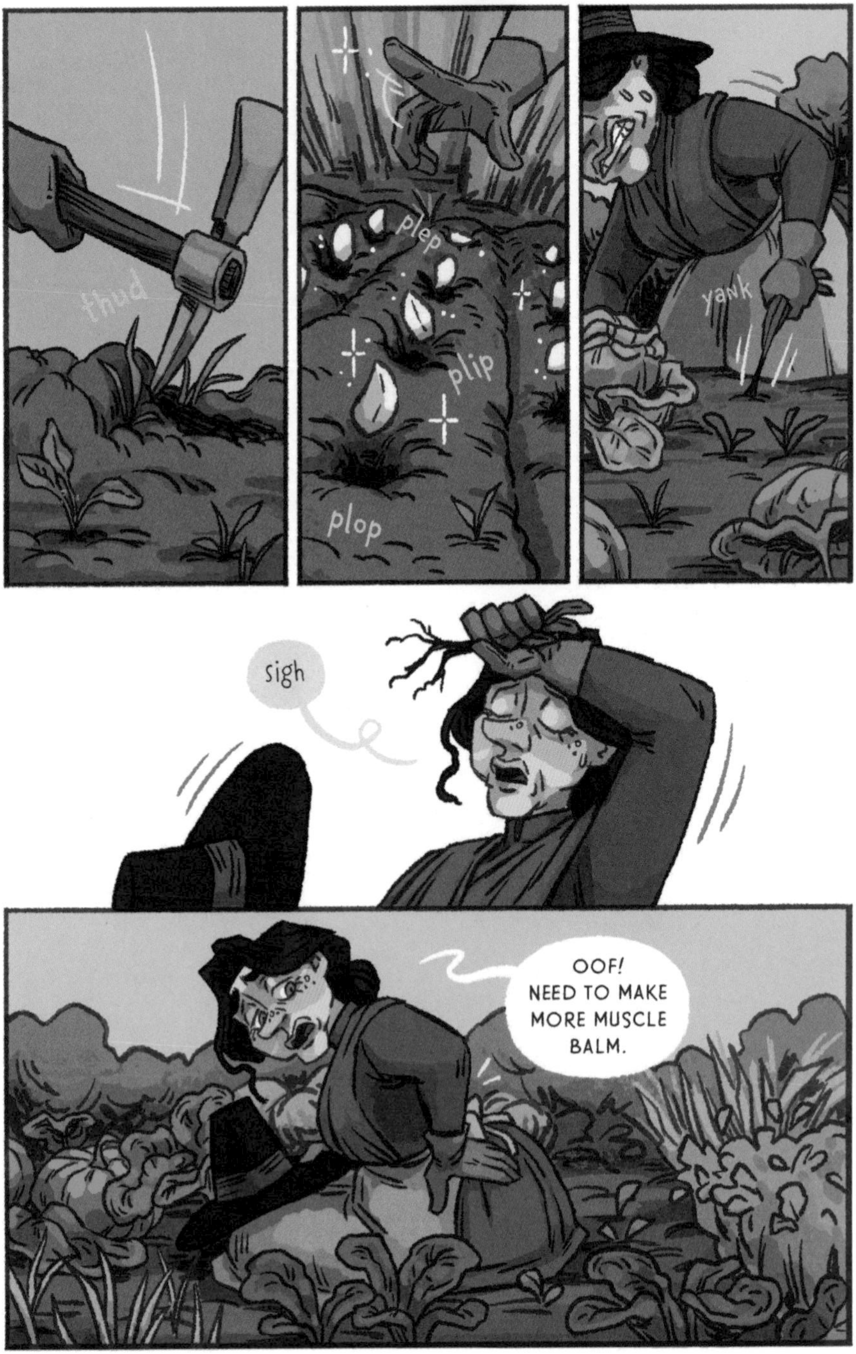
thud
plep
plip
plop
yank
sigh
OOF!
NEED TO MAKE
MORE MUSCLE
BALM.

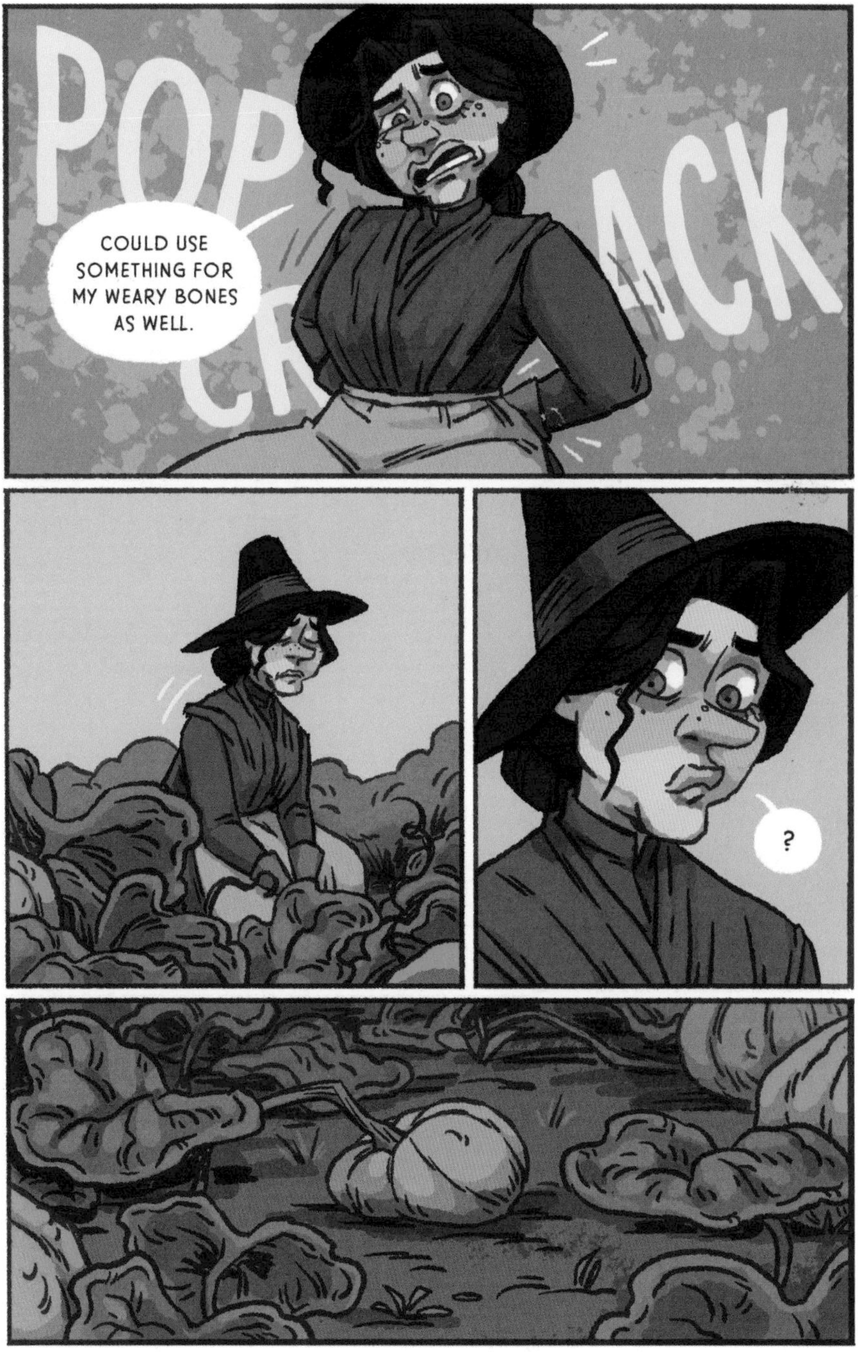
POP
COULD USE SOMETHING FOR MY WEARY BONES AS WELL.
CRACK
?

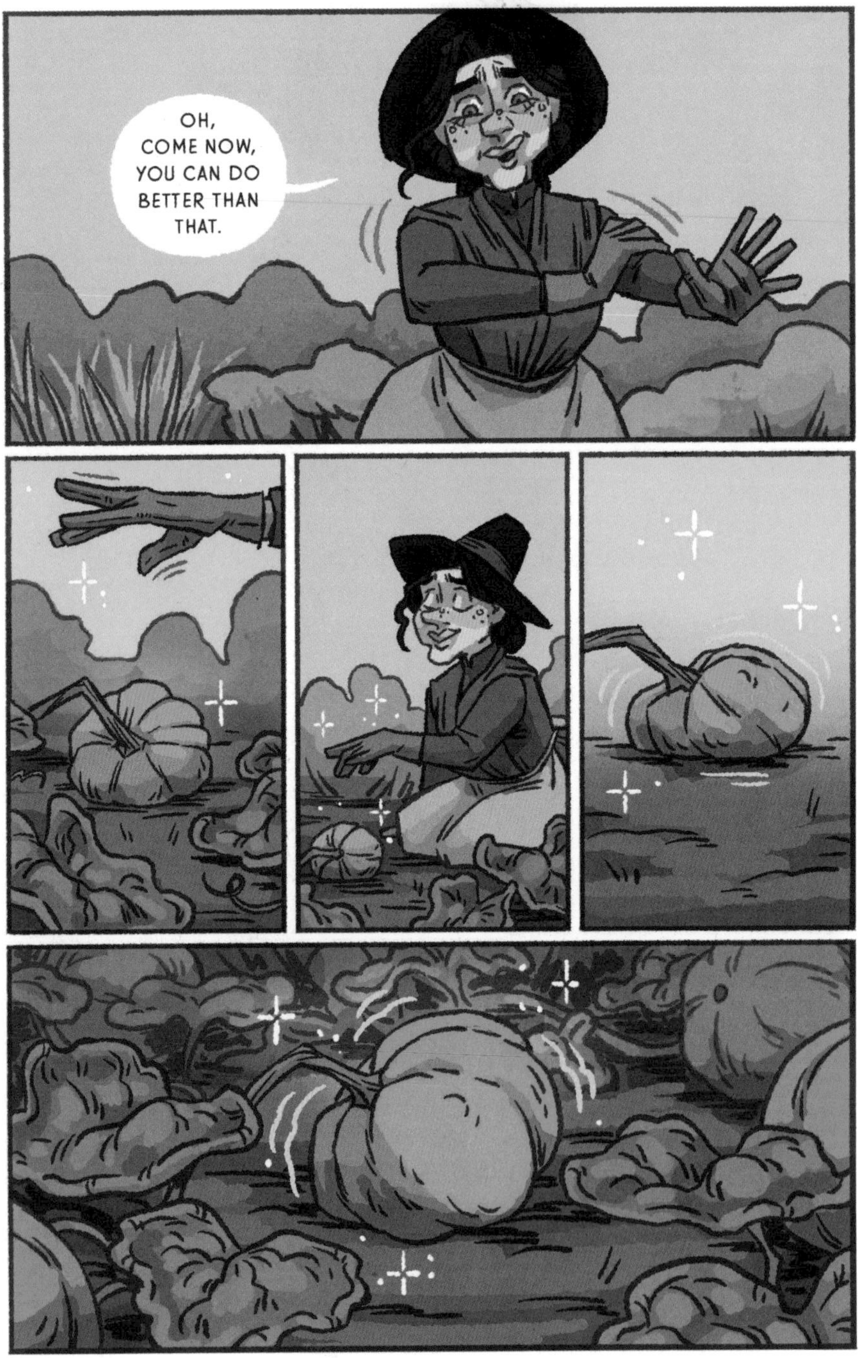
OH, COME NOW, YOU CAN DO BETTER THAN THAT.

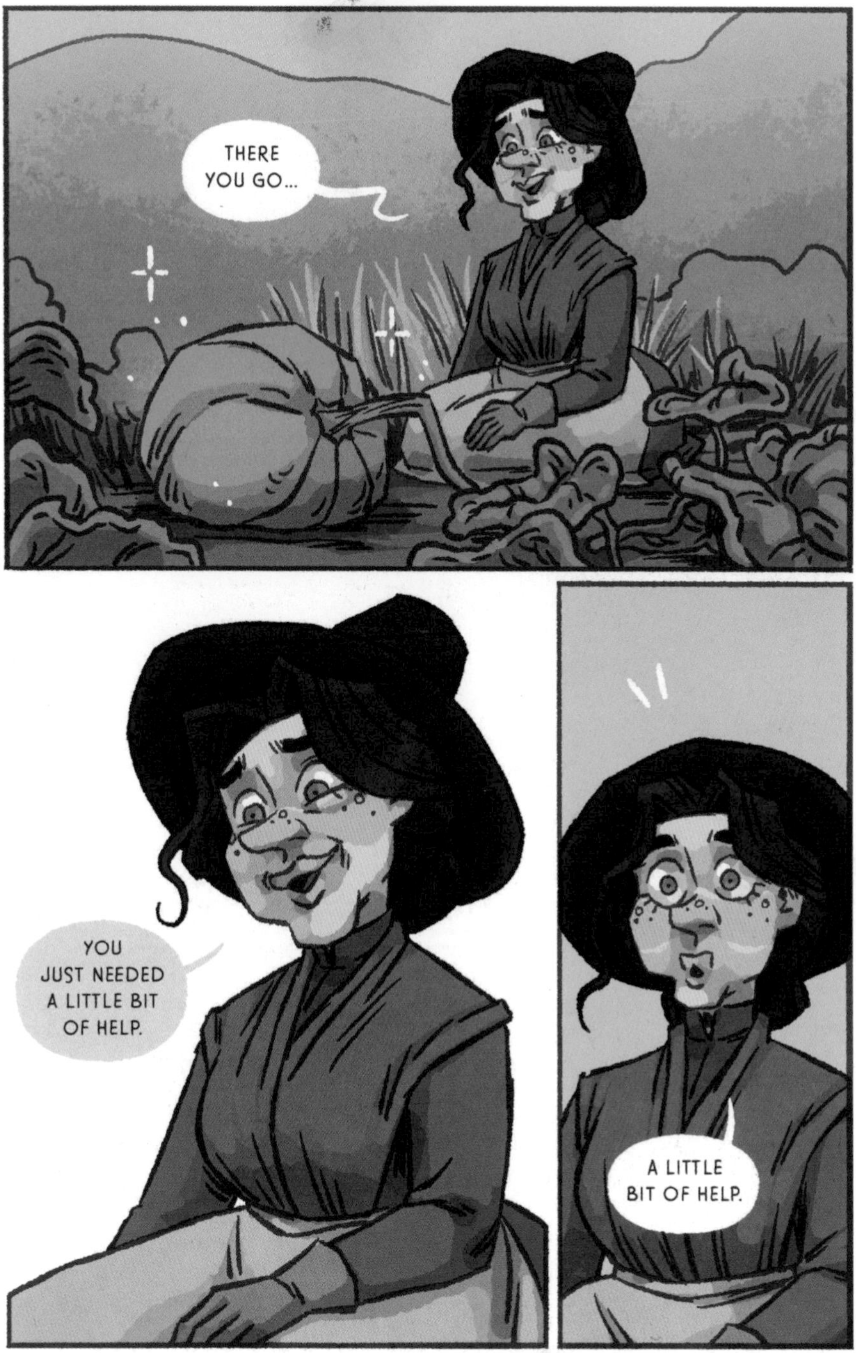
THERE YOU GO...
YOU JUST NEEDED A LITTLE BIT OF HELP.
A LITTLE BIT OF HELP.

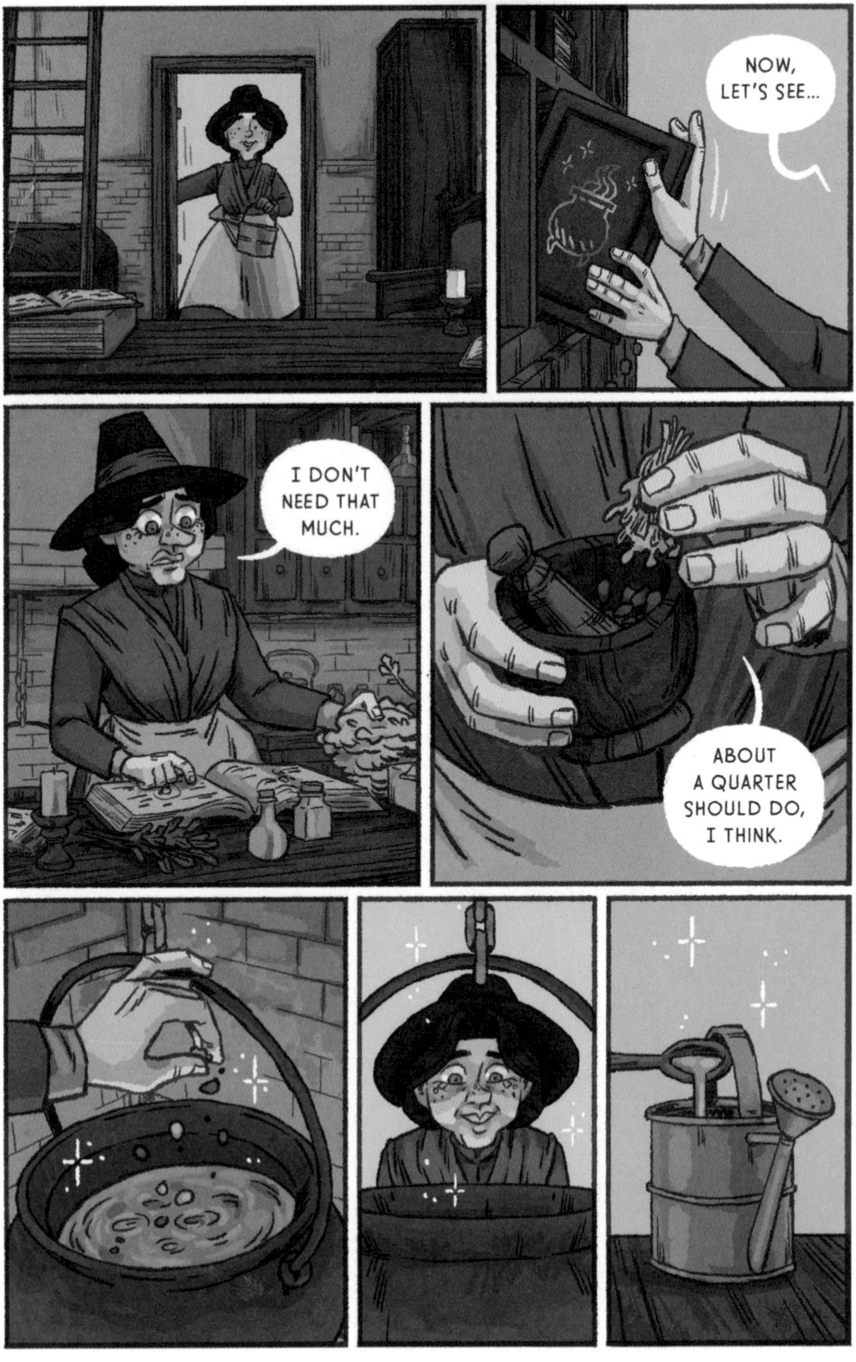
NOW, LET'S SEE...
I DON'T NEED THAT MUCH.
ABOUT A QUARTER SHOULD DO, I THINK.

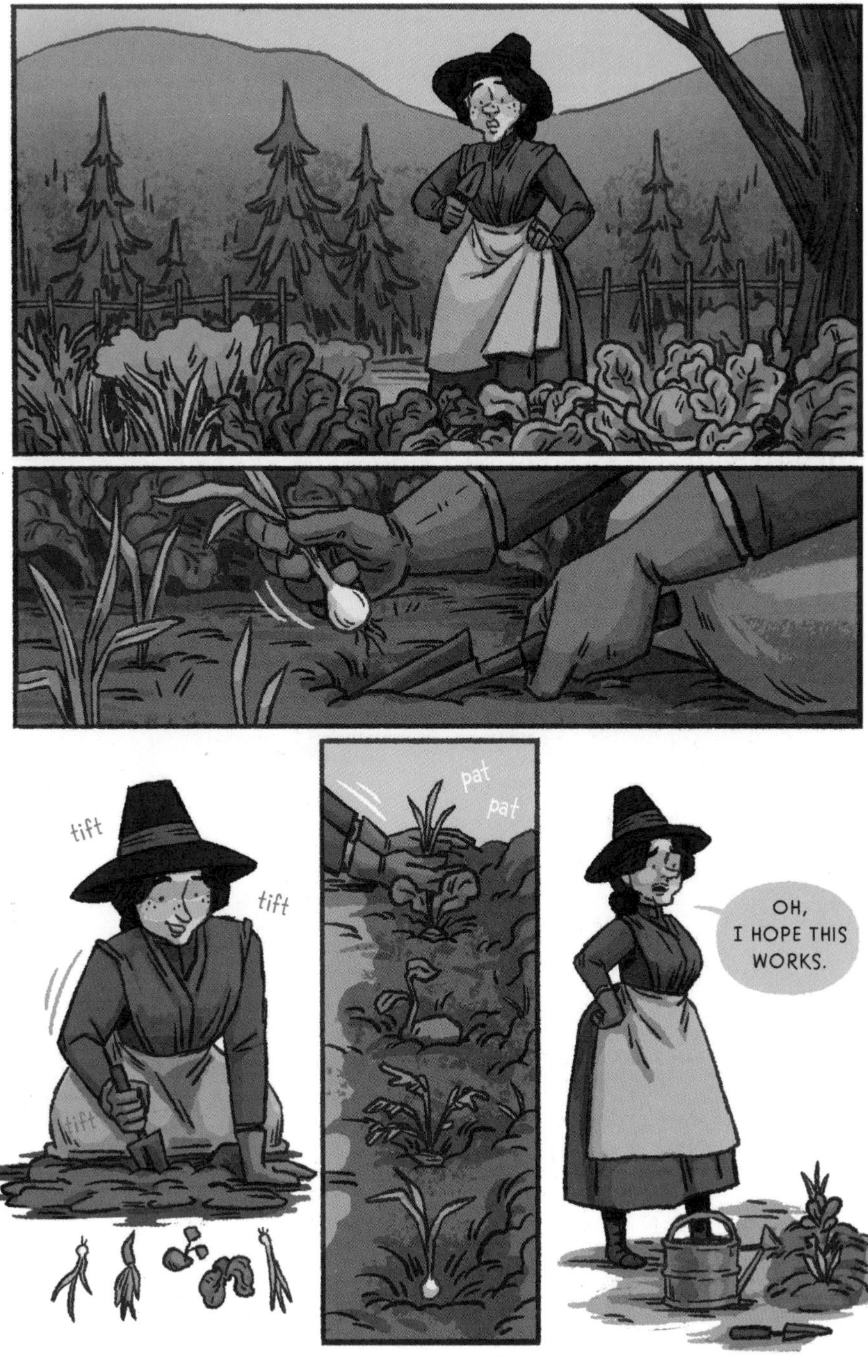
tift
tift
tift
pat
pat
OH,
I HOPE THIS
WORKS.

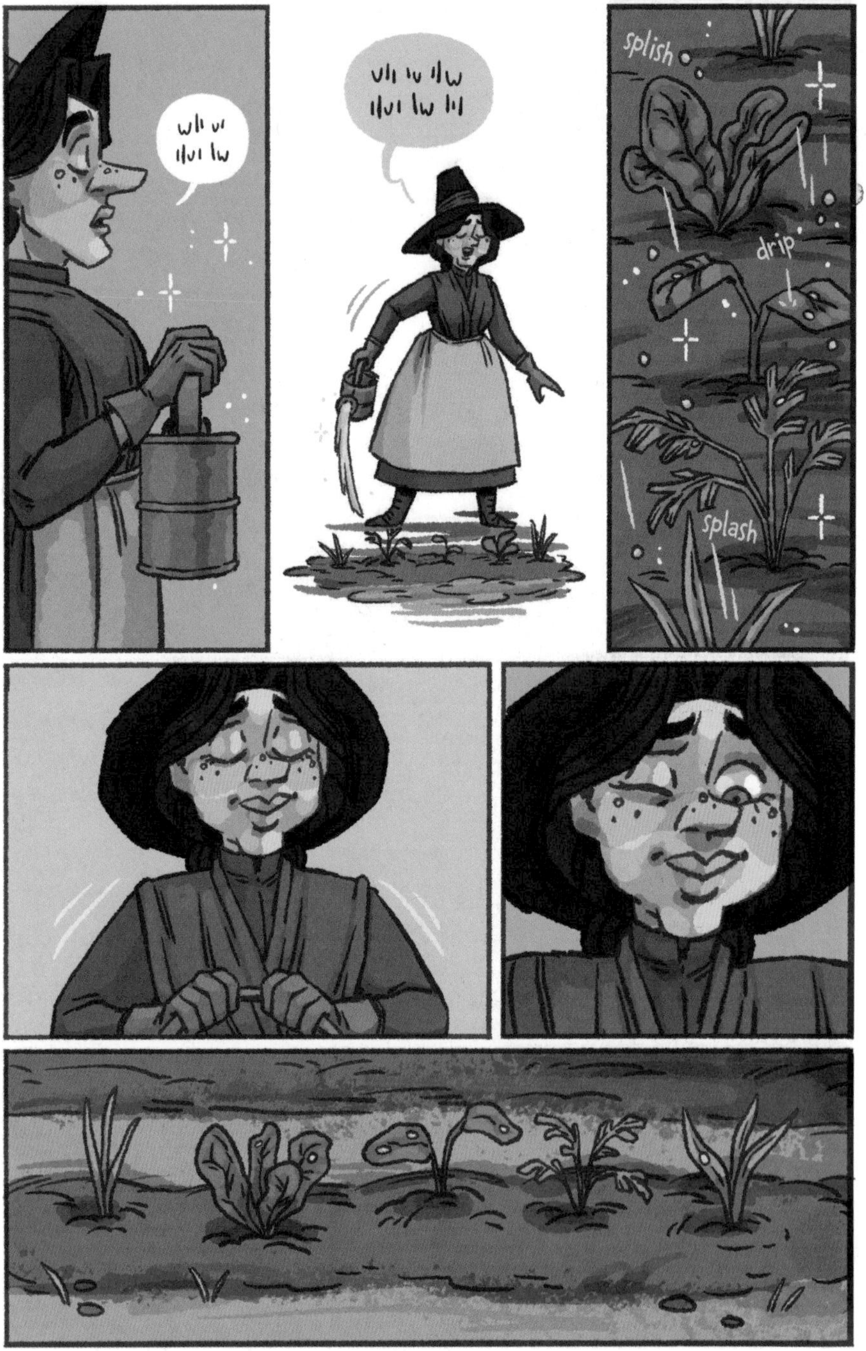
splish
drip
splash

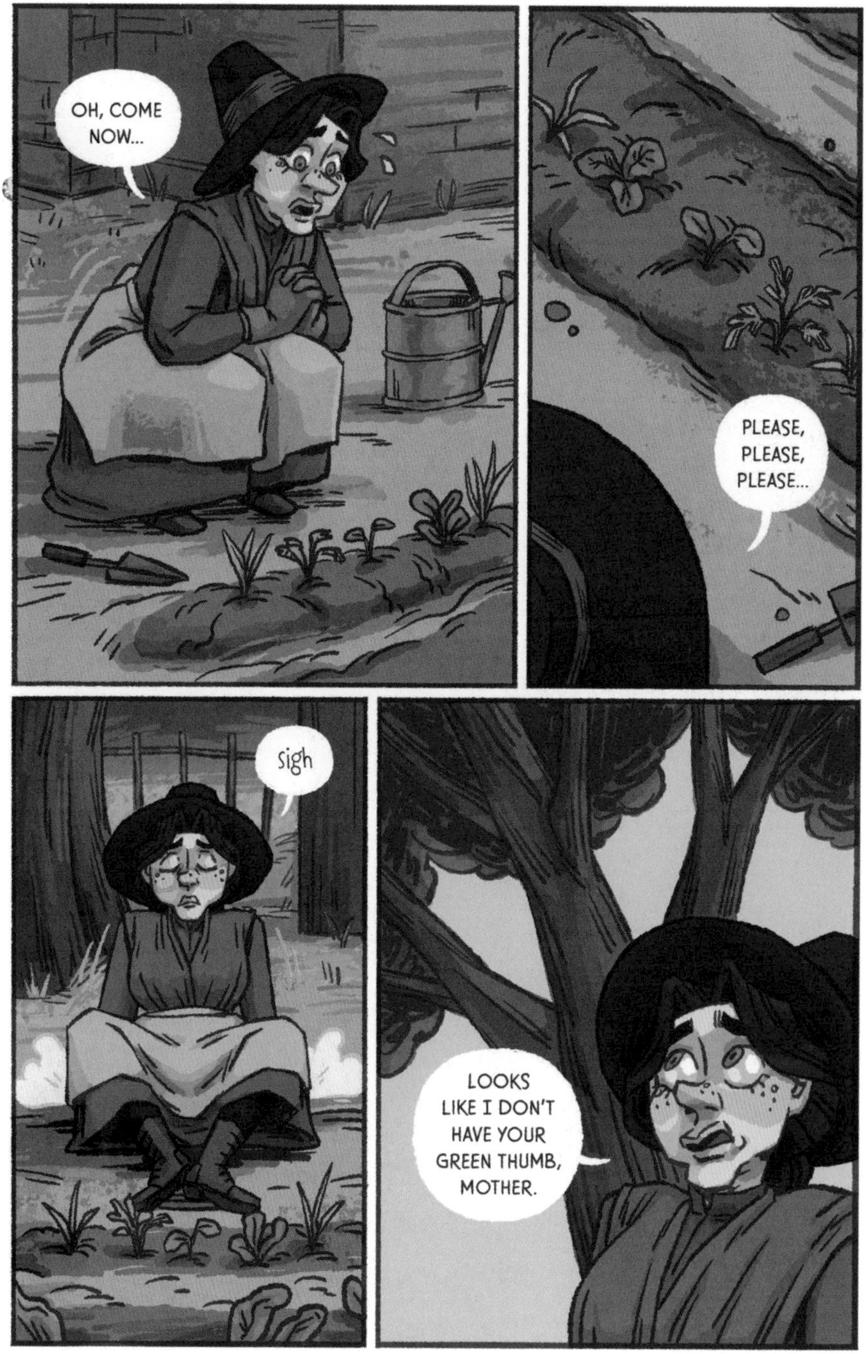
OH, COME NOW...
PLEASE, PLEASE, PLEASE...
Sigh
LOOKS LIKE I DON'T HAVE YOUR GREEN THUMB, MOTHER.

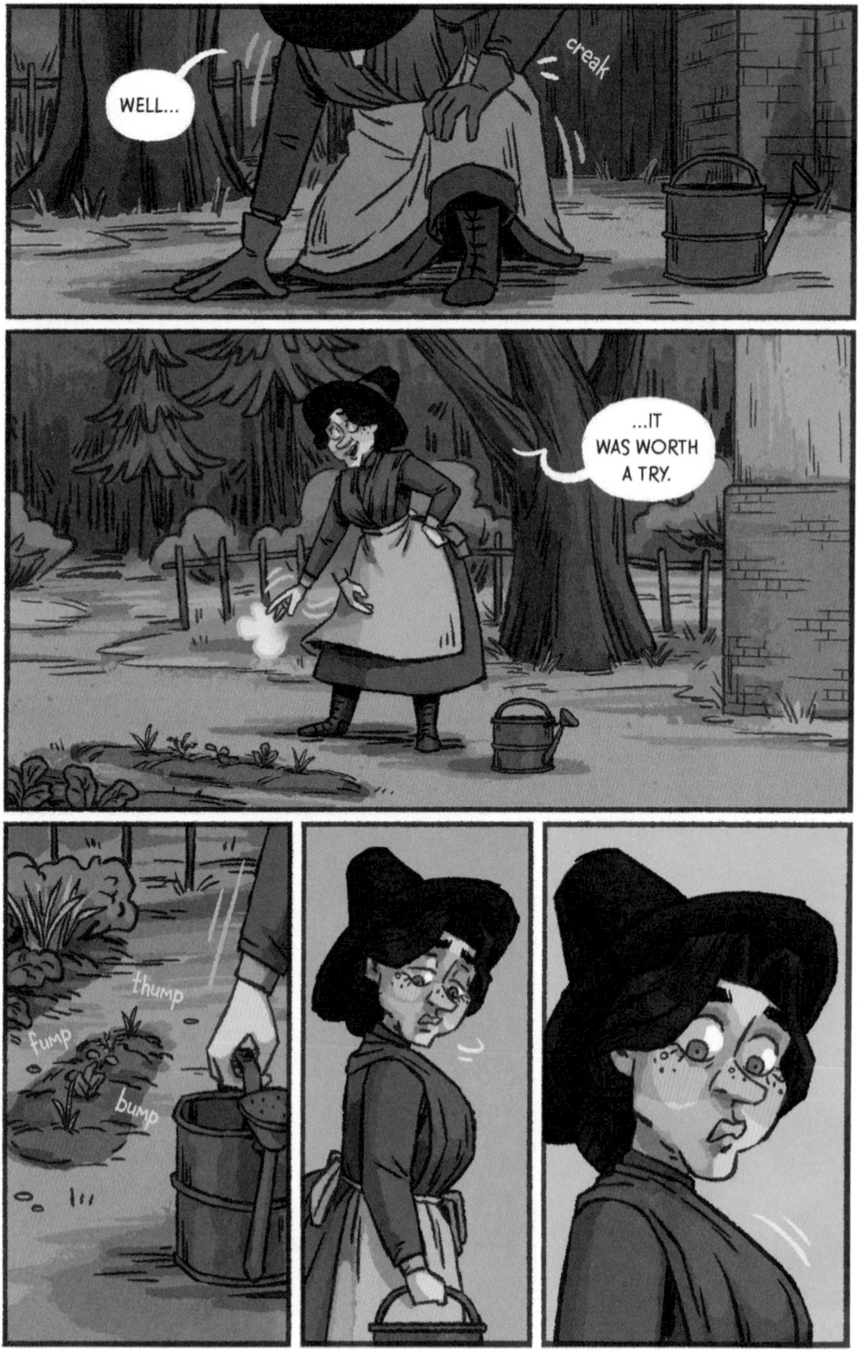
WELL...
creak
...IT WAS WORTH A TRY.
thump
fump
bump

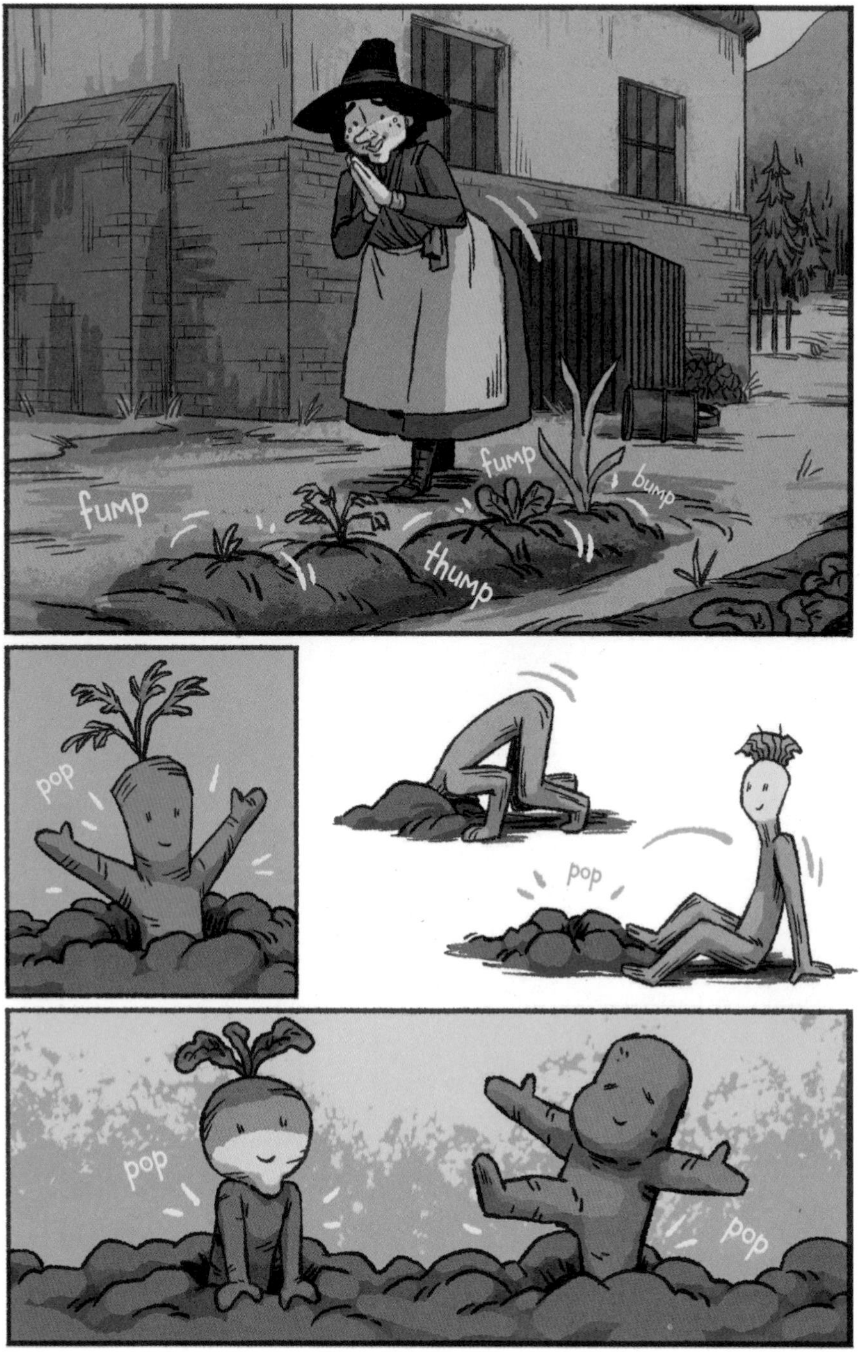
fump
fump
bump
thump
pop
pop
pop
pop

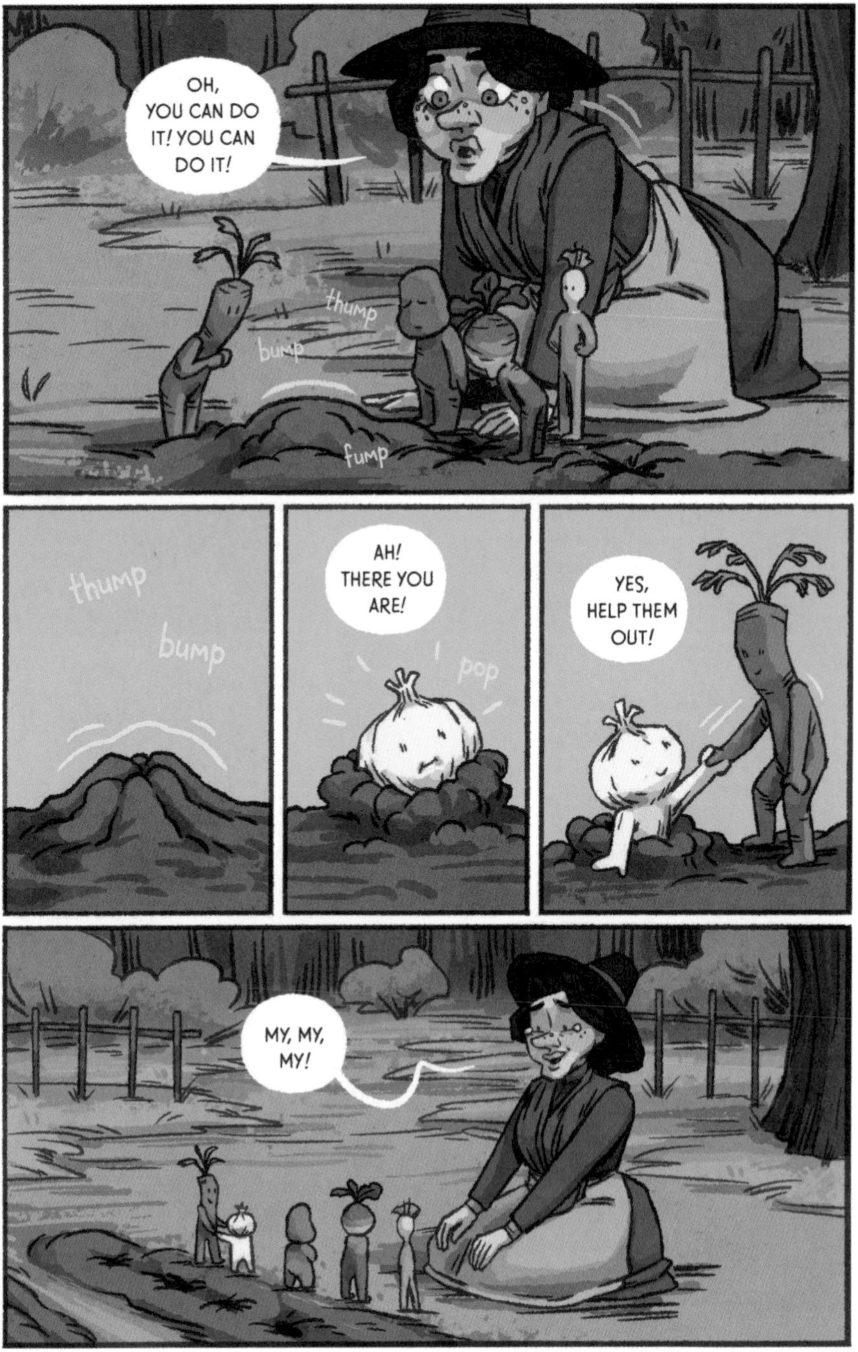
OH, YOU CAN DO IT! YOU CAN DO IT!
thump
bump
fump
thump
bump
AH! THERE YOU ARE!
pop
YES, HELP THEM OUT!
MY, MY, MY!

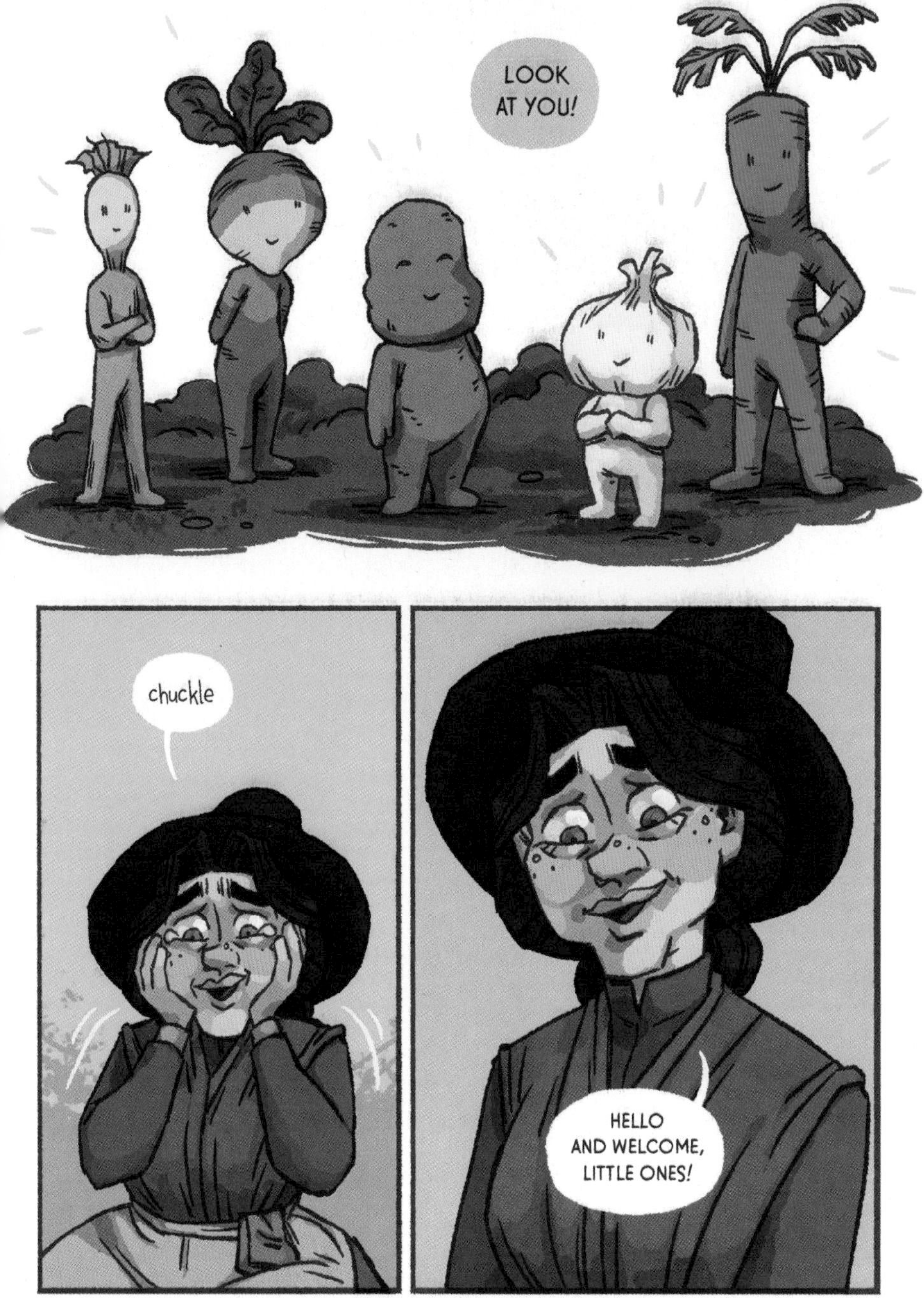
LOOK AT YOU!
chuckle
HELLO AND WELCOME, LITTLE ONES!

chapter two

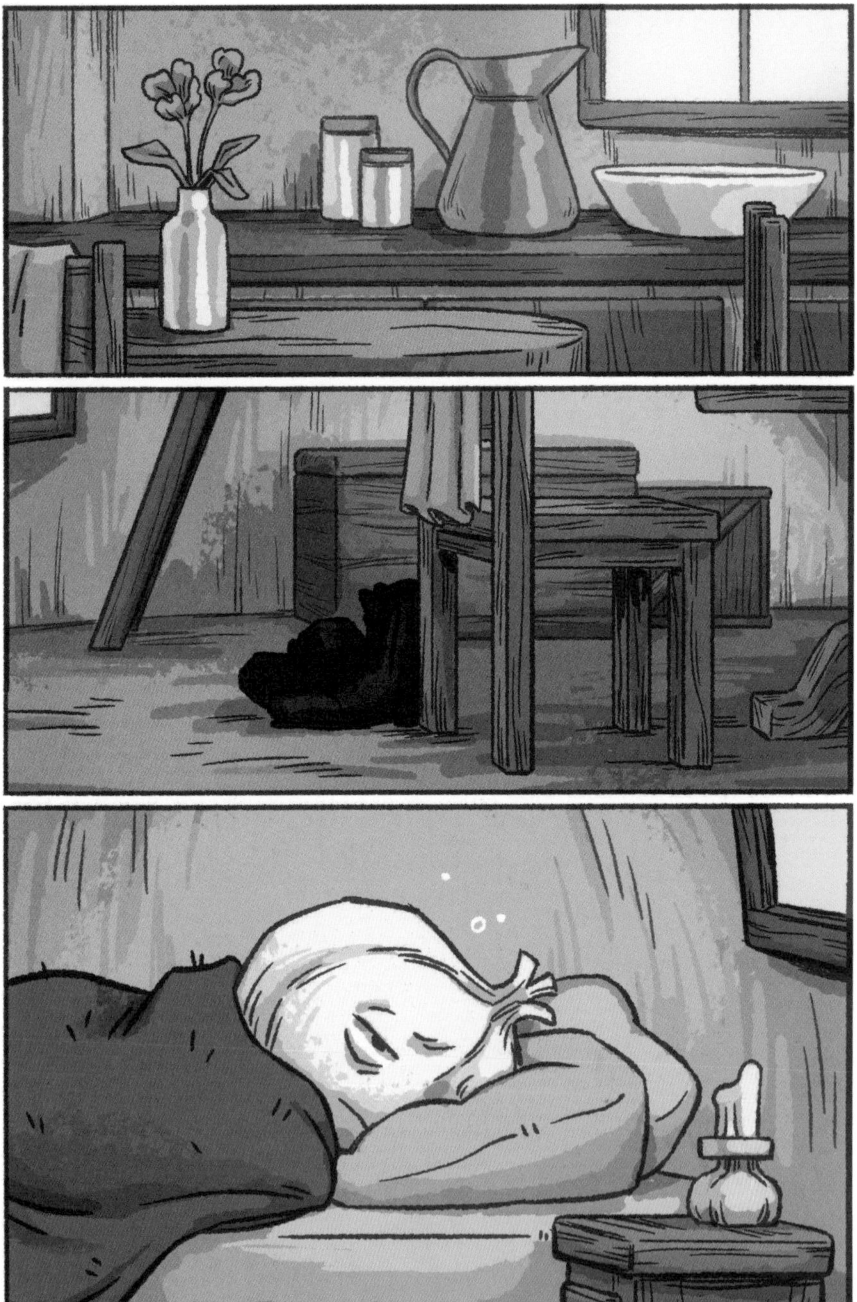

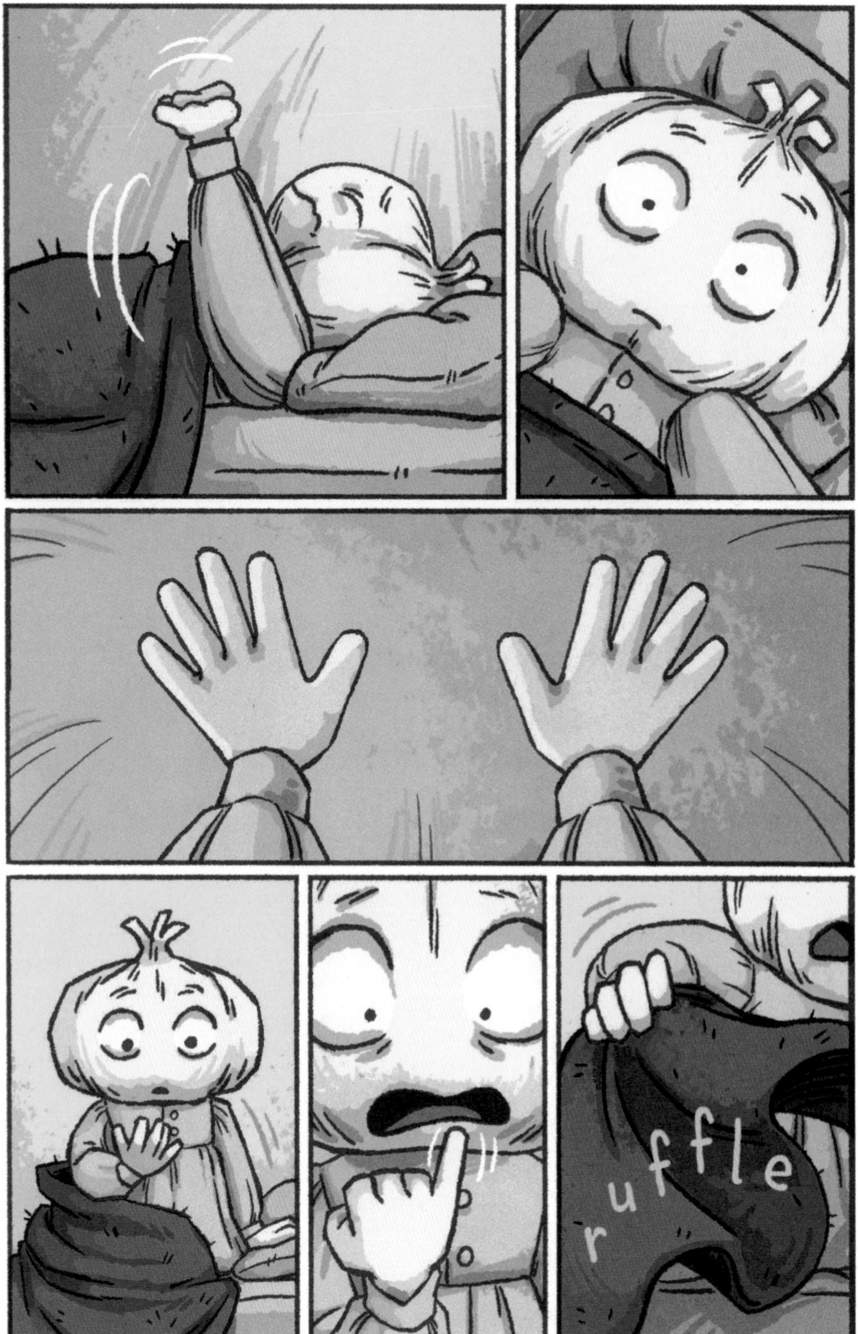
ruffle

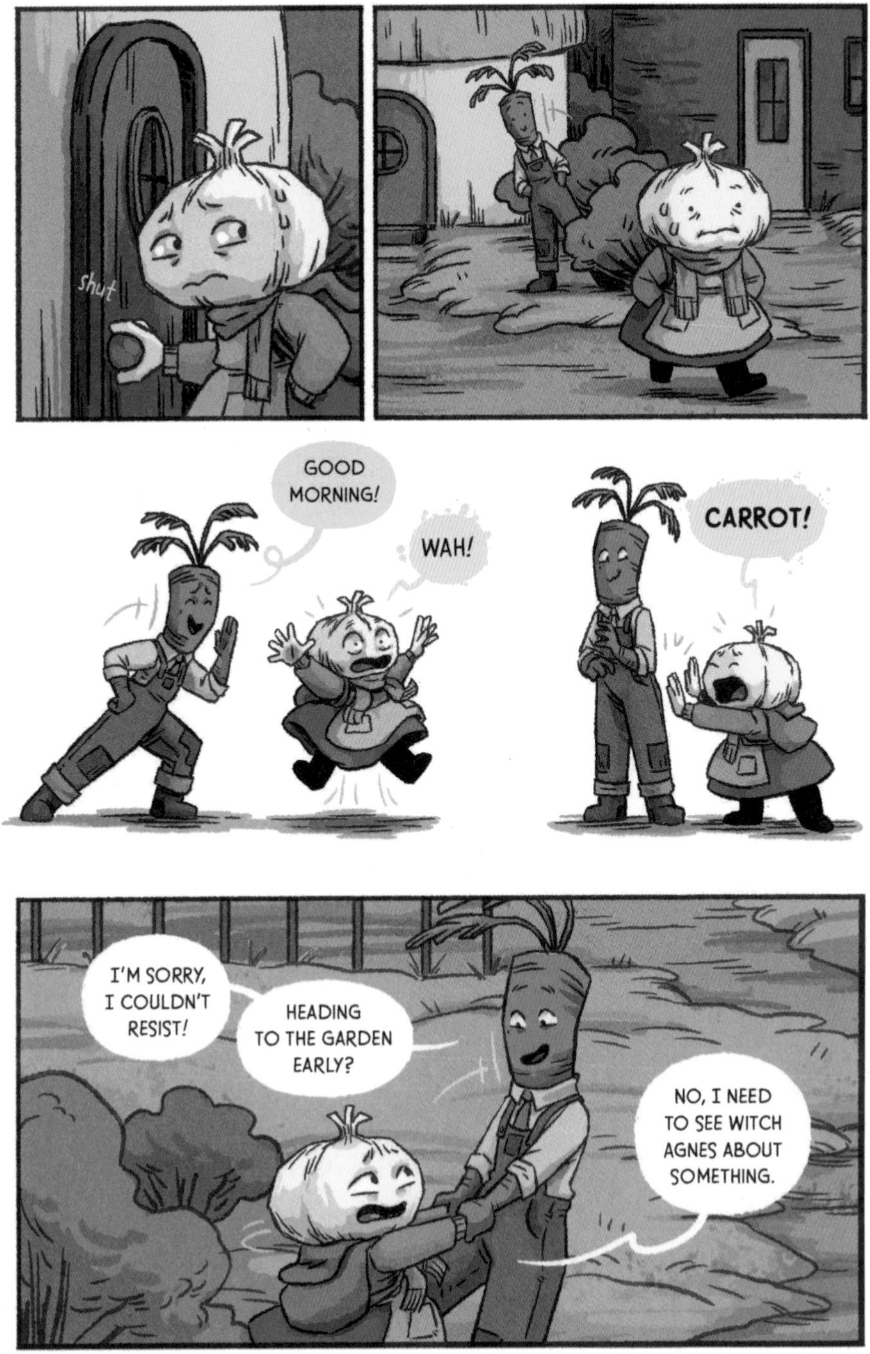
shut
GOOD MORNING!
WAH!
CARROT!
I'M SORRY, I COULDN'T RESIST!
HEADING TO THE GARDEN EARLY?
NO, I NEED TO SEE WITCH AGNES ABOUT SOMETHING.

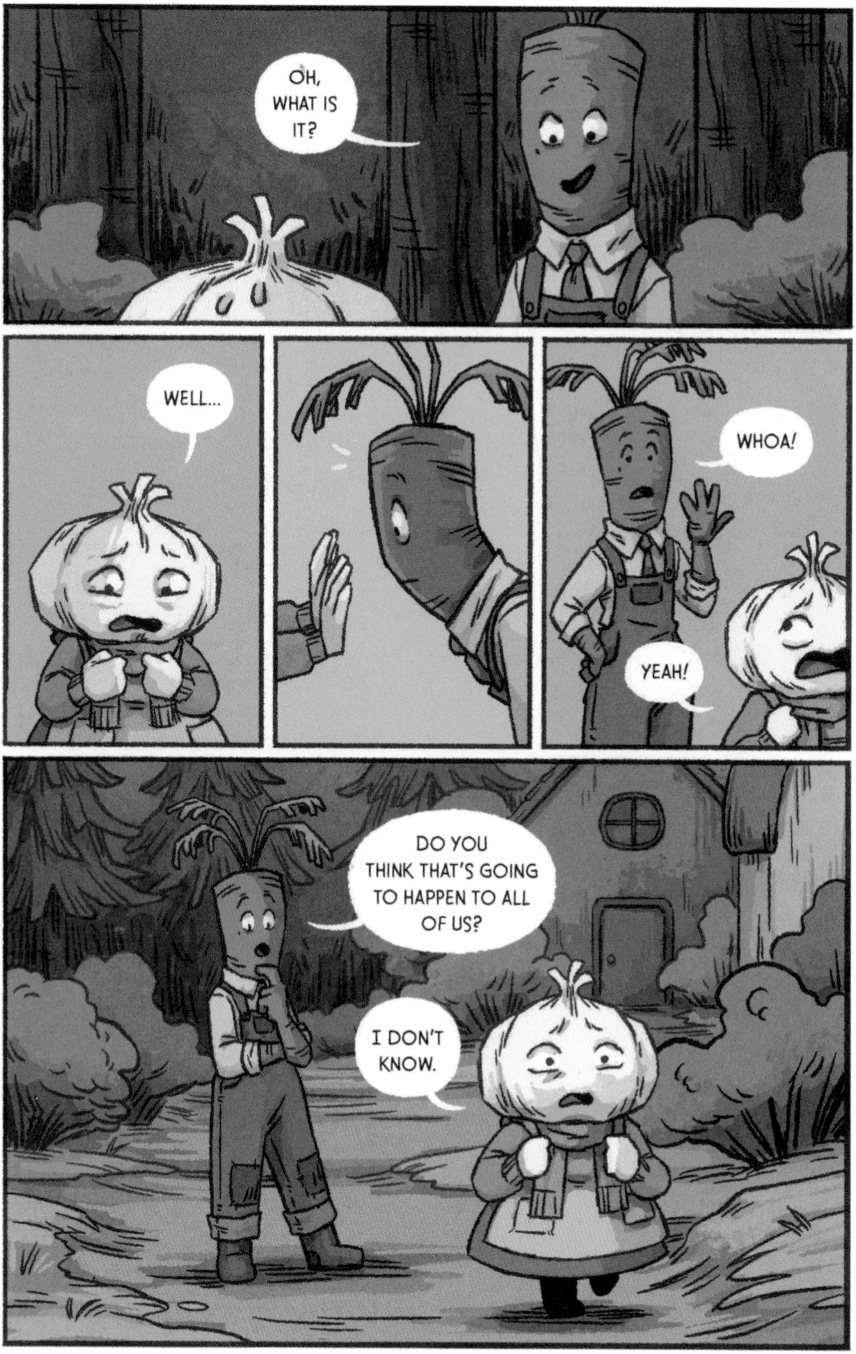
OH, WHAT IS IT?
WELL...
WHOA!
YEAH!
DO YOU THINK THAT'S GOING TO HAPPEN TO ALL OF US?
I DON'T KNOW.

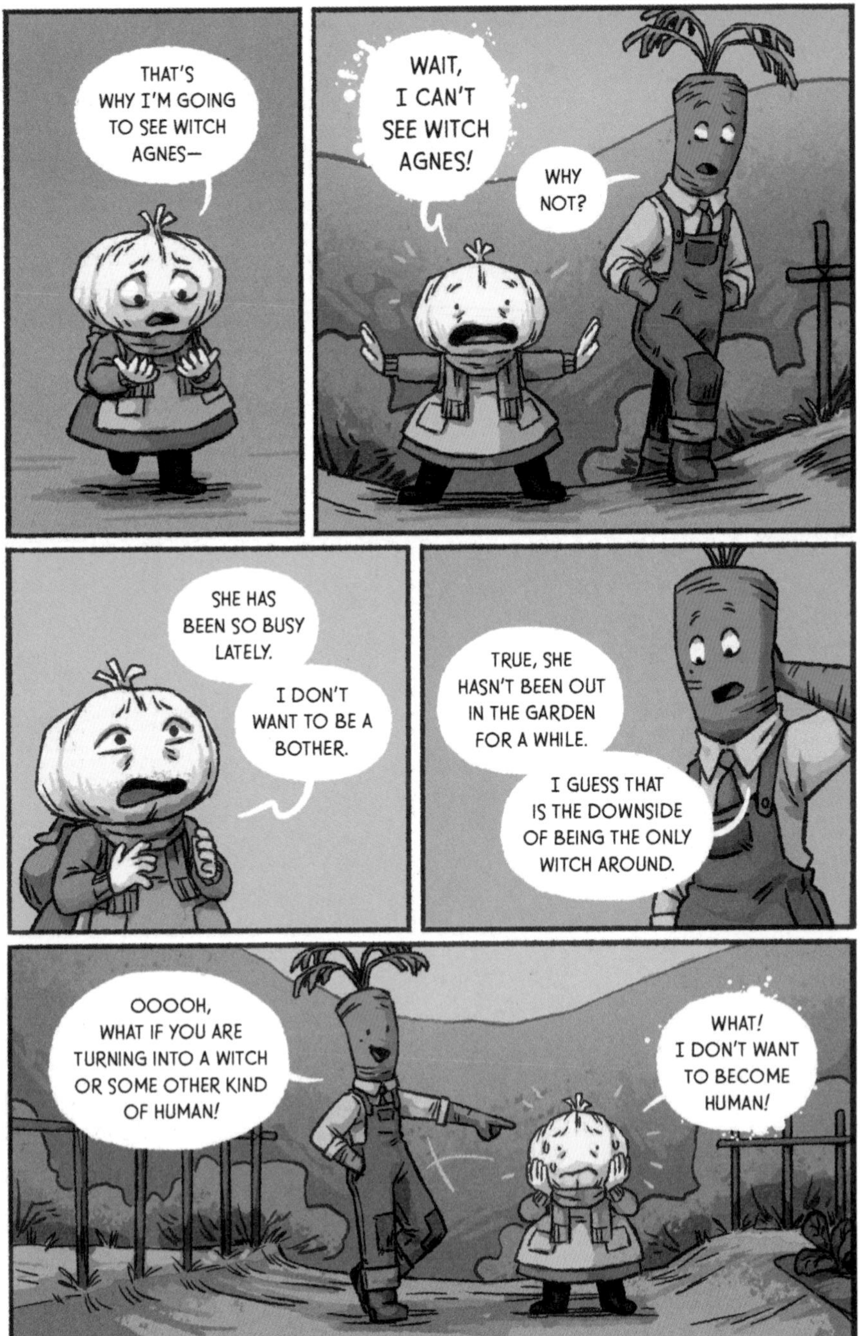
THAT'S WHY I'M GOING TO SEE WITCH AGNES—
WAIT, I CAN'T SEE WITCH AGNES!
WHY NOT?
SHE HAS BEEN SO BUSY LATELY.
I DON'T WANT TO BE A BOTHER.
TRUE, SHE HASN'T BEEN OUT IN THE GARDEN FOR A WHILE.
I GUESS THAT IS THE DOWNSIDE OF BEING THE ONLY WITCH AROUND.
OOOOH, WHAT IF YOU ARE TURNING INTO A WITCH OR SOME OTHER KIND OF HUMAN!
WHAT! I DON'T WANT TO BECOME HUMAN!

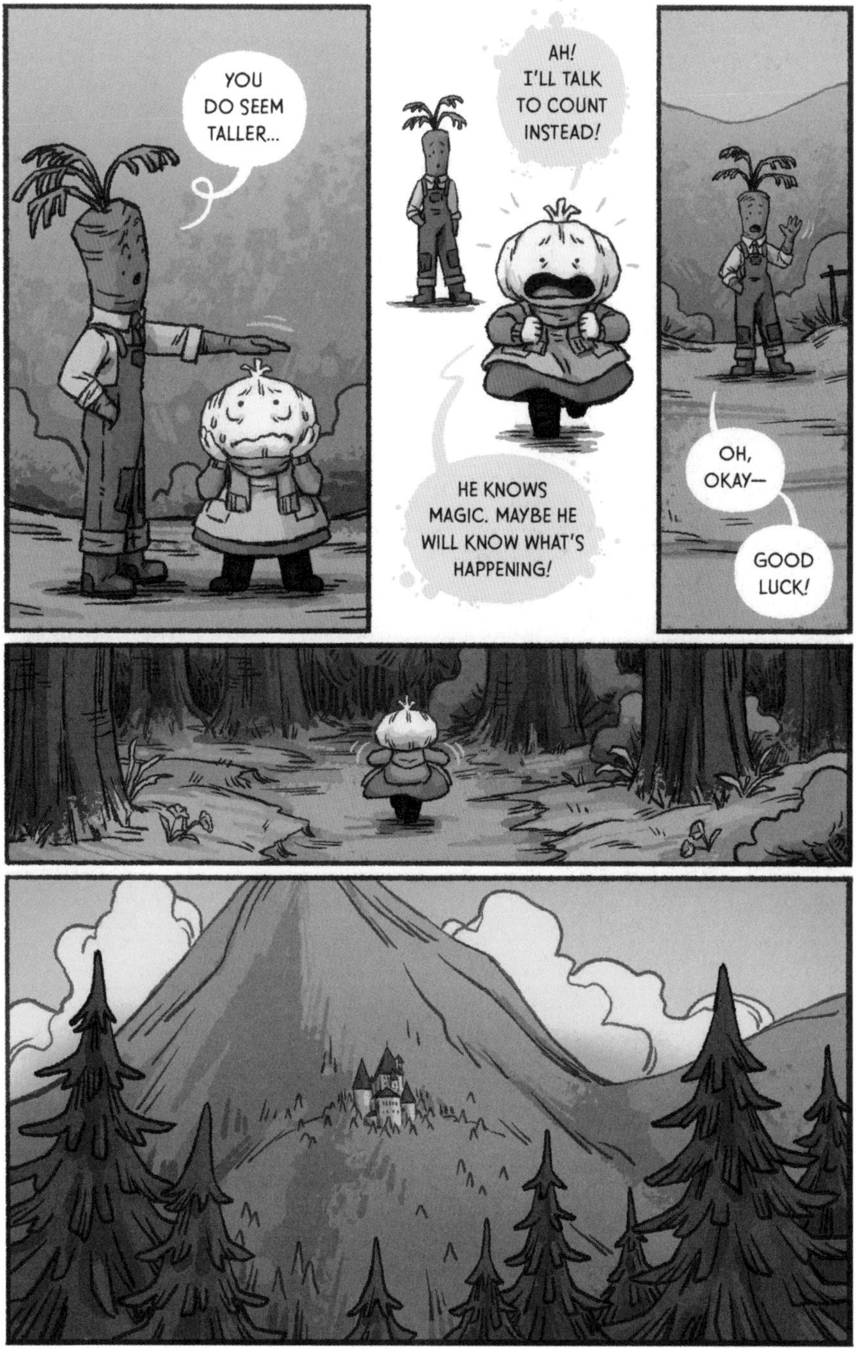

YOU DO SEEM TALLER...
AH! I'LL TALK TO COUNT INSTEAD!
HE KNOWS MAGIC. MAYBE HE WILL KNOW WHAT'S HAPPENING!
OH, OKAY—
GOOD LUCK!

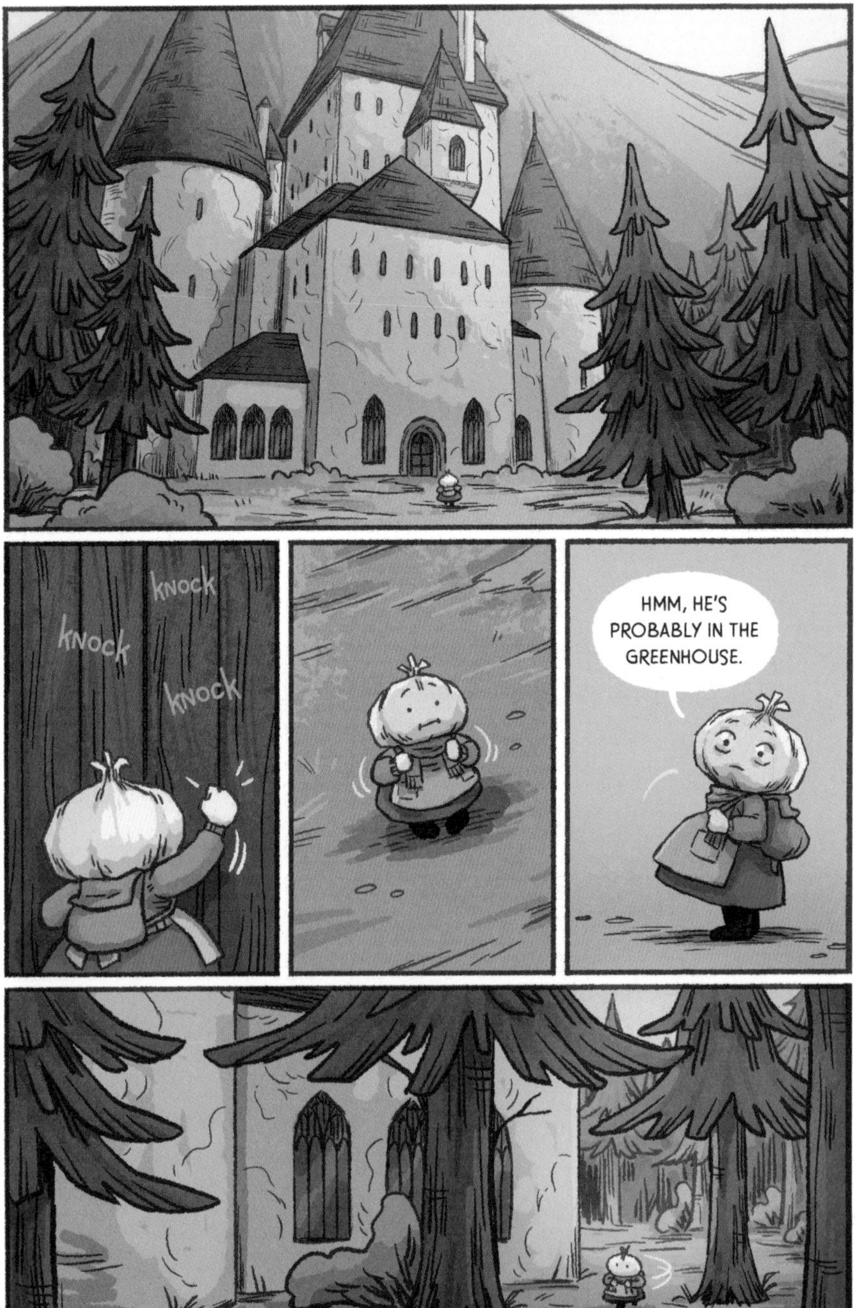
knock
knock
knock
HMM, HE'S PROBABLY IN THE GREENHOUSE.

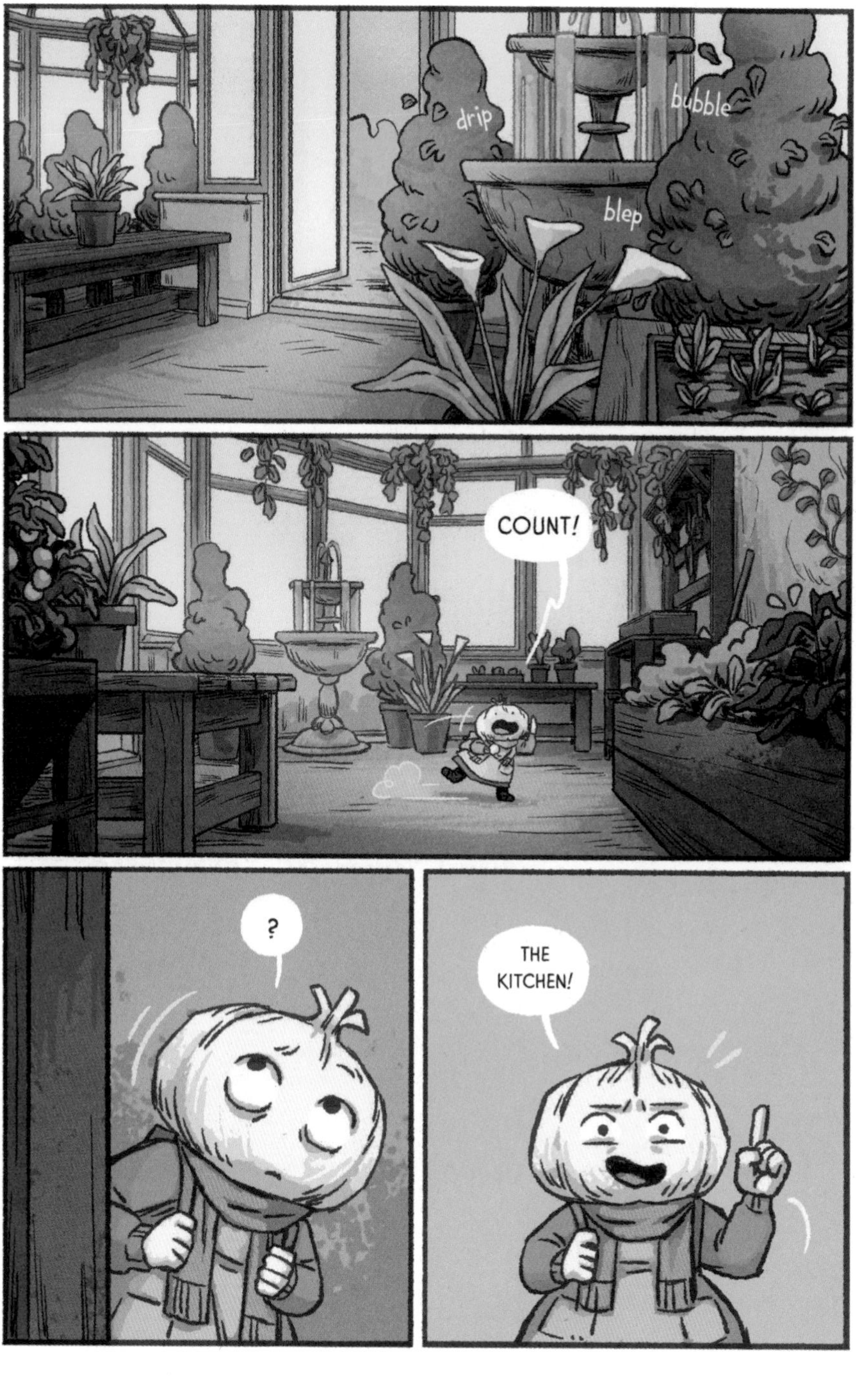
drip
bubble
blep
COUNT!
?
THE KITCHEN!

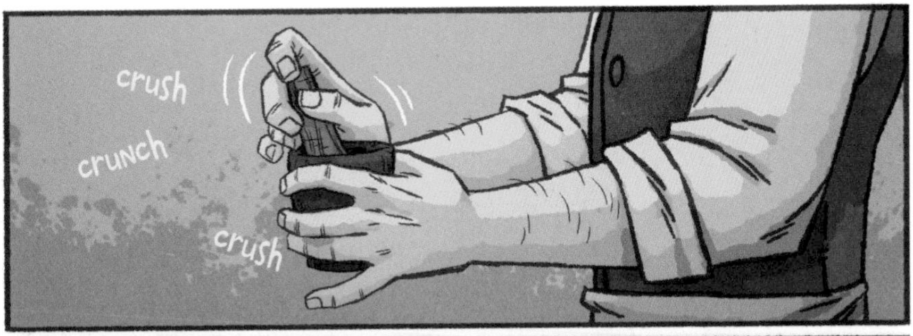
crush
crunch
crush

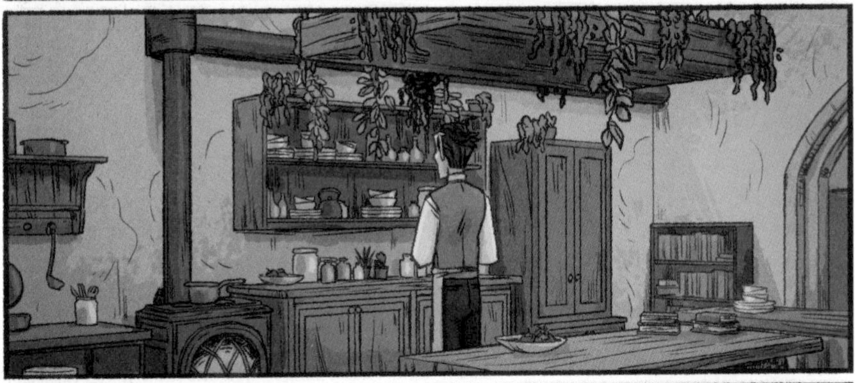

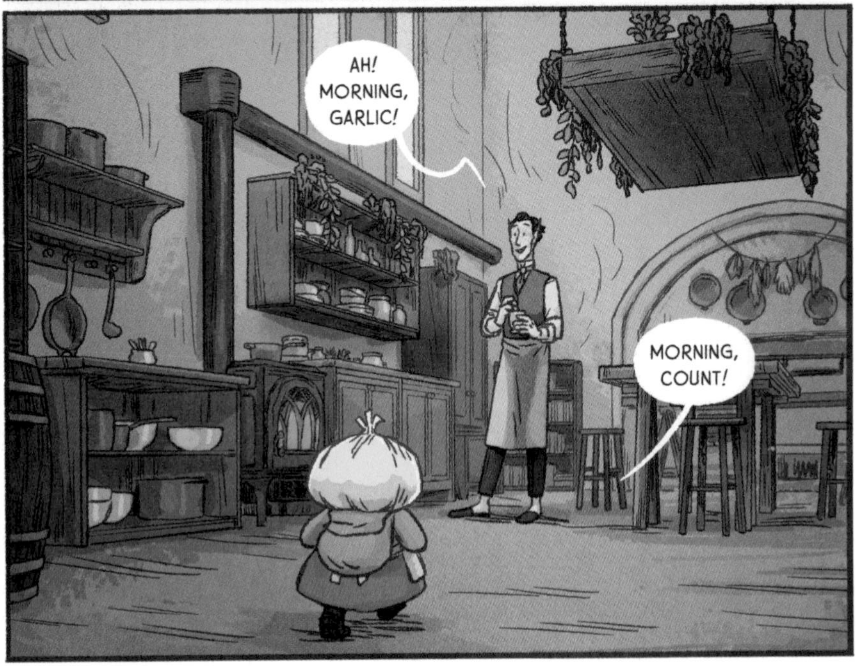
AH! MORNING, GARLIC!
MORNING, COUNT!

YOU JUST MISSED AGNES.
SHE DROPPED OFF A NEW BLEND OF HERBS FOR MY BLOOD SUBSTITUTE POTION.
GRAPES, SHE WAS HERE?
I HAVE A QUESTION FOR HER...OH WELL, MAYBE I'LL VISIT HER LATER.
NOW, LET'S SEE IF WE FINALLY GOT IT.

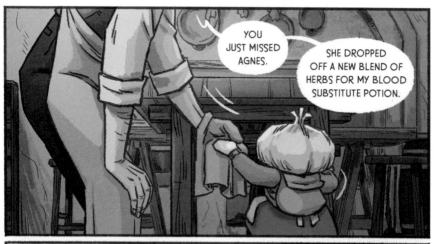

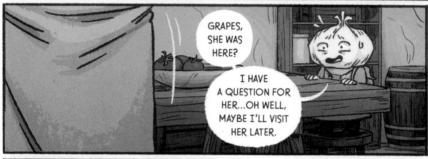

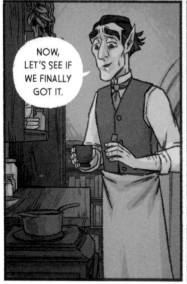

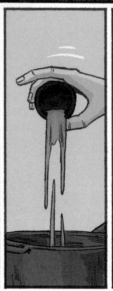

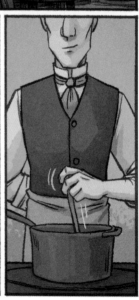

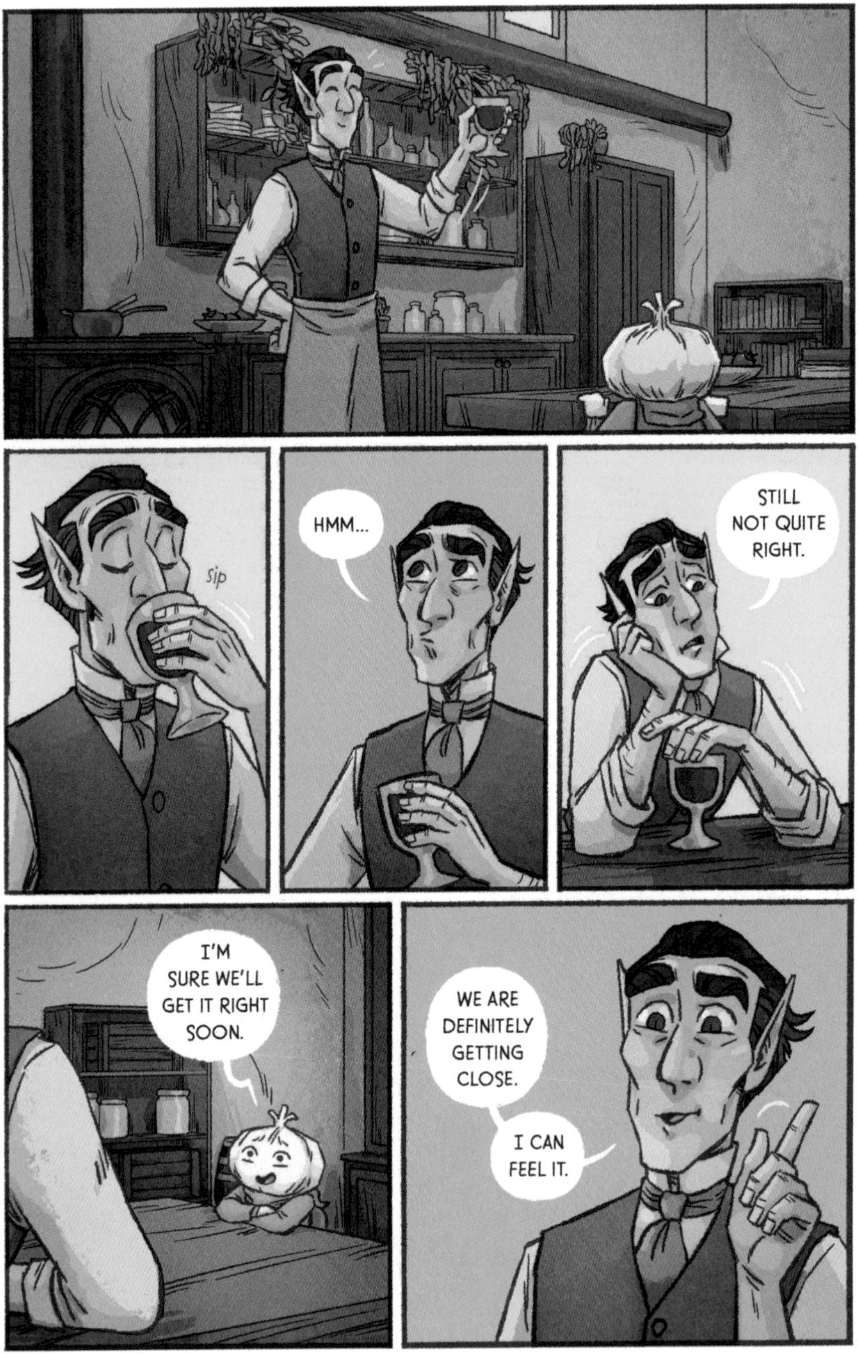
Sip
HMM...
STILL NOT QUITE RIGHT.
I'M SURE WE'LL GET IT RIGHT SOON.
WE ARE DEFINITELY GETTING CLOSE.
I CAN FEEL IT.

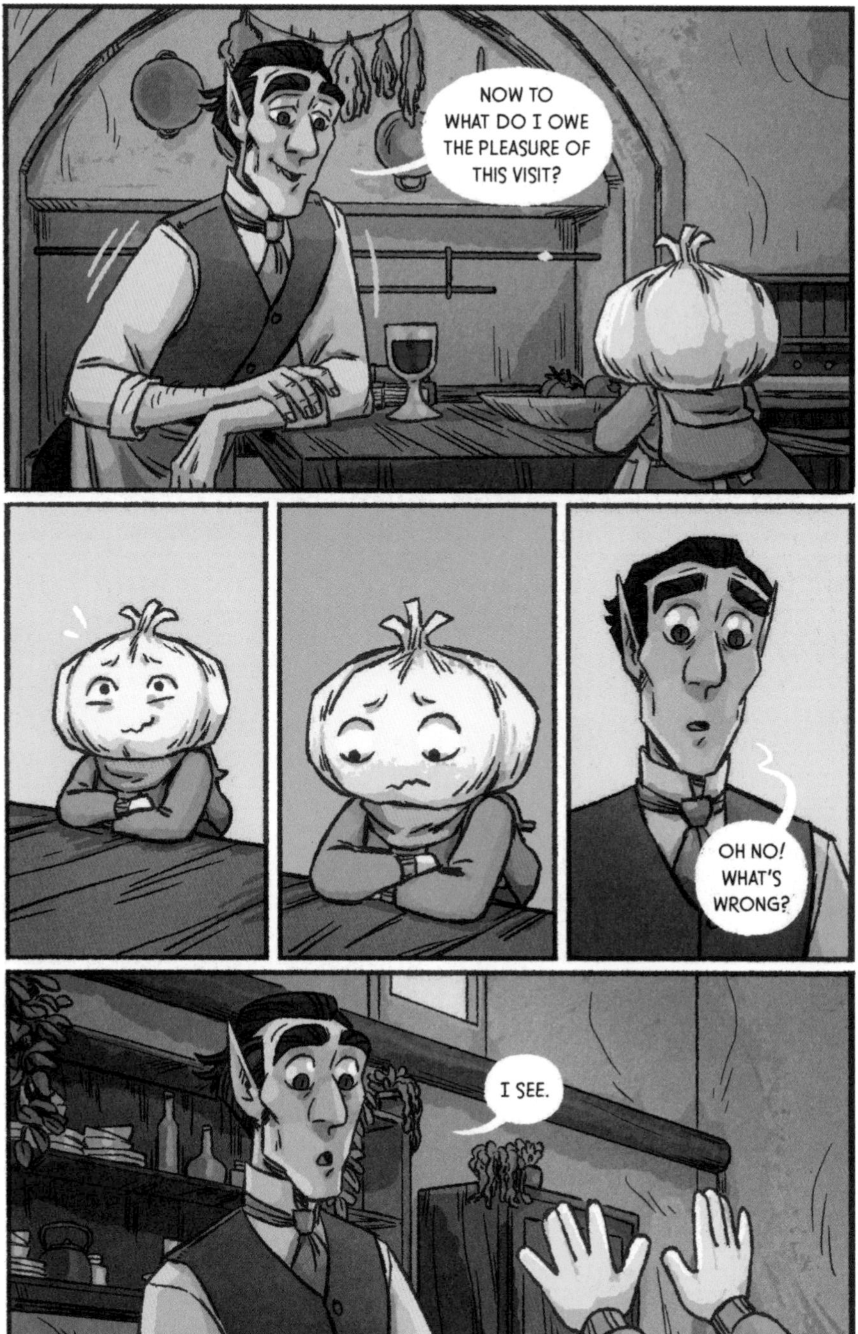
NOW TO WHAT DO I OWE THE PLEASURE OF THIS VISIT?
OH NO! WHAT'S WRONG?
I SEE.

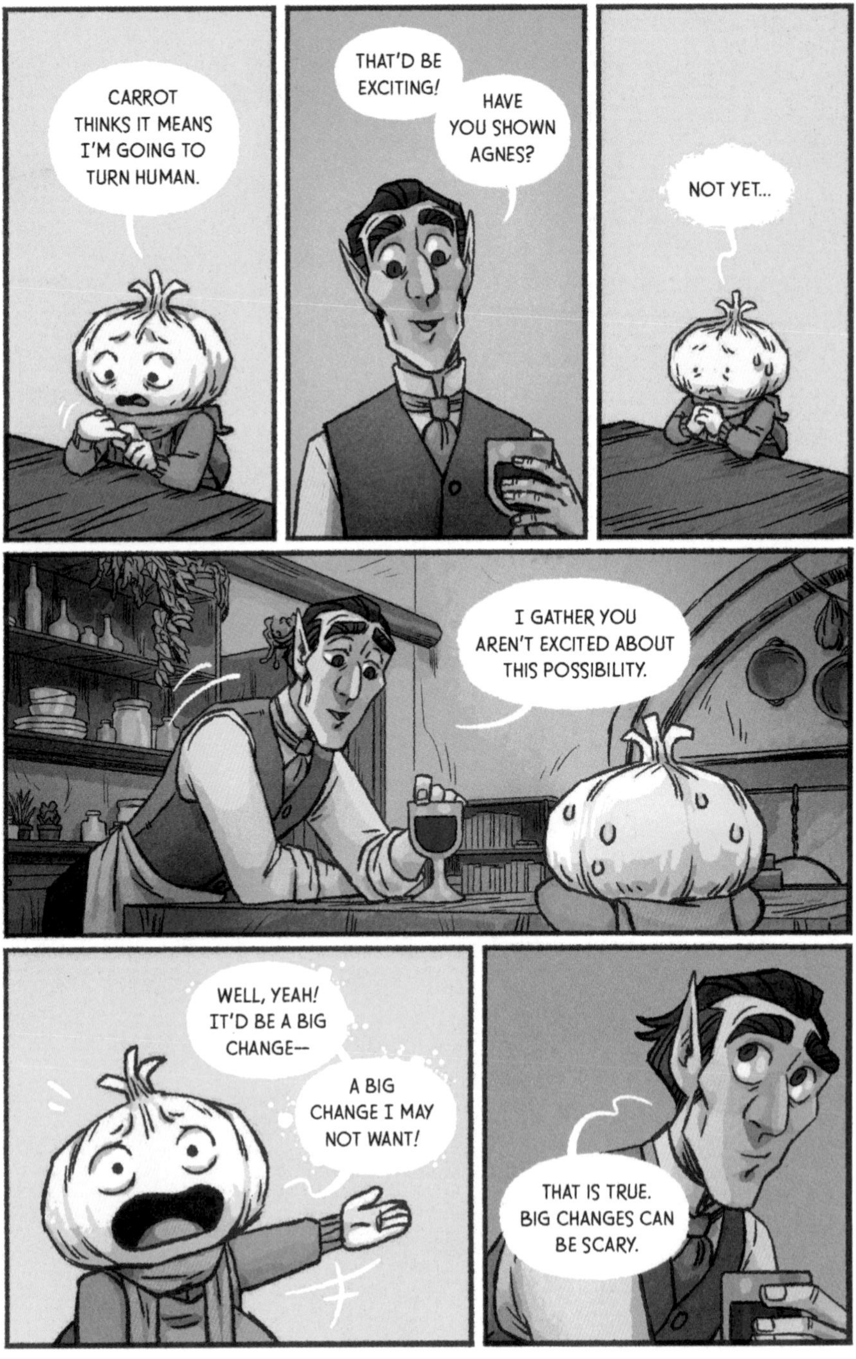
CARROT THINKS IT MEANS I'M GOING TO TURN HUMAN.
THAT'D BE EXCITING!
HAVE YOU SHOWN AGNES?
NOT YET...
I GATHER YOU AREN'T EXCITED ABOUT THIS POSSIBILITY.
WELL, YEAH! IT'D BE A BIG CHANGE--
A BIG CHANGE I MAY NOT WANT!
THAT IS TRUE. BIG CHANGES CAN BE SCARY.

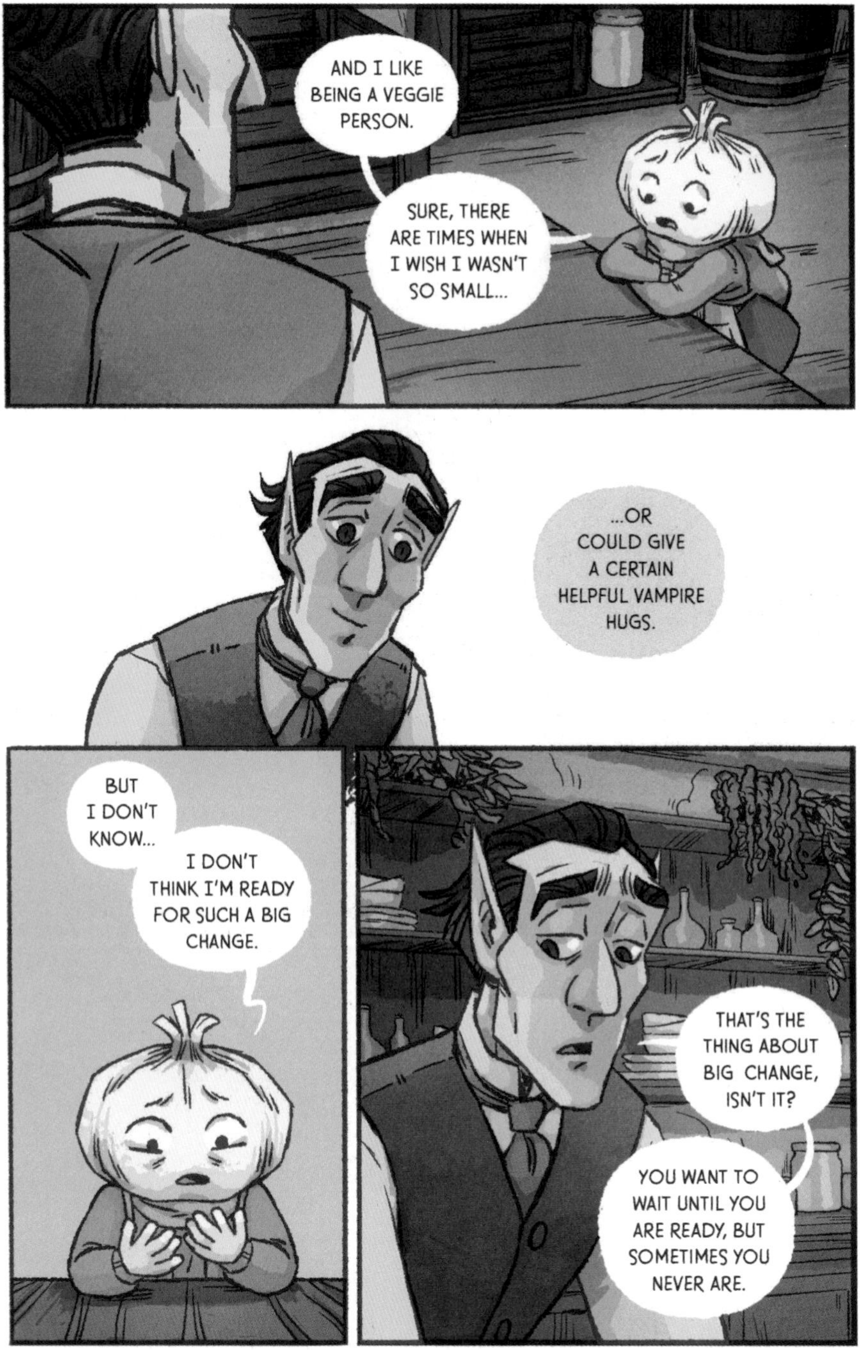
AND I LIKE BEING A VEGGIE PERSON.
SURE, THERE ARE TIMES WHEN I WISH I WASN'T SO SMALL...
...OR COULD GIVE A CERTAIN HELPFUL VAMPIRE HUGS.
BUT I DON'T KNOW...
I DON'T THINK I'M READY FOR SUCH A BIG CHANGE.
THAT'S THE THING ABOUT BIG CHANGE, ISN'T IT?
YOU WANT TO WAIT UNTIL YOU ARE READY, BUT SOMETIMES YOU NEVER ARE.

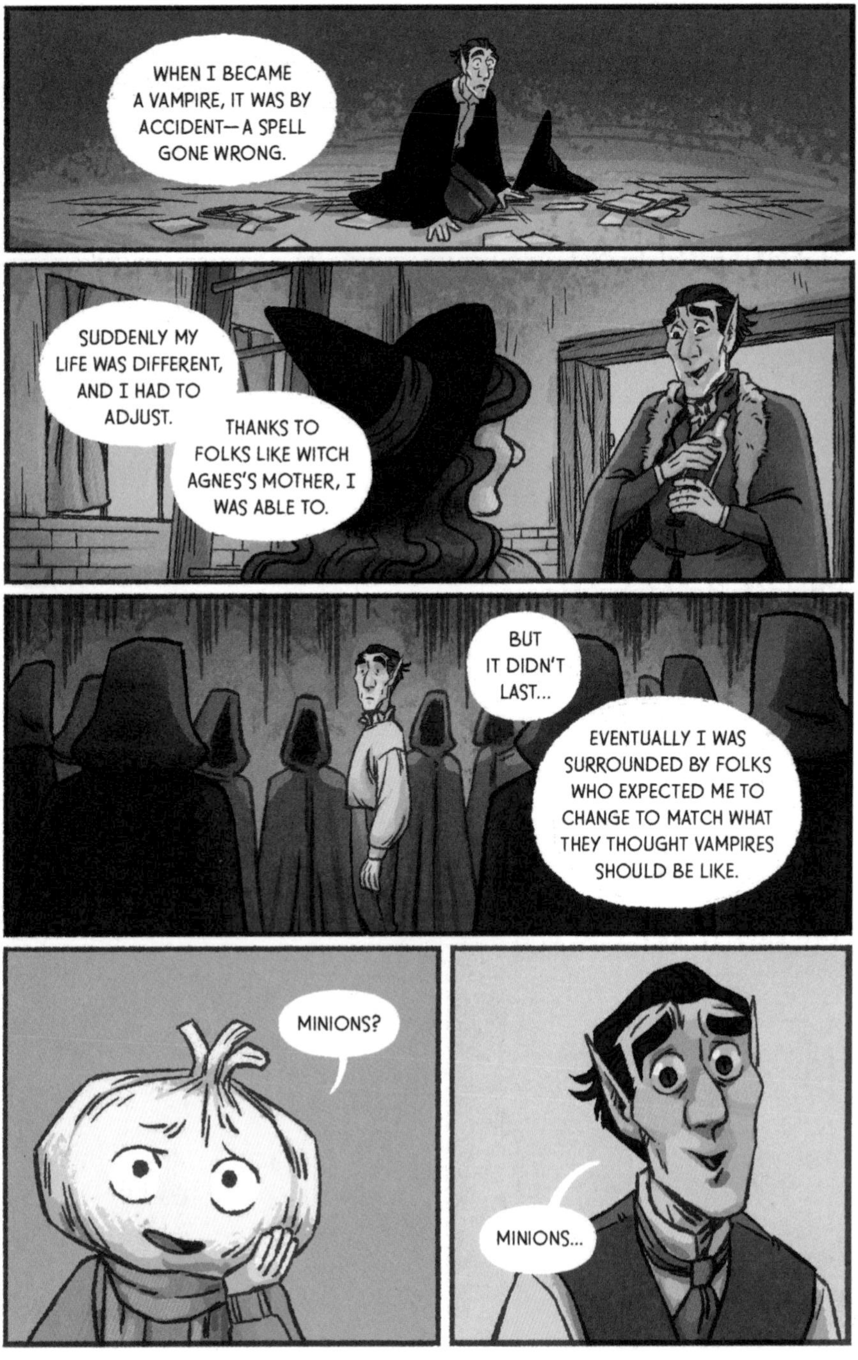
WHEN I BECAME A VAMPIRE, IT WAS BY ACCIDENT—A SPELL GONE WRONG.
SUDDENLY MY LIFE WAS DIFFERENT, AND I HAD TO ADJUST.
THANKS TO FOLKS LIKE WITCH AGNES'S MOTHER, I WAS ABLE TO.
BUT IT DIDN'T LAST...
EVENTUALLY I WAS SURROUNDED BY FOLKS WHO EXPECTED ME TO CHANGE TO MATCH WHAT THEY THOUGHT VAMPIRES SHOULD BE LIKE.
MINIONS?
MINIONS...

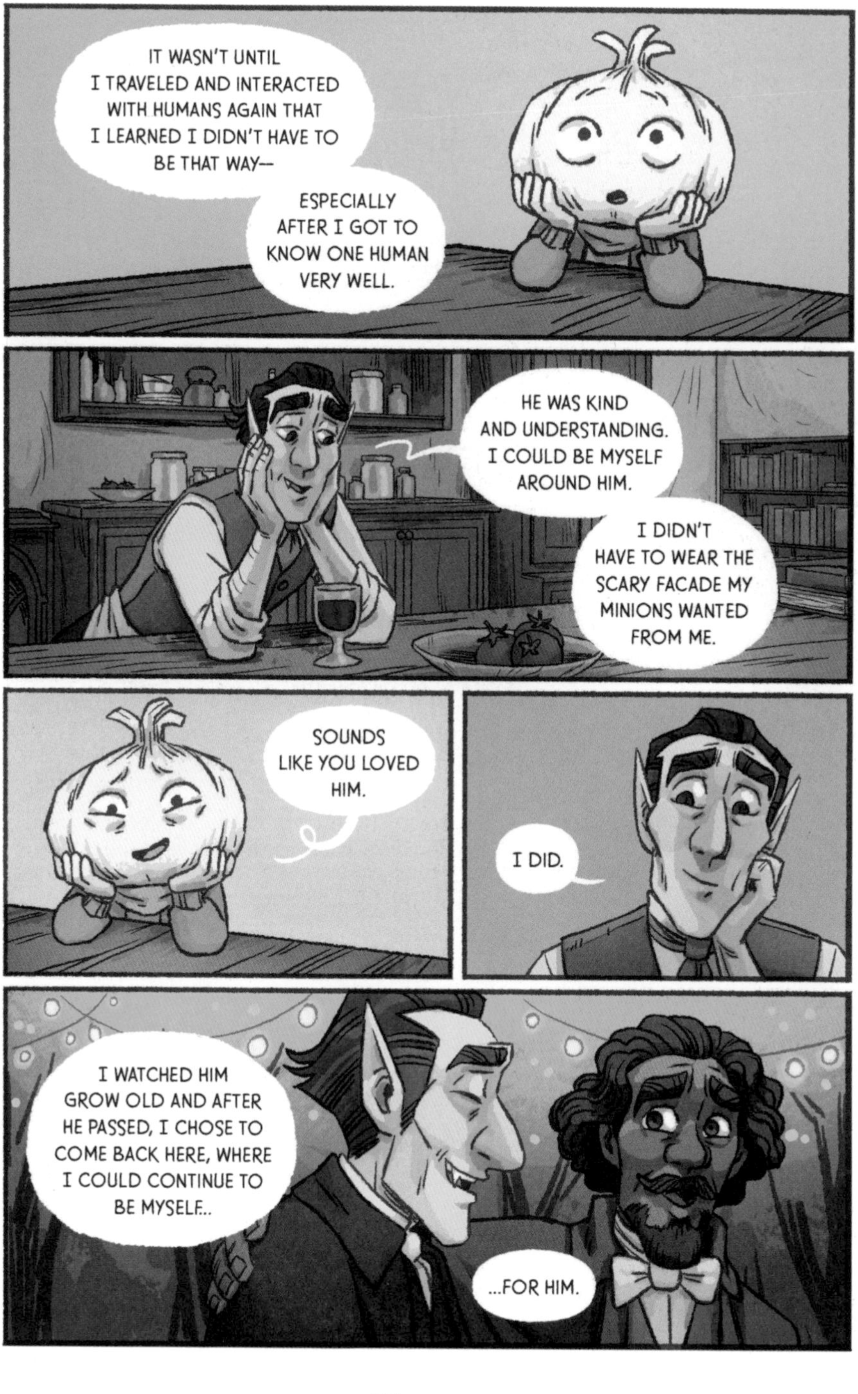
IT WASN'T UNTIL I TRAVELED AND INTERACTED WITH HUMANS AGAIN THAT I LEARNED I DIDN'T HAVE TO BE THAT WAY--
ESPECIALLY AFTER I GOT TO KNOW ONE HUMAN VERY WELL.
HE WAS KIND AND UNDERSTANDING. I COULD BE MYSELF AROUND HIM.
I DIDN'T HAVE TO WEAR THE SCARY FACADE MY MINIONS WANTED FROM ME.
SOUNDS LIKE YOU LOVED HIM.
I DID.
I WATCHED HIM GROW OLD AND AFTER HE PASSED, I CHOSE TO COME BACK HERE, WHERE I COULD CONTINUE TO BE MYSELF...
...FOR HIM.

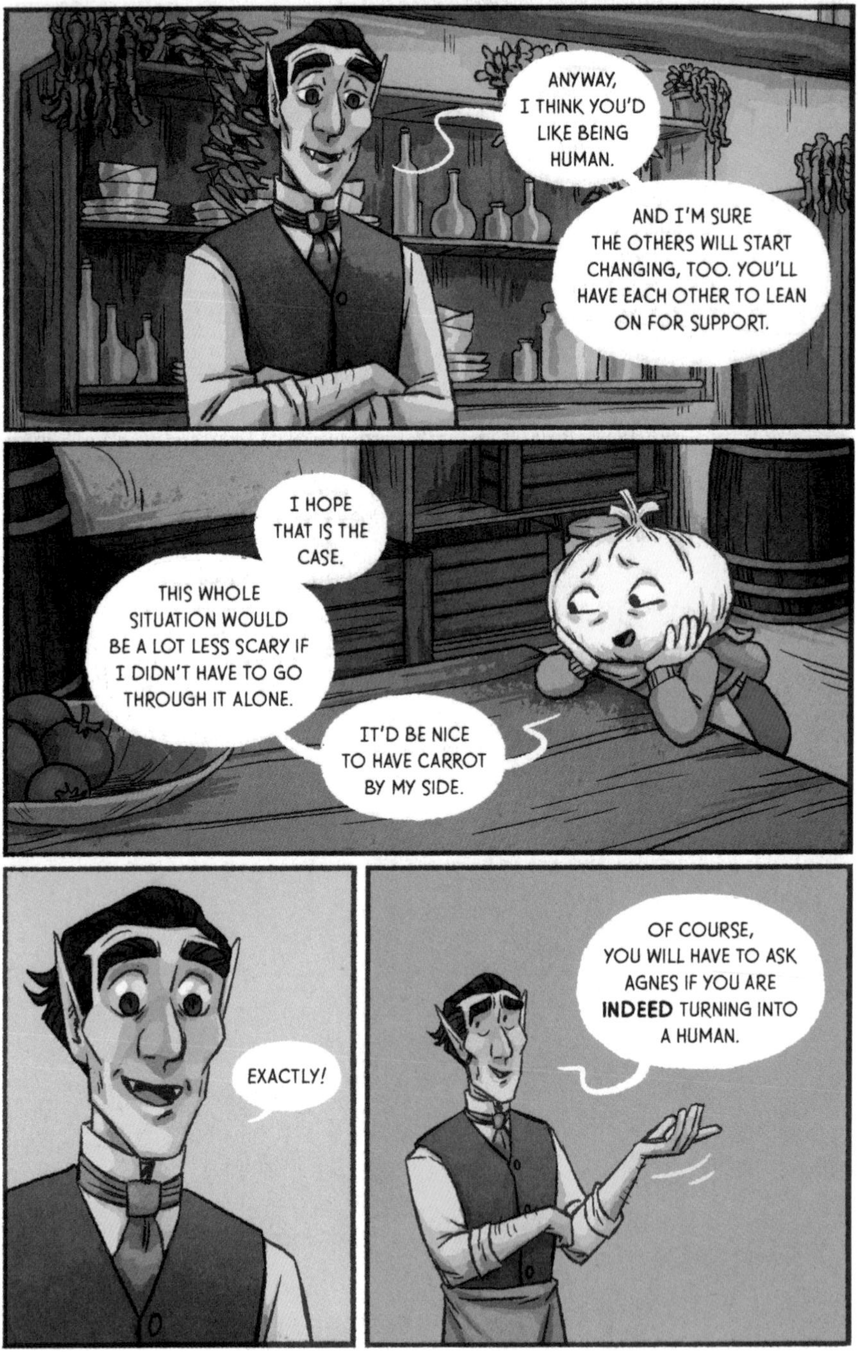
ANYWAY, I THINK YOU'D LIKE BEING HUMAN.
AND I'M SURE THE OTHERS WILL START CHANGING, TOO. YOU'LL HAVE EACH OTHER TO LEAN ON FOR SUPPORT.
I HOPE THAT IS THE CASE.
THIS WHOLE SITUATION WOULD BE A LOT LESS SCARY IF I DIDN'T HAVE TO GO THROUGH IT ALONE.
IT'D BE NICE TO HAVE CARROT BY MY SIDE.
EXACTLY!
OF COURSE, YOU WILL HAVE TO ASK AGNES IF YOU ARE **INDEED** TURNING INTO A HUMAN.

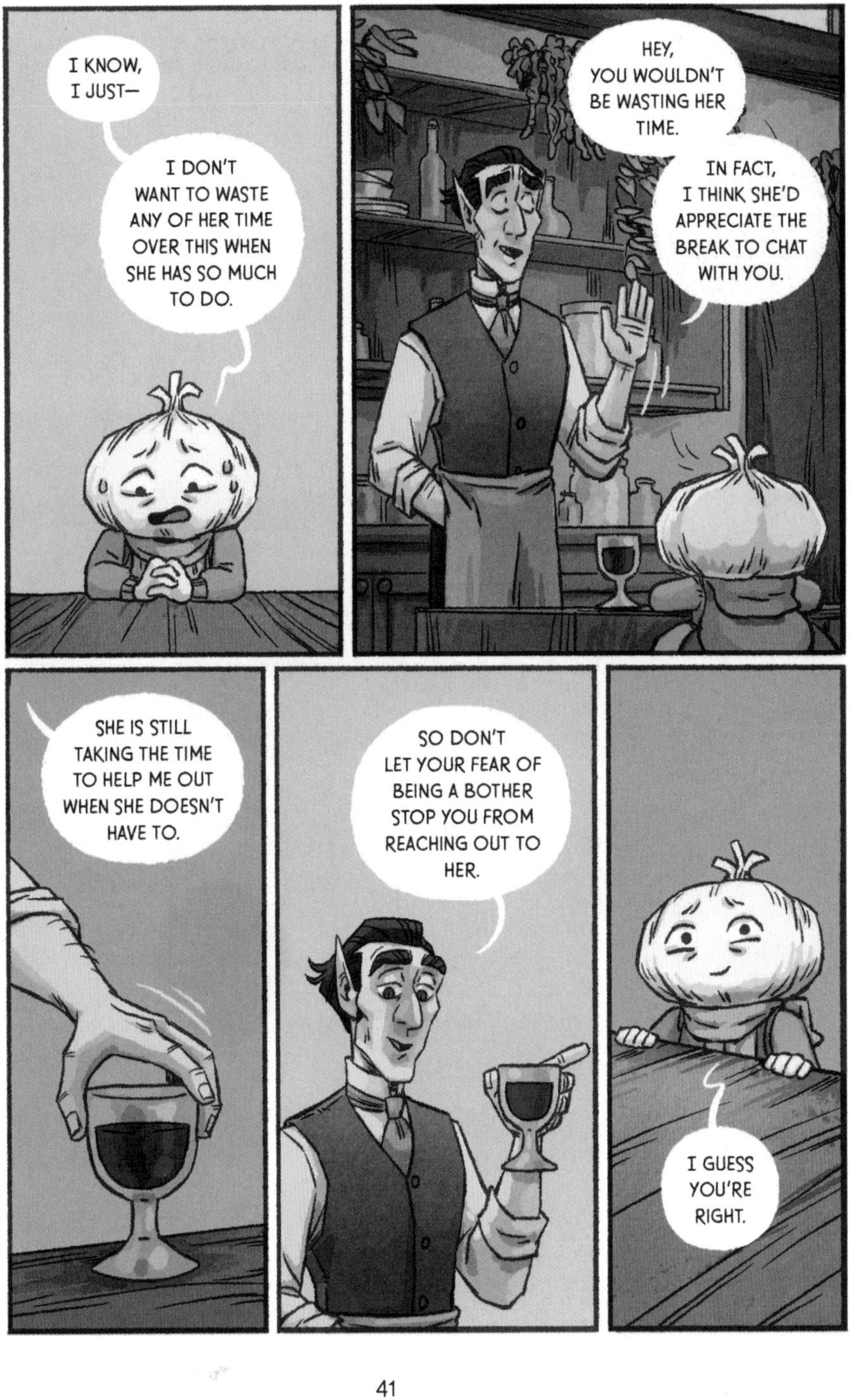
I KNOW, I JUST—
I DON'T WANT TO WASTE ANY OF HER TIME OVER THIS WHEN SHE HAS SO MUCH TO DO.
HEY, YOU WOULDN'T BE WASTING HER TIME.
IN FACT, I THINK SHE'D APPRECIATE THE BREAK TO CHAT WITH YOU.
SHE IS STILL TAKING THE TIME TO HELP ME OUT WHEN SHE DOESN'T HAVE TO.
SO DON'T LET YOUR FEAR OF BEING A BOTHER STOP YOU FROM REACHING OUT TO HER.
I GUESS YOU'RE RIGHT.

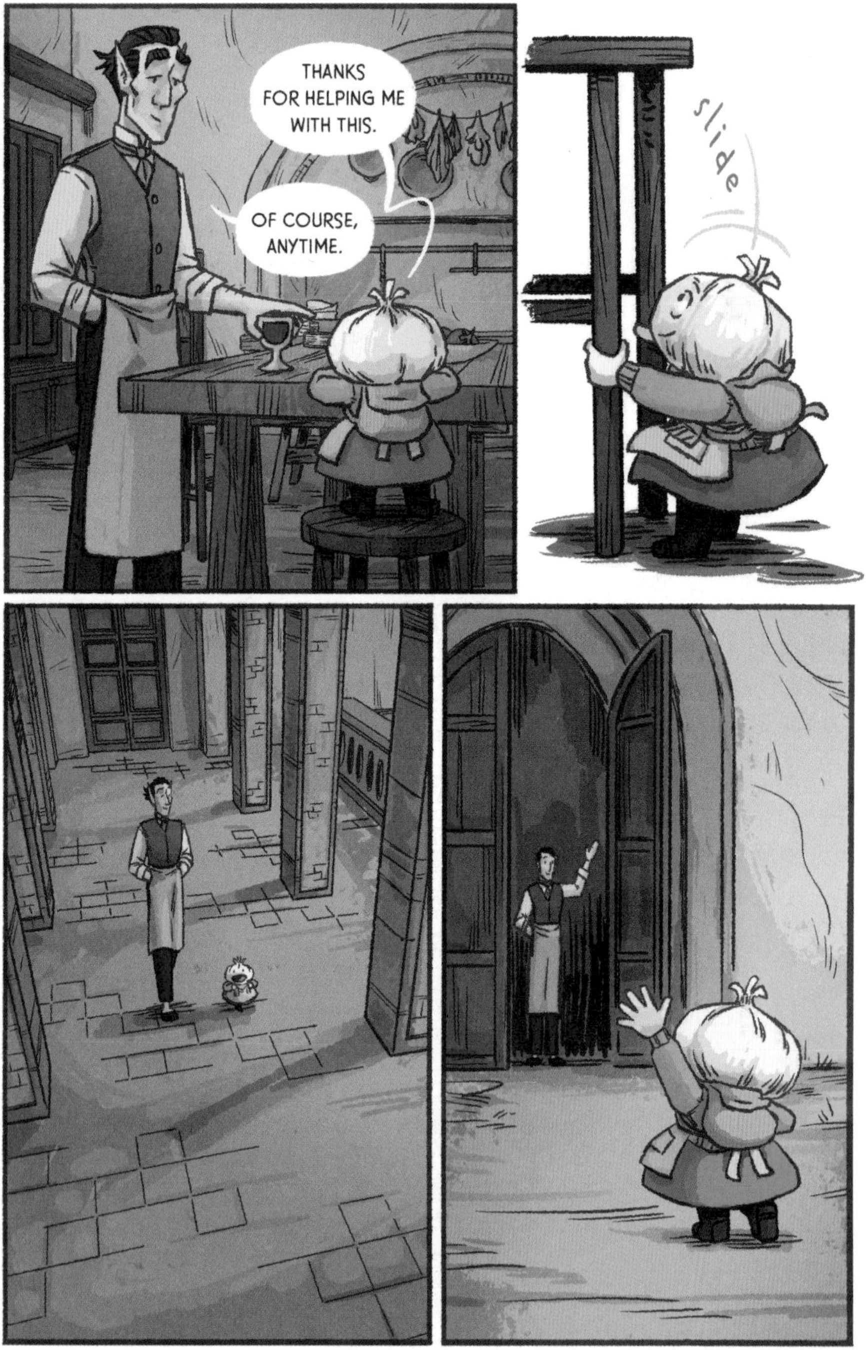
THANKS FOR HELPING ME WITH THIS.
OF COURSE, ANYTIME.
slide

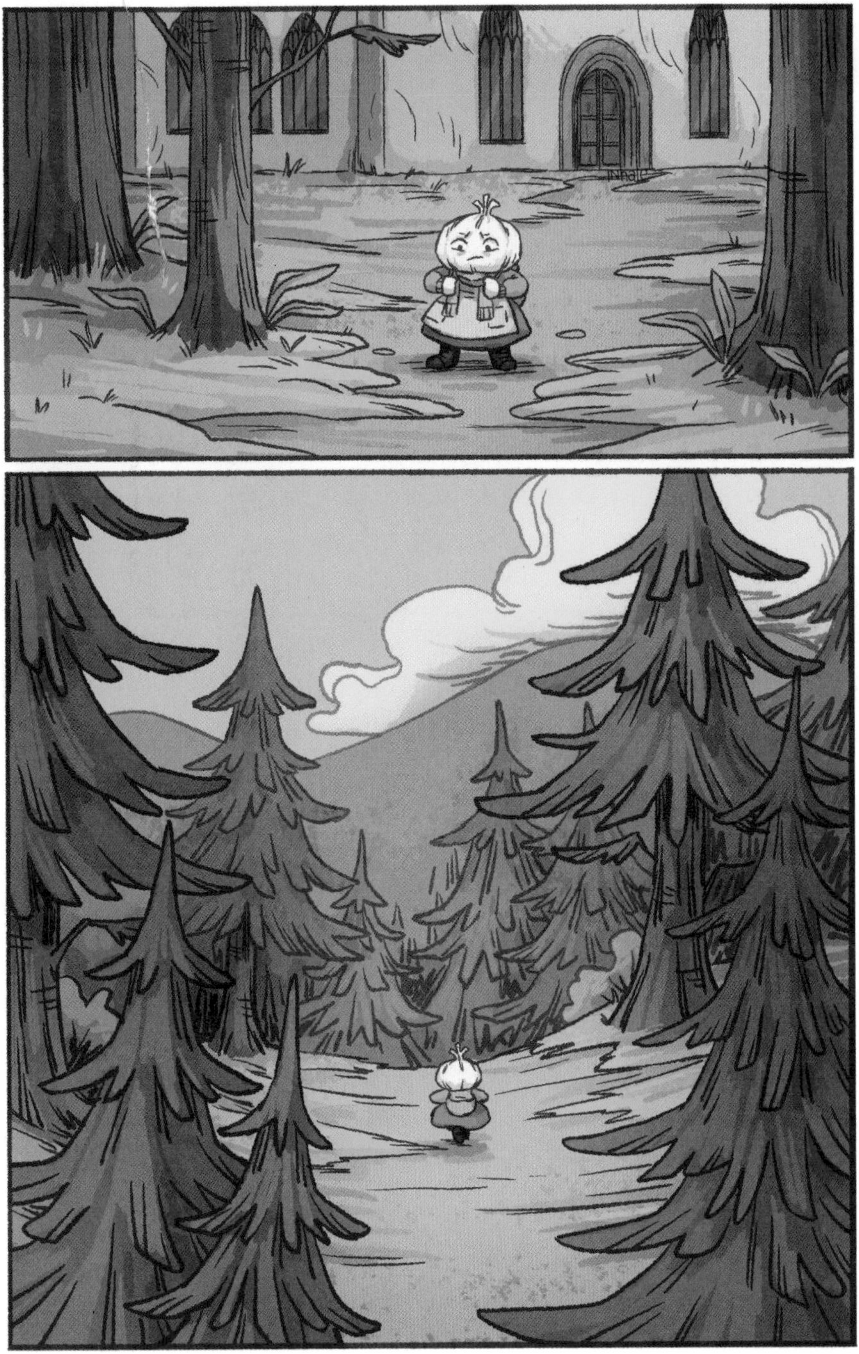

chapter three

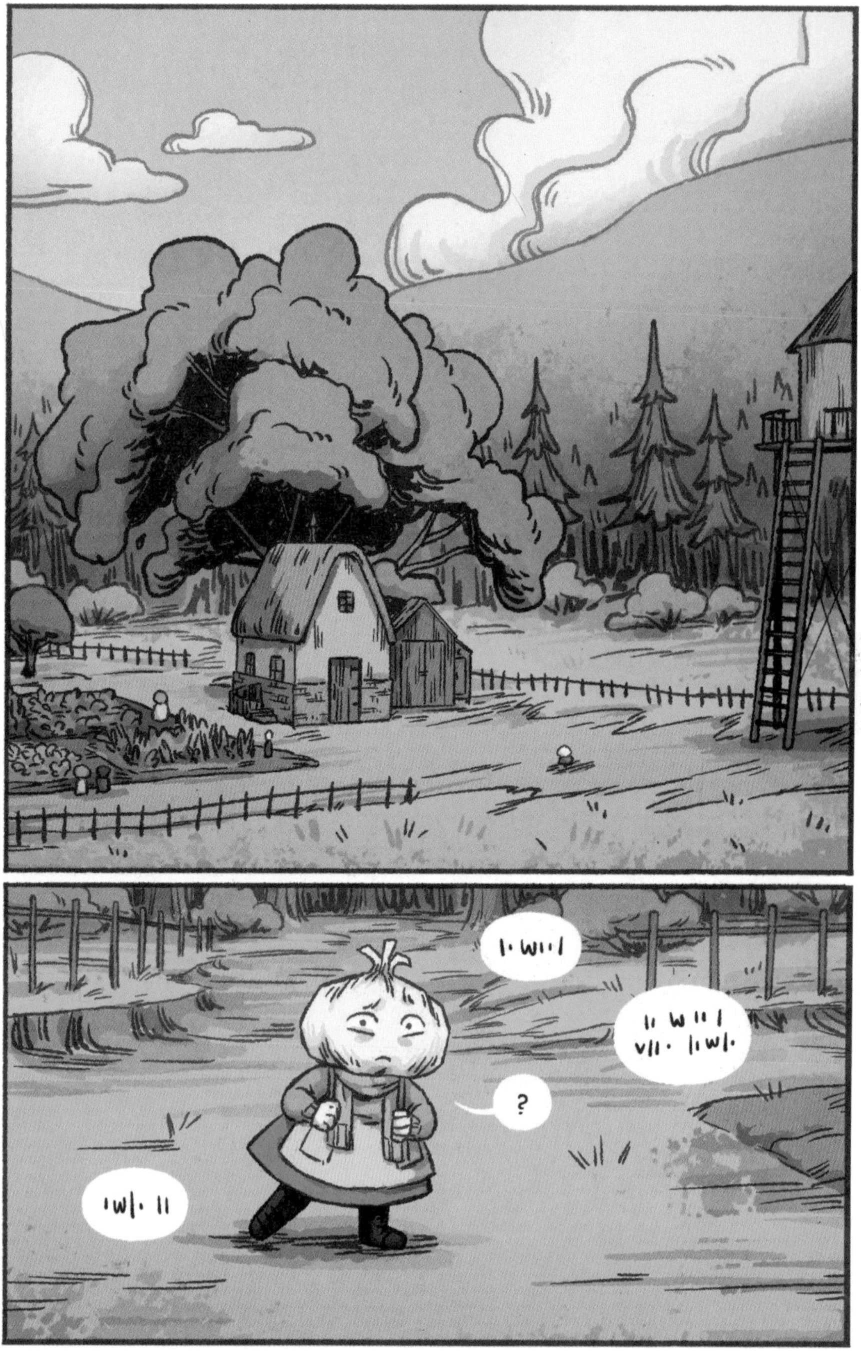
?

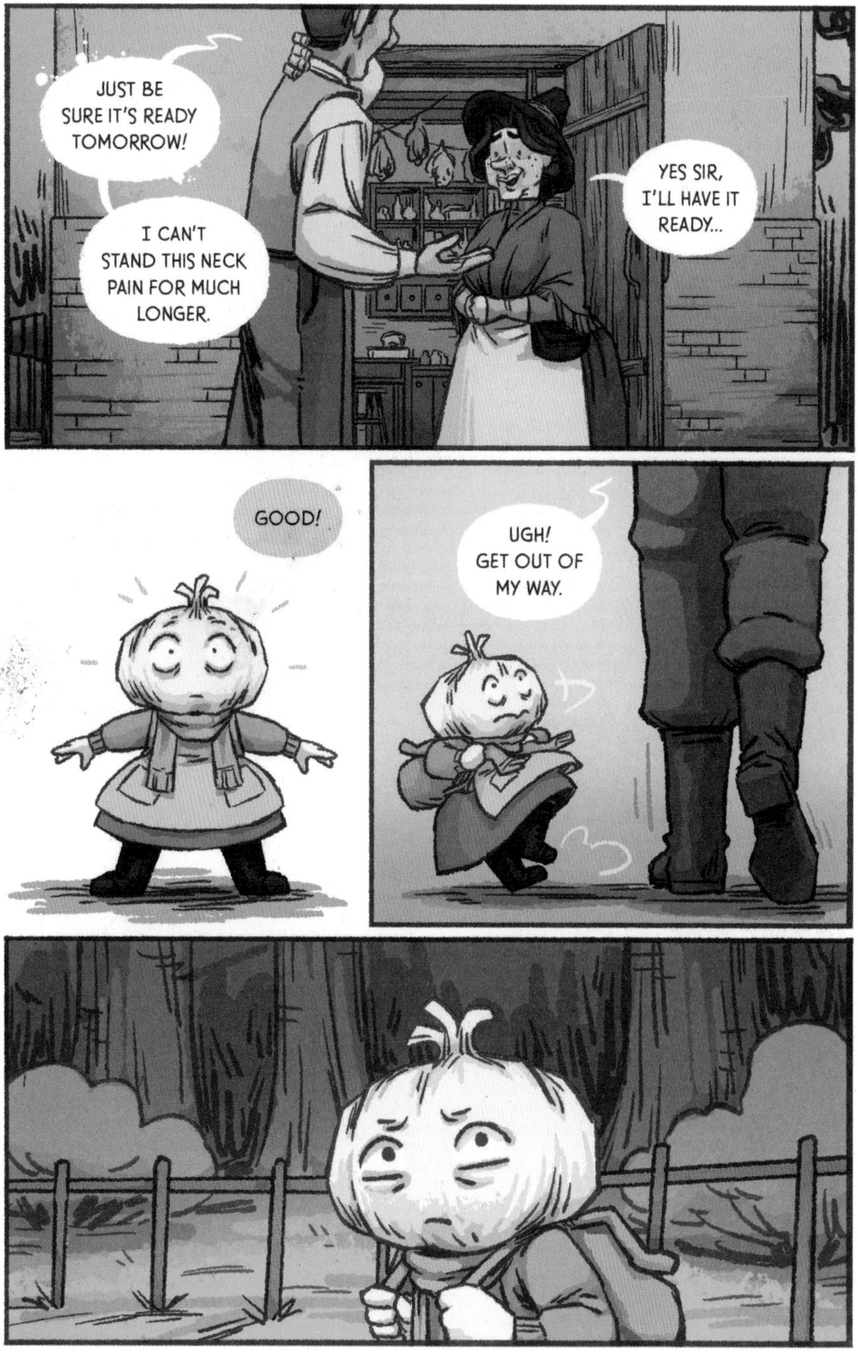
JUST BE SURE IT'S READY TOMORROW!
I CAN'T STAND THIS NECK PAIN FOR MUCH LONGER.
YES SIR, I'LL HAVE IT READY...
GOOD!
UGH! GET OUT OF MY WAY.

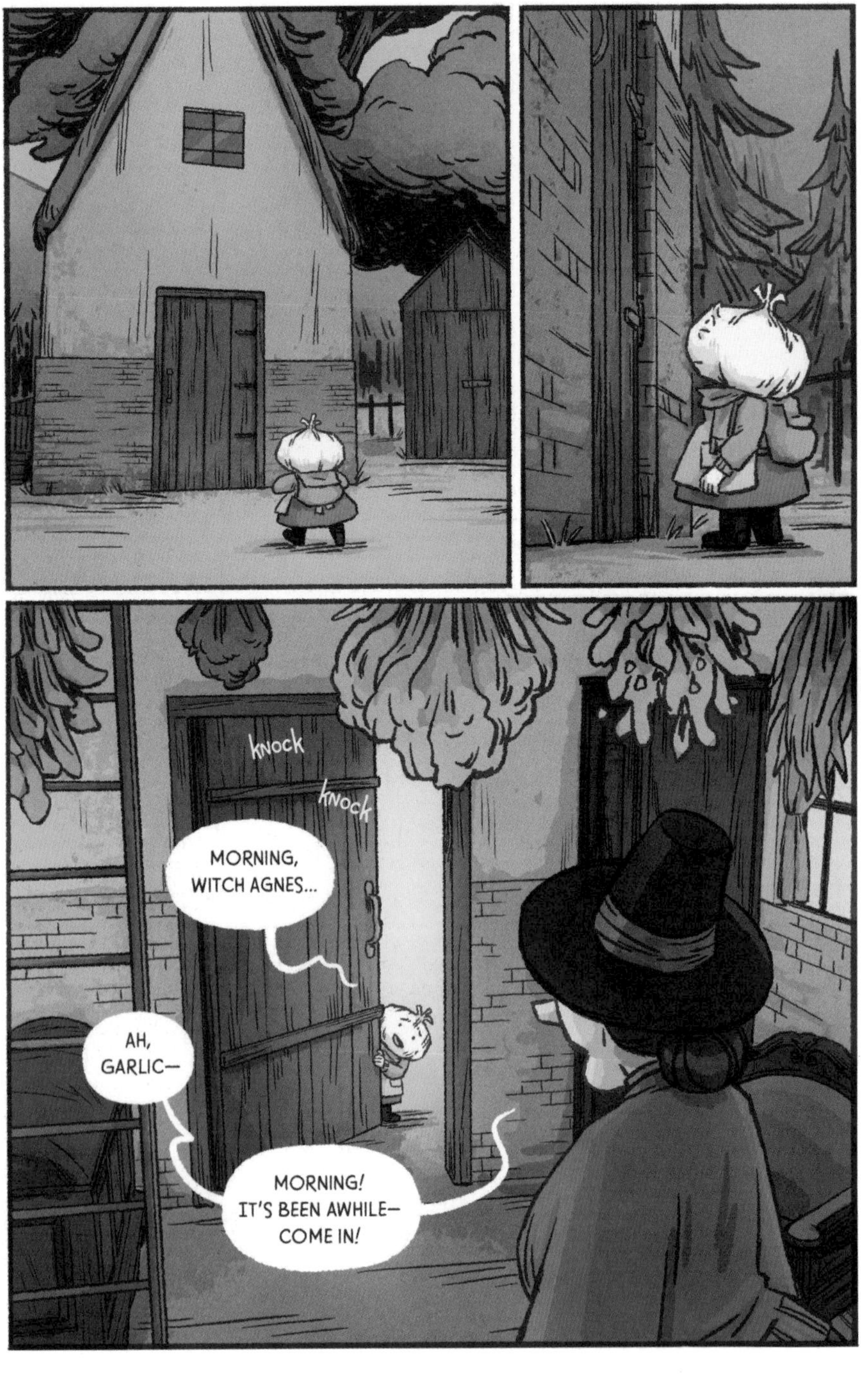
KNOCK
KNOCK
MORNING, WITCH AGNES...
AH, GARLIC—
MORNING! IT'S BEEN AWHILE— COME IN!

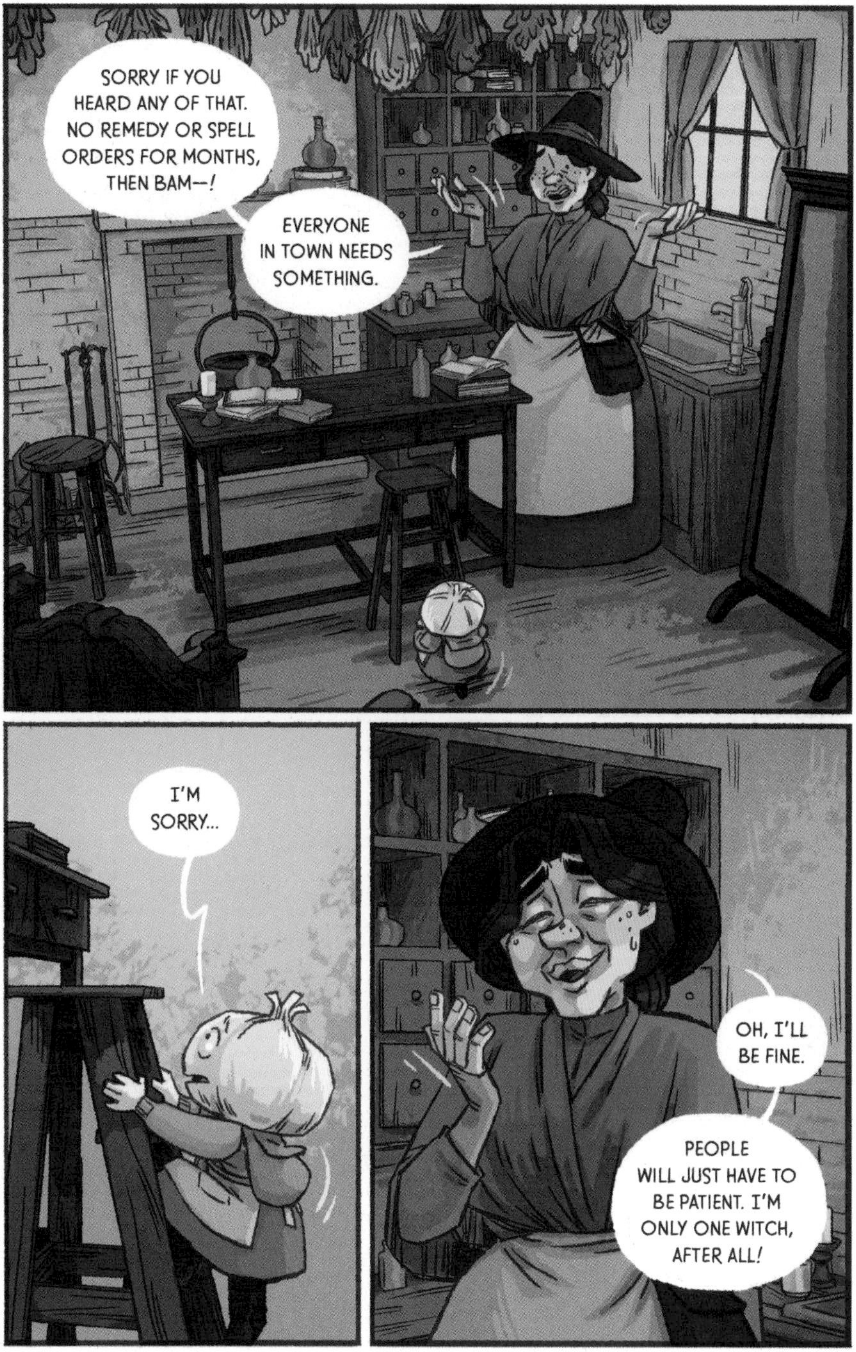
SORRY IF YOU HEARD ANY OF THAT. NO REMEDY OR SPELL ORDERS FOR MONTHS, THEN BAM—!
EVERYONE IN TOWN NEEDS SOMETHING.
I'M SORRY...
OH, I'LL BE FINE.
PEOPLE WILL JUST HAVE TO BE PATIENT. I'M ONLY ONE WITCH, AFTER ALL!

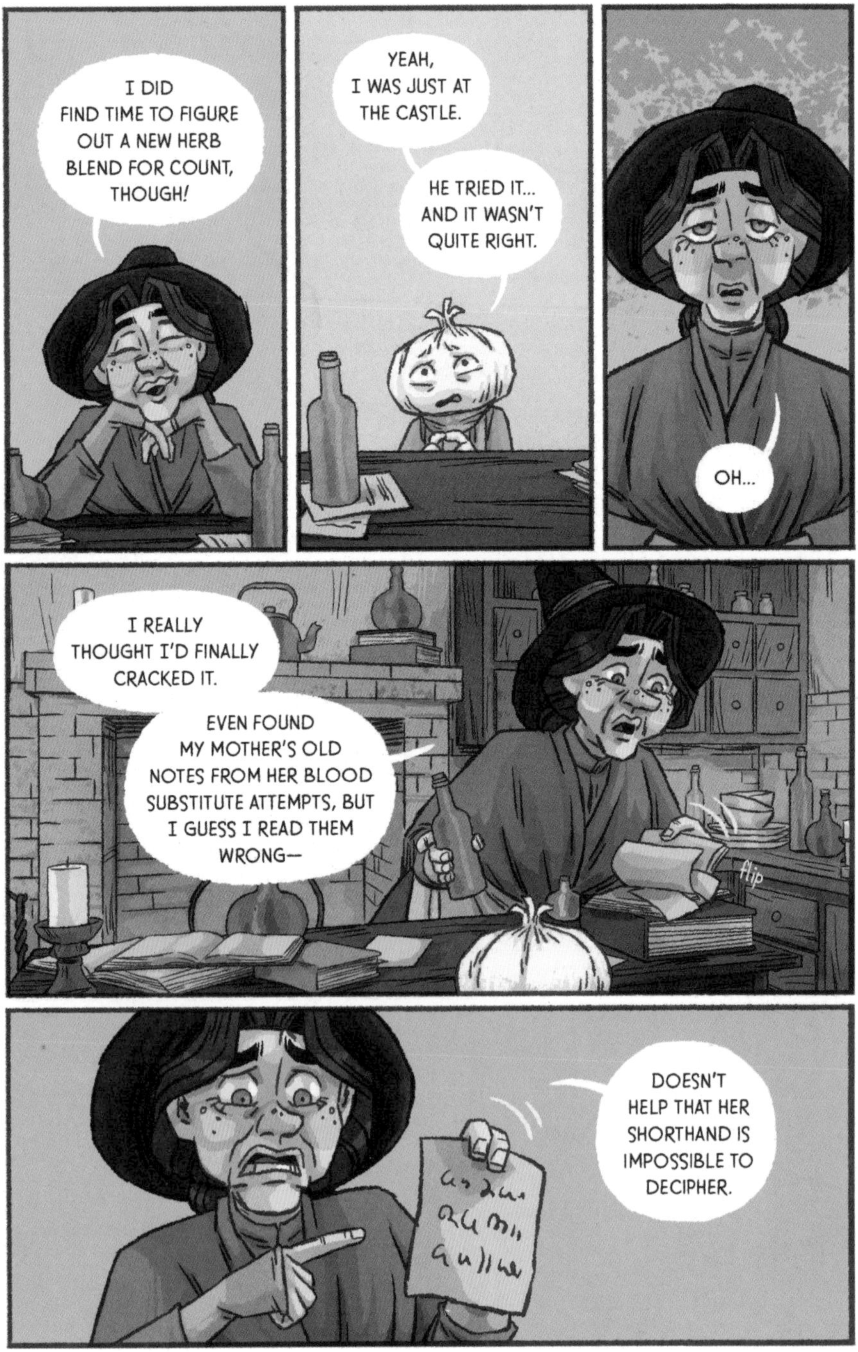
I DID FIND TIME TO FIGURE OUT A NEW HERB BLEND FOR COUNT, THOUGH!
YEAH, I WAS JUST AT THE CASTLE.
HE TRIED IT... AND IT WASN'T QUITE RIGHT.
OH...
I REALLY THOUGHT I'D FINALLY CRACKED IT.
EVEN FOUND MY MOTHER'S OLD NOTES FROM HER BLOOD SUBSTITUTE ATTEMPTS, BUT I GUESS I READ THEM WRONG—
flip
DOESN'T HELP THAT HER SHORTHAND IS IMPOSSIBLE TO DECIPHER.

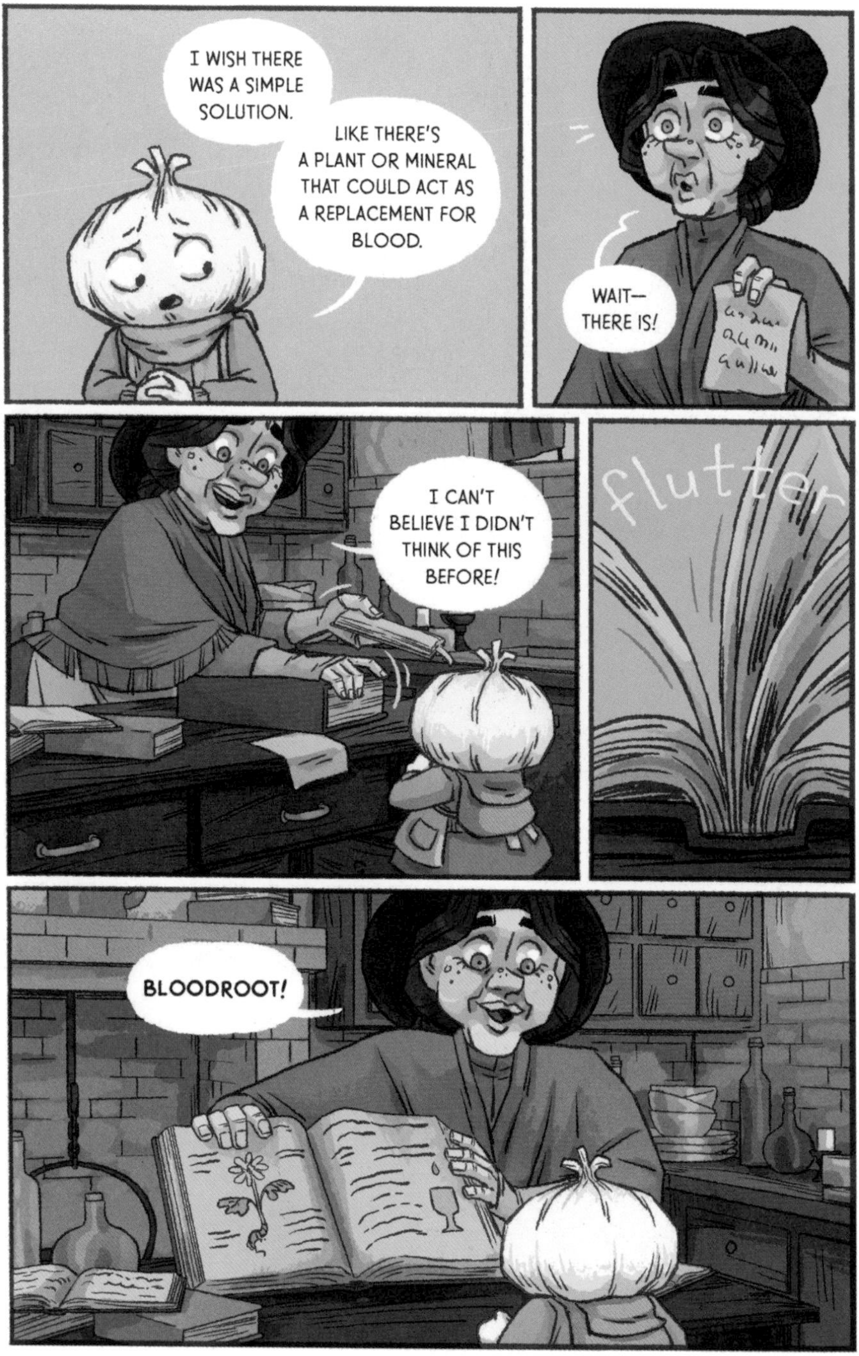
I WISH THERE WAS A SIMPLE SOLUTION.
LIKE THERE'S A PLANT OR MINERAL THAT COULD ACT AS A REPLACEMENT FOR BLOOD.
WAIT— THERE IS!
I CAN'T BELIEVE I DIDN'T THINK OF THIS BEFORE!
flutter
BLOODROOT!

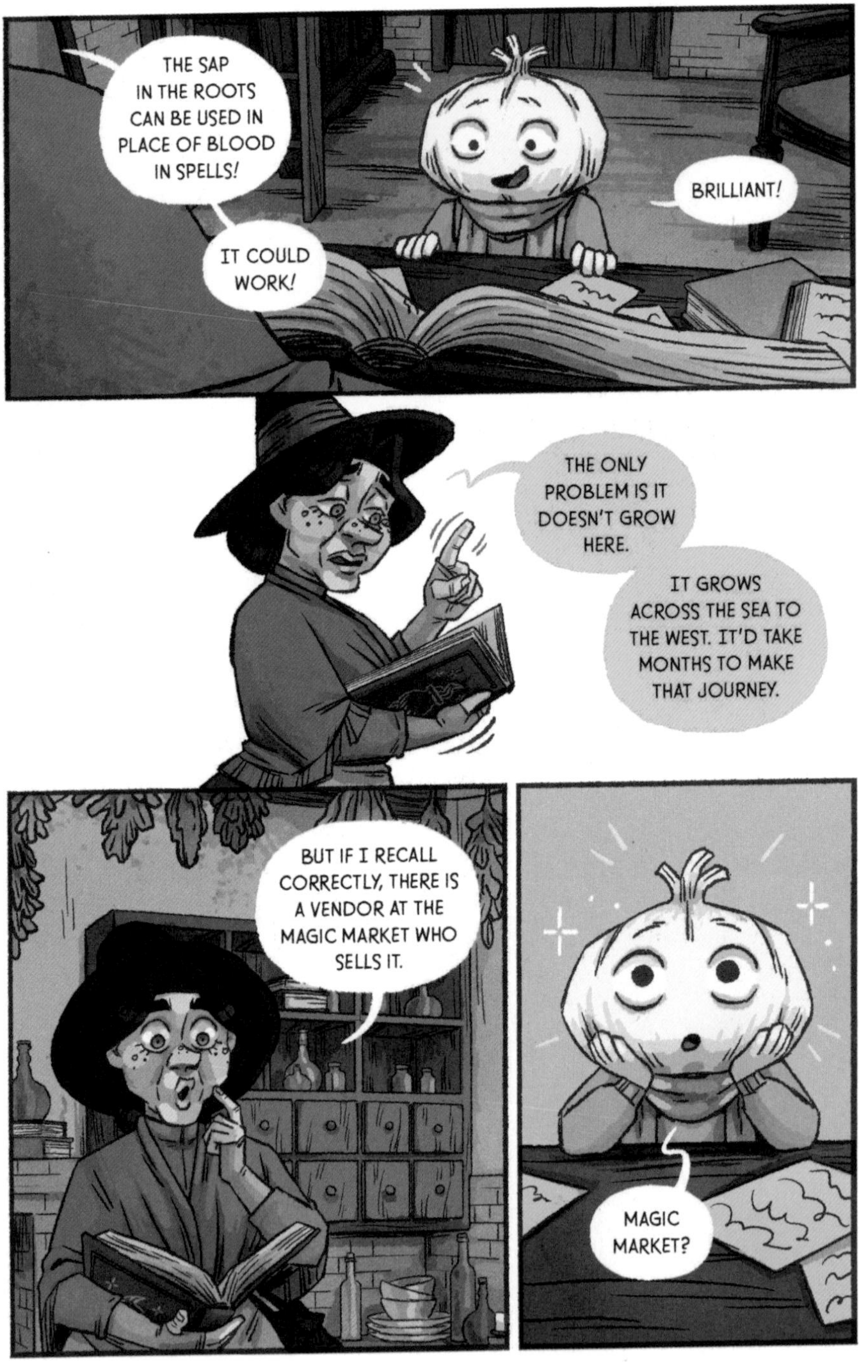
THE SAP IN THE ROOTS CAN BE USED IN PLACE OF BLOOD IN SPELLS!
IT COULD WORK!
BRILLIANT!
THE ONLY PROBLEM IS IT DOESN'T GROW HERE.
IT GROWS ACROSS THE SEA TO THE WEST. IT'D TAKE MONTHS TO MAKE THAT JOURNEY.
BUT IF I RECALL CORRECTLY, THERE IS A VENDOR AT THE MAGIC MARKET WHO SELLS IT.
MAGIC MARKET?

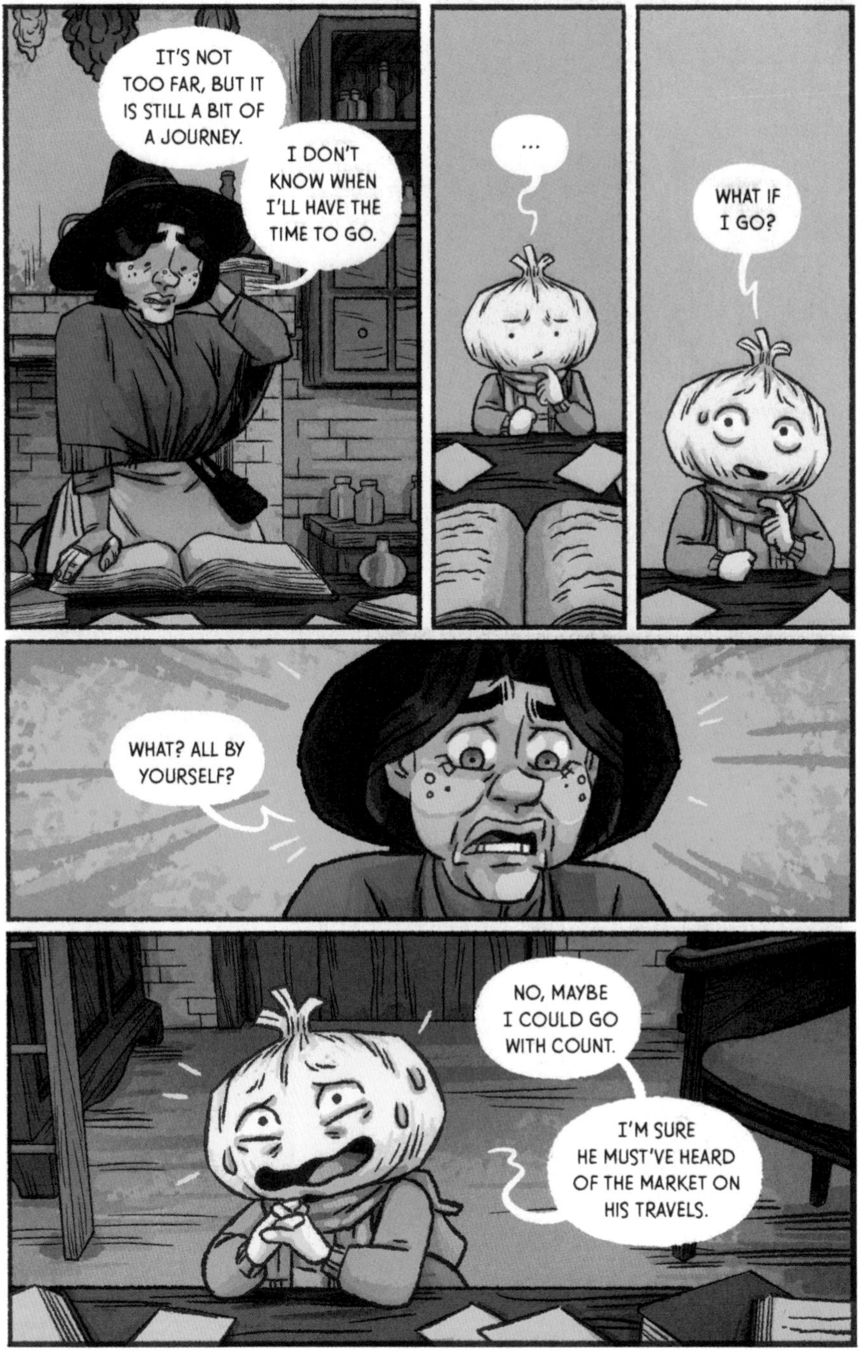
IT'S NOT TOO FAR, BUT IT IS STILL A BIT OF A JOURNEY.
I DON'T KNOW WHEN I'LL HAVE THE TIME TO GO.
...
WHAT IF I GO?
WHAT? ALL BY YOURSELF?
NO, MAYBE I COULD GO WITH COUNT.
I'M SURE HE MUST'VE HEARD OF THE MARKET ON HIS TRAVELS.

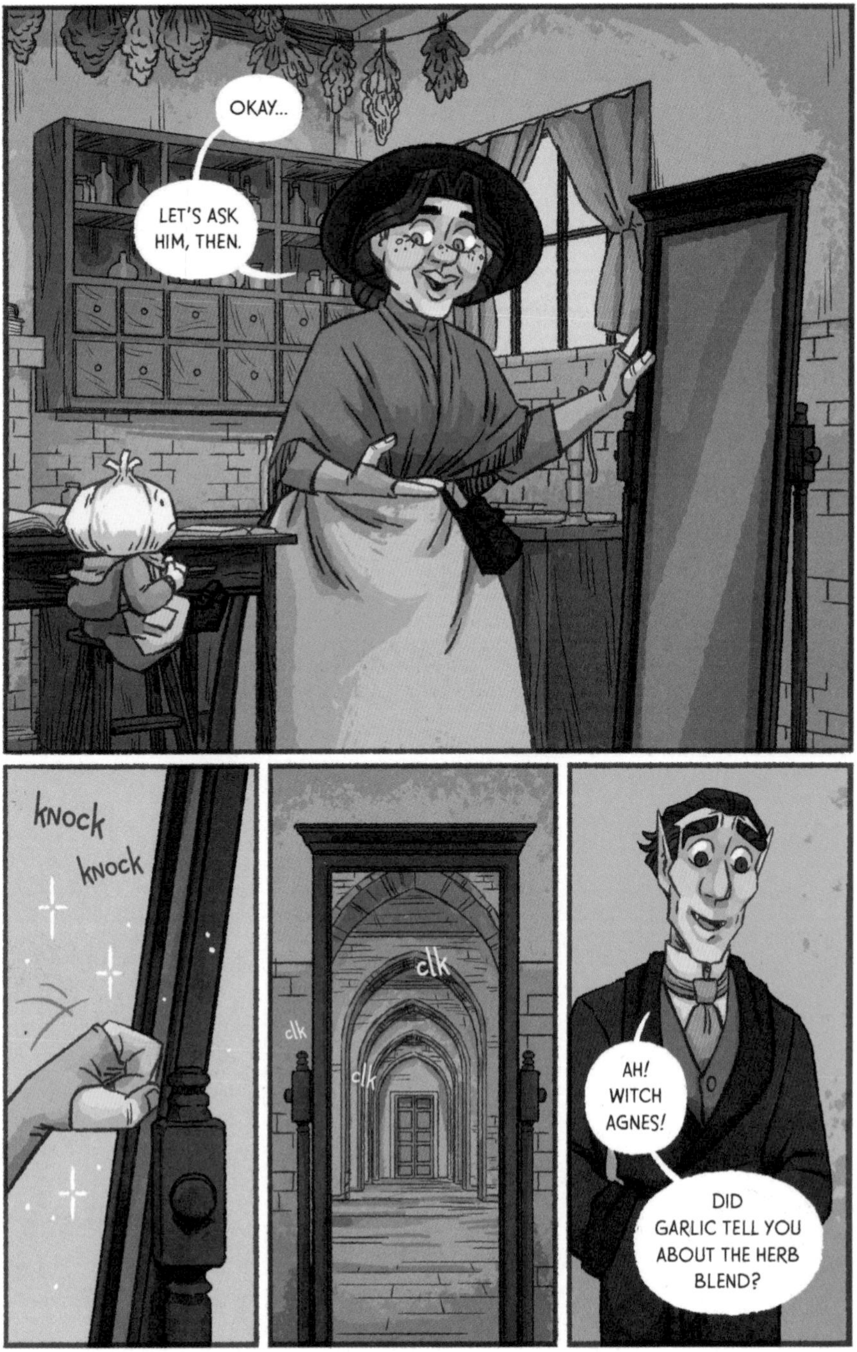
OKAY...
LET'S ASK HIM, THEN.
knock
knock
clk
clk
clk
AH! WITCH AGNES!
DID GARLIC TELL YOU ABOUT THE HERB BLEND?

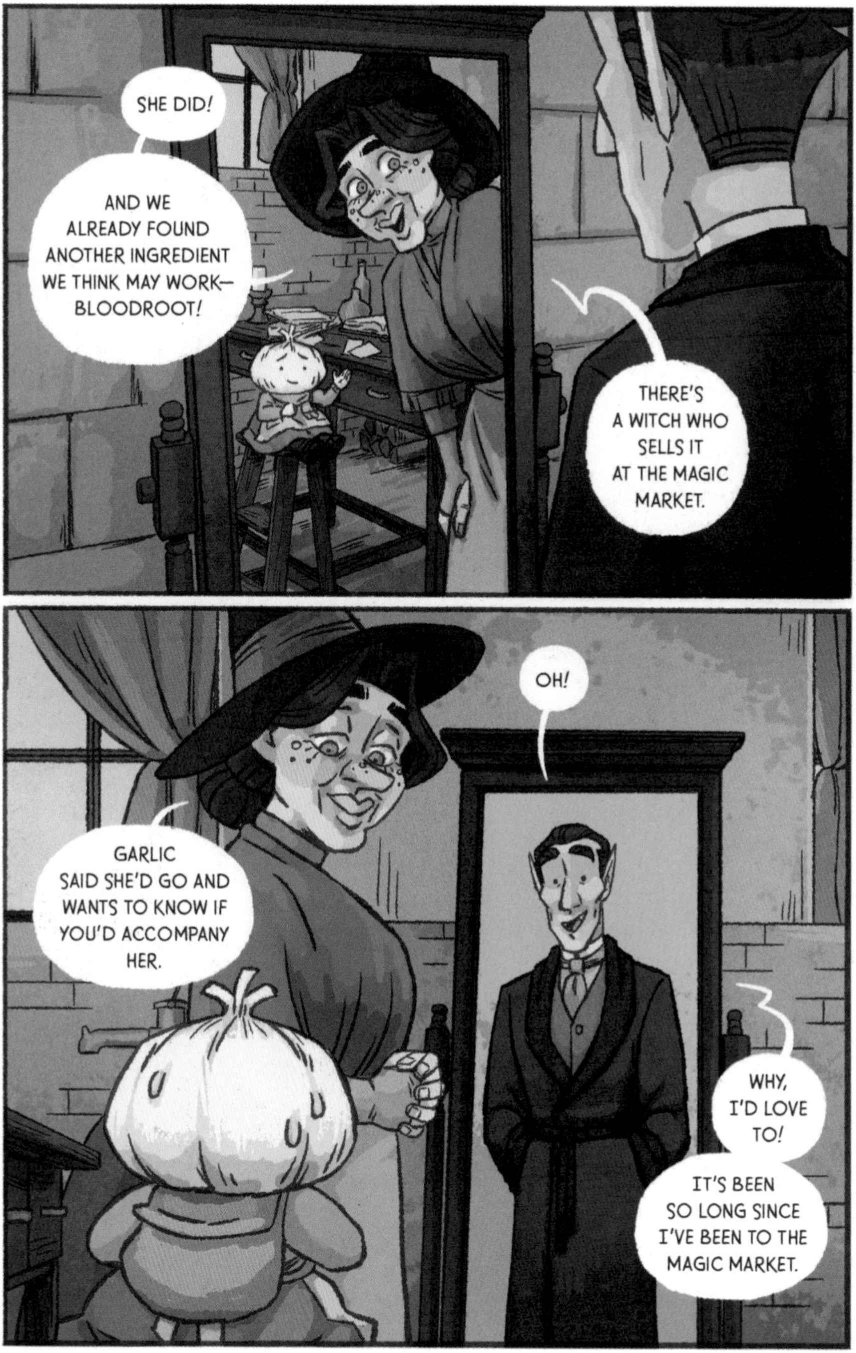
SHE DID!
AND WE ALREADY FOUND ANOTHER INGREDIENT WE THINK MAY WORK—BLOODROOT!
THERE'S A WITCH WHO SELLS IT AT THE MAGIC MARKET.
OH!
GARLIC SAID SHE'D GO AND WANTS TO KNOW IF YOU'D ACCOMPANY HER.
WHY, I'D LOVE TO!
IT'S BEEN SO LONG SINCE I'VE BEEN TO THE MAGIC MARKET.

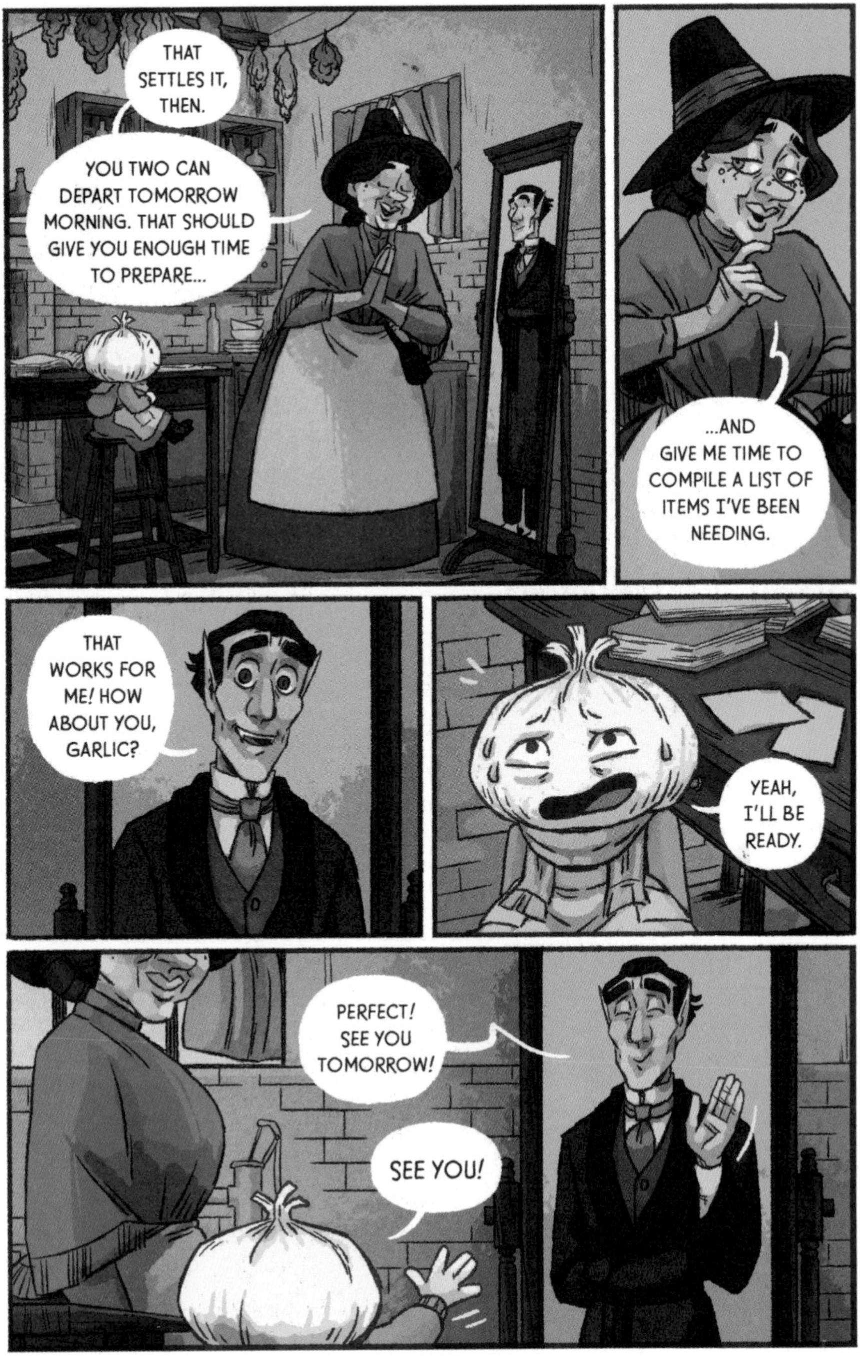
THAT SETTLES IT, THEN.
YOU TWO CAN DEPART TOMORROW MORNING. THAT SHOULD GIVE YOU ENOUGH TIME TO PREPARE...
...AND GIVE ME TIME TO COMPILE A LIST OF ITEMS I'VE BEEN NEEDING.
THAT WORKS FOR ME! HOW ABOUT YOU, GARLIC?
YEAH, I'LL BE READY.
PERFECT! SEE YOU TOMORROW!
SEE YOU!

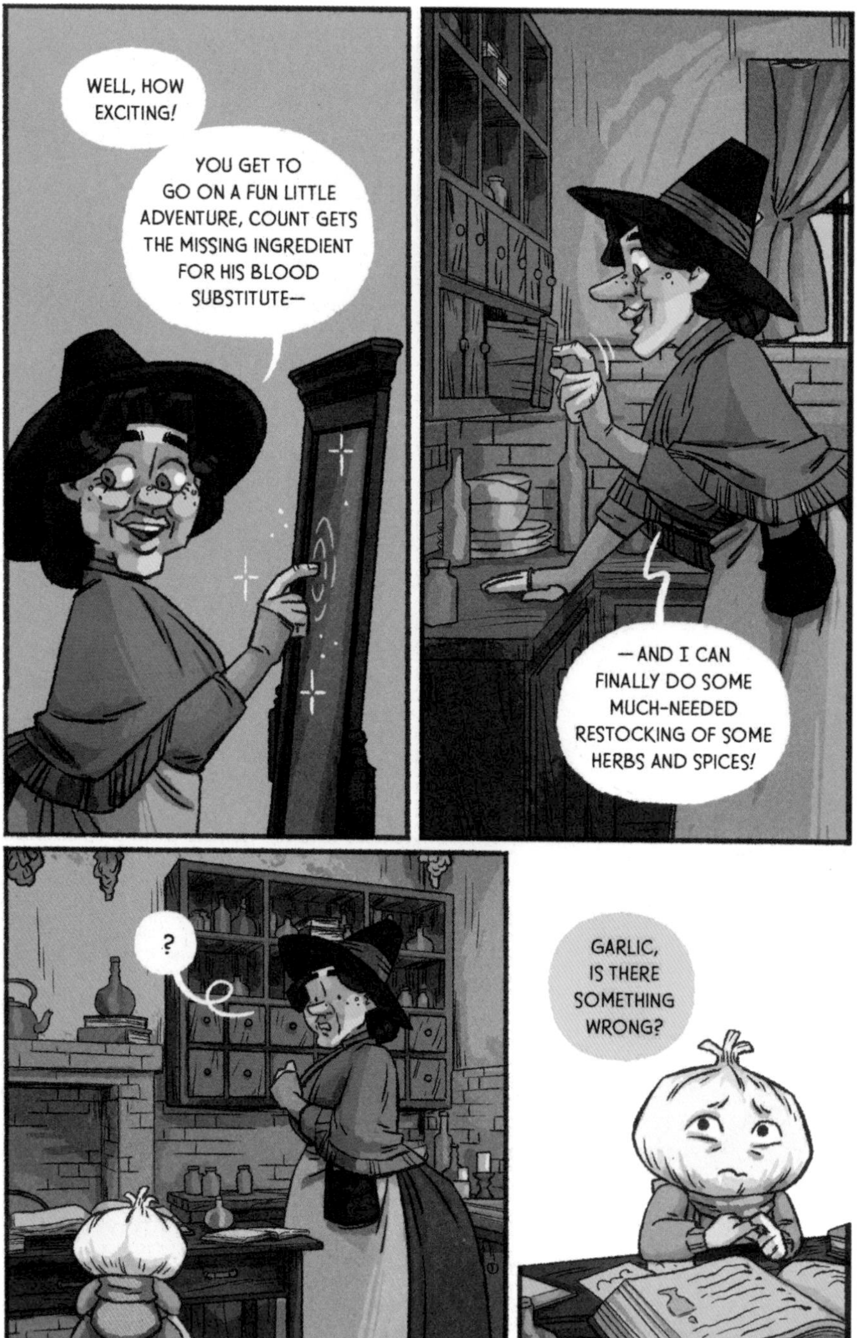
WELL, HOW EXCITING!
YOU GET TO GO ON A FUN LITTLE ADVENTURE, COUNT GETS THE MISSING INGREDIENT FOR HIS BLOOD SUBSTITUTE—
—AND I CAN FINALLY DO SOME MUCH-NEEDED RESTOCKING OF SOME HERBS AND SPICES!
?
GARLIC, IS THERE SOMETHING WRONG?

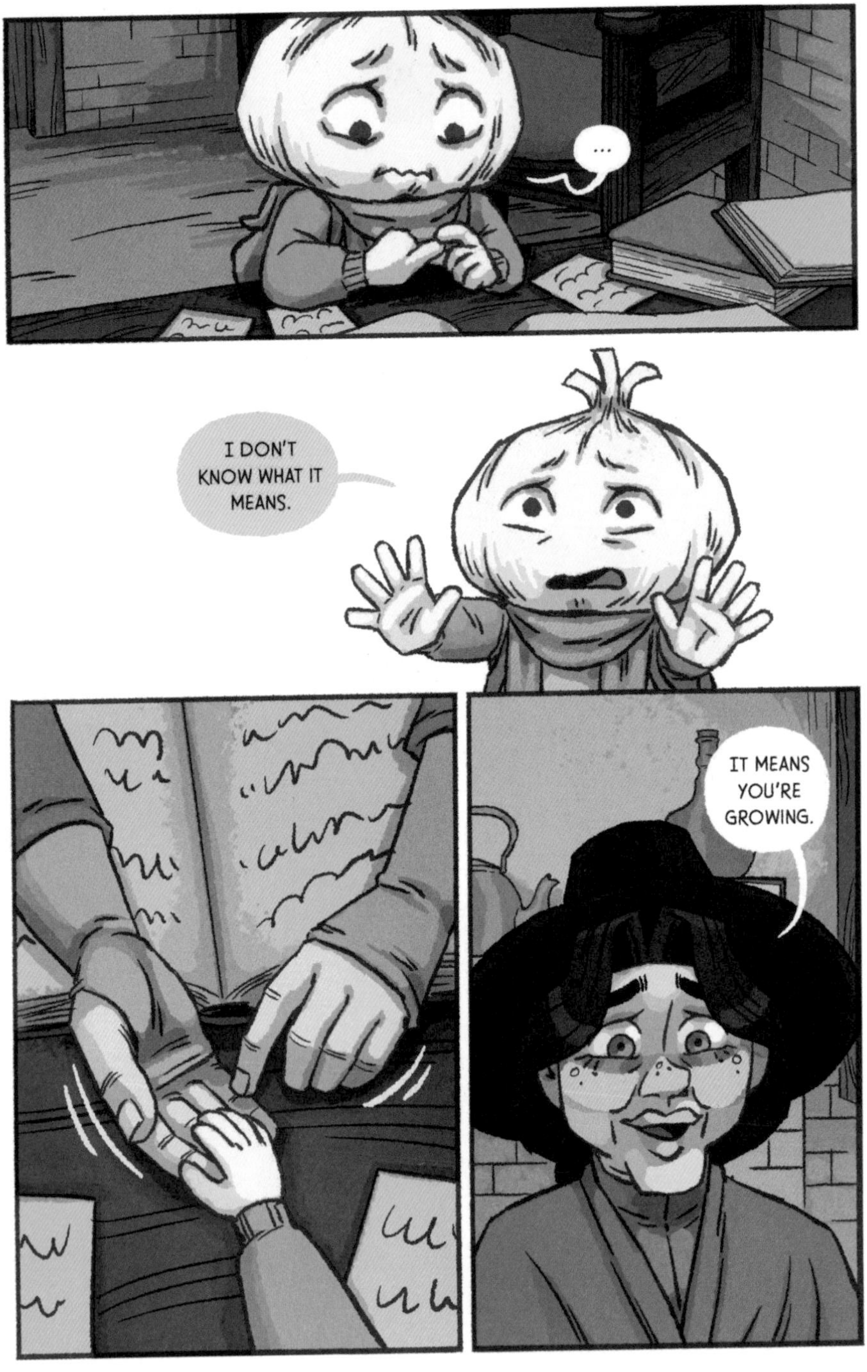
...
I DON'T KNOW WHAT IT MEANS.
IT MEANS YOU'RE GROWING.

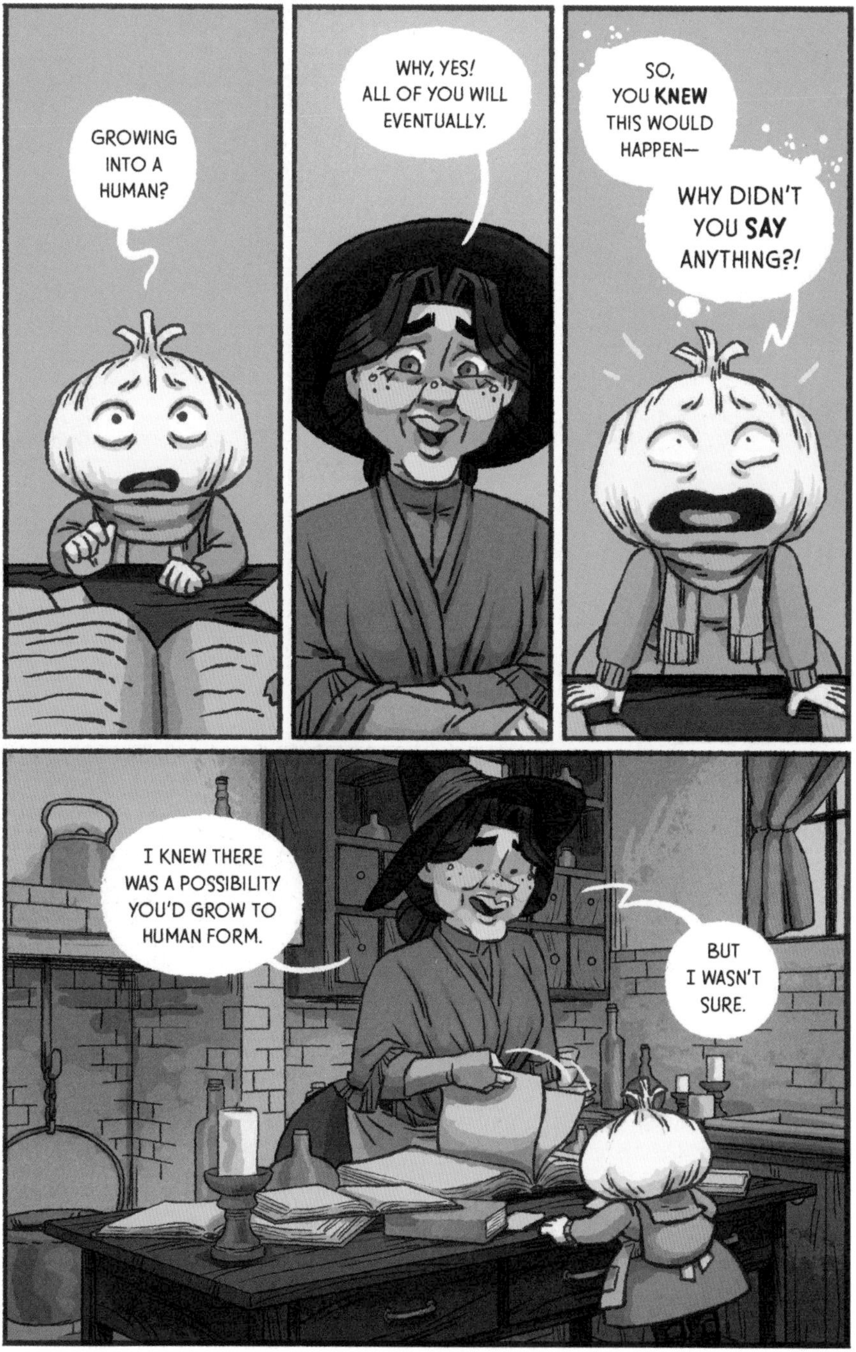
GROWING INTO A HUMAN?
WHY, YES! ALL OF YOU WILL EVENTUALLY.
SO, YOU **KNEW** THIS WOULD HAPPEN—
WHY DIDN'T YOU **SAY** ANYTHING?!
I KNEW THERE WAS A POSSIBILITY YOU'D GROW TO HUMAN FORM.
BUT I WASN'T SURE.

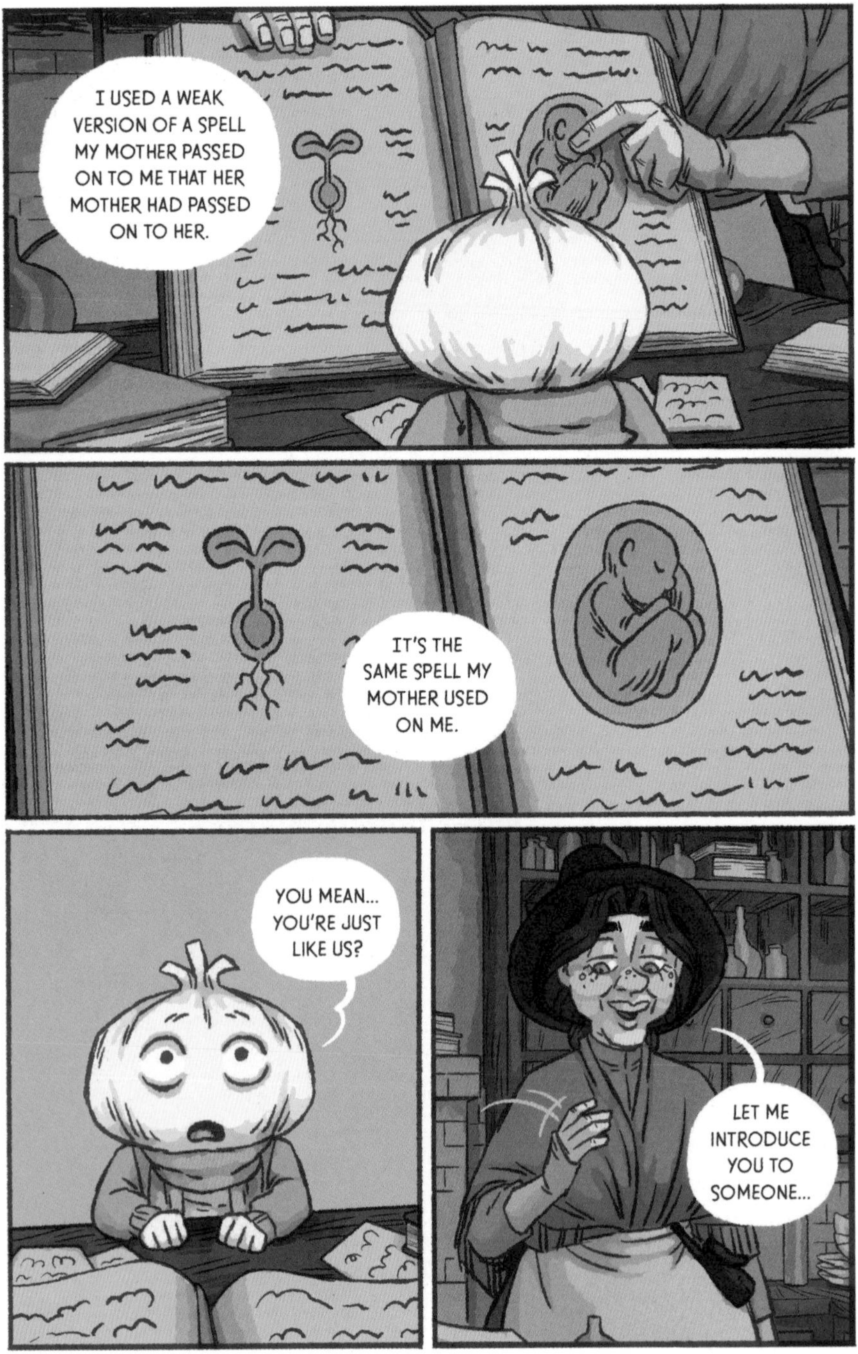
I USED A WEAK VERSION OF A SPELL MY MOTHER PASSED ON TO ME THAT HER MOTHER HAD PASSED ON TO HER.
IT'S THE SAME SPELL MY MOTHER USED ON ME.
YOU MEAN... YOU'RE JUST LIKE US?
LET ME INTRODUCE YOU TO SOMEONE...

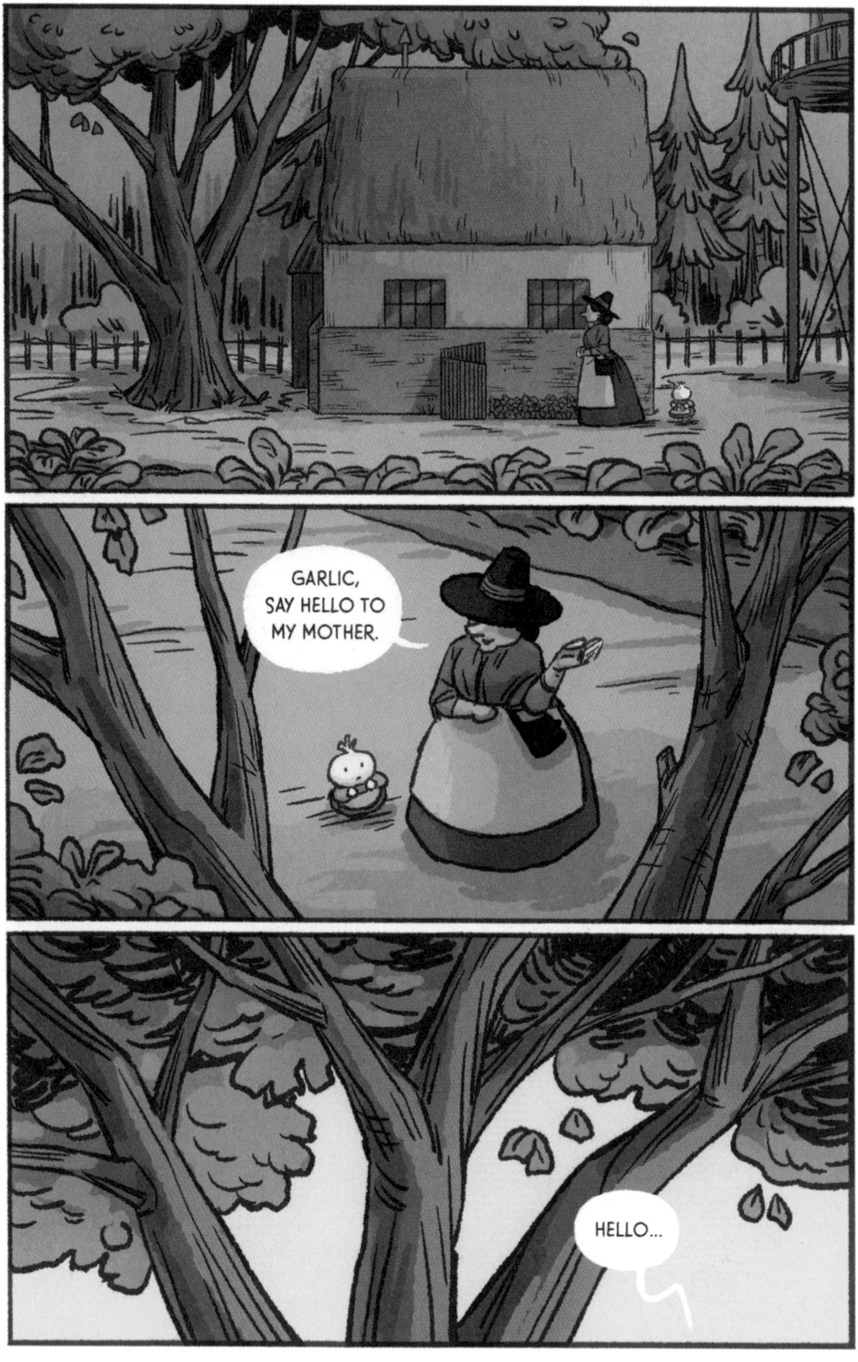
GARLIC,
SAY HELLO TO
MY MOTHER.
HELLO...

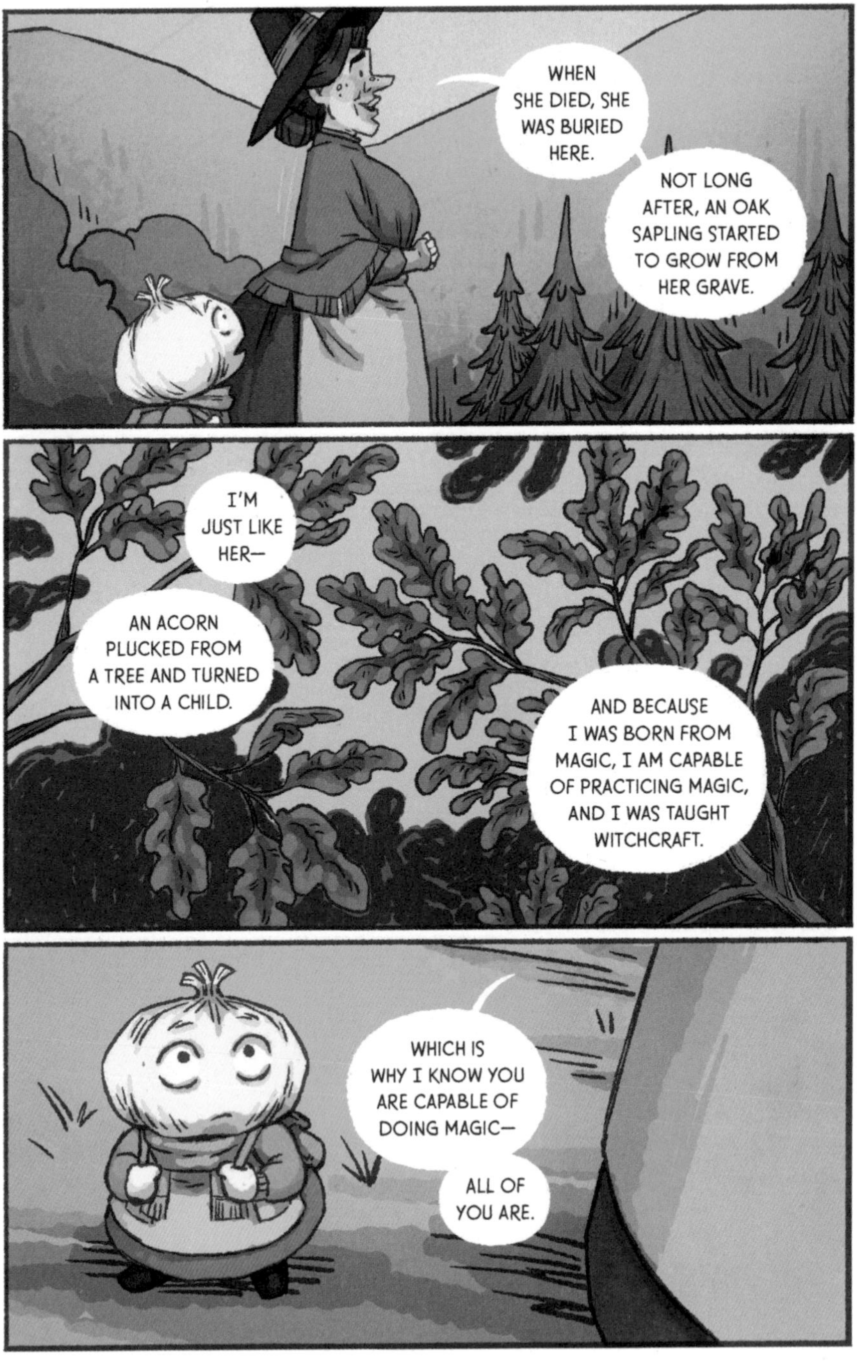
WHEN SHE DIED, SHE WAS BURIED HERE.
NOT LONG AFTER, AN OAK SAPLING STARTED TO GROW FROM HER GRAVE.
I'M JUST LIKE HER—
AN ACORN PLUCKED FROM A TREE AND TURNED INTO A CHILD.
AND BECAUSE I WAS BORN FROM MAGIC, I AM CAPABLE OF PRACTICING MAGIC, AND I WAS TAUGHT WITCHCRAFT.
WHICH IS WHY I KNOW YOU ARE CAPABLE OF DOING MAGIC—
ALL OF YOU ARE.

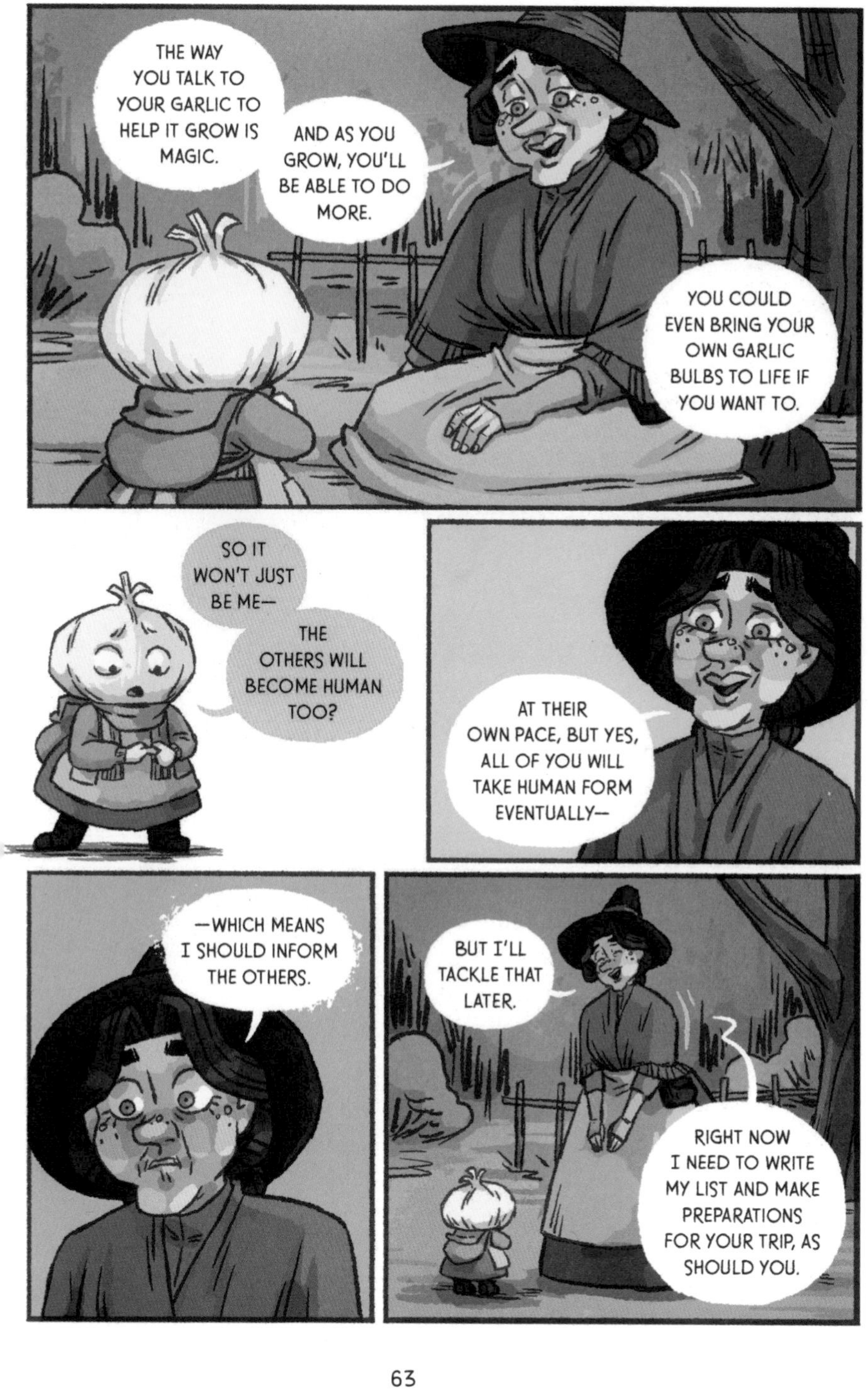

THE WAY YOU TALK TO YOUR GARLIC TO HELP IT GROW IS MAGIC.
AND AS YOU GROW, YOU'LL BE ABLE TO DO MORE.
YOU COULD EVEN BRING YOUR OWN GARLIC BULBS TO LIFE IF YOU WANT TO.
SO IT WON'T JUST BE ME—
THE OTHERS WILL BECOME HUMAN TOO?
AT THEIR OWN PACE, BUT YES, ALL OF YOU WILL TAKE HUMAN FORM EVENTUALLY—
—WHICH MEANS I SHOULD INFORM THE OTHERS.
BUT I'LL TACKLE THAT LATER.
RIGHT NOW I NEED TO WRITE MY LIST AND MAKE PREPARATIONS FOR YOUR TRIP, AS SHOULD YOU.

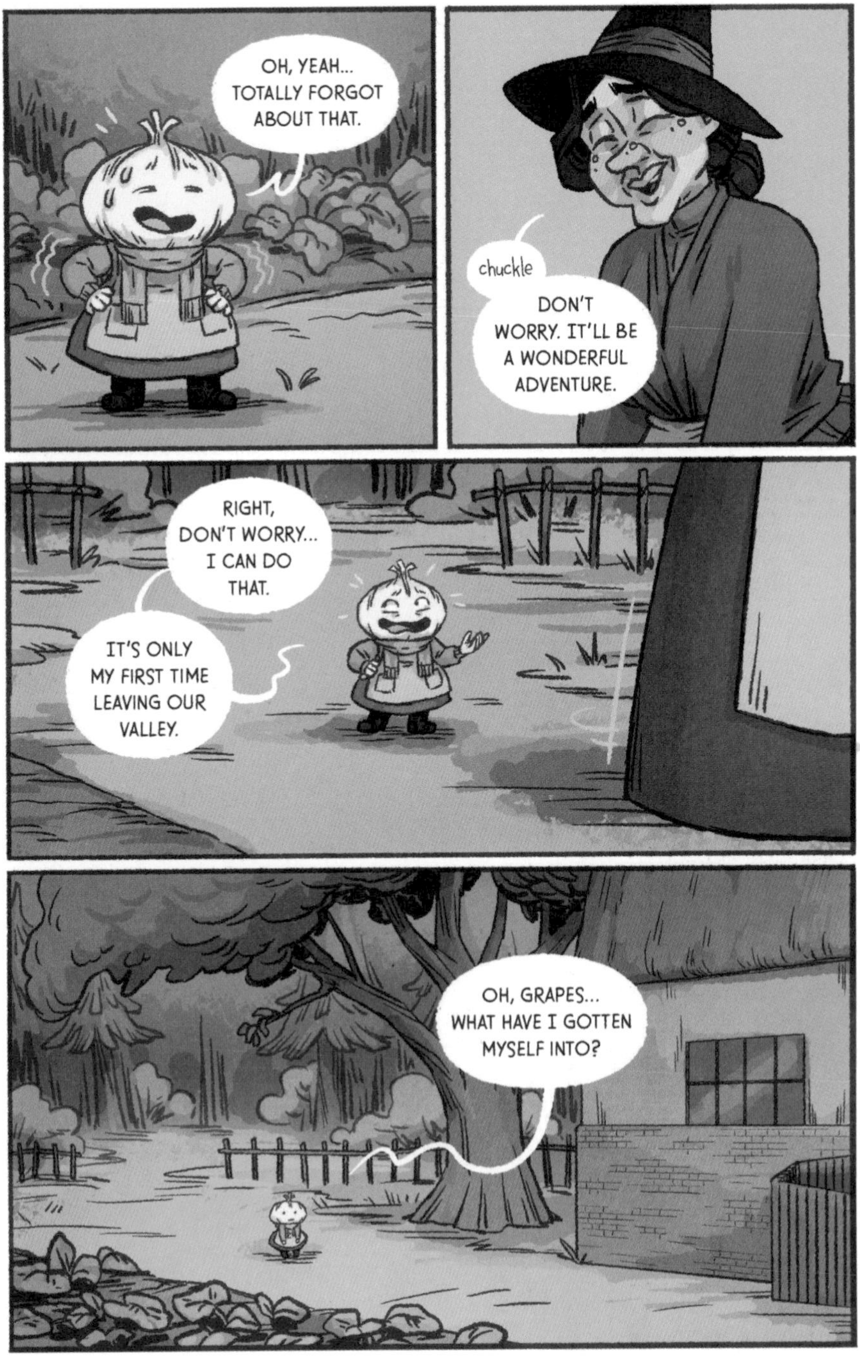
OH, YEAH... TOTALLY FORGOT ABOUT THAT.
chuckle
DON'T WORRY. IT'LL BE A WONDERFUL ADVENTURE.
RIGHT, DON'T WORRY... I CAN DO THAT.
IT'S ONLY MY FIRST TIME LEAVING OUR VALLEY.
OH, GRAPES... WHAT HAVE I GOTTEN MYSELF INTO?

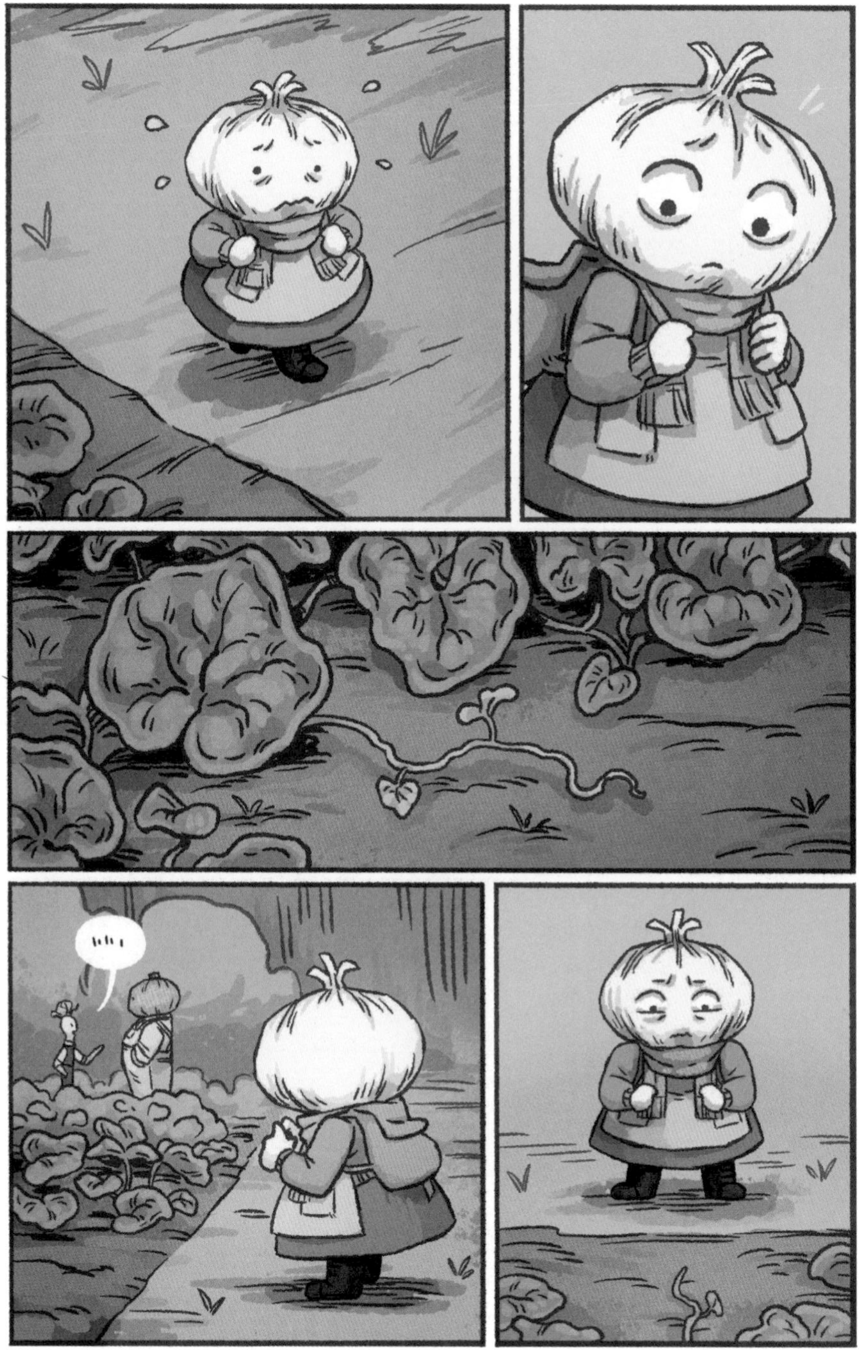

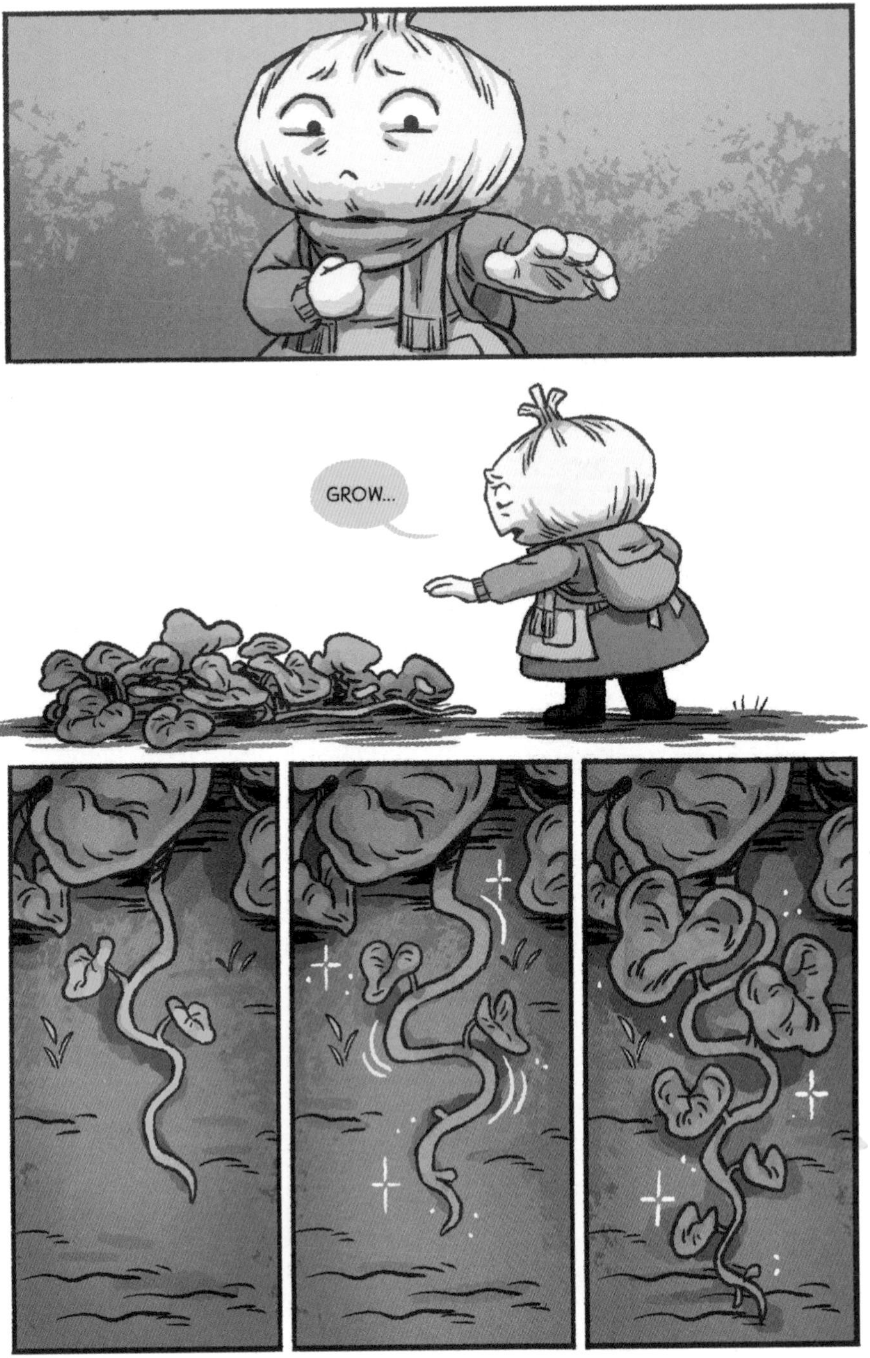
GROW...

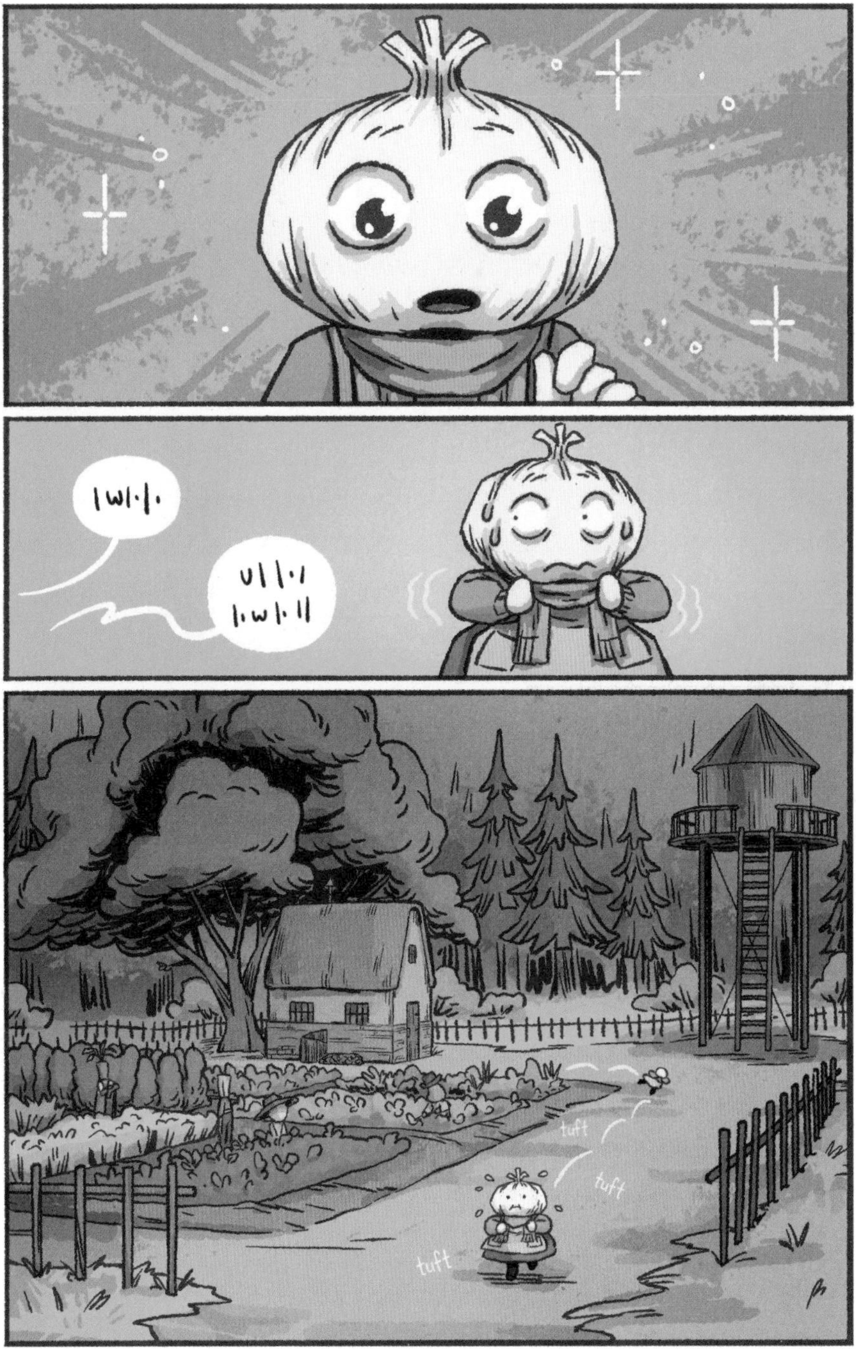
tuft
tuft
tuft

chapter four

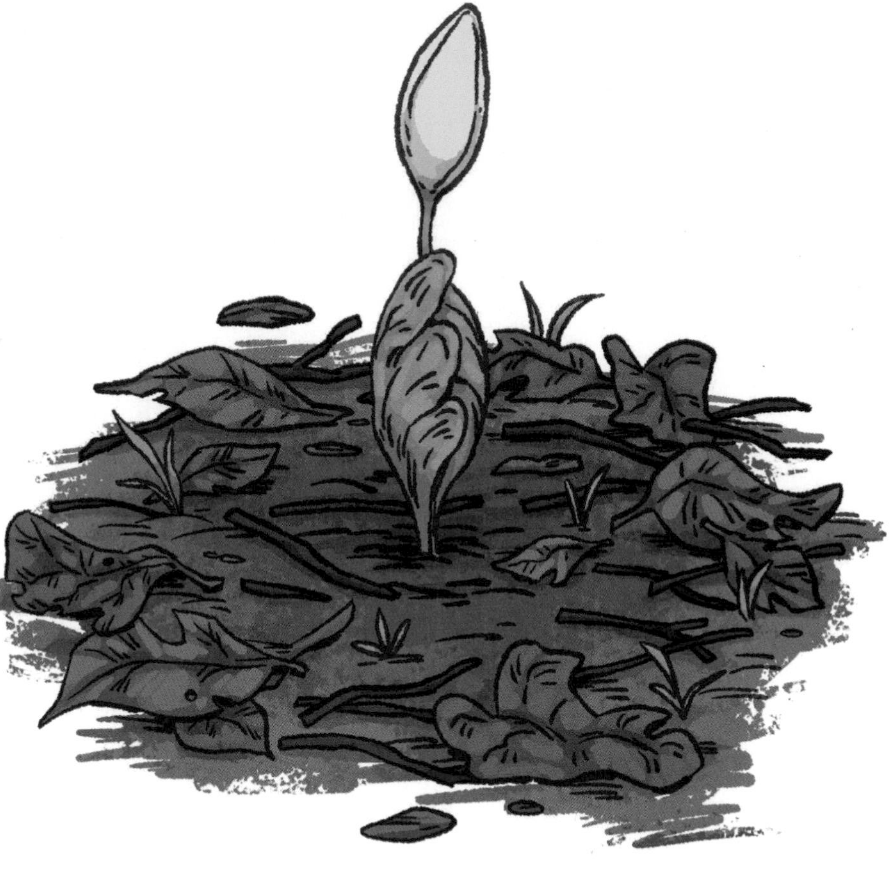

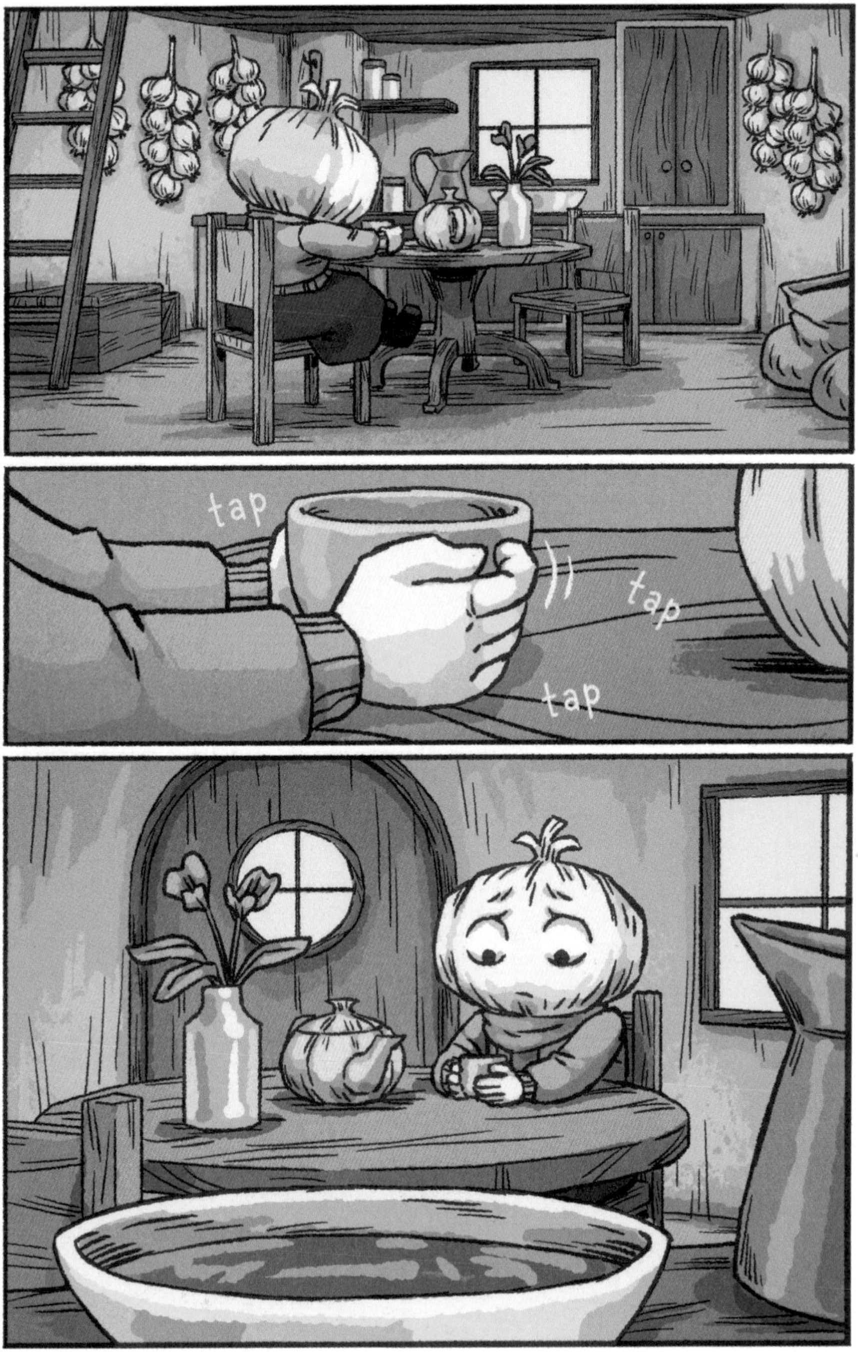
tap
tap
tap

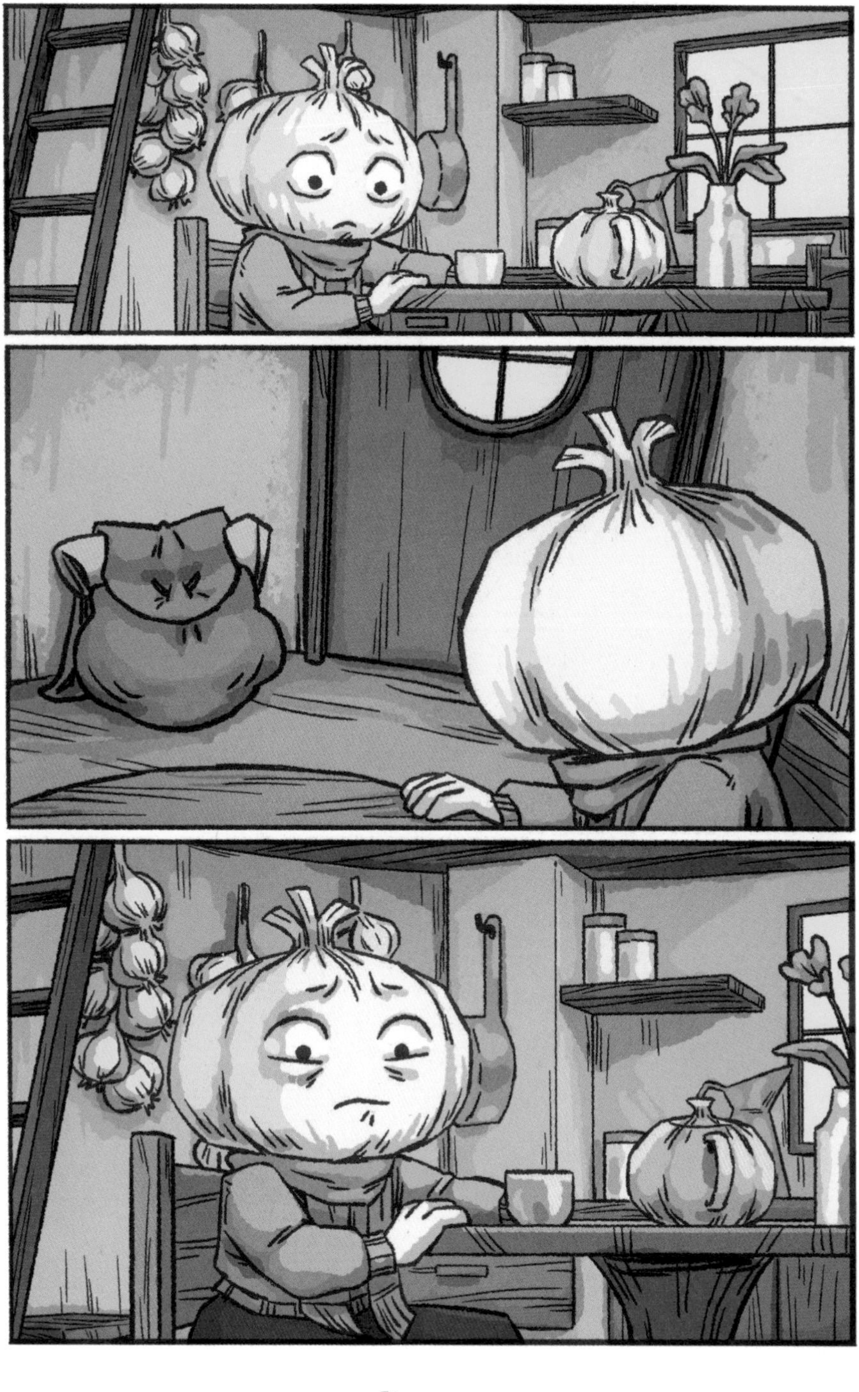

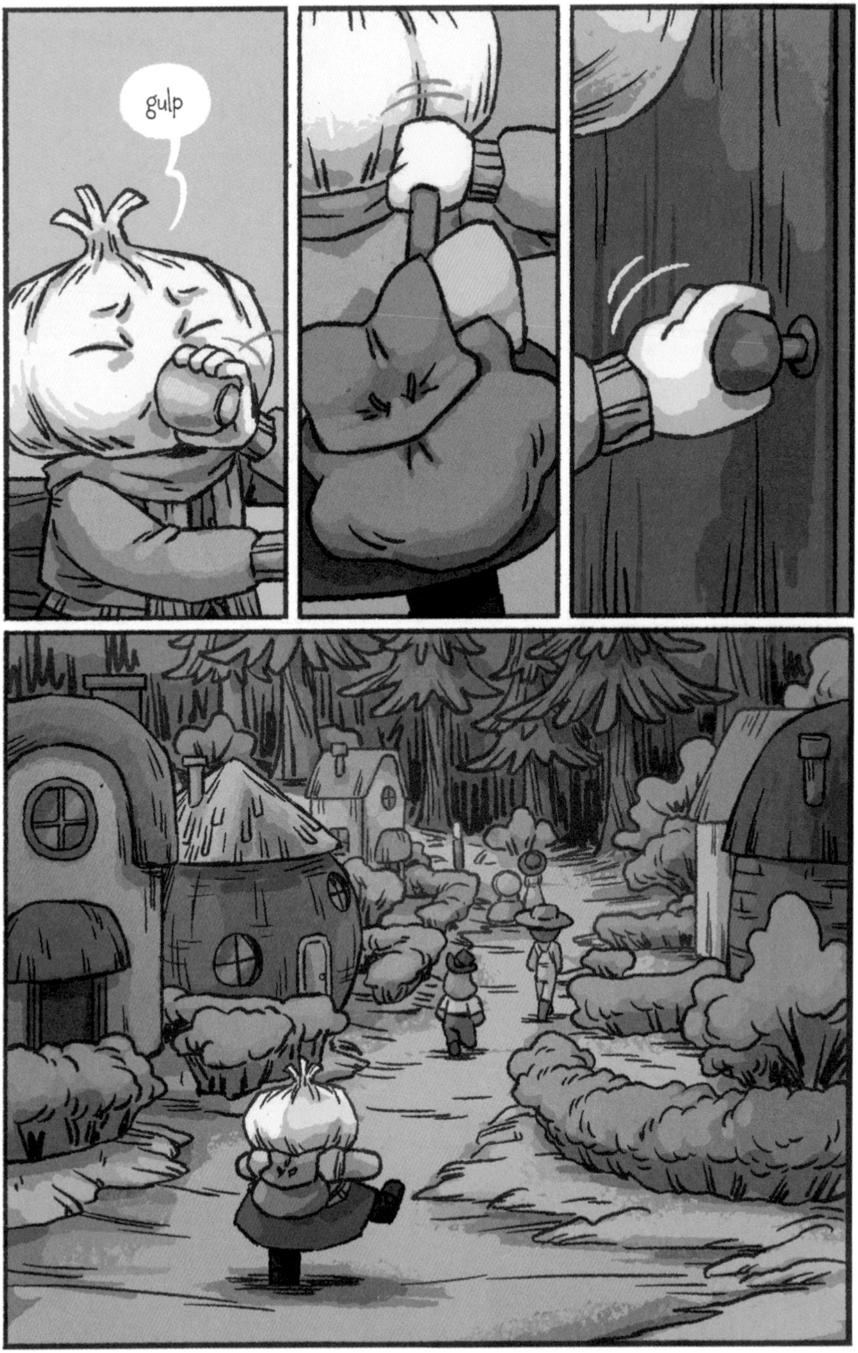
gulp

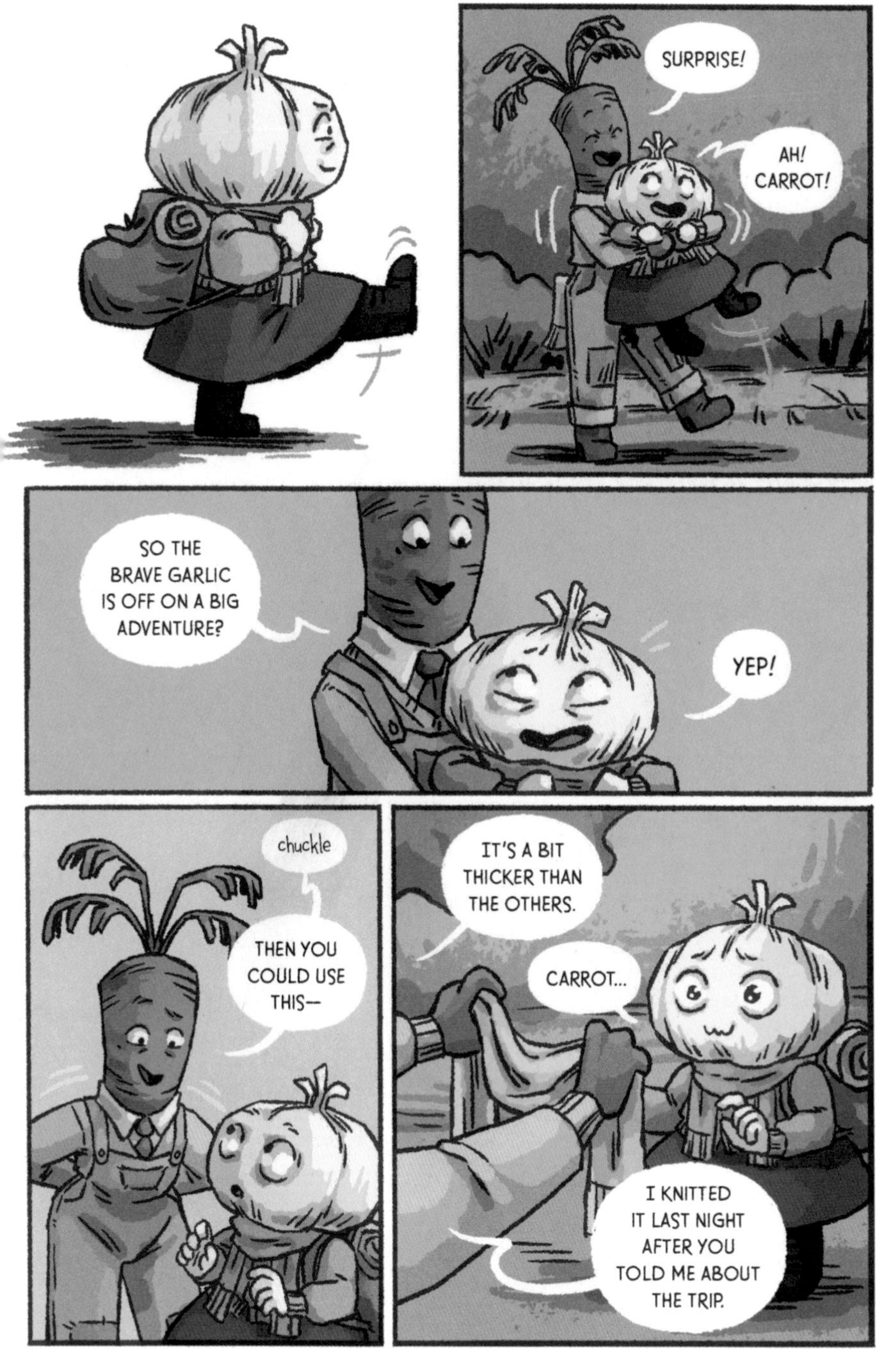
SURPRISE!
AH! CARROT!
SO THE BRAVE GARLIC IS OFF ON A BIG ADVENTURE?
YEP!
chuckle
THEN YOU COULD USE THIS--
IT'S A BIT THICKER THAN THE OTHERS.
CARROT...
I KNITTED IT LAST NIGHT AFTER YOU TOLD ME ABOUT THE TRIP.

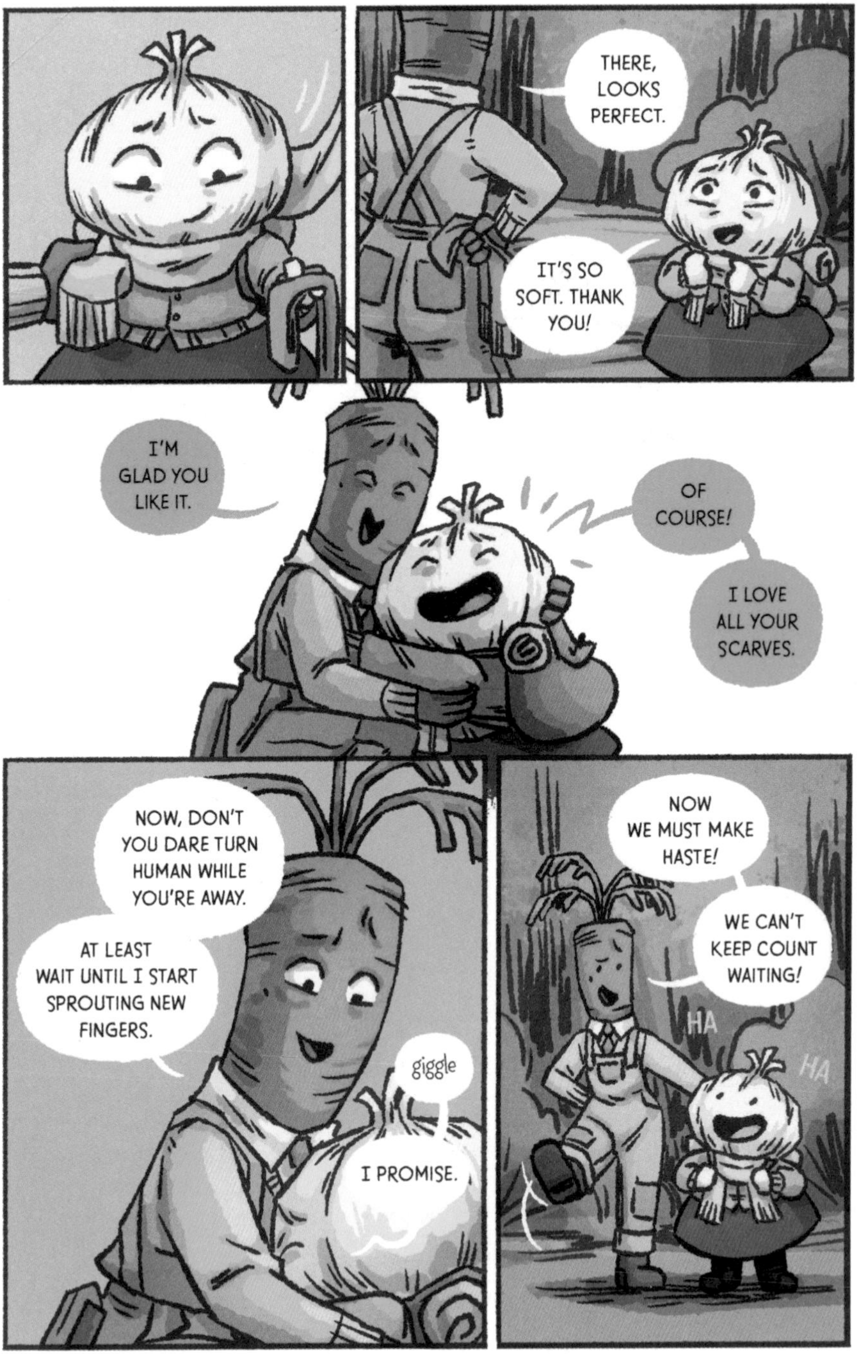
THERE, LOOKS PERFECT.
IT'S SO SOFT. THANK YOU!
I'M GLAD YOU LIKE IT.
OF COURSE!
I LOVE ALL YOUR SCARVES.
NOW, DON'T YOU DARE TURN HUMAN WHILE YOU'RE AWAY.
AT LEAST WAIT UNTIL I START SPROUTING NEW FINGERS.
giggle
I PROMISE.
NOW WE MUST MAKE HASTE!
WE CAN'T KEEP COUNT WAITING!
HA
HA

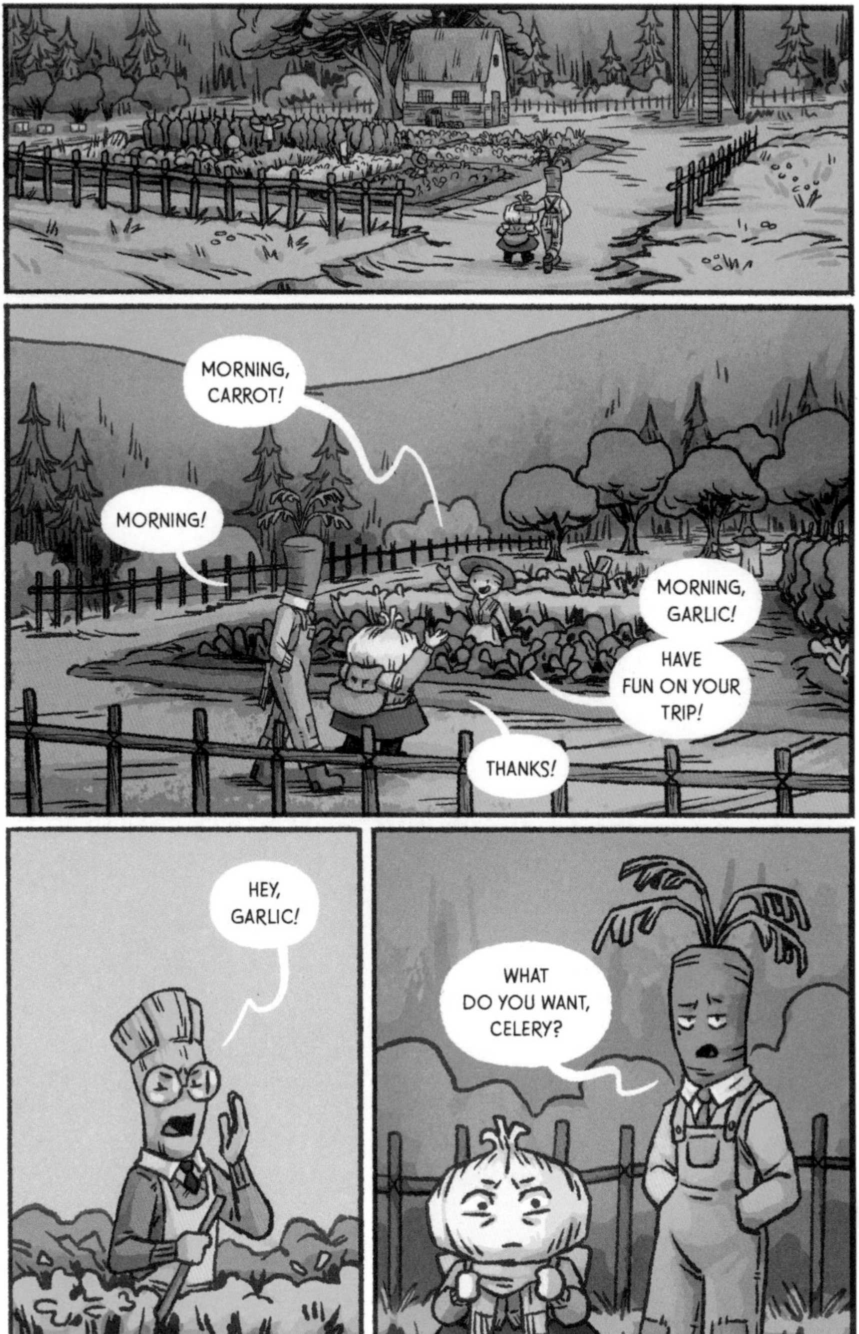
MORNING, CARROT!
MORNING!
MORNING, GARLIC!
HAVE FUN ON YOUR TRIP!
THANKS!
HEY, GARLIC!
WHAT DO YOU WANT, CELERY?

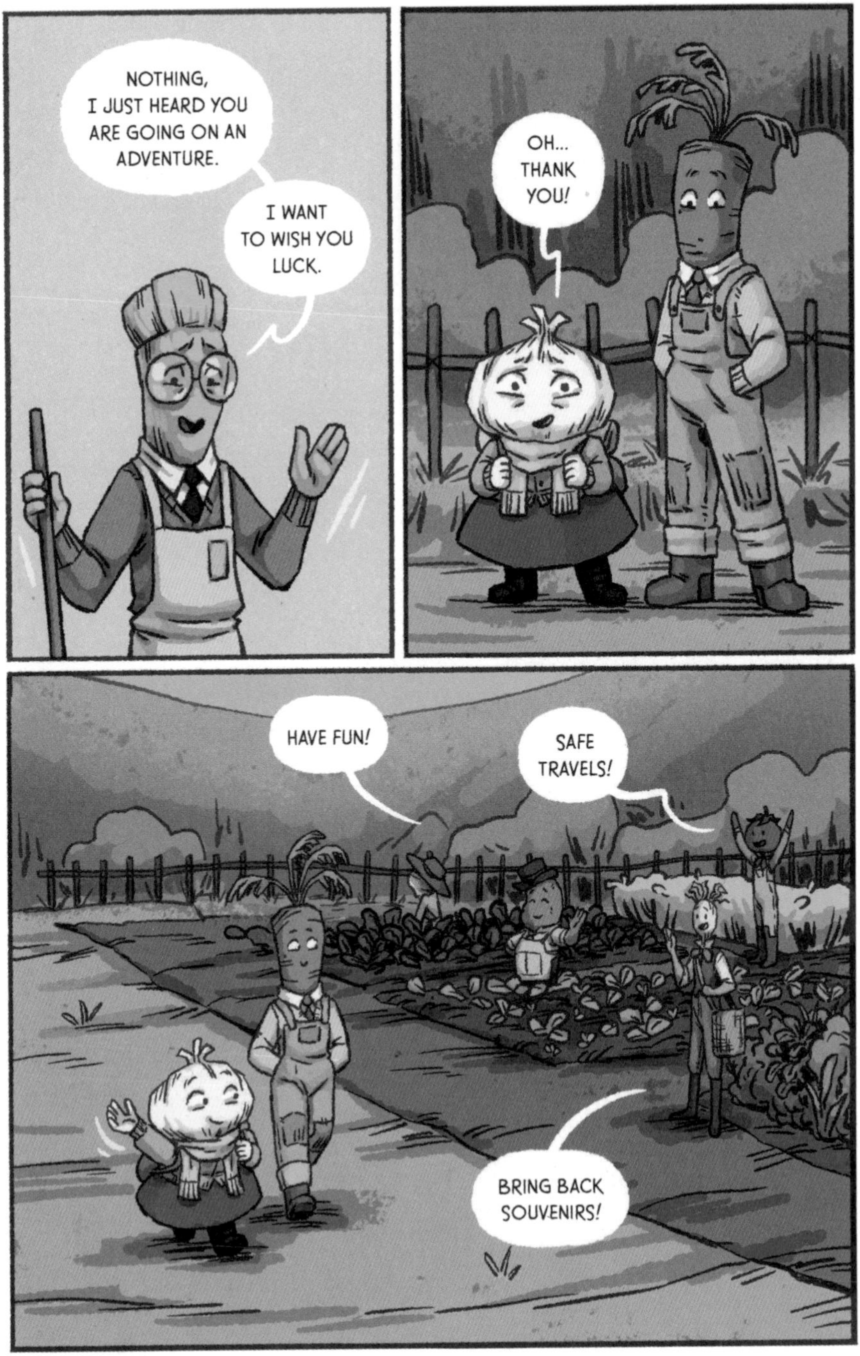
NOTHING, I JUST HEARD YOU ARE GOING ON AN ADVENTURE.
I WANT TO WISH YOU LUCK.
OH... THANK YOU!
HAVE FUN!
SAFE TRAVELS!
BRING BACK SOUVENIRS!

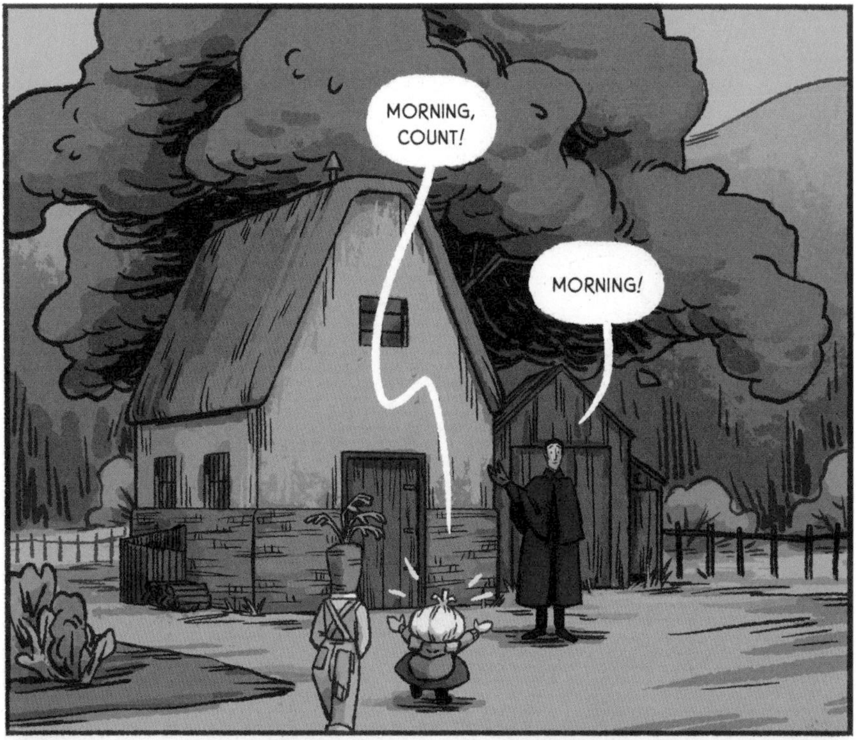
MORNING, COUNT!
MORNING!
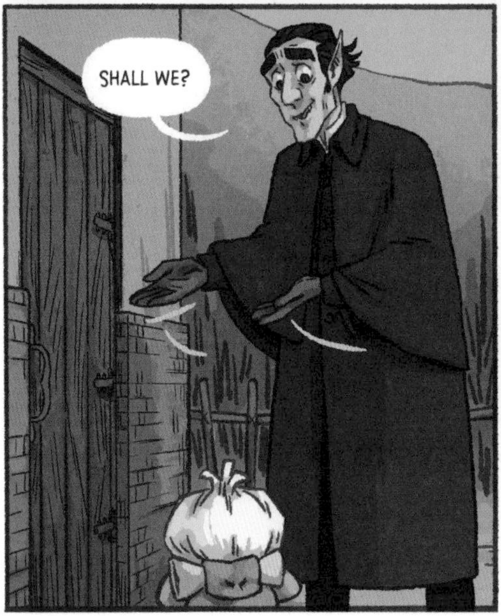
SHALL WE?
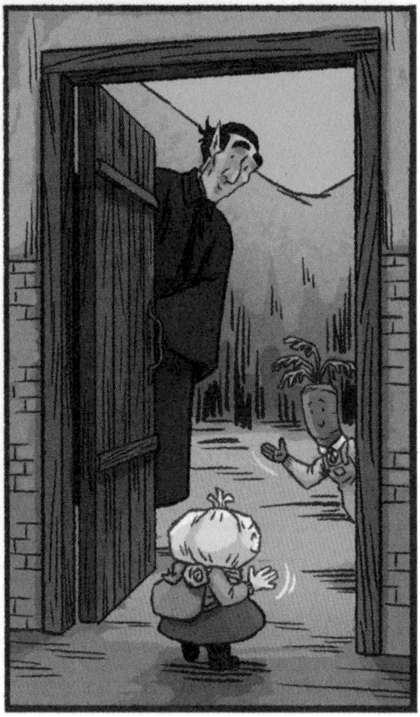

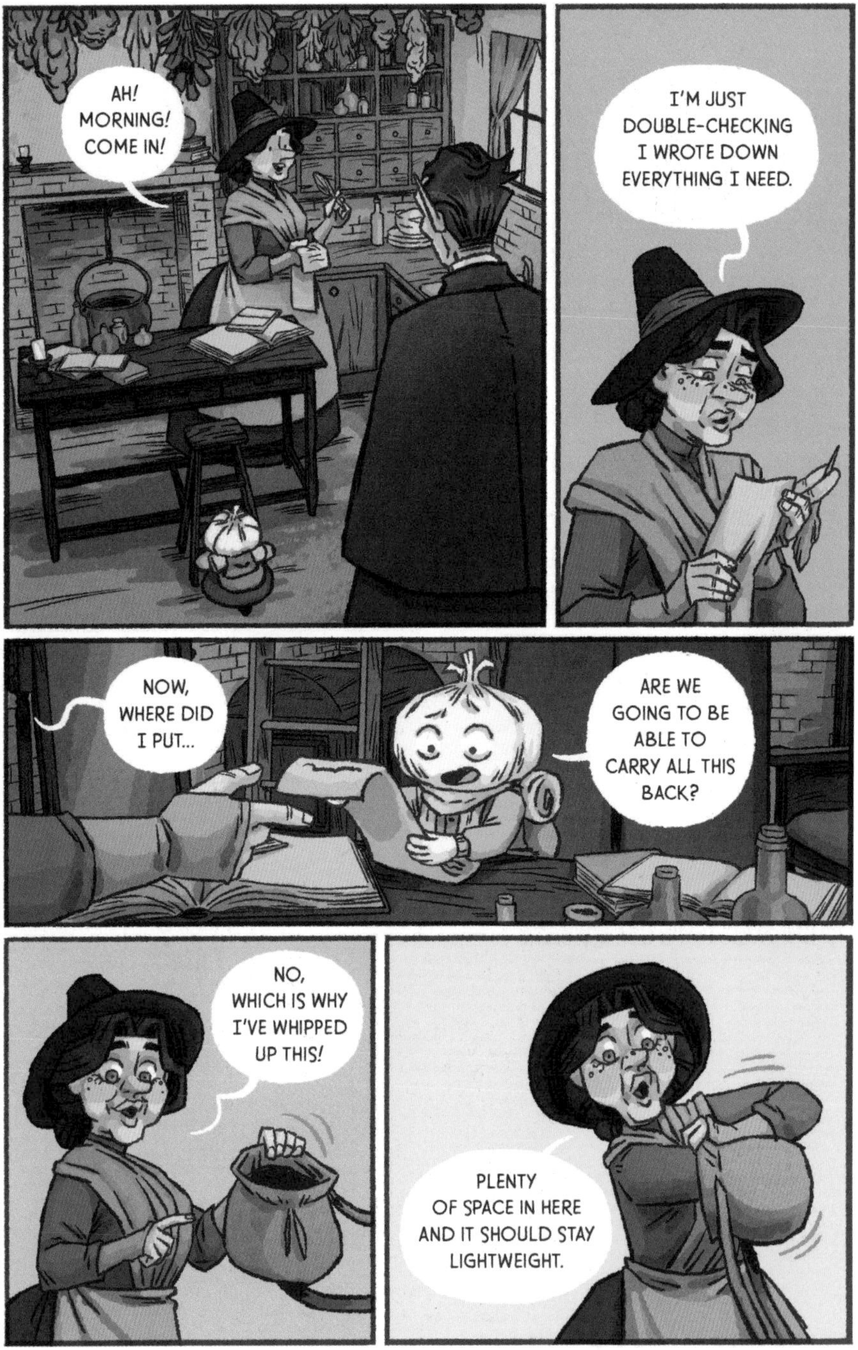
AH! MORNING! COME IN!
I'M JUST DOUBLE-CHECKING I WROTE DOWN EVERYTHING I NEED.
NOW, WHERE DID I PUT...
ARE WE GOING TO BE ABLE TO CARRY ALL THIS BACK?
NO, WHICH IS WHY I'VE WHIPPED UP THIS!
PLENTY OF SPACE IN HERE AND IT SHOULD STAY LIGHTWEIGHT.

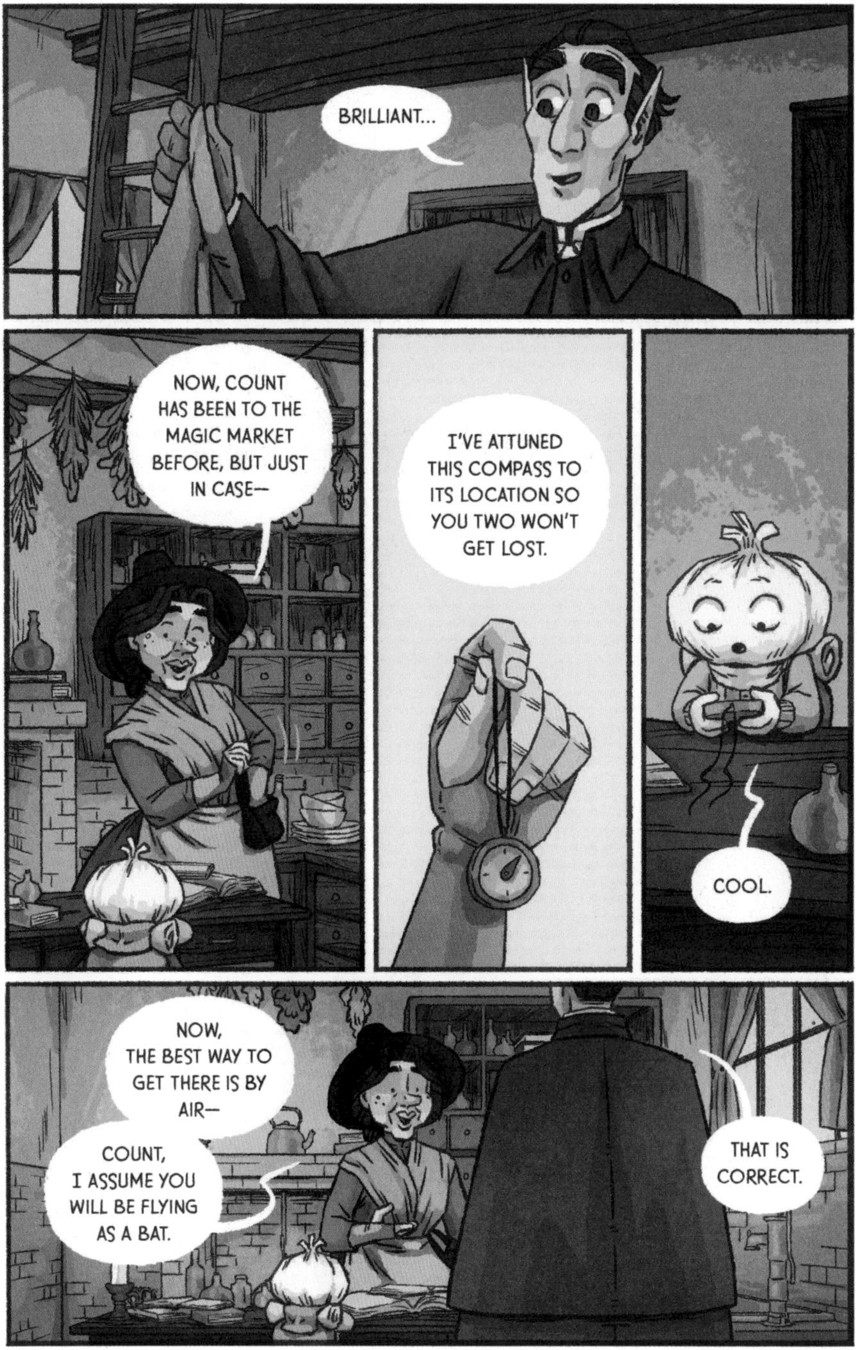
BRILLIANT...
NOW, COUNT HAS BEEN TO THE MAGIC MARKET BEFORE, BUT JUST IN CASE—
I'VE ATTUNED THIS COMPASS TO ITS LOCATION SO YOU TWO WON'T GET LOST.
COOL.
NOW, THE BEST WAY TO GET THERE IS BY AIR—
COUNT, I ASSUME YOU WILL BE FLYING AS A BAT.
THAT IS CORRECT.

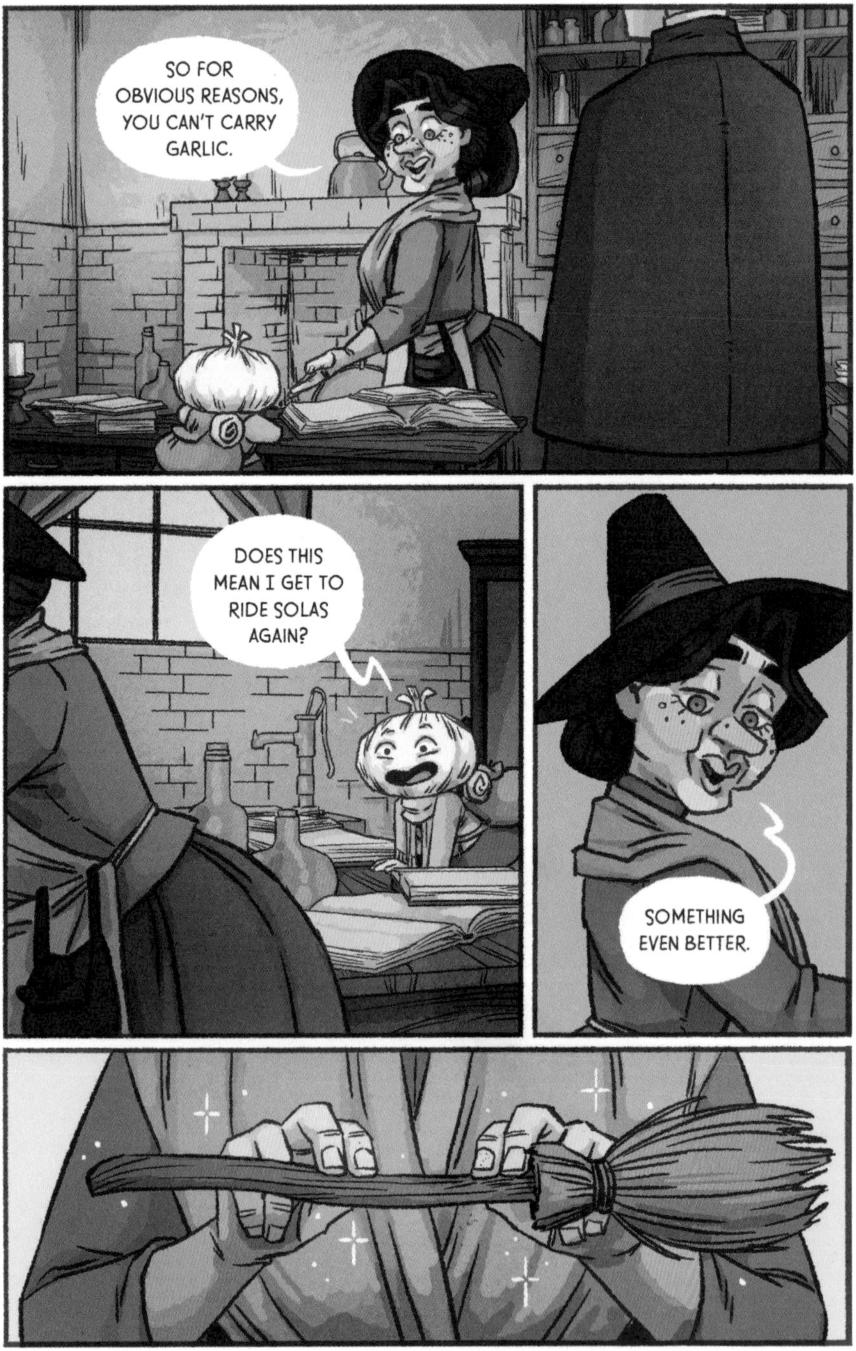
SO FOR OBVIOUS REASONS, YOU CAN'T CARRY GARLIC.
DOES THIS MEAN I GET TO RIDE SOLAS AGAIN?
SOMETHING EVEN BETTER.

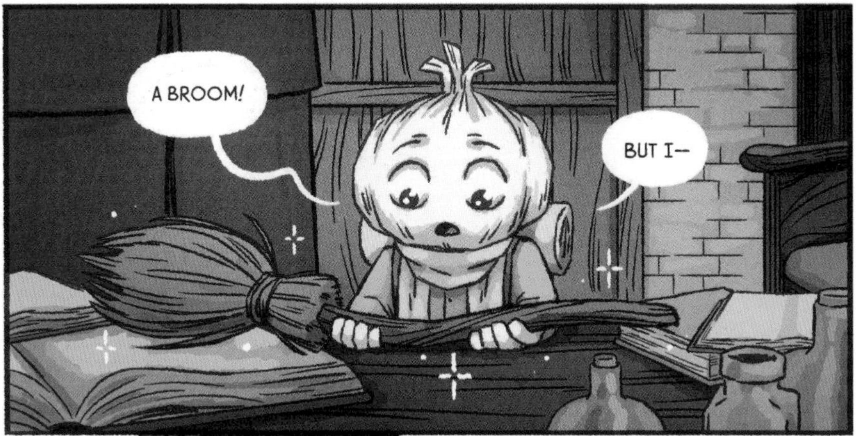
A BROOM!
BUT I--

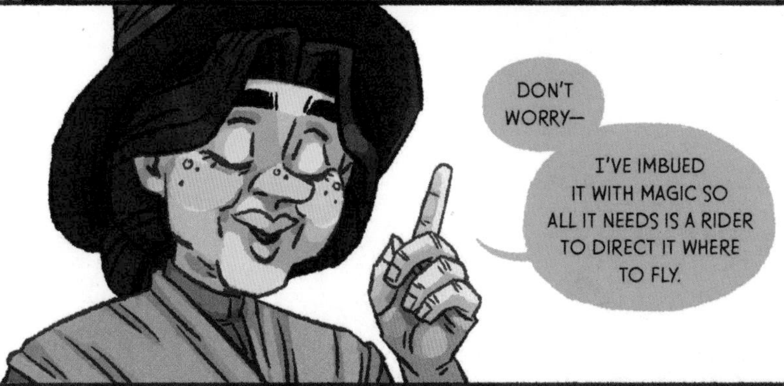
DON'T WORRY--
I'VE IMBUED IT WITH MAGIC SO ALL IT NEEDS IS A RIDER TO DIRECT IT WHERE TO FLY.

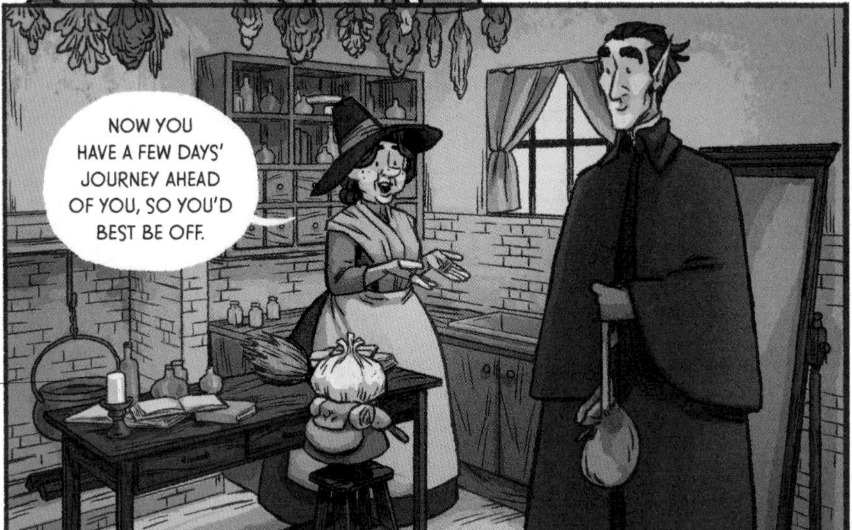
NOW YOU HAVE A FEW DAYS' JOURNEY AHEAD OF YOU, SO YOU'D BEST BE OFF.

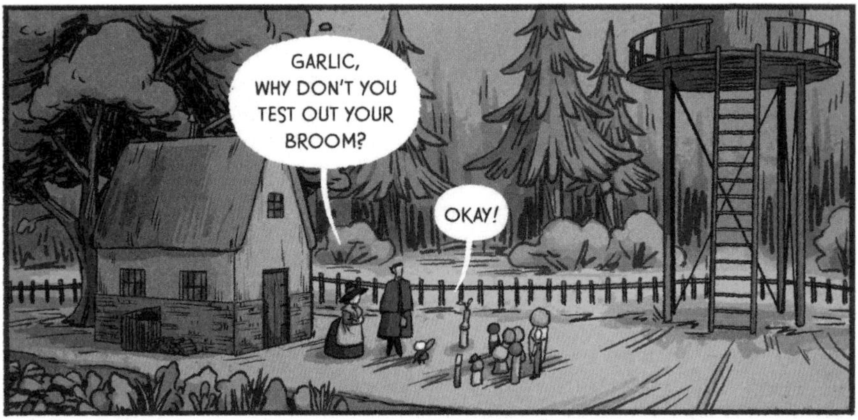
GARLIC, WHY DON'T YOU TEST OUT YOUR BROOM?
OKAY!

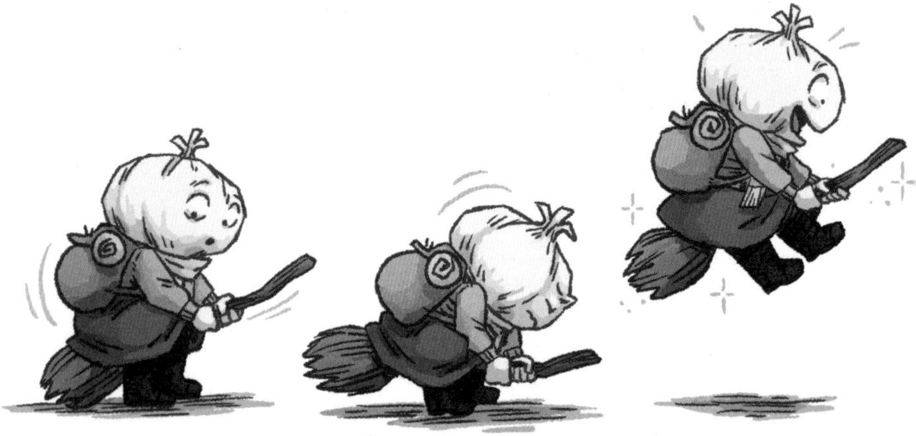

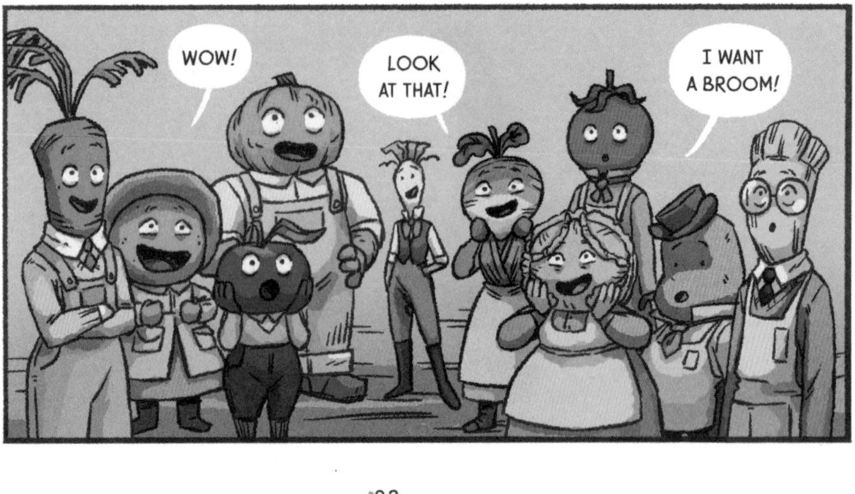
WOW!
LOOK AT THAT!
I WANT A BROOM!

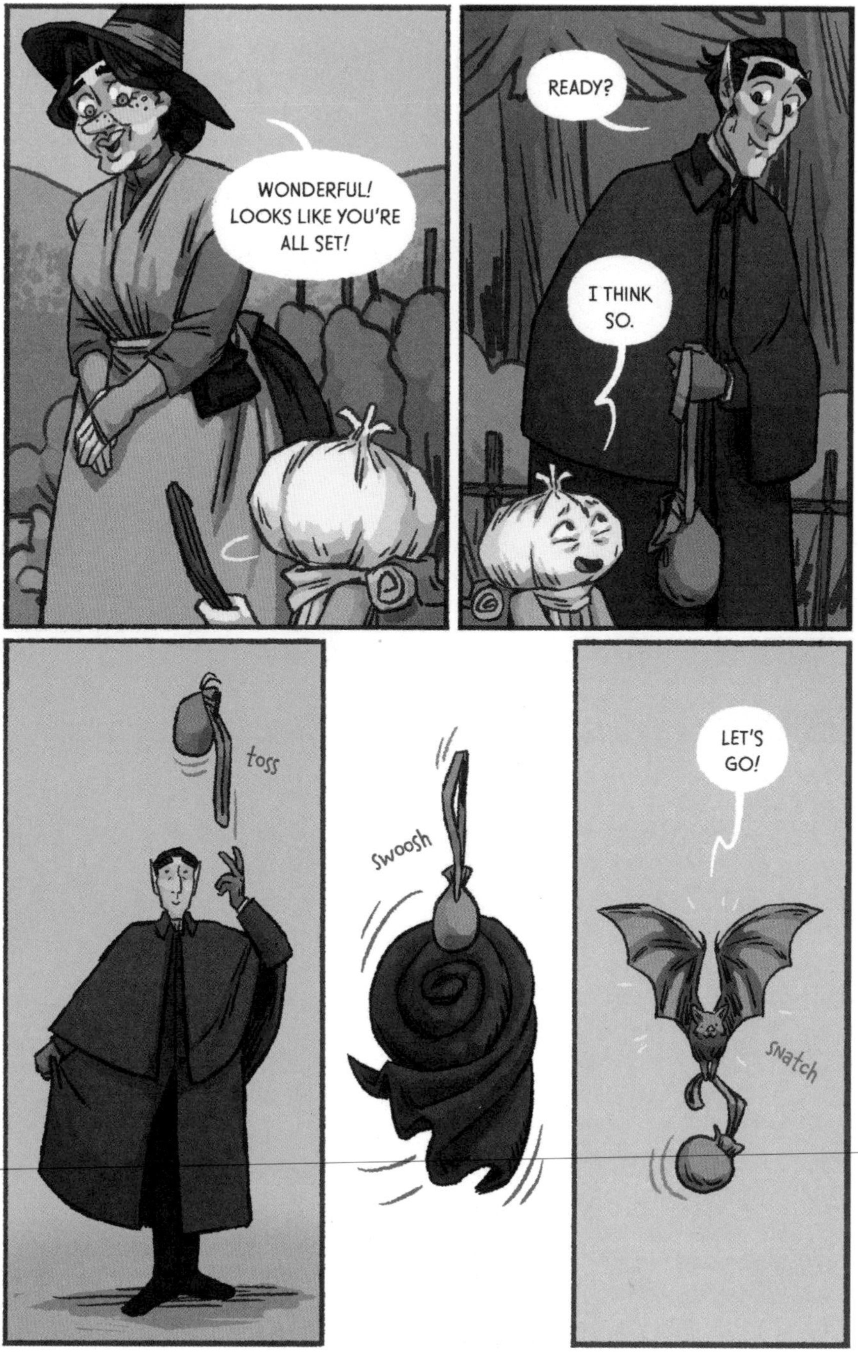
WONDERFUL! LOOKS LIKE YOU'RE ALL SET!
READY?
I THINK SO.
toss
swoosh
LET'S GO!
snatch

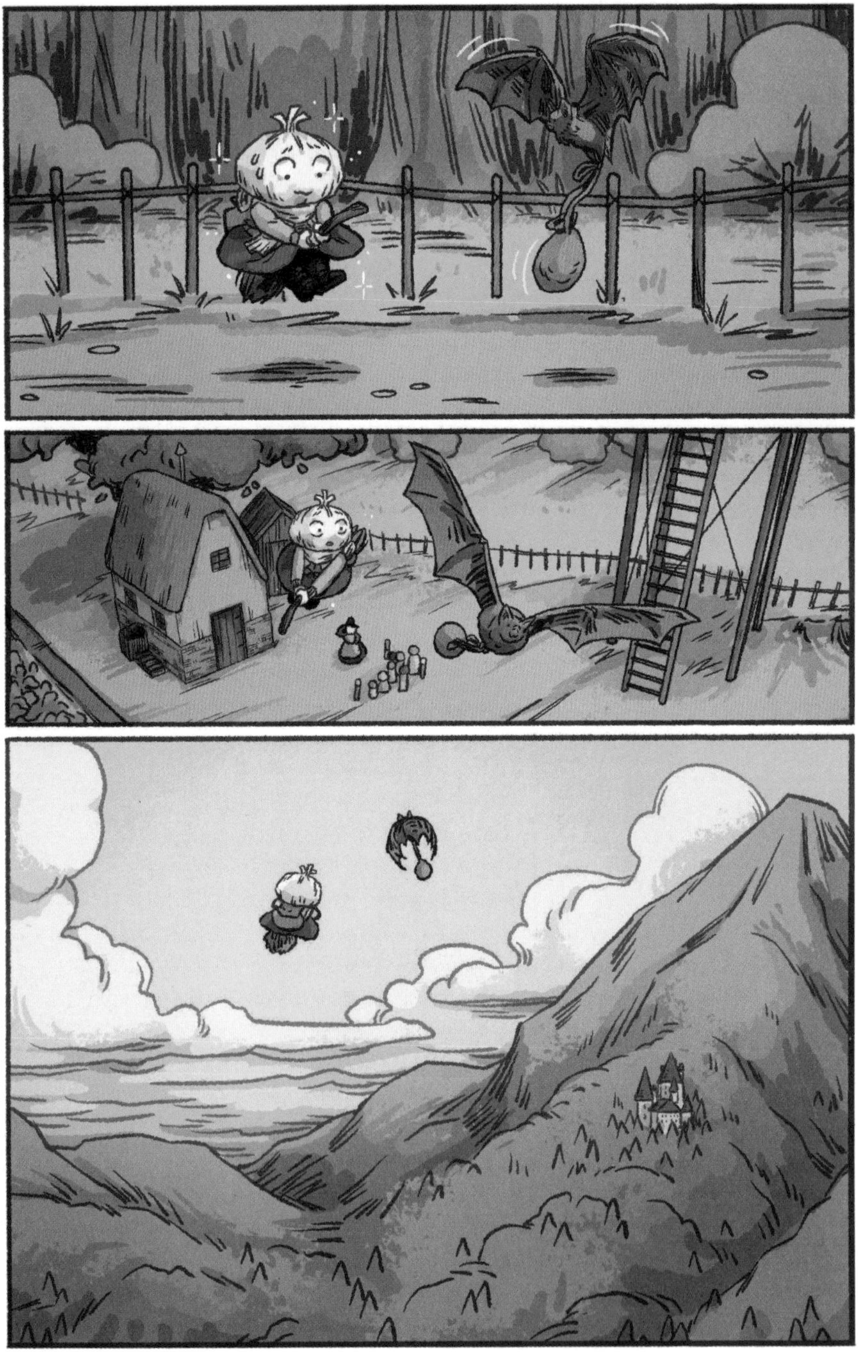

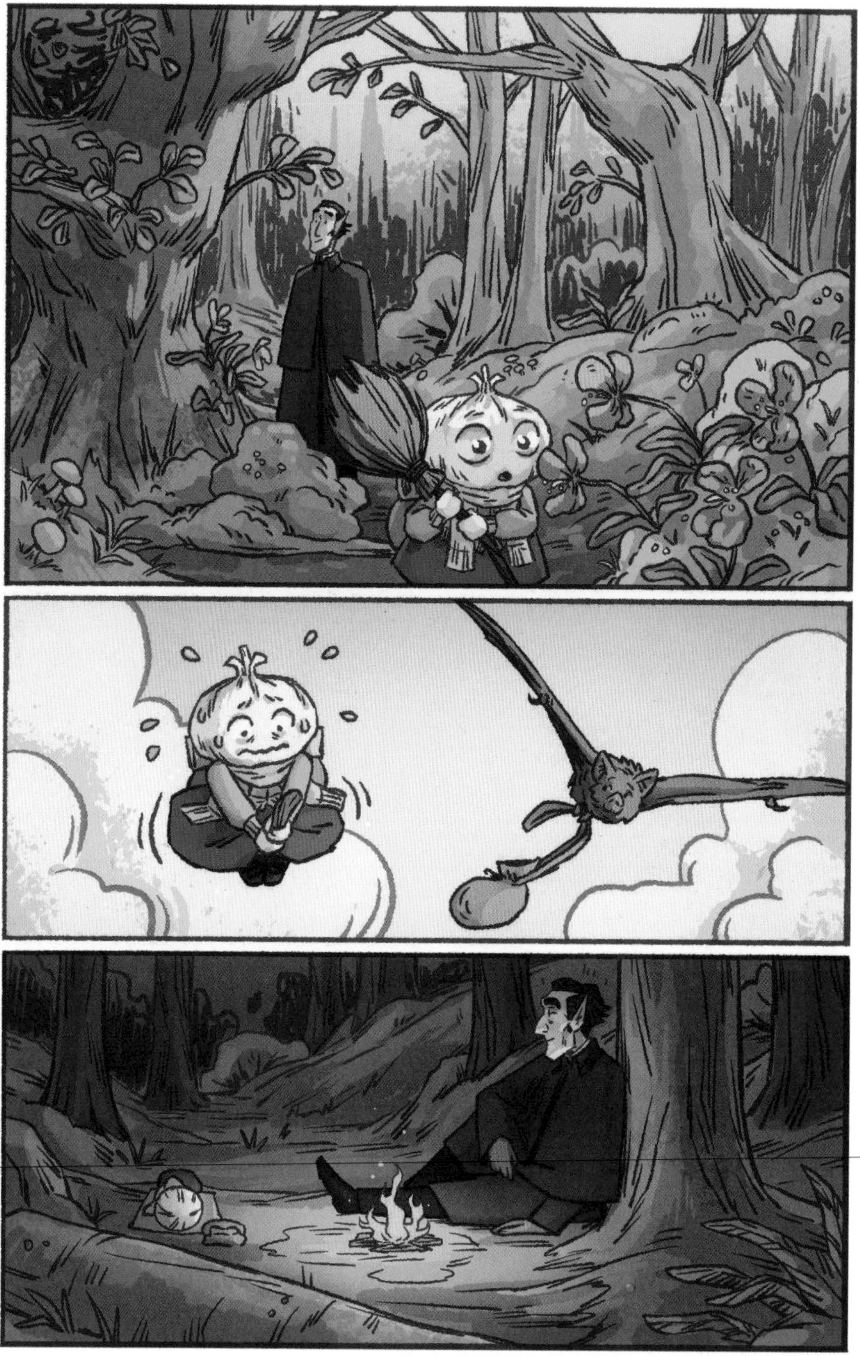

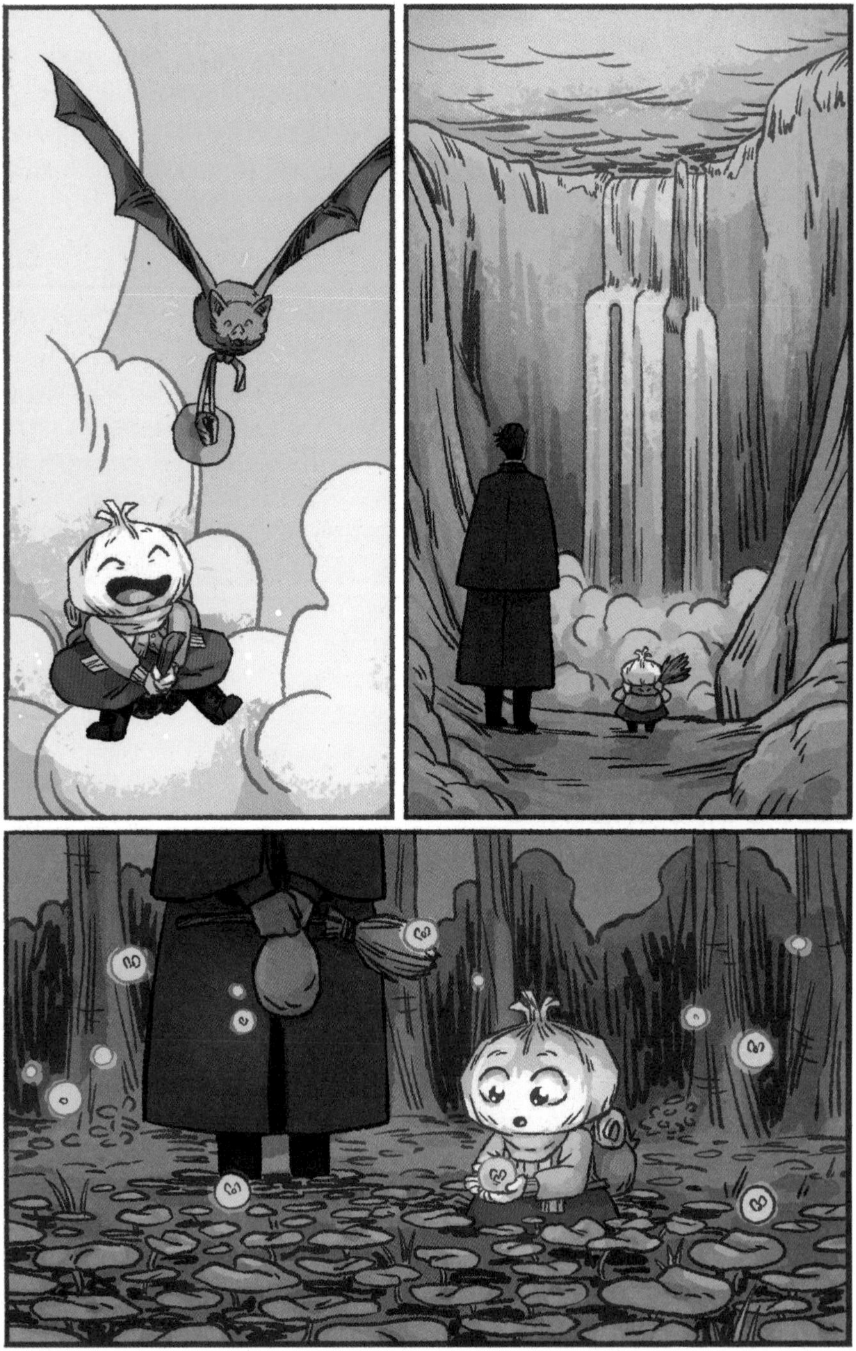

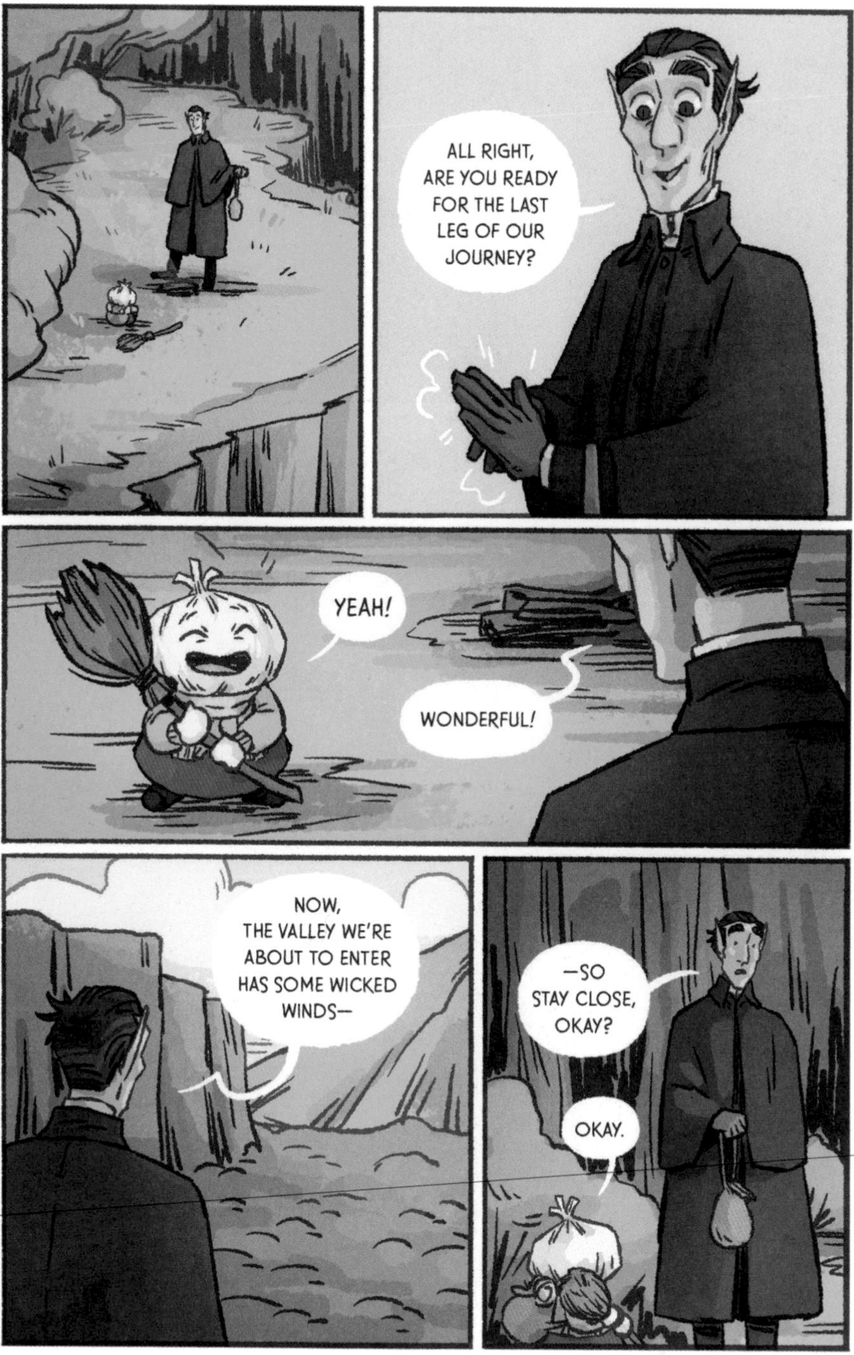
ALL RIGHT, ARE YOU READY FOR THE LAST LEG OF OUR JOURNEY?
YEAH!
WONDERFUL!
NOW, THE VALLEY WE'RE ABOUT TO ENTER HAS SOME WICKED WINDS—
—SO STAY CLOSE, OKAY?
OKAY.

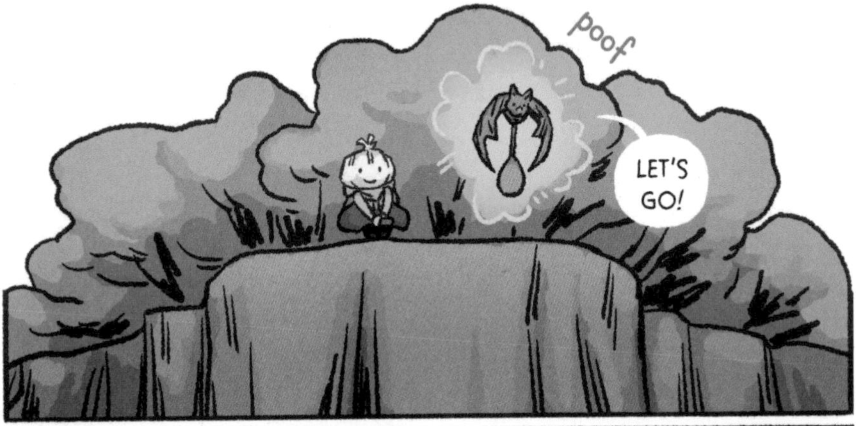
poof
LET'S GO!

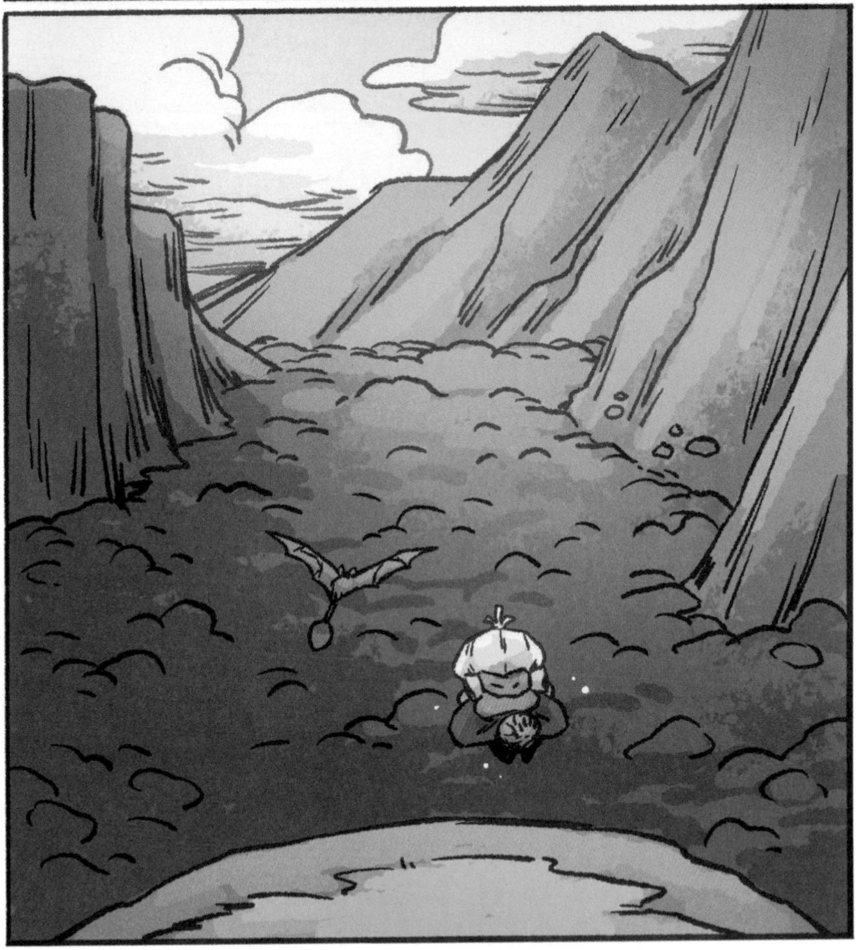

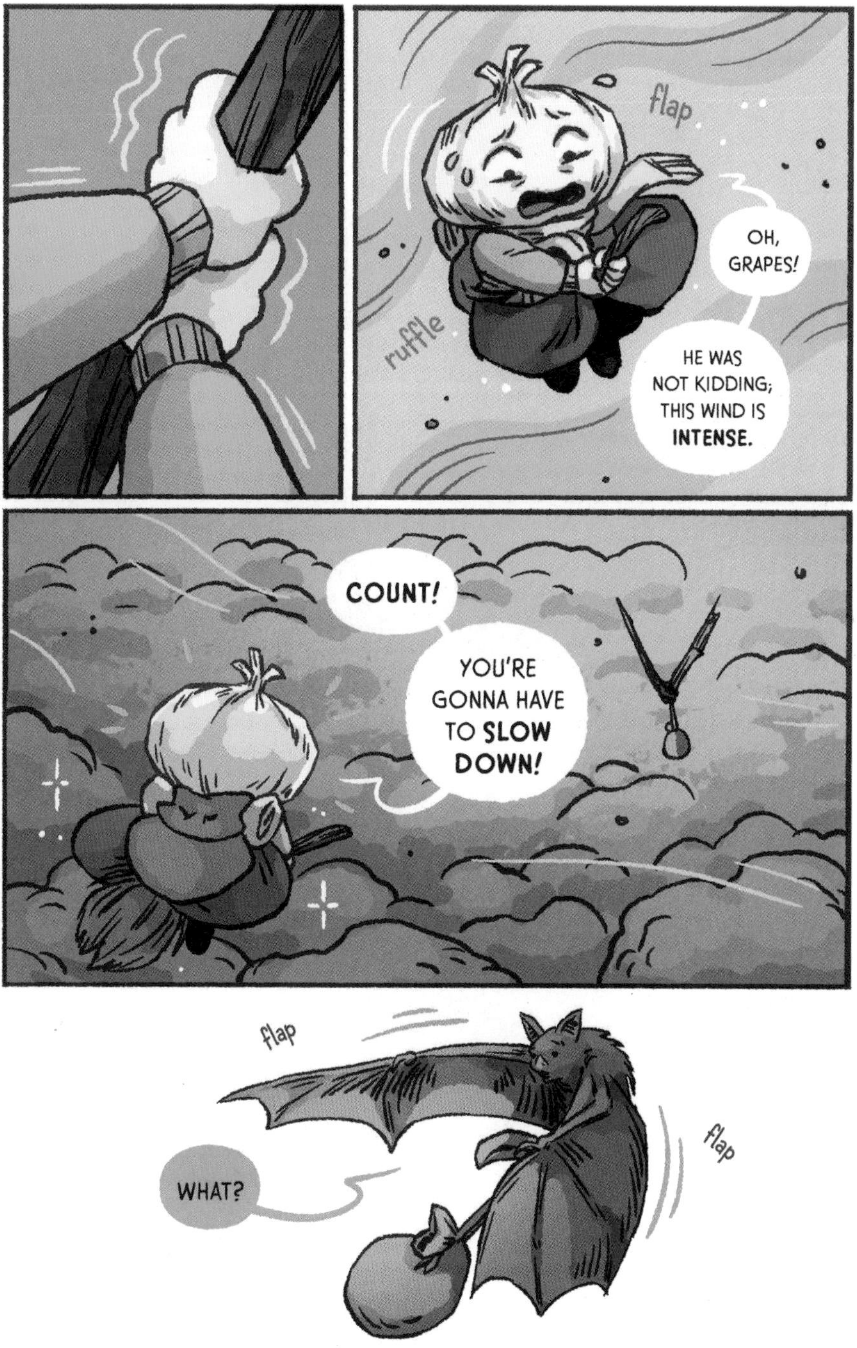
flap
ruffle
OH, GRAPES!
HE WAS NOT KIDDING; THIS WIND IS **INTENSE.**
COUNT!
YOU'RE GONNA HAVE TO **SLOW DOWN!**
flap
flap
WHAT?

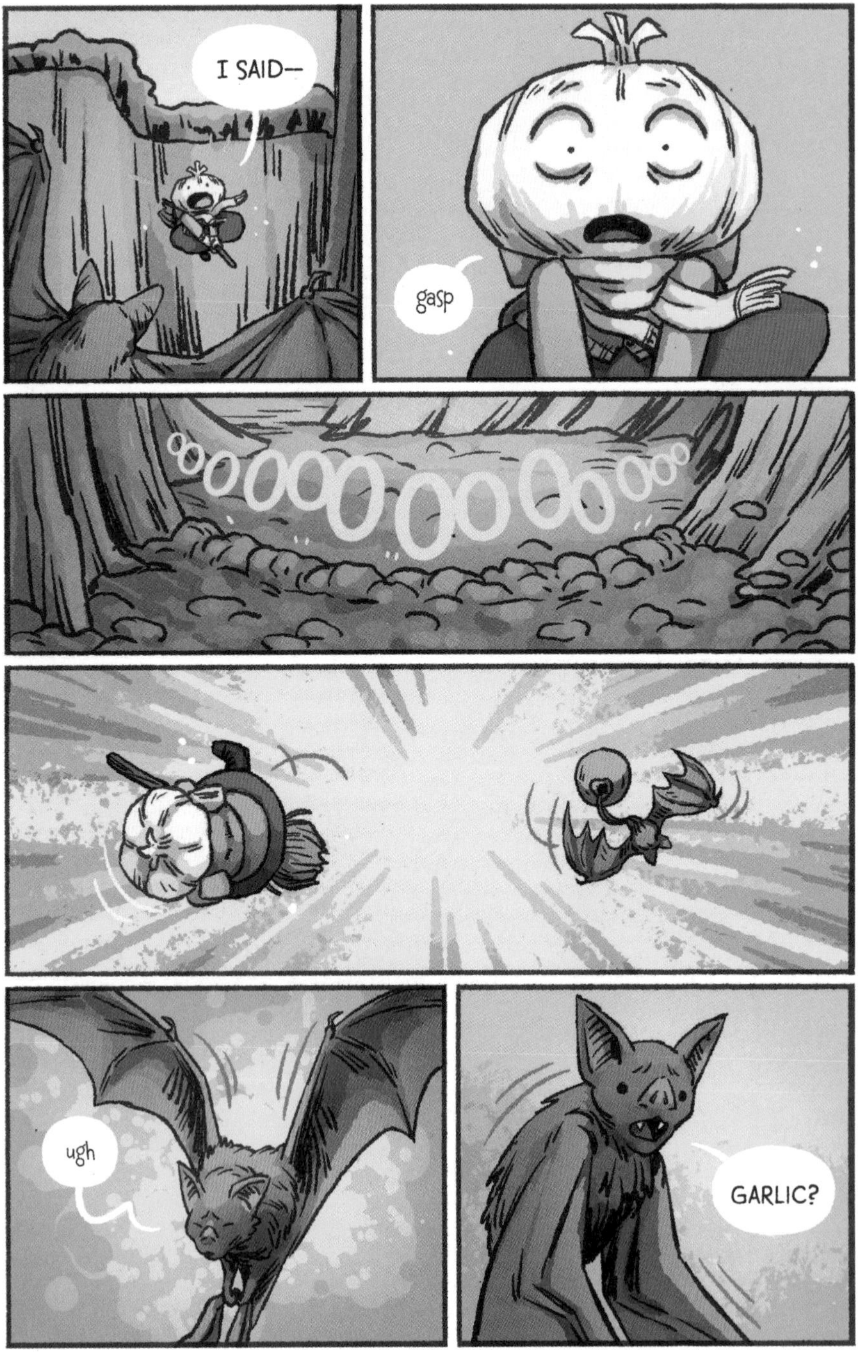
I SAID--
gasp
ugh
GARLIC?

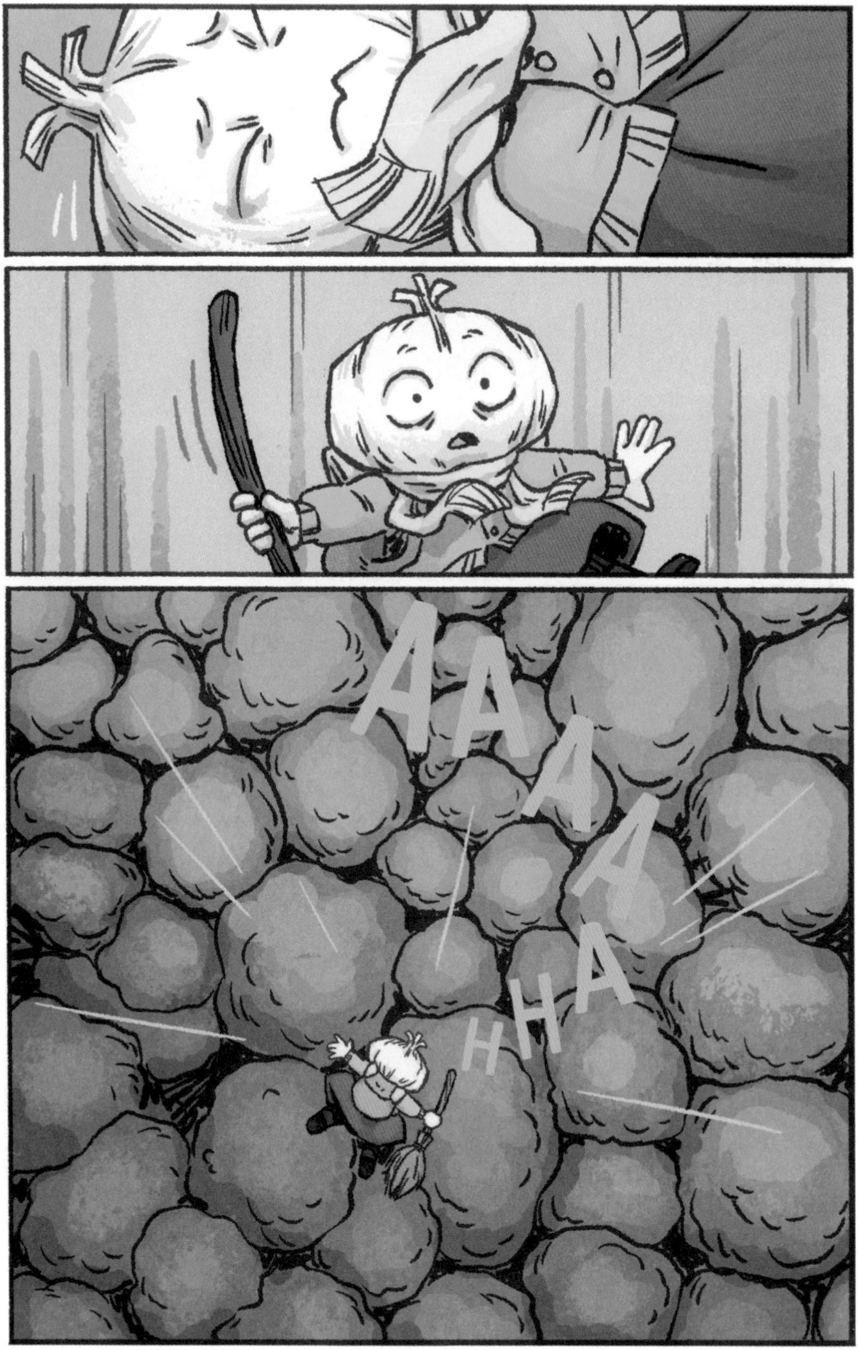
AAAAAHHA

chapter five

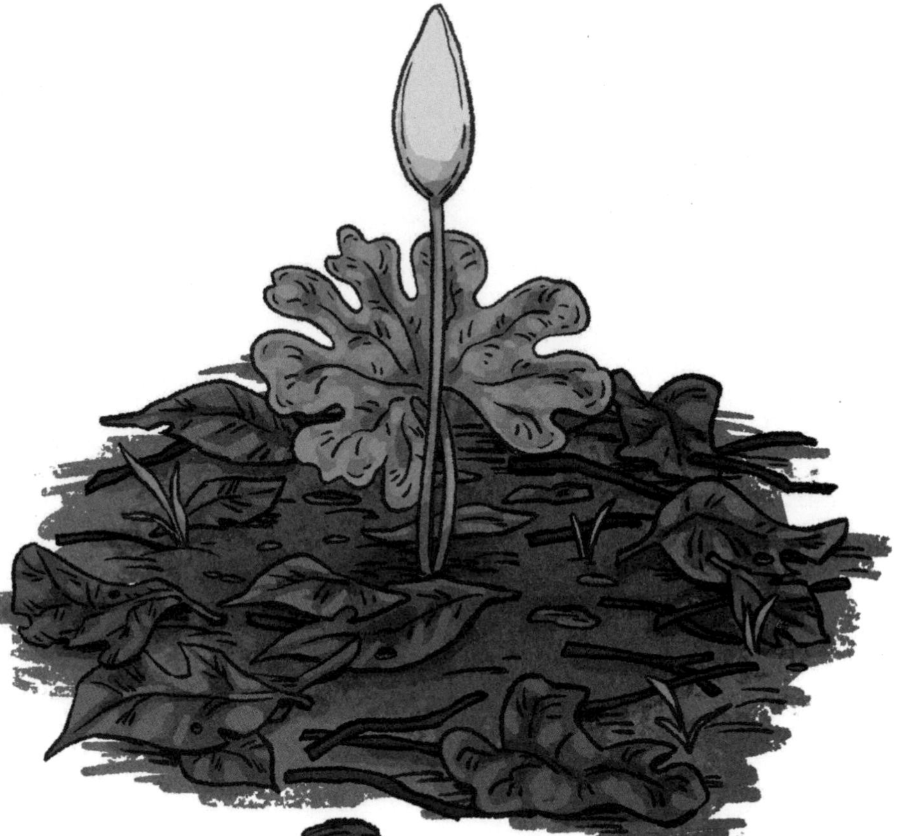

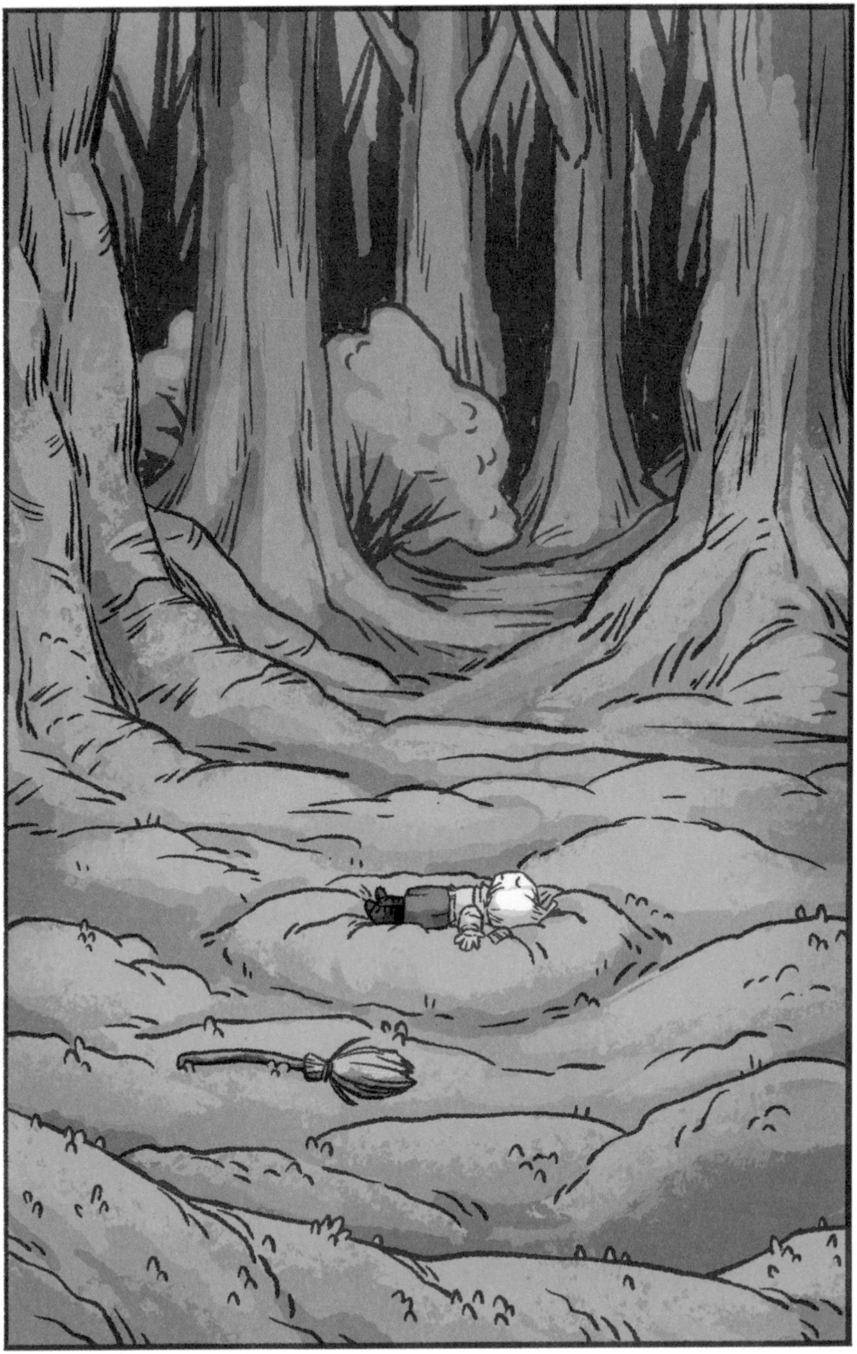

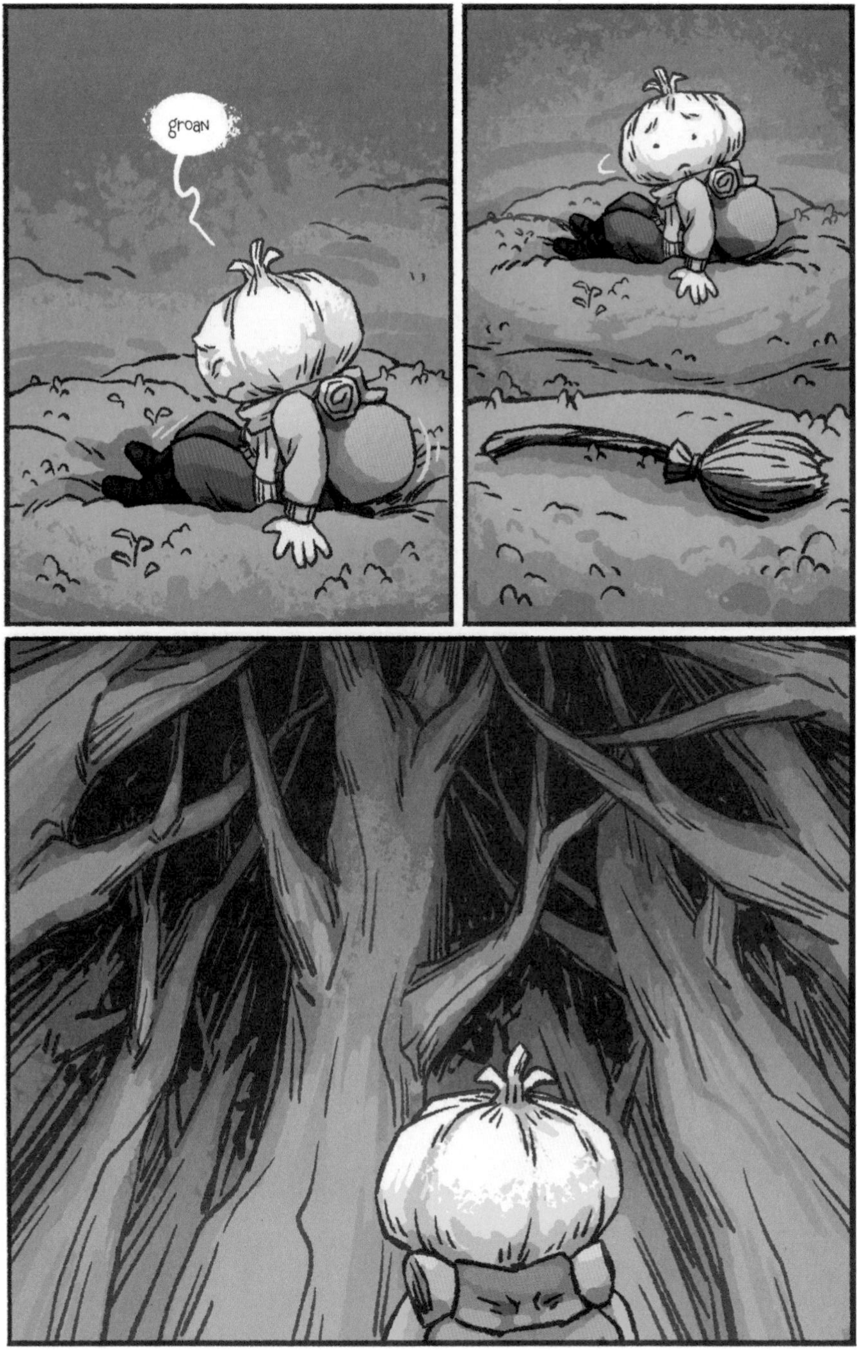
groan

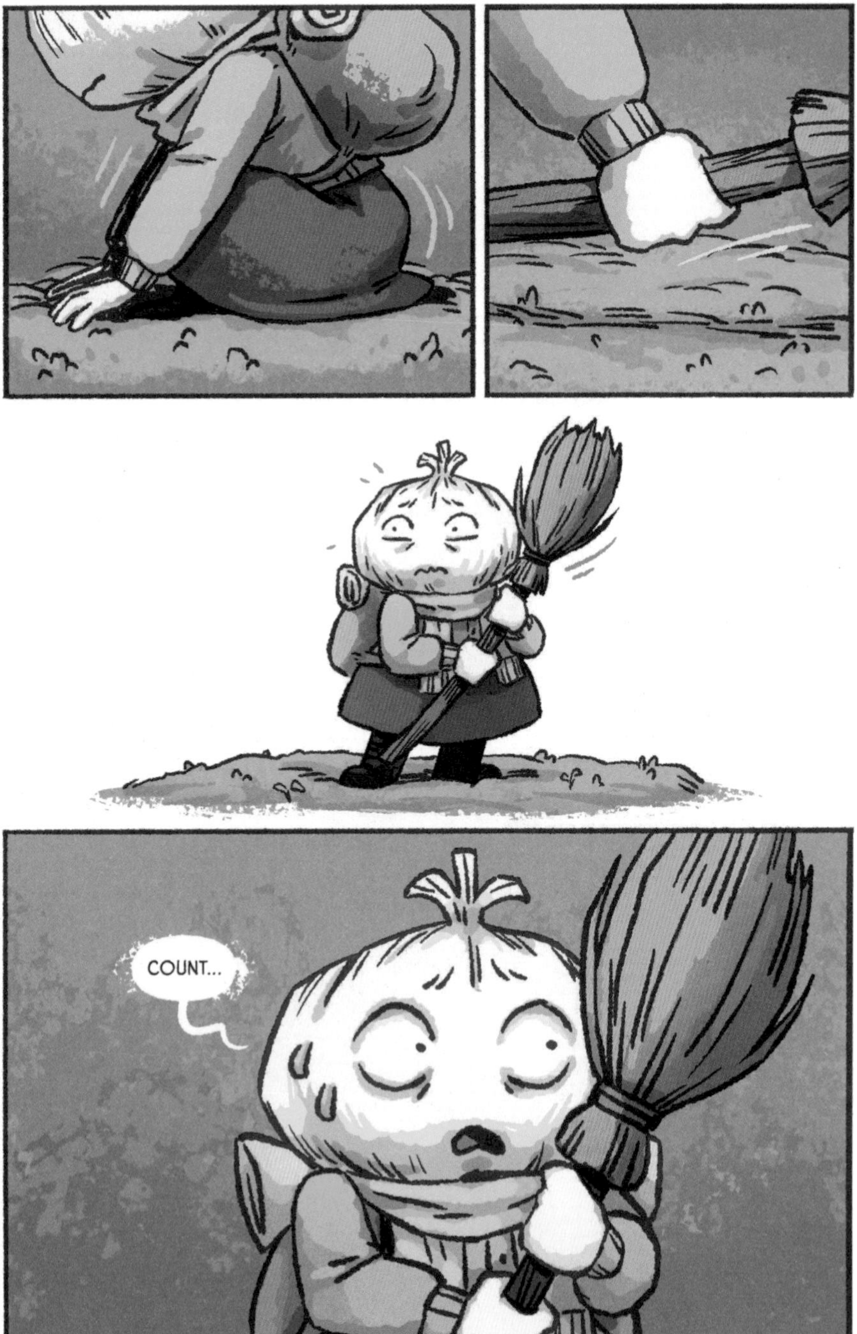
COUNT...

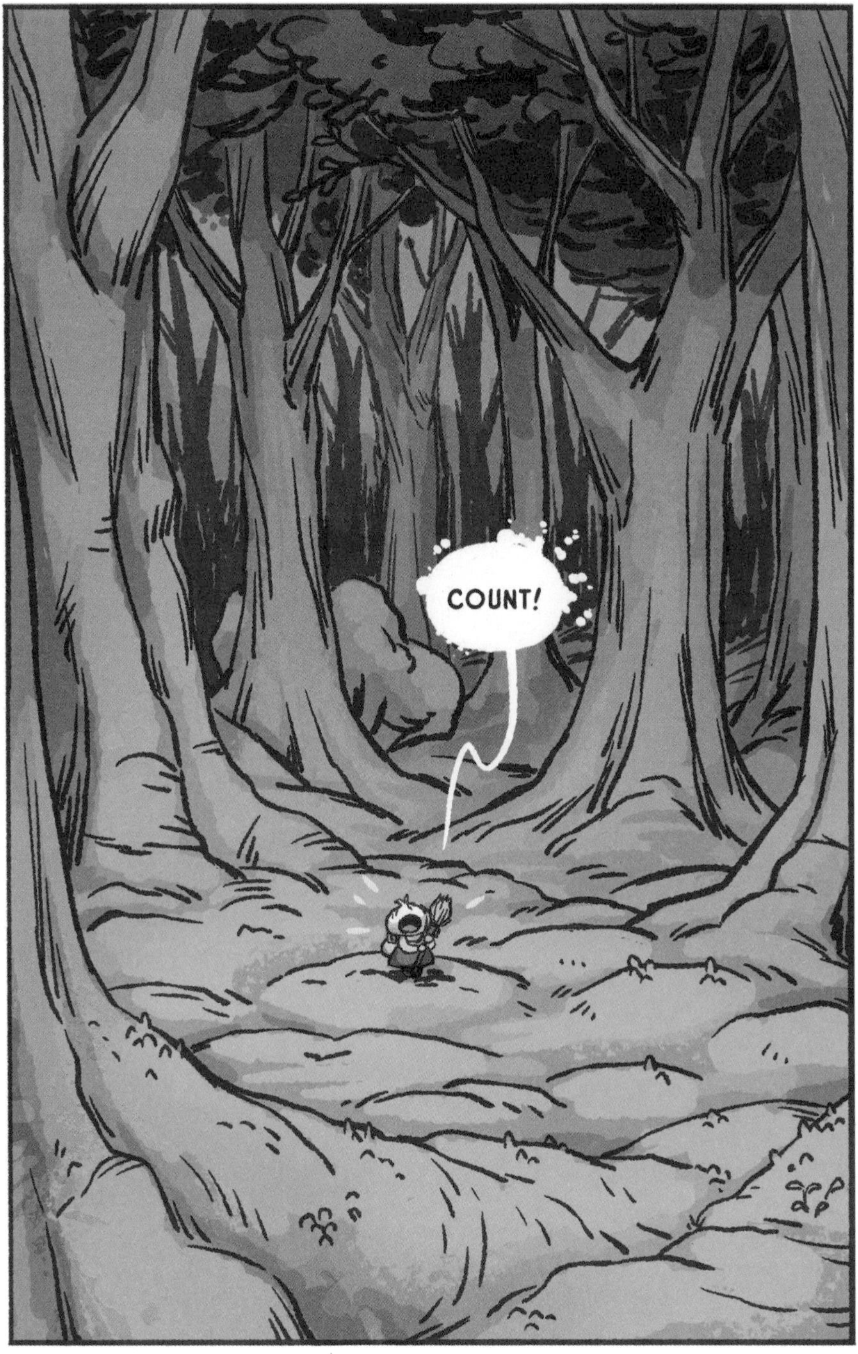
COUNT!

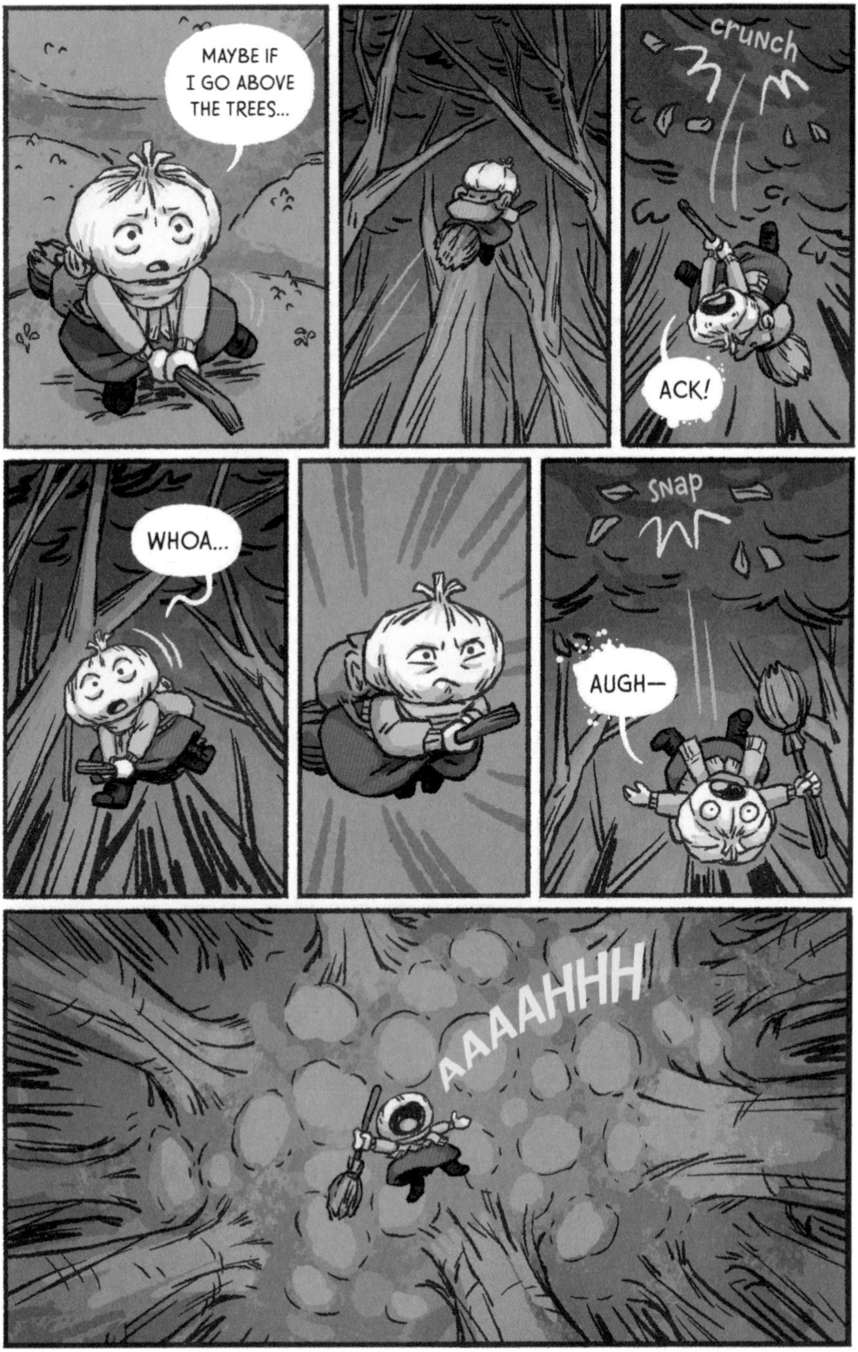
MAYBE IF I GO ABOVE THE TREES...
crunch
ACK!
WHOA...
snap
AUGH—
AAAAHHH

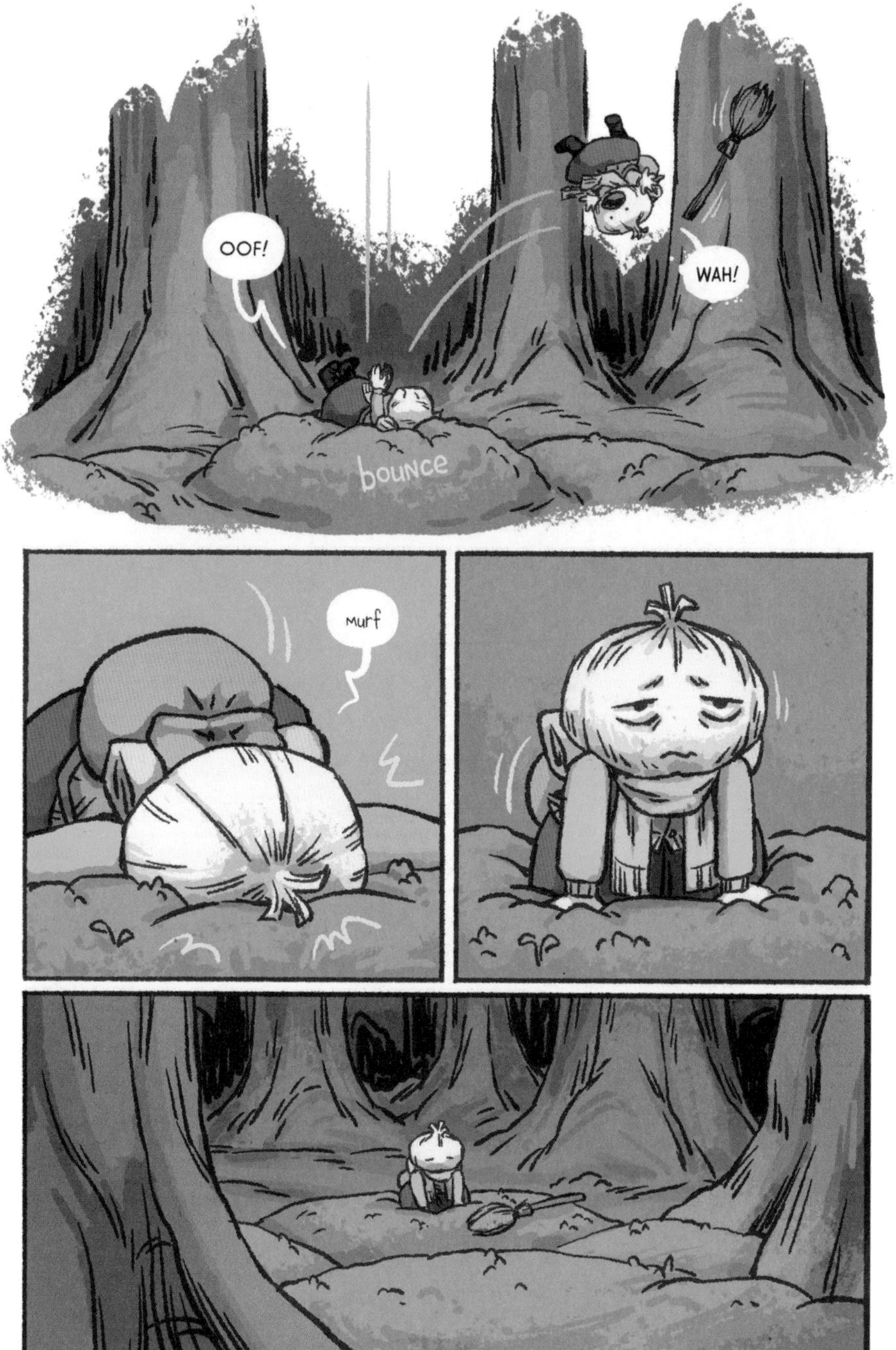
OOF!
WAH!
bounce
Murf

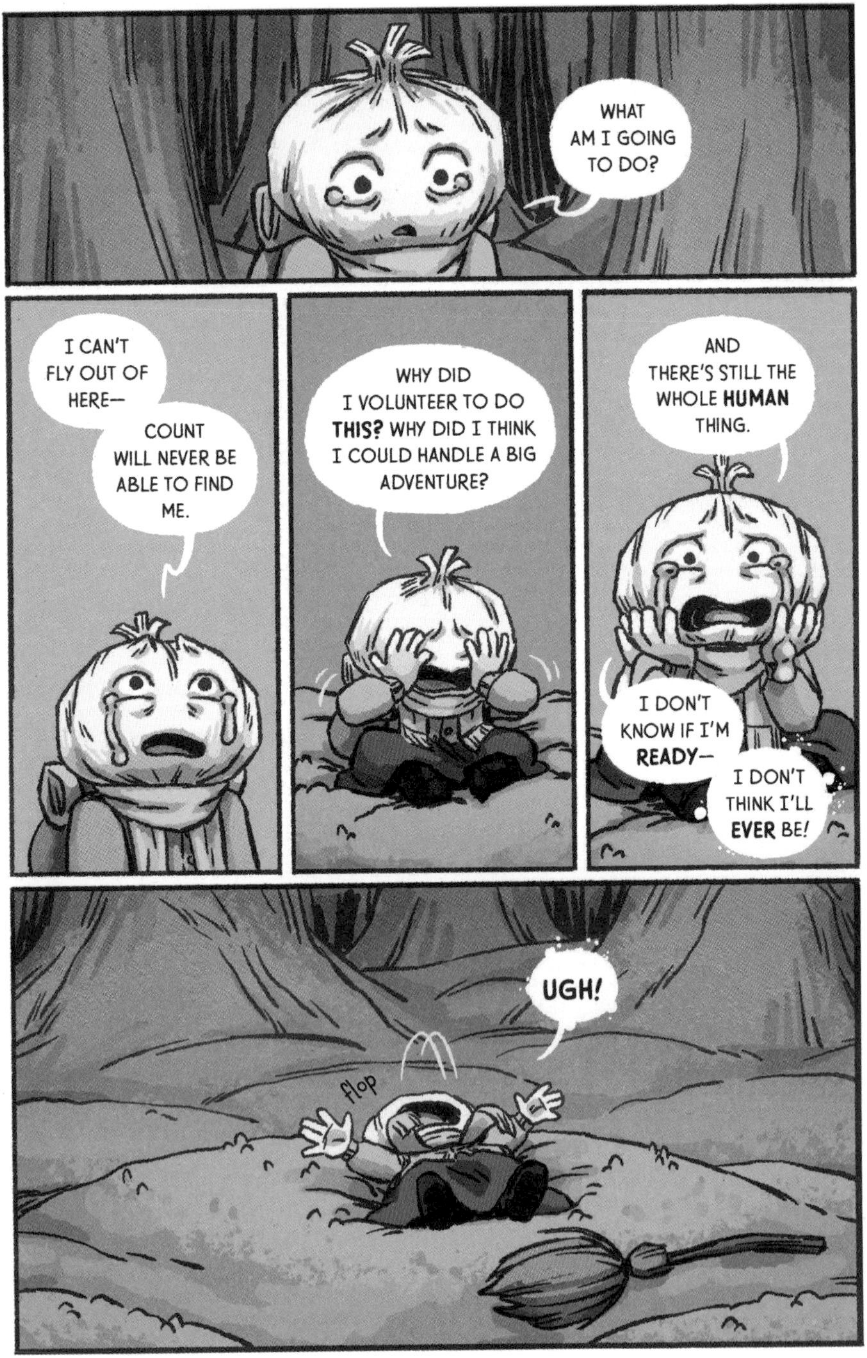
WHAT AM I GOING TO DO?
I CAN'T FLY OUT OF HERE—
COUNT WILL NEVER BE ABLE TO FIND ME.
WHY DID I VOLUNTEER TO DO **THIS?** WHY DID I THINK I COULD HANDLE A BIG ADVENTURE?
AND THERE'S STILL THE WHOLE **HUMAN** THING.
I DON'T KNOW IF I'M **READY**—
I DON'T THINK I'LL **EVER** BE!
UGH!
flop

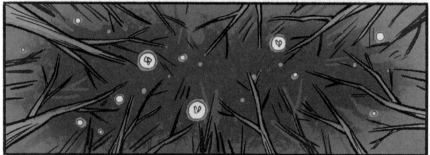

I HAVE SEEN A LOT OF AMAZING, BEAUTIFUL THINGS, THOUGH.

THINGS I WOULD NEVER HAVE SEEN IF I HADN'T LEFT HOME.

MAYBE THAT'S WHAT BEING HUMAN WILL BE LIKE...

IT'LL BE SCARY BUT NOT ALL THE TIME.

THAT WOULDN'T BE SO BAD.

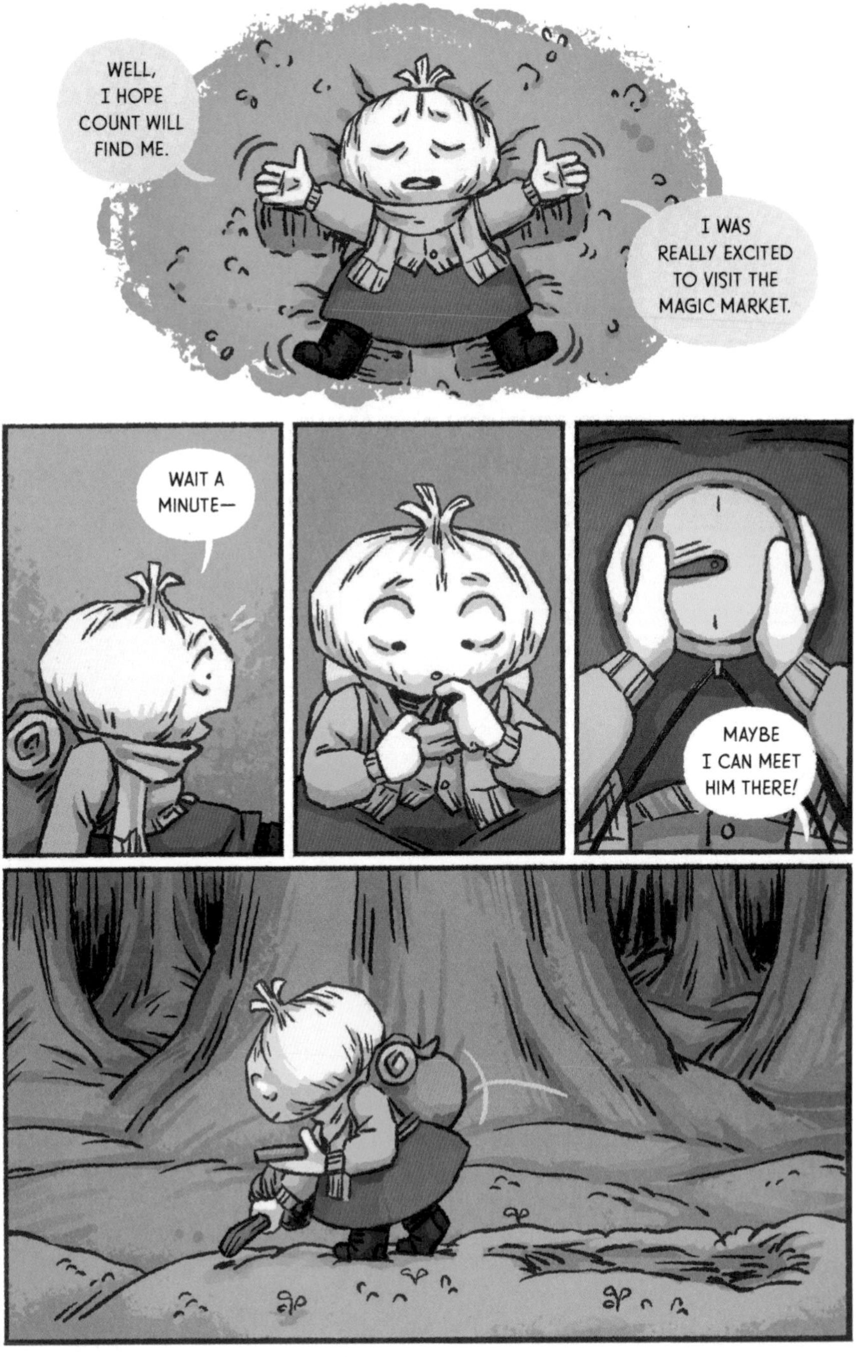

WELL, I HOPE COUNT WILL FIND ME.
I WAS REALLY EXCITED TO VISIT THE MAGIC MARKET.
WAIT A MINUTE—
MAYBE I CAN MEET HIM THERE!

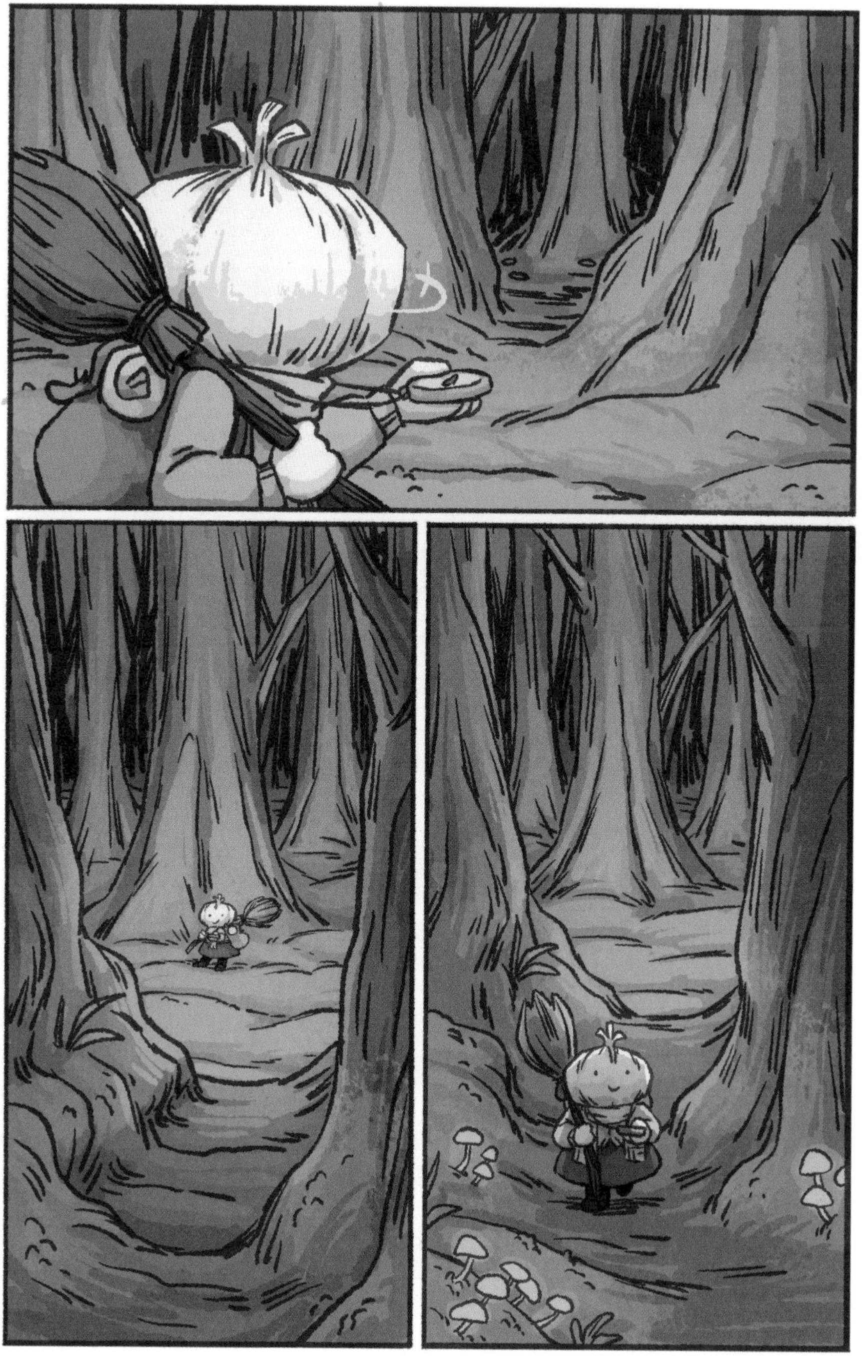

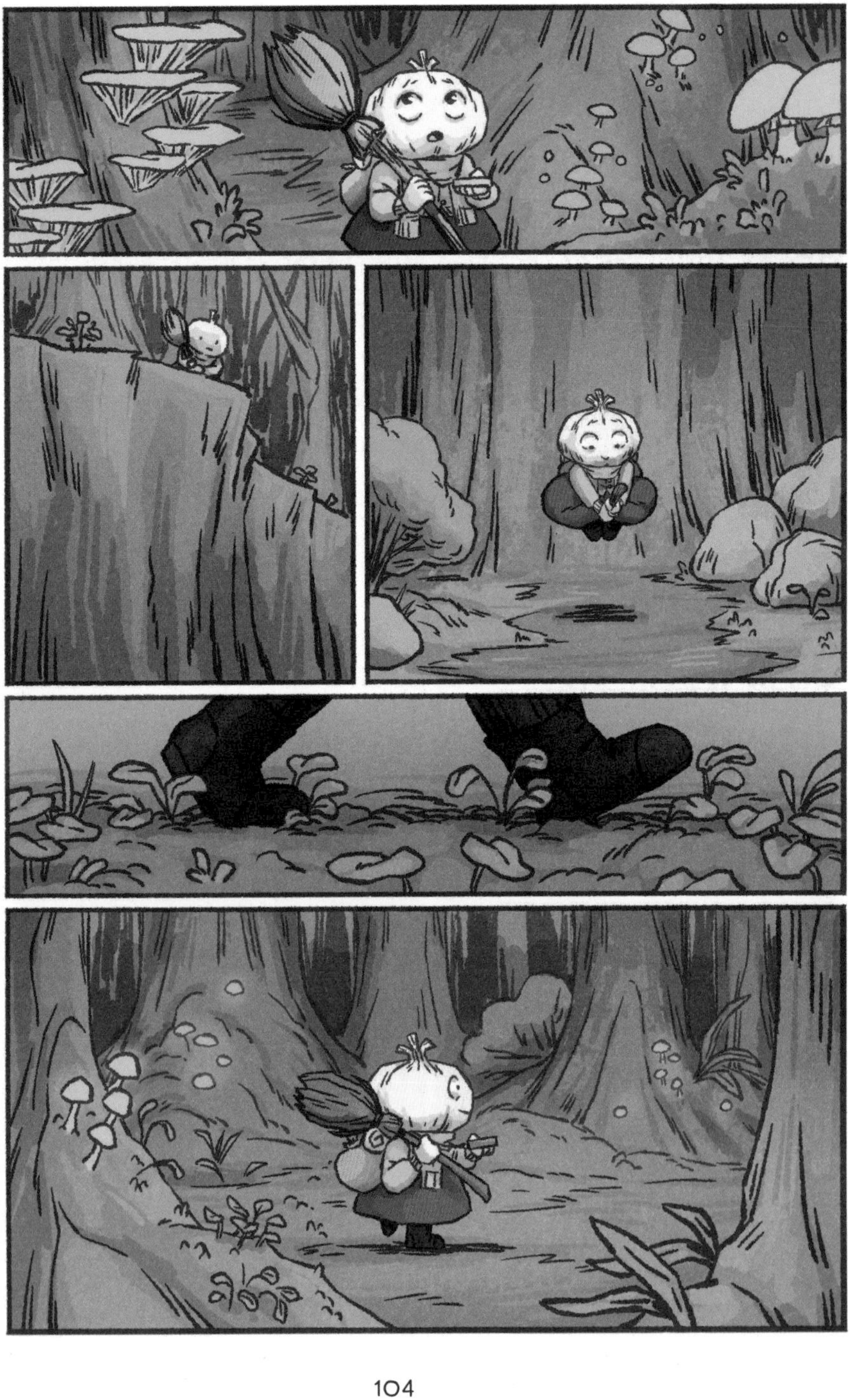

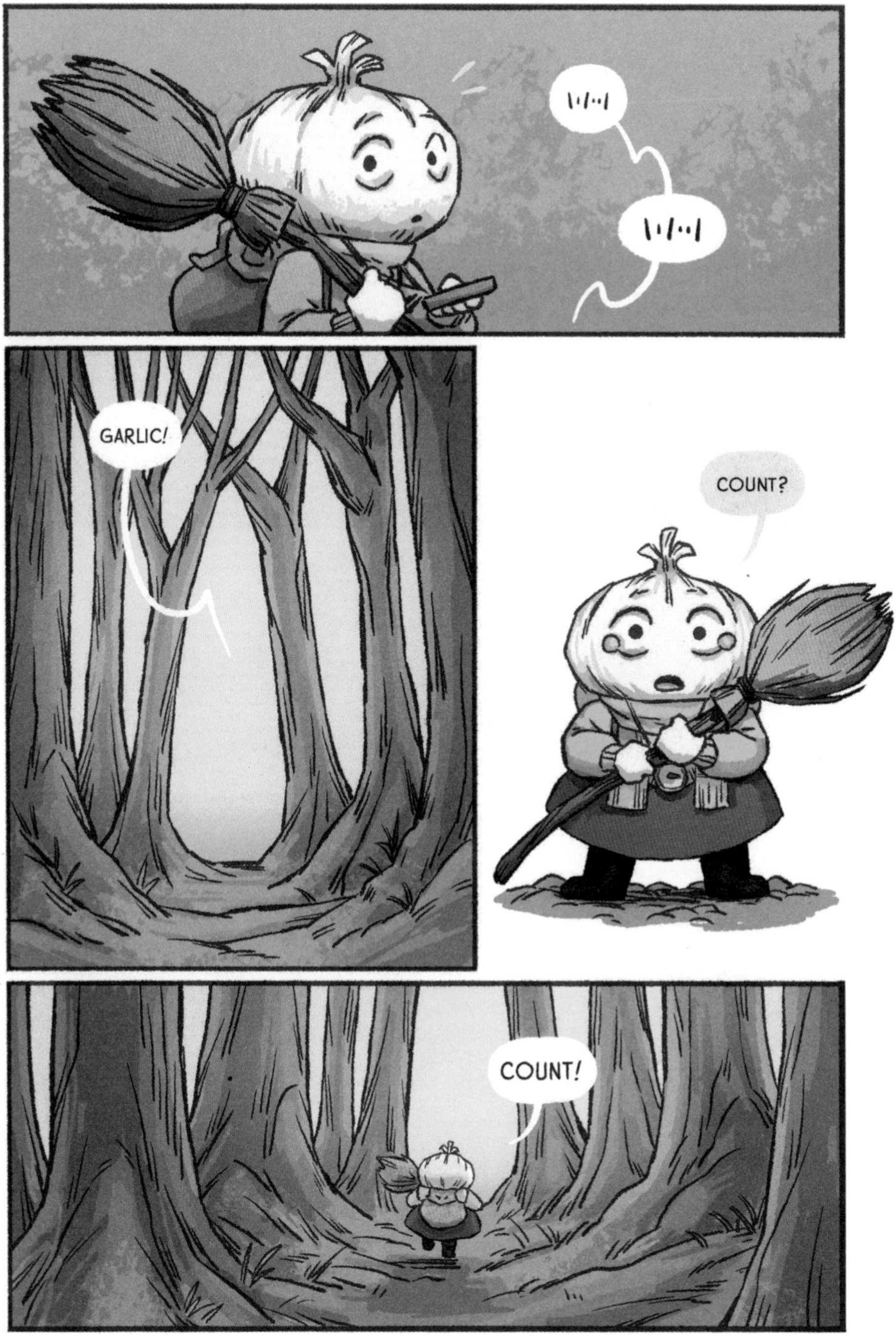
GARLIC!
COUNT?
COUNT!

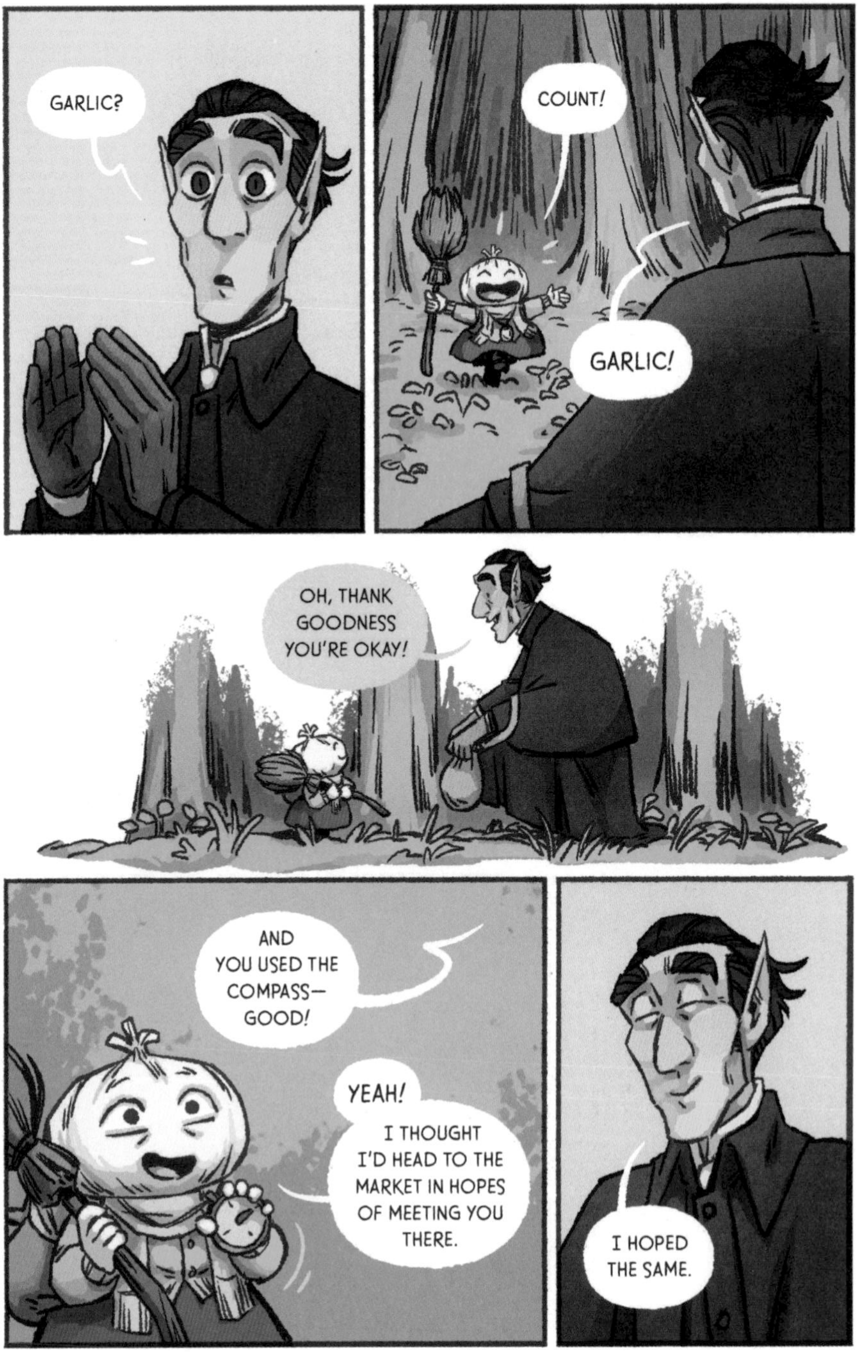
GARLIC?
COUNT!
GARLIC!
OH, THANK GOODNESS YOU'RE OKAY!
AND YOU USED THE COMPASS—GOOD!
YEAH!
I THOUGHT I'D HEAD TO THE MARKET IN HOPES OF MEETING YOU THERE.
I HOPED THE SAME.

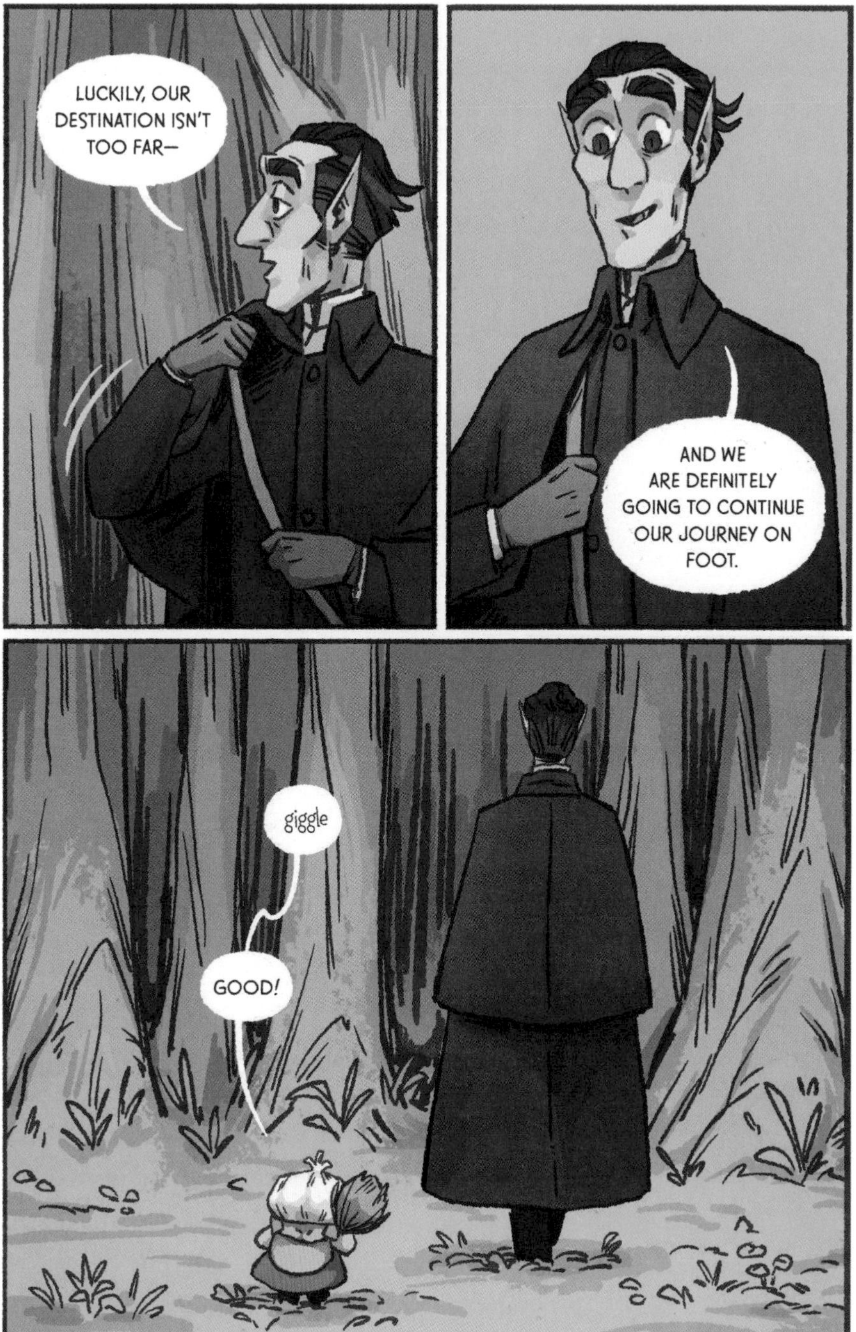
LUCKILY, OUR DESTINATION ISN'T TOO FAR—
AND WE ARE DEFINITELY GOING TO CONTINUE OUR JOURNEY ON FOOT.
giggle
GOOD!

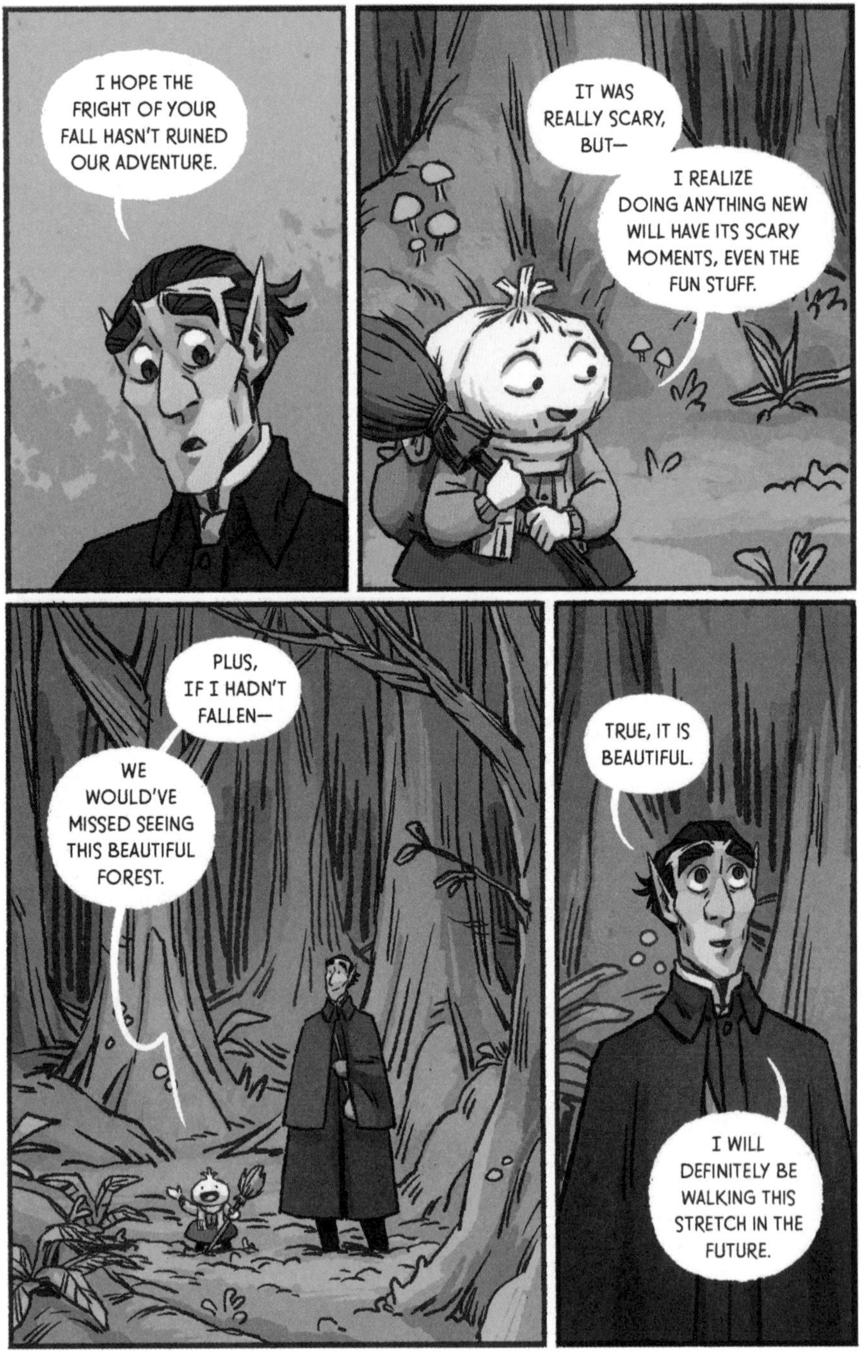
I HOPE THE FRIGHT OF YOUR FALL HASN'T RUINED OUR ADVENTURE.
IT WAS REALLY SCARY, BUT—
I REALIZE DOING ANYTHING NEW WILL HAVE ITS SCARY MOMENTS, EVEN THE FUN STUFF.
PLUS, IF I HADN'T FALLEN—
WE WOULD'VE MISSED SEEING THIS BEAUTIFUL FOREST.
TRUE, IT IS BEAUTIFUL.
I WILL DEFINITELY BE WALKING THIS STRETCH IN THE FUTURE.

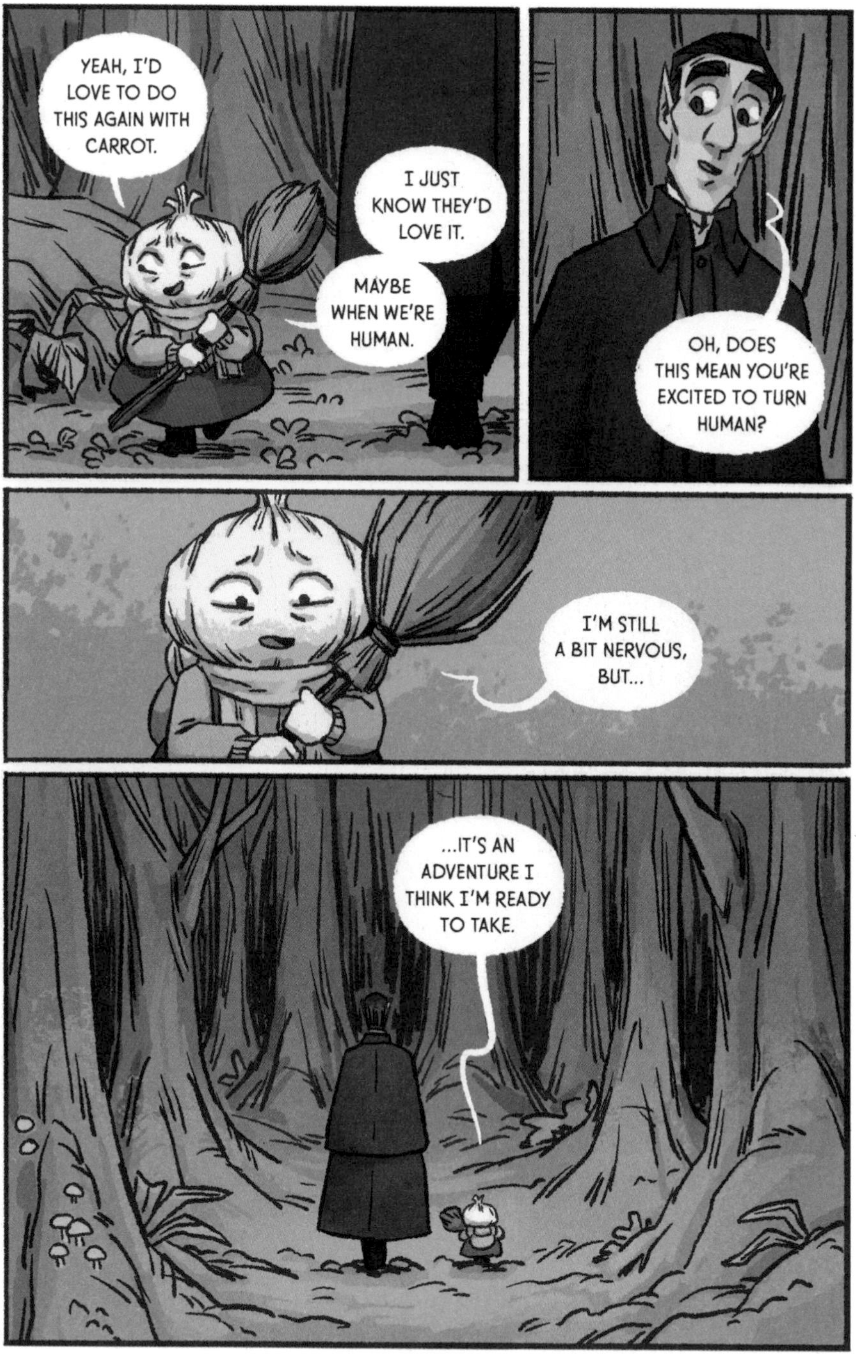
YEAH, I'D LOVE TO DO THIS AGAIN WITH CARROT.
I JUST KNOW THEY'D LOVE IT.
MAYBE WHEN WE'RE HUMAN.
OH, DOES THIS MEAN YOU'RE EXCITED TO TURN HUMAN?
I'M STILL A BIT NERVOUS, BUT...
...IT'S AN ADVENTURE I THINK I'M READY TO TAKE.

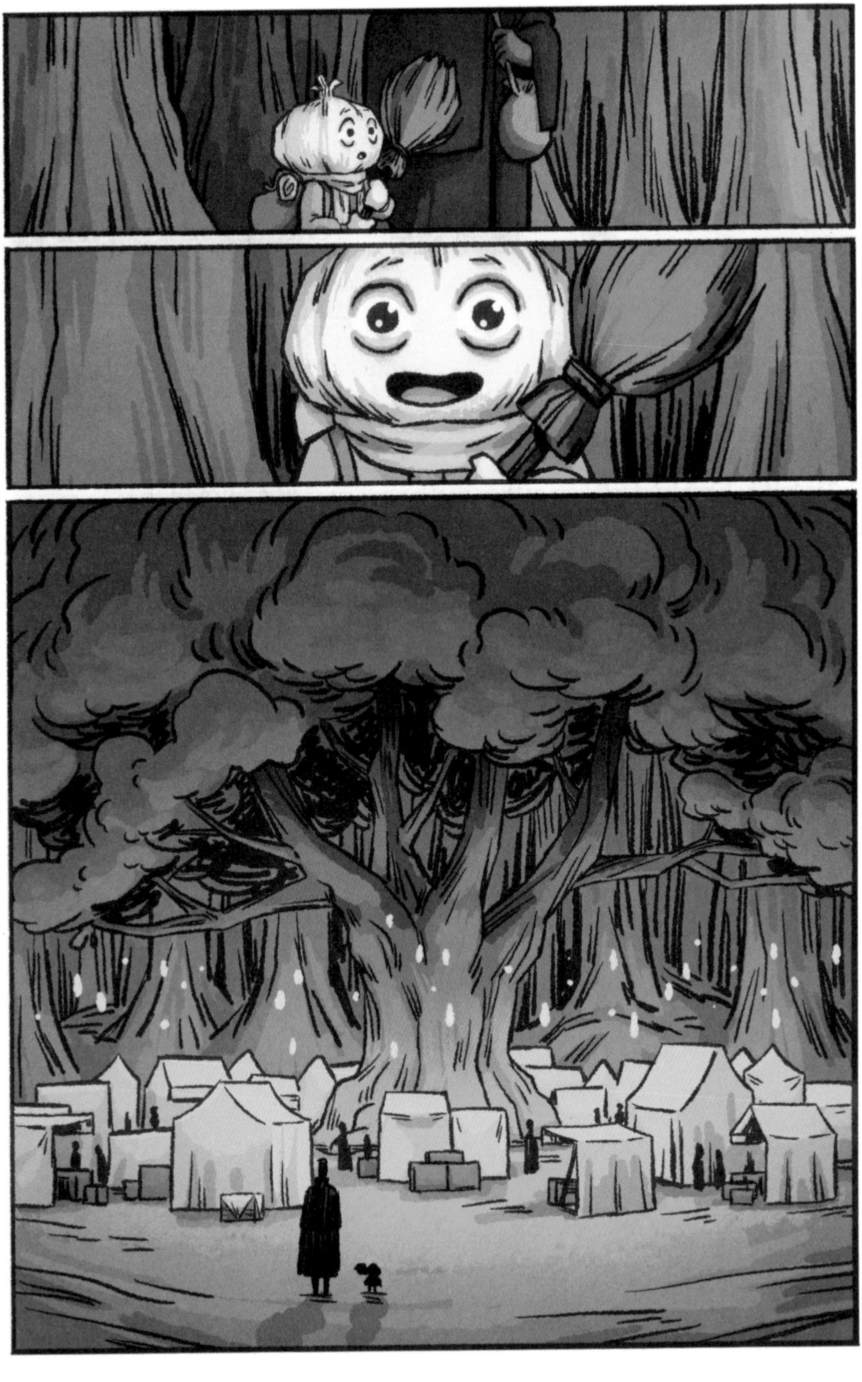

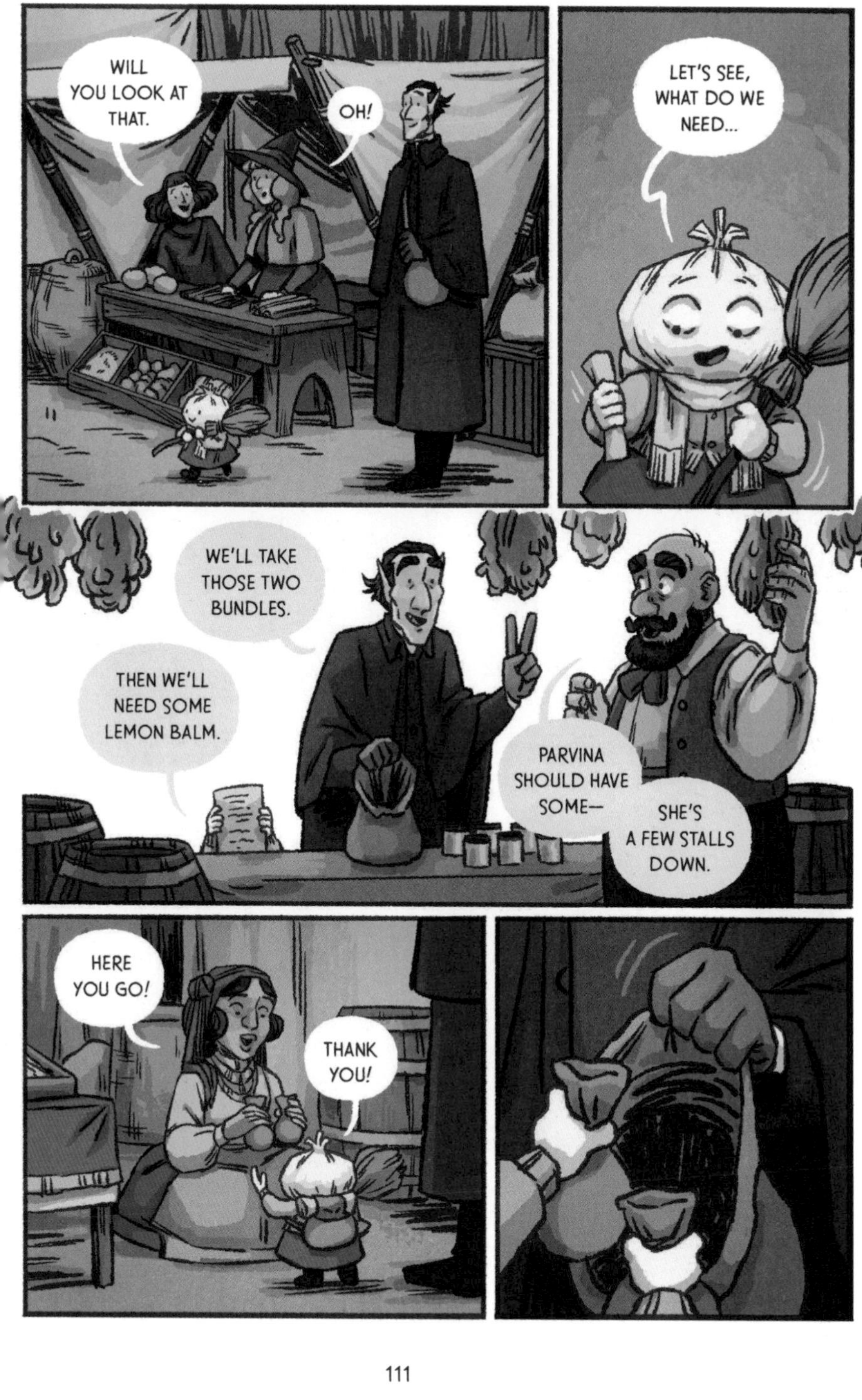

WILL YOU LOOK AT THAT.
OH!
LET'S SEE, WHAT DO WE NEED...
WE'LL TAKE THOSE TWO BUNDLES.
THEN WE'LL NEED SOME LEMON BALM.
PARVINA SHOULD HAVE SOME—
SHE'S A FEW STALLS DOWN.
HERE YOU GO!
THANK YOU!

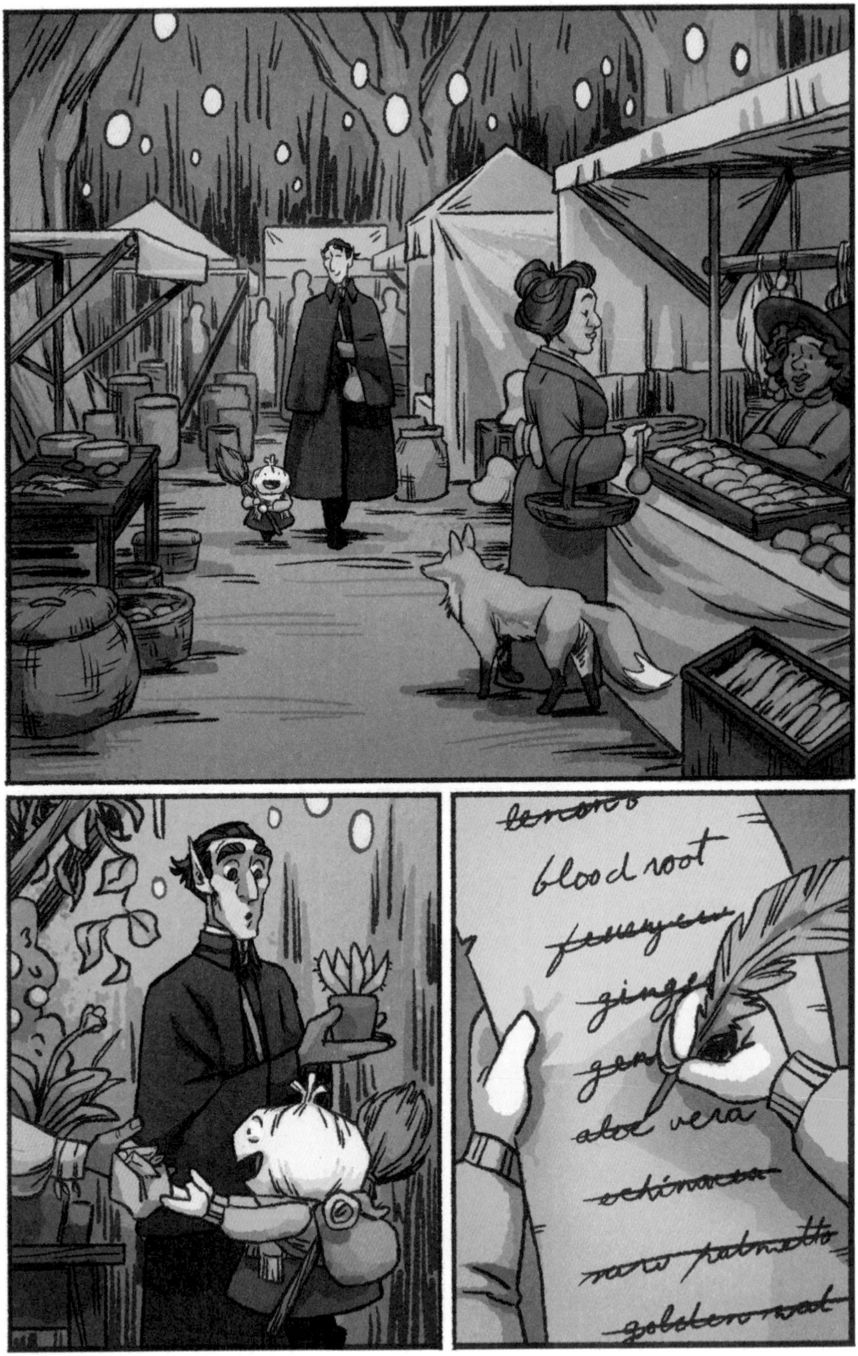
blood root
aloe vera

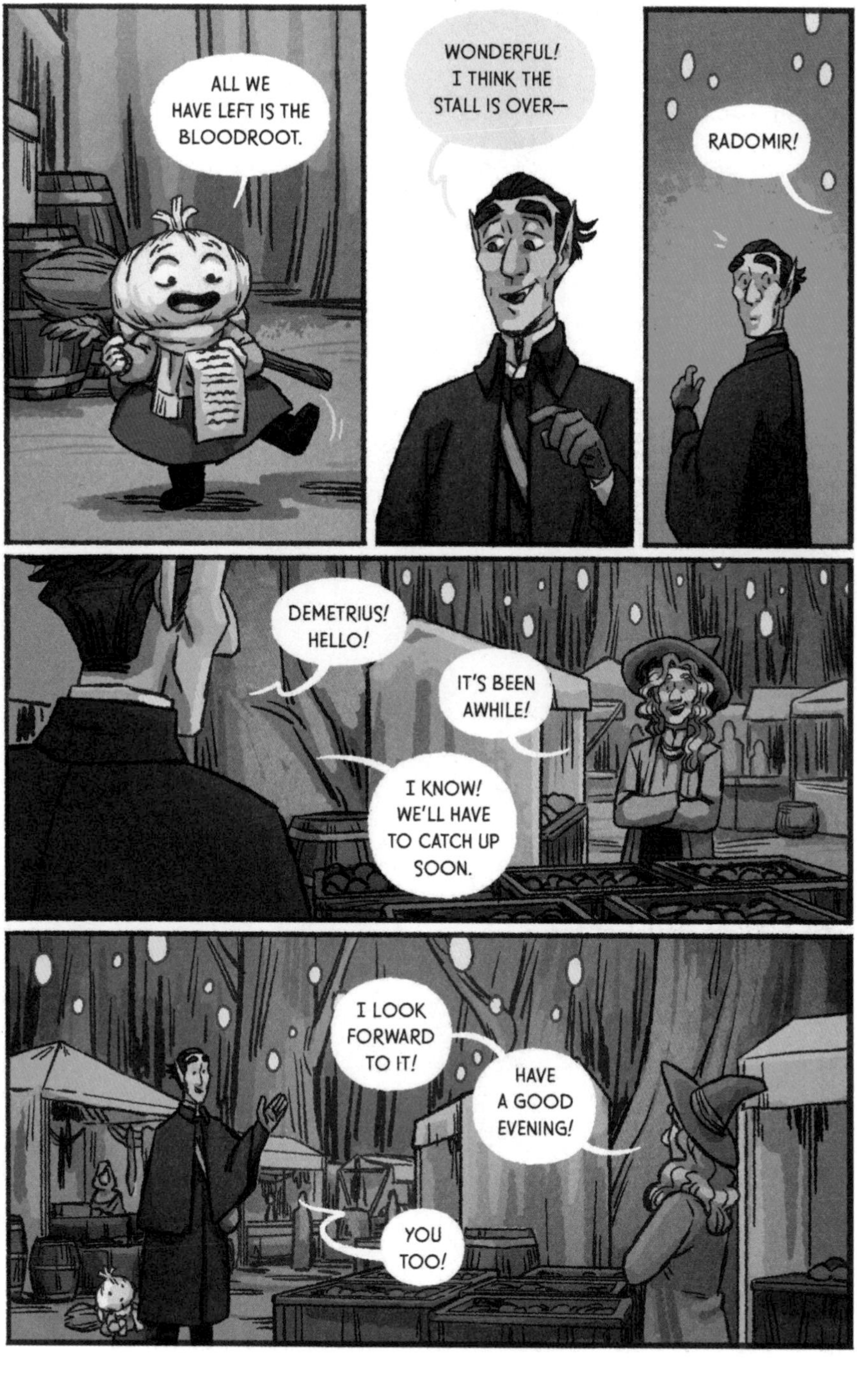
ALL WE HAVE LEFT IS THE BLOODROOT.
WONDERFUL! I THINK THE STALL IS OVER—
RADOMIR!
DEMETRIUS! HELLO!
IT'S BEEN AWHILE!
I KNOW! WE'LL HAVE TO CATCH UP SOON.
I LOOK FORWARD TO IT!
HAVE A GOOD EVENING!
YOU TOO!

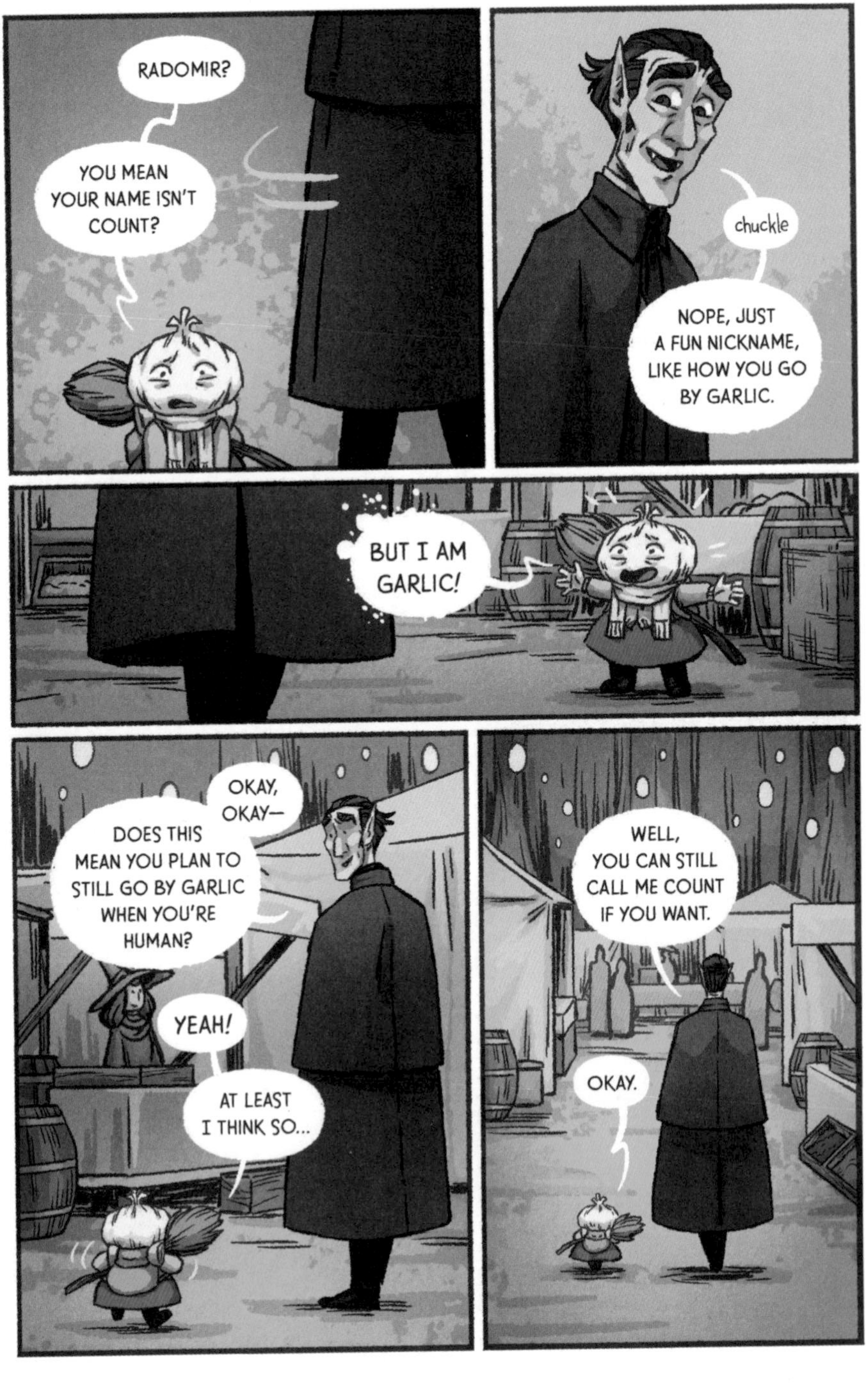

RADOMIR?
YOU MEAN YOUR NAME ISN'T COUNT?
chuckle
NOPE, JUST A FUN NICKNAME, LIKE HOW YOU GO BY GARLIC.
BUT I AM GARLIC!
OKAY, OKAY—
DOES THIS MEAN YOU PLAN TO STILL GO BY GARLIC WHEN YOU'RE HUMAN?
YEAH!
AT LEAST I THINK SO...
WELL, YOU CAN STILL CALL ME COUNT IF YOU WANT.
OKAY.

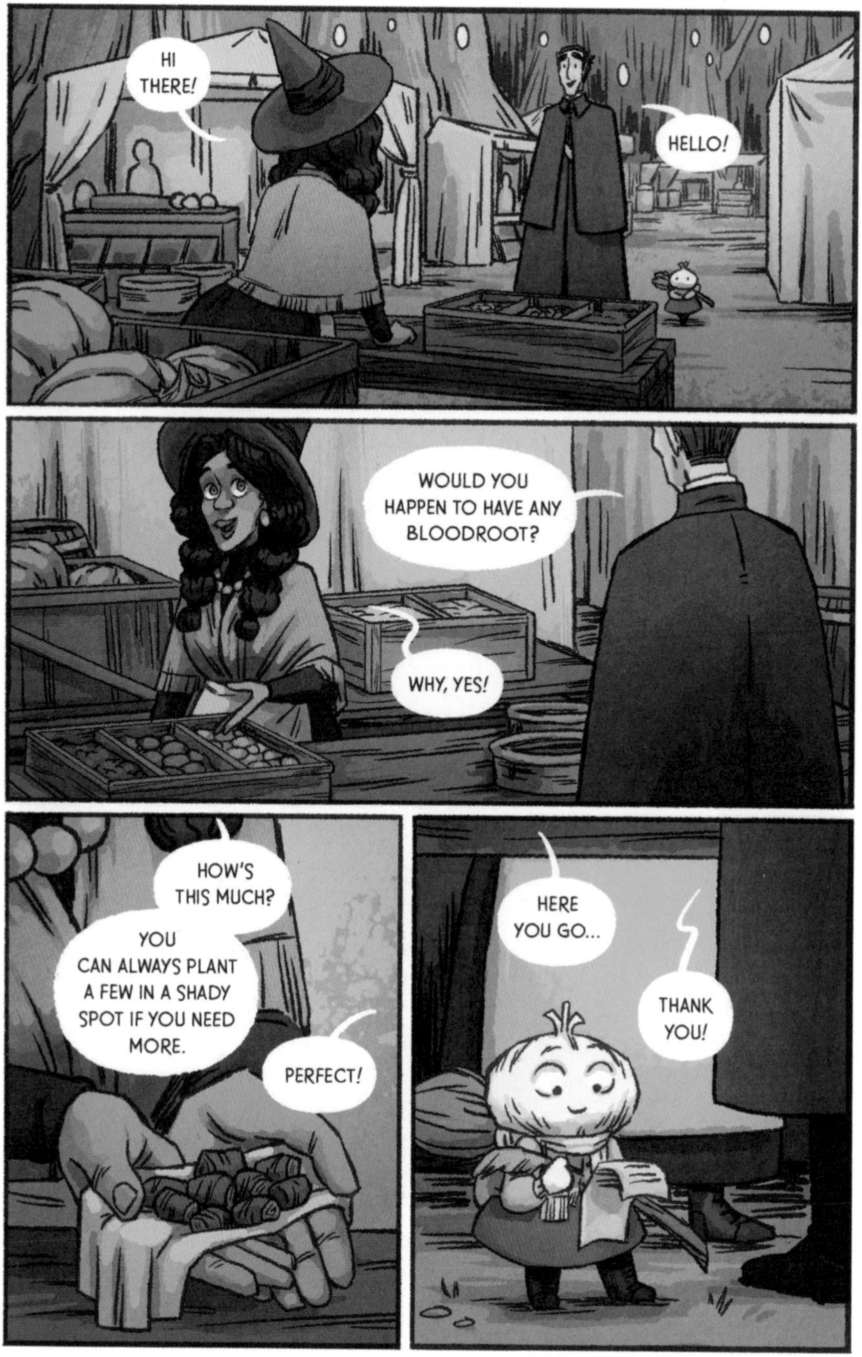
HI THERE!
HELLO!
WOULD YOU HAPPEN TO HAVE ANY BLOODROOT?
WHY, YES!
HOW'S THIS MUCH?
YOU CAN ALWAYS PLANT A FEW IN A SHADY SPOT IF YOU NEED MORE.
PERFECT!
HERE YOU GO...
THANK YOU!

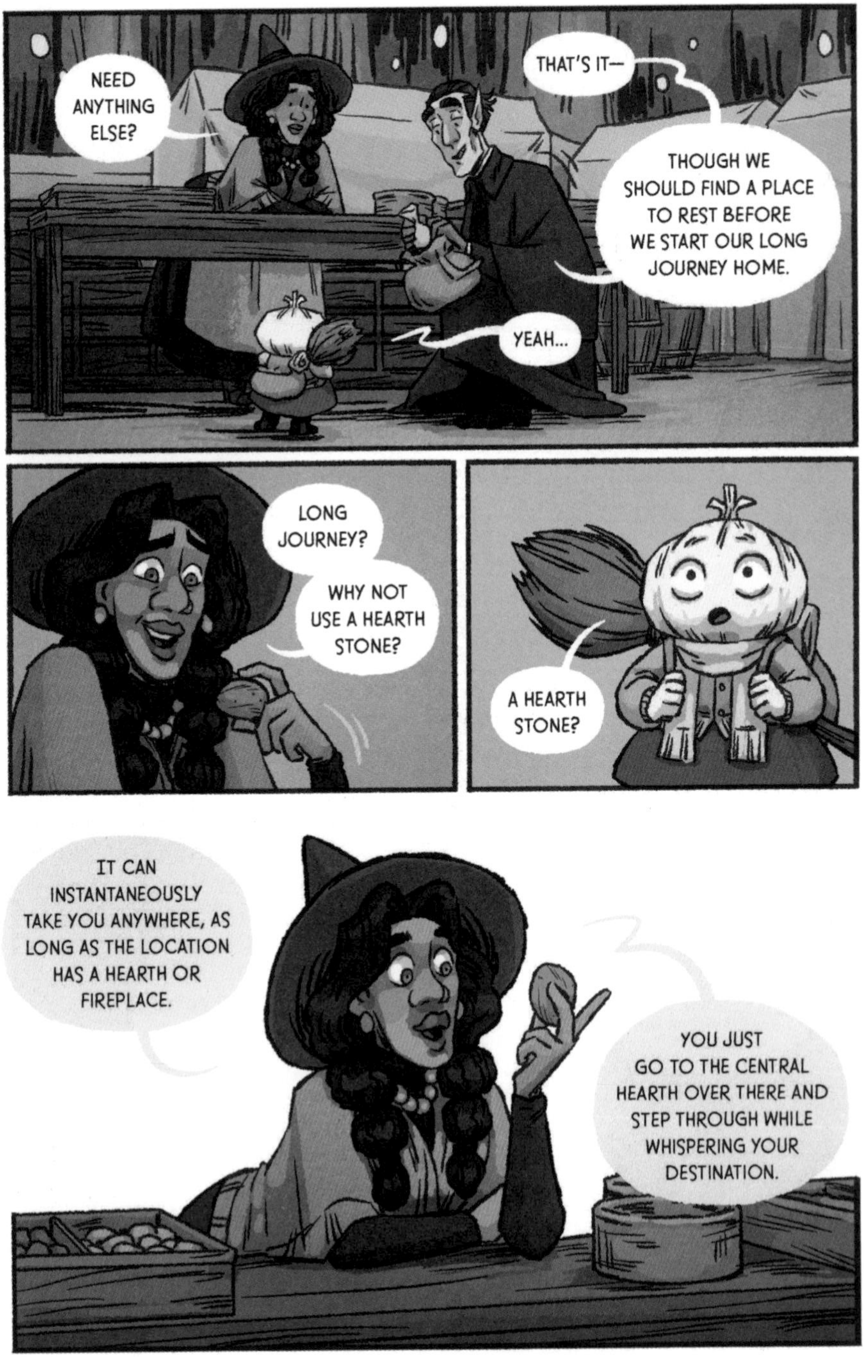
NEED ANYTHING ELSE?
THAT'S IT—
THOUGH WE SHOULD FIND A PLACE TO REST BEFORE WE START OUR LONG JOURNEY HOME.
YEAH...
LONG JOURNEY?
WHY NOT USE A HEARTH STONE?
A HEARTH STONE?
IT CAN INSTANTANEOUSLY TAKE YOU ANYWHERE, AS LONG AS THE LOCATION HAS A HEARTH OR FIREPLACE.
YOU JUST GO TO THE CENTRAL HEARTH OVER THERE AND STEP THROUGH WHILE WHISPERING YOUR DESTINATION.

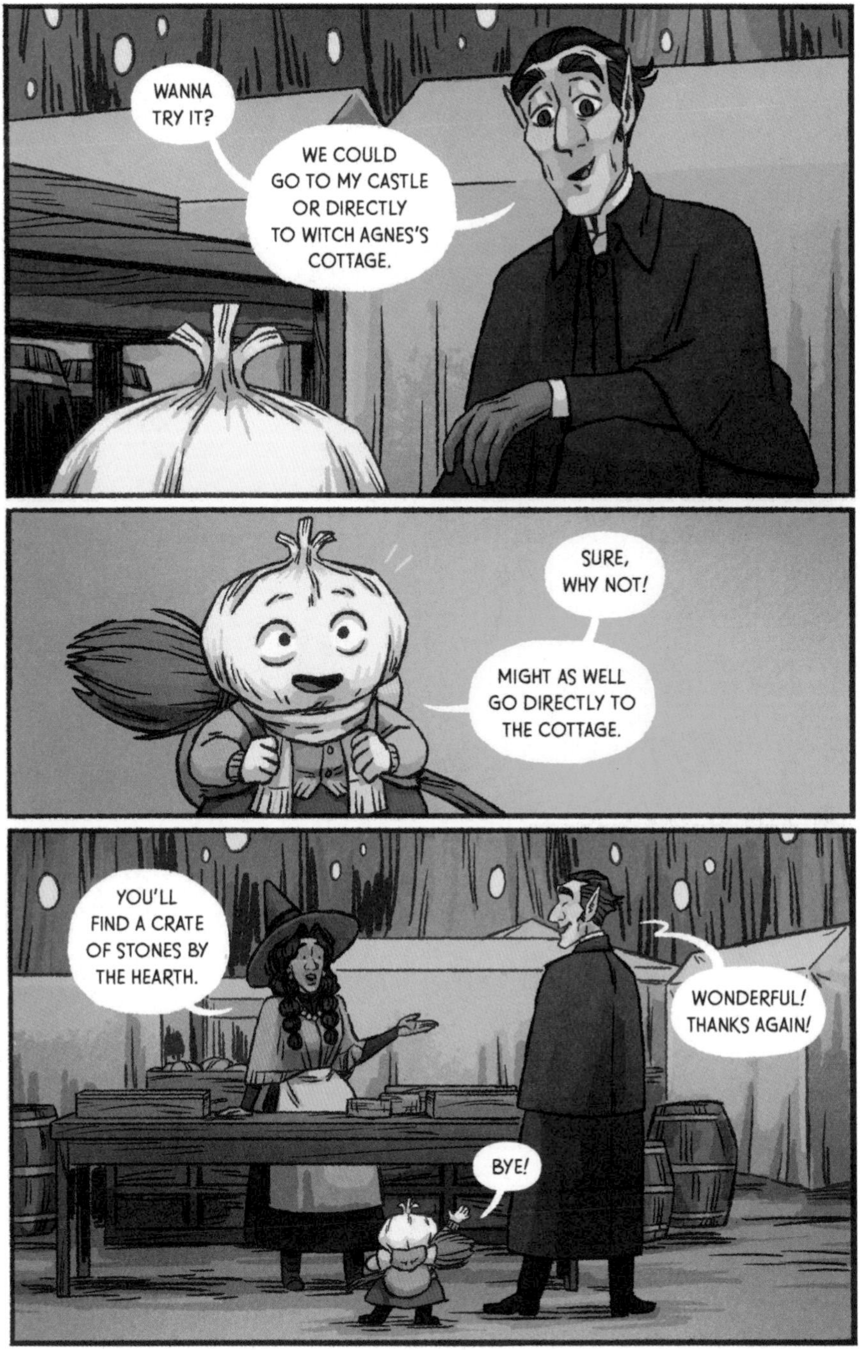
WANNA TRY IT?
WE COULD GO TO MY CASTLE OR DIRECTLY TO WITCH AGNES'S COTTAGE.
SURE, WHY NOT!
MIGHT AS WELL GO DIRECTLY TO THE COTTAGE.
YOU'LL FIND A CRATE OF STONES BY THE HEARTH.
WONDERFUL! THANKS AGAIN!
BYE!

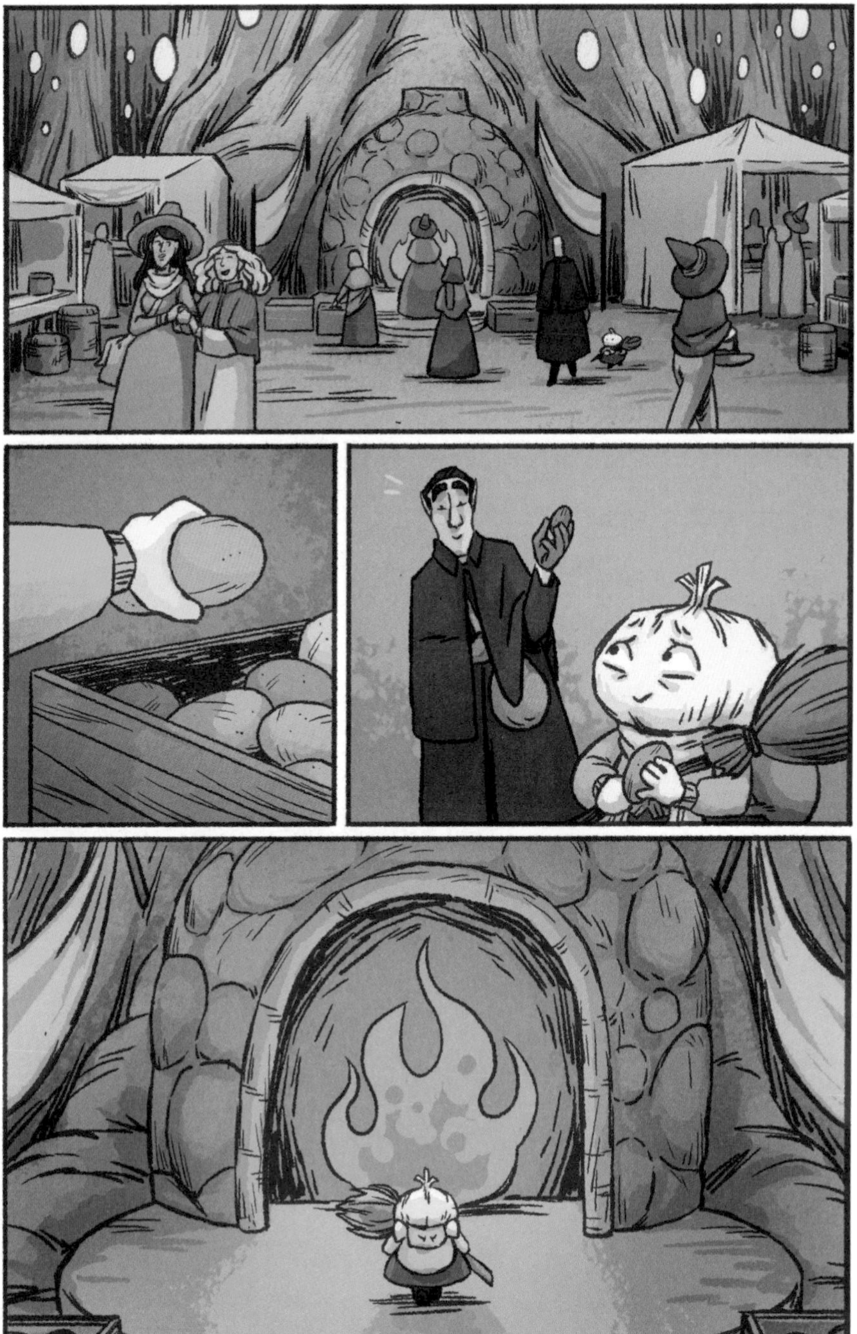

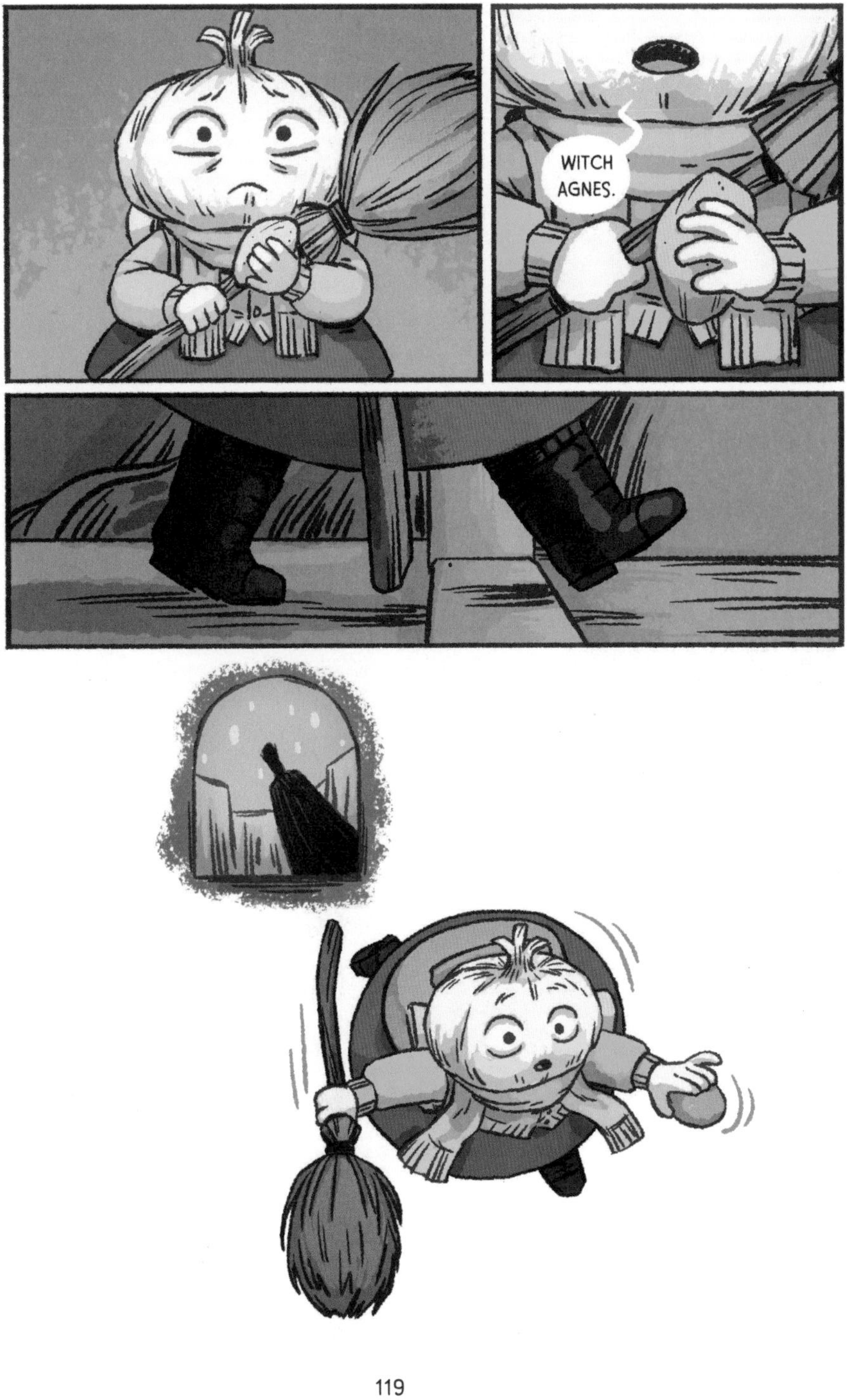
WITCH
AGNES.

chapter six

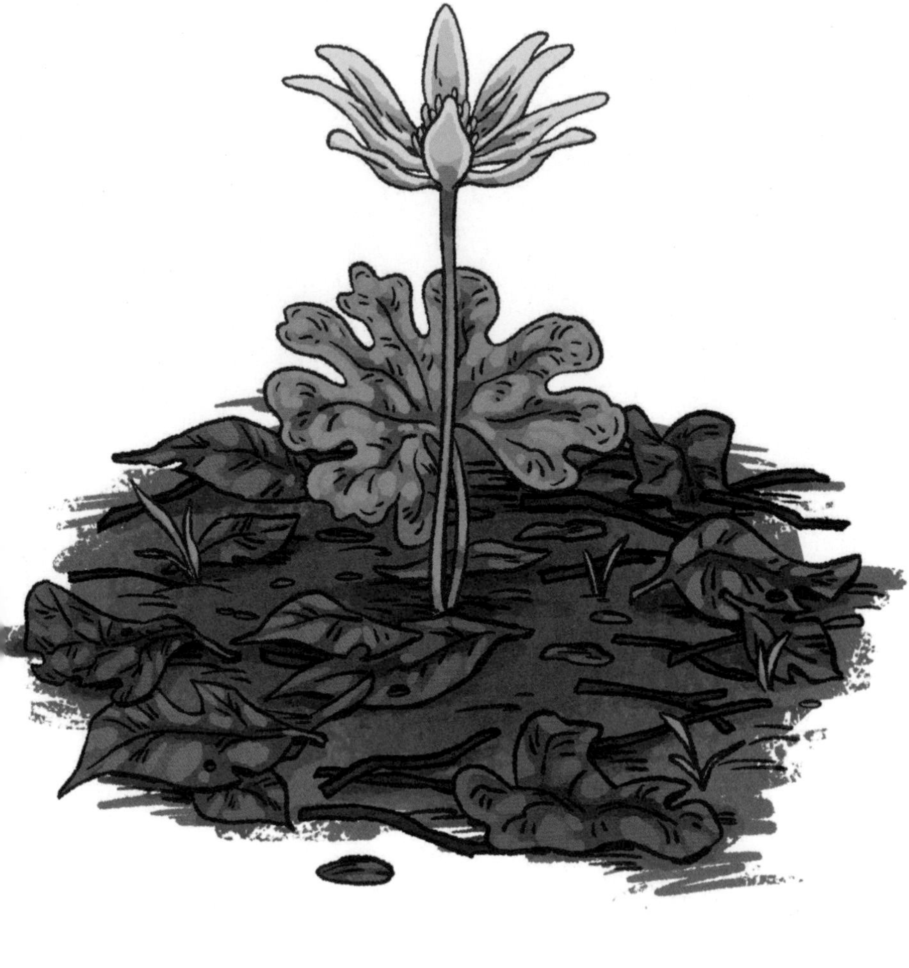

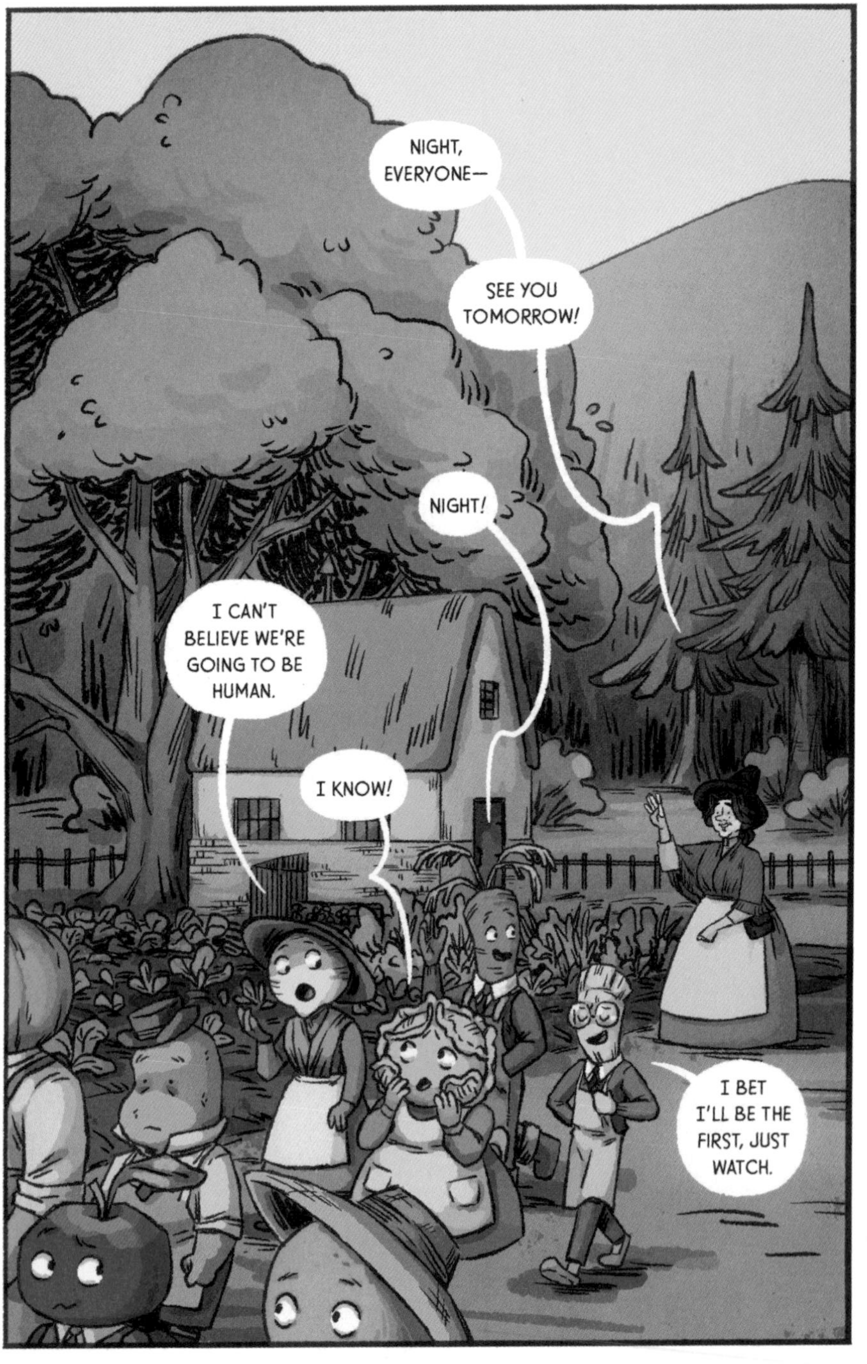
NIGHT, EVERYONE—
SEE YOU TOMORROW!
NIGHT!
I CAN'T BELIEVE WE'RE GOING TO BE HUMAN.
I KNOW!
I BET I'LL BE THE FIRST, JUST WATCH.

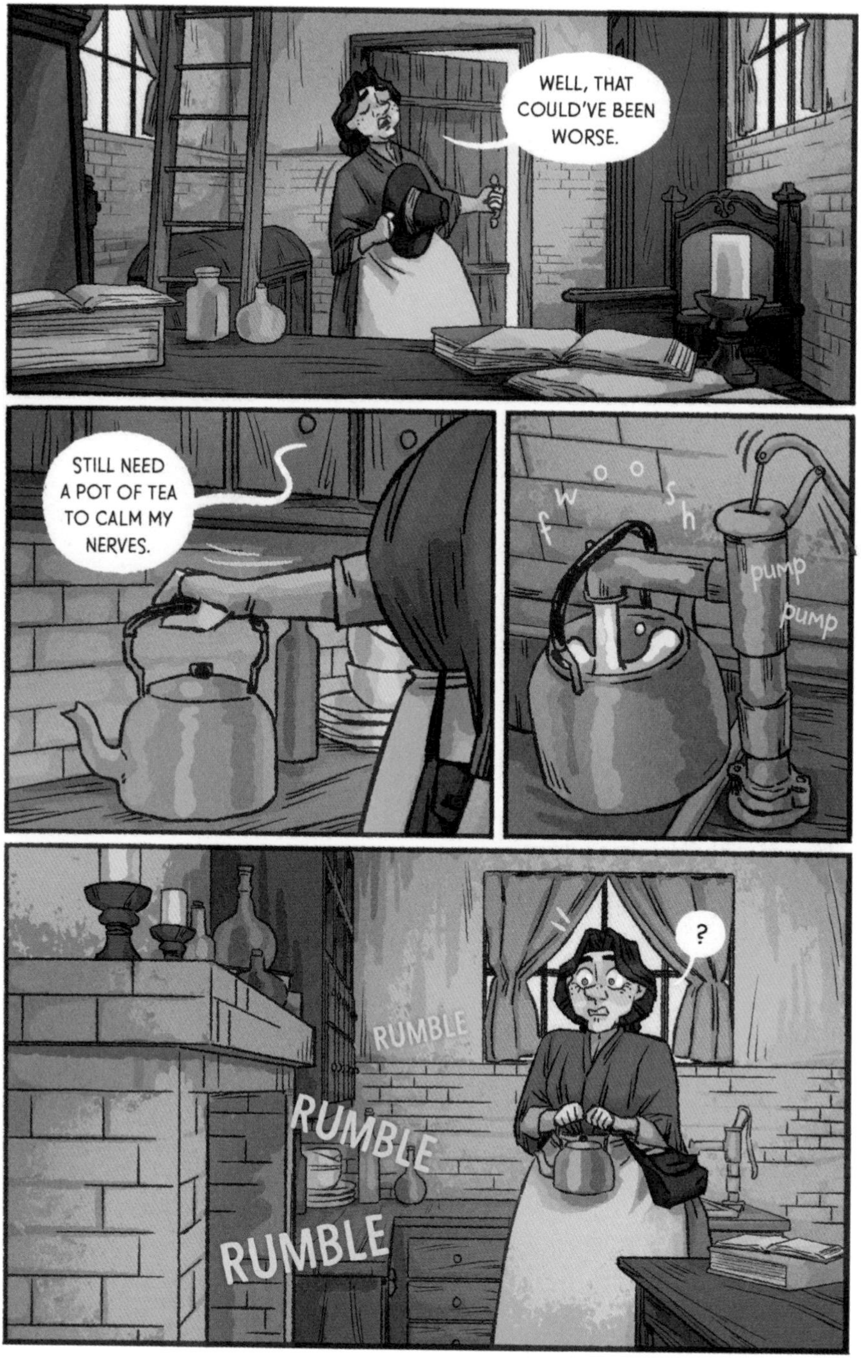
WELL, THAT COULD'VE BEEN WORSE.
STILL NEED A POT OF TEA TO CALM MY NERVES.
fwoosh
pump
pump
?
RUMBLE
RUMBLE
RUMBLE

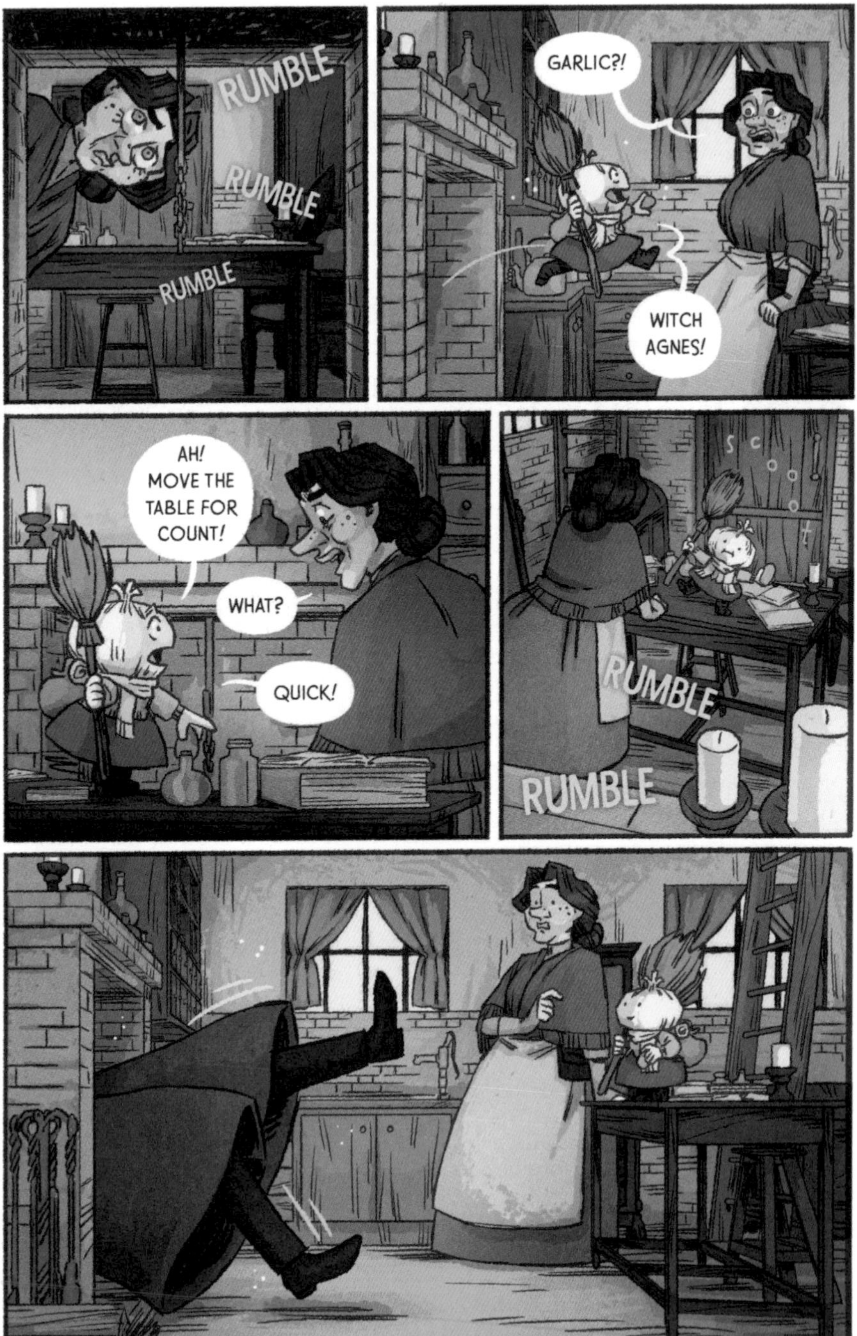
RUMBLE
RUMBLE
RUMBLE
GARLIC?!
WITCH AGNES!
AH! MOVE THE TABLE FOR COUNT!
WHAT?
QUICK!
RUMBLE
RUMBLE

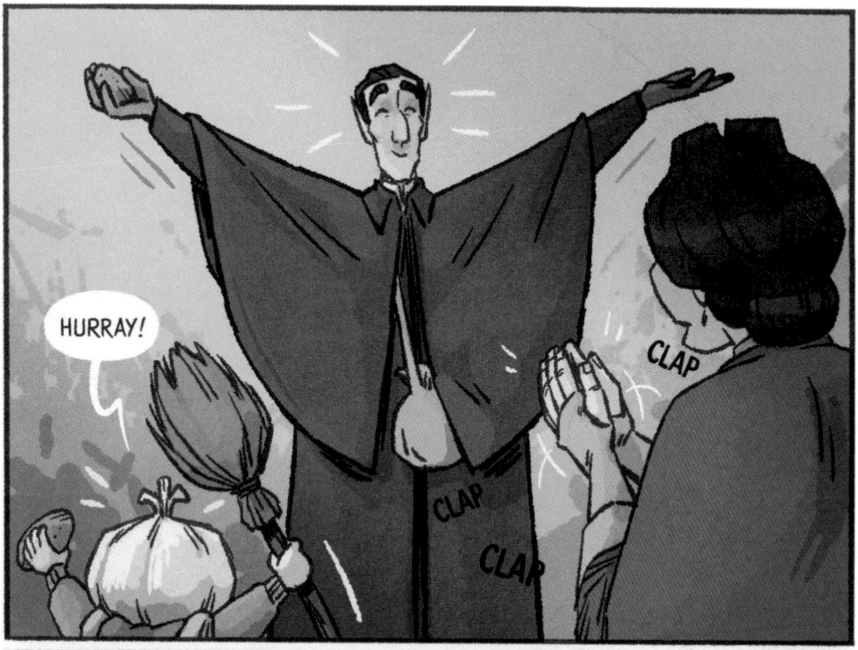
HURRAY!
CLAP
CLAP
CLAP

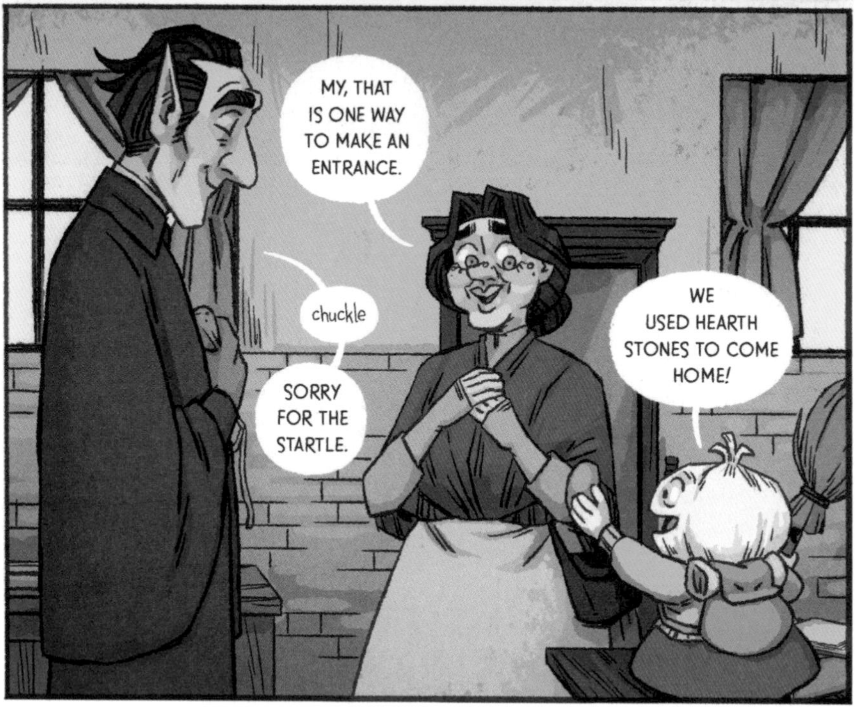
MY, THAT IS ONE WAY TO MAKE AN ENTRANCE.
chuckle
SORRY FOR THE STARTLE.
WE USED HEARTH STONES TO COME HOME!

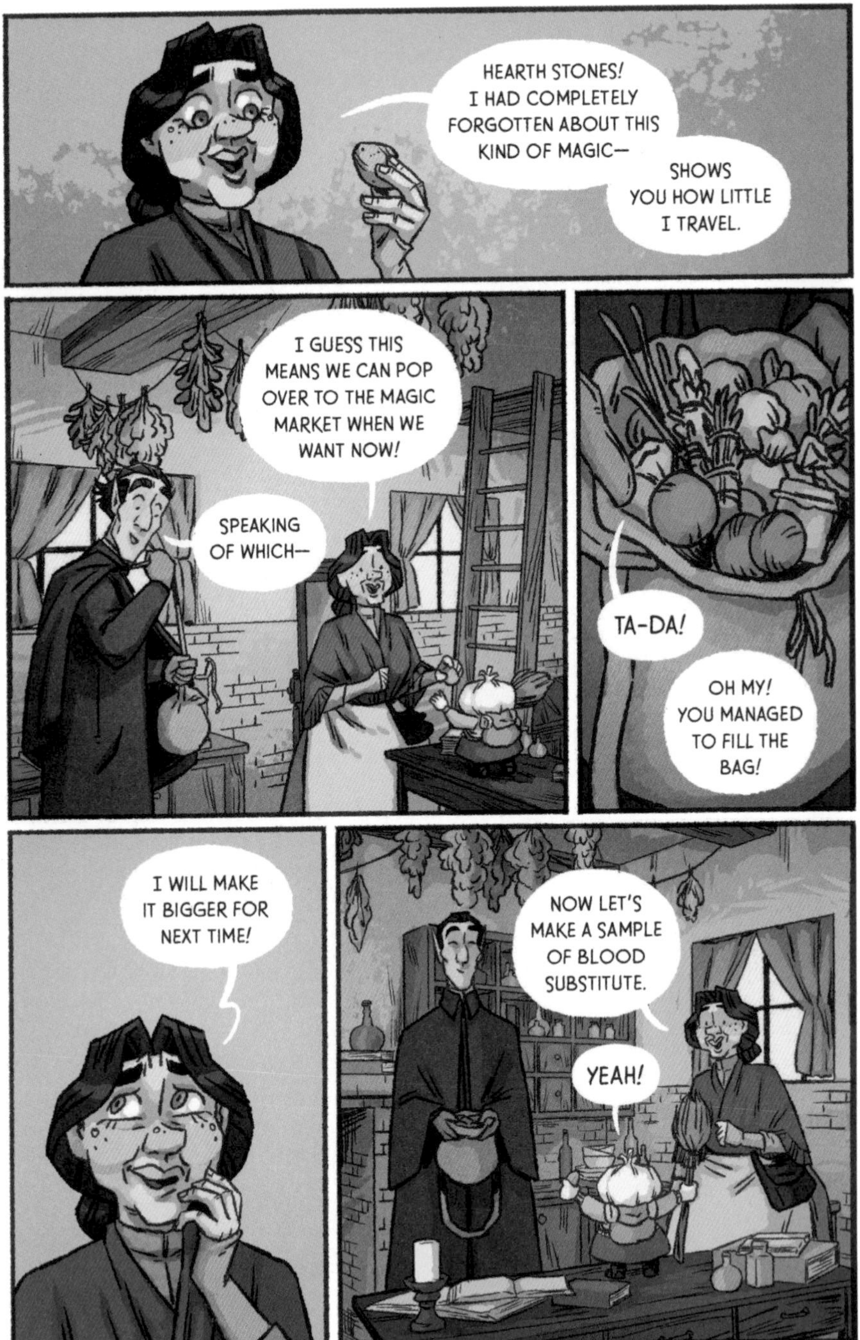
HEARTH STONES! I HAD COMPLETELY FORGOTTEN ABOUT THIS KIND OF MAGIC—
SHOWS YOU HOW LITTLE I TRAVEL.
I GUESS THIS MEANS WE CAN POP OVER TO THE MAGIC MARKET WHEN WE WANT NOW!
SPEAKING OF WHICH--
TA-DA!
OH MY! YOU MANAGED TO FILL THE BAG!
I WILL MAKE IT BIGGER FOR NEXT TIME!
NOW LET'S MAKE A SAMPLE OF BLOOD SUBSTITUTE.
YEAH!

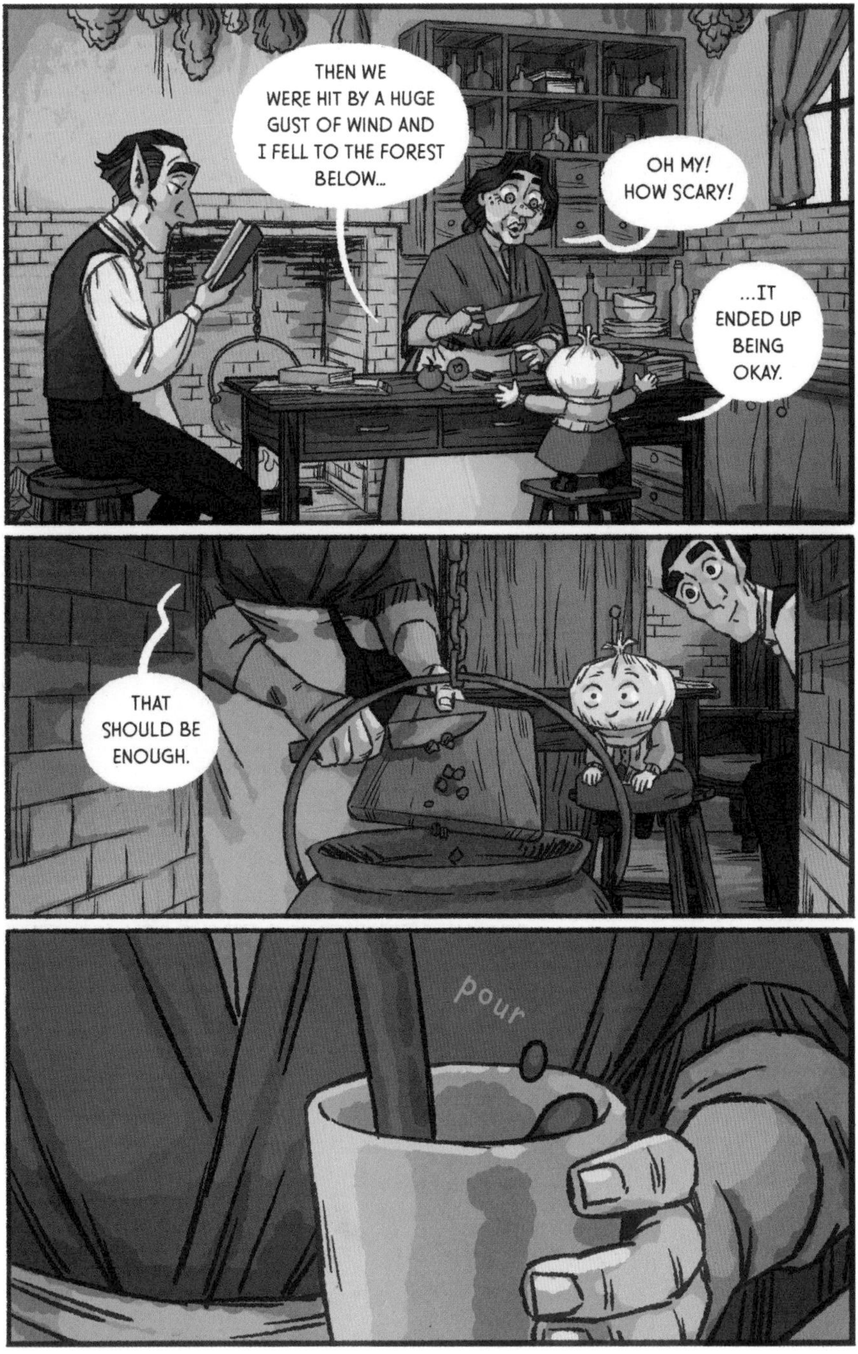
THEN WE WERE HIT BY A HUGE GUST OF WIND AND I FELL TO THE FOREST BELOW...
OH MY! HOW SCARY!
...IT ENDED UP BEING OKAY.
THAT SHOULD BE ENOUGH.
pour

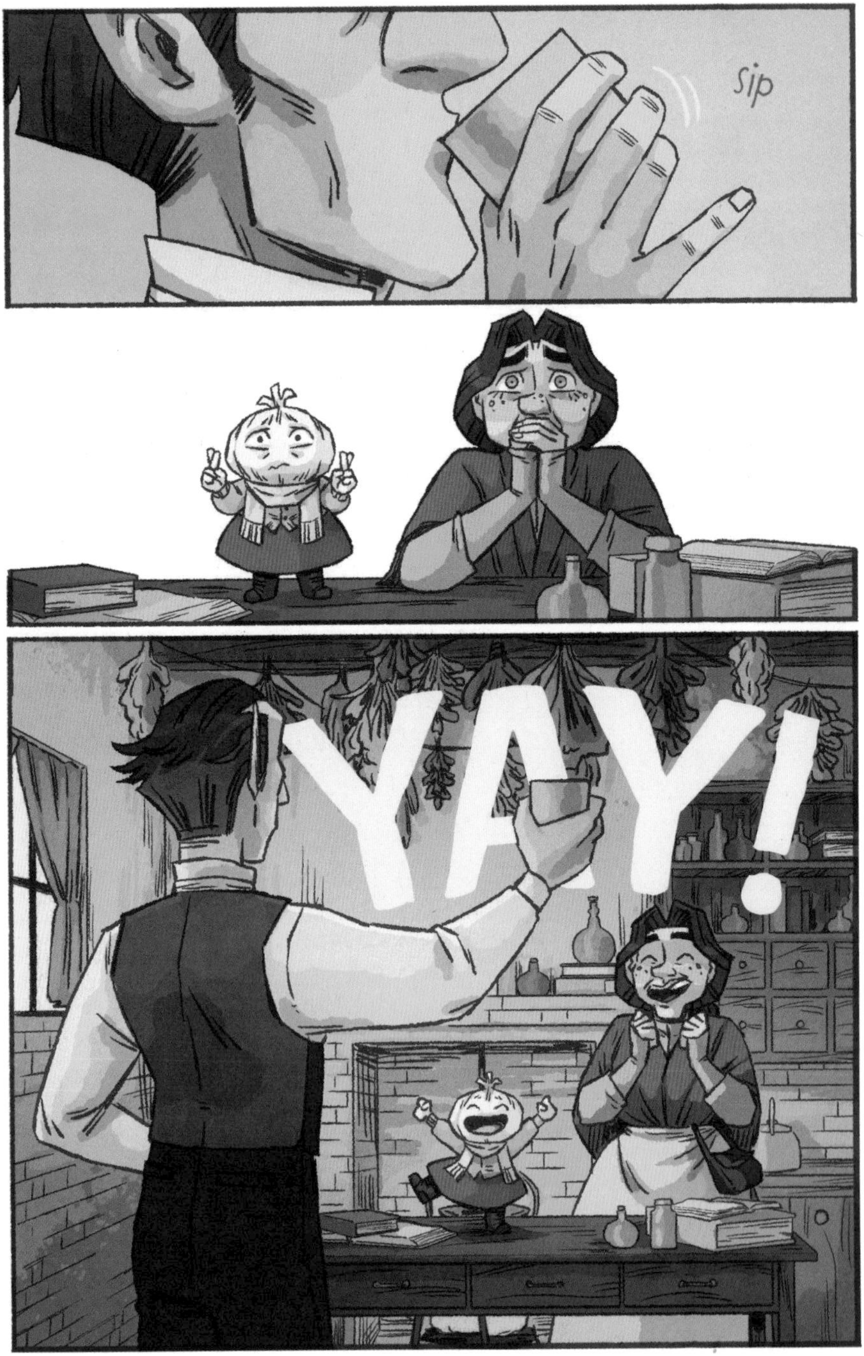
Sip
YAY!

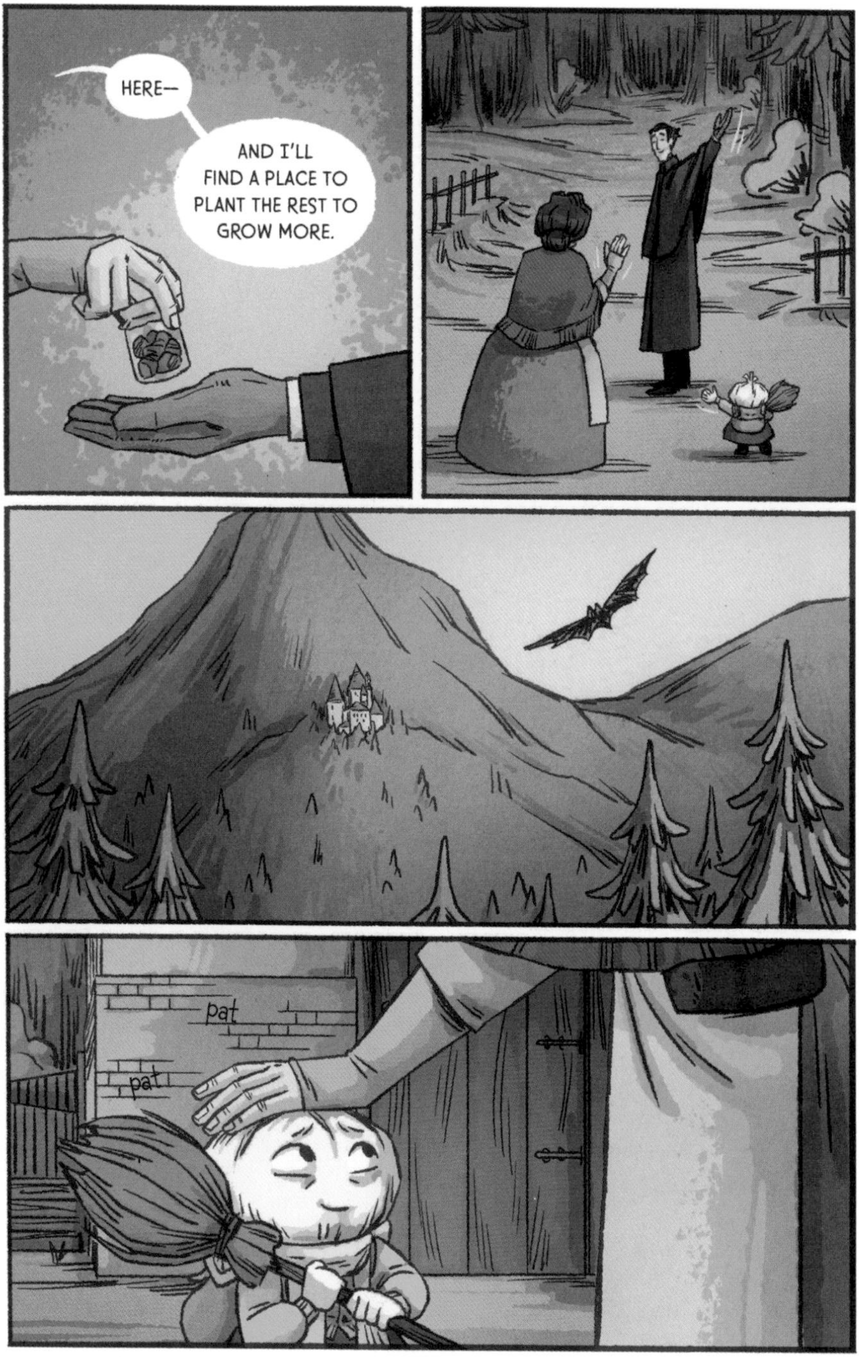
HERE—
AND I'LL FIND A PLACE TO PLANT THE REST TO GROW MORE.
pat
pat

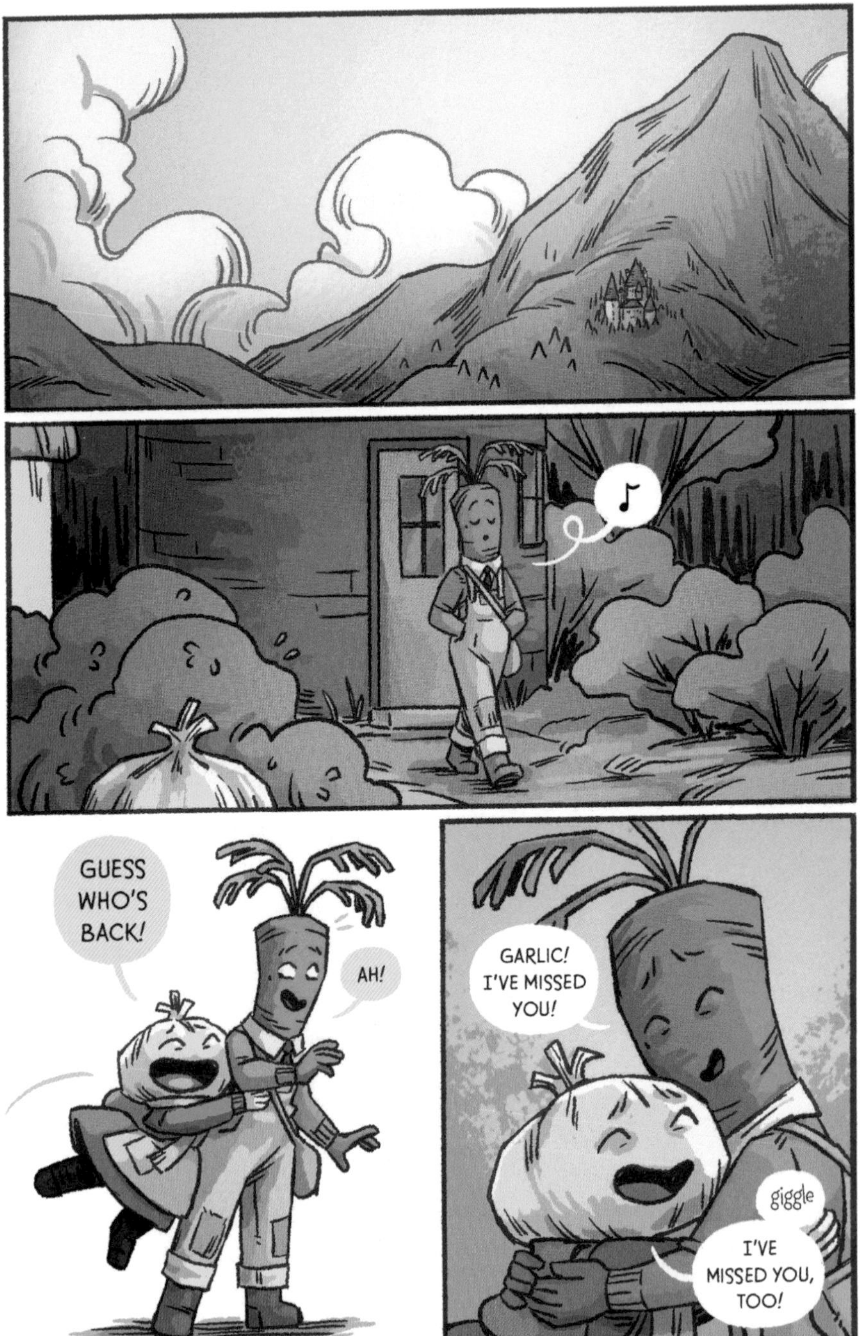
♪
GUESS WHO'S BACK!
AH!
GARLIC! I'VE MISSED YOU!
giggle
I'VE MISSED YOU, TOO!

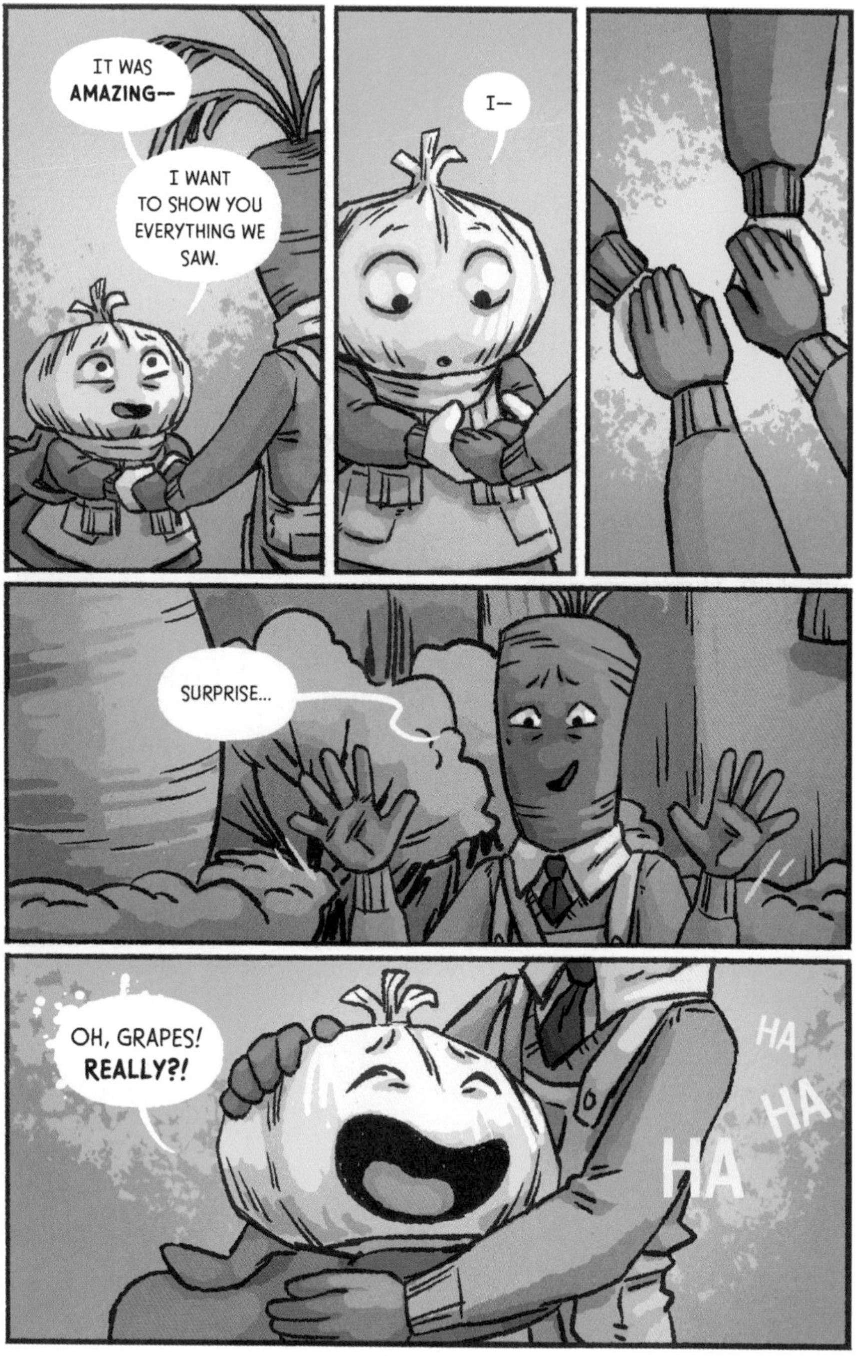
IT WAS AMAZING—
I WANT TO SHOW YOU EVERYTHING WE SAW.
I—
SURPRISE...
OH, GRAPES! REALLY?!
HA HA HA

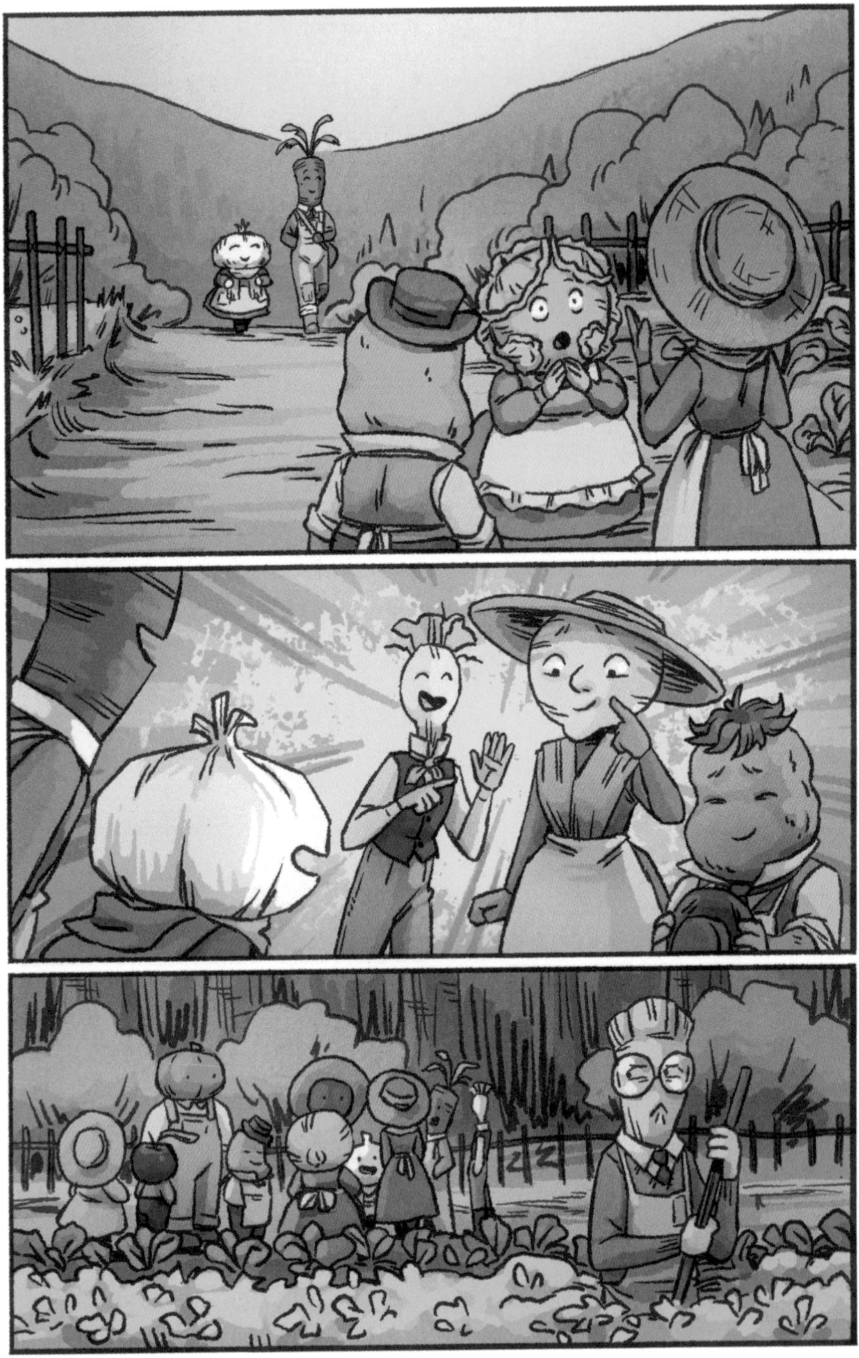

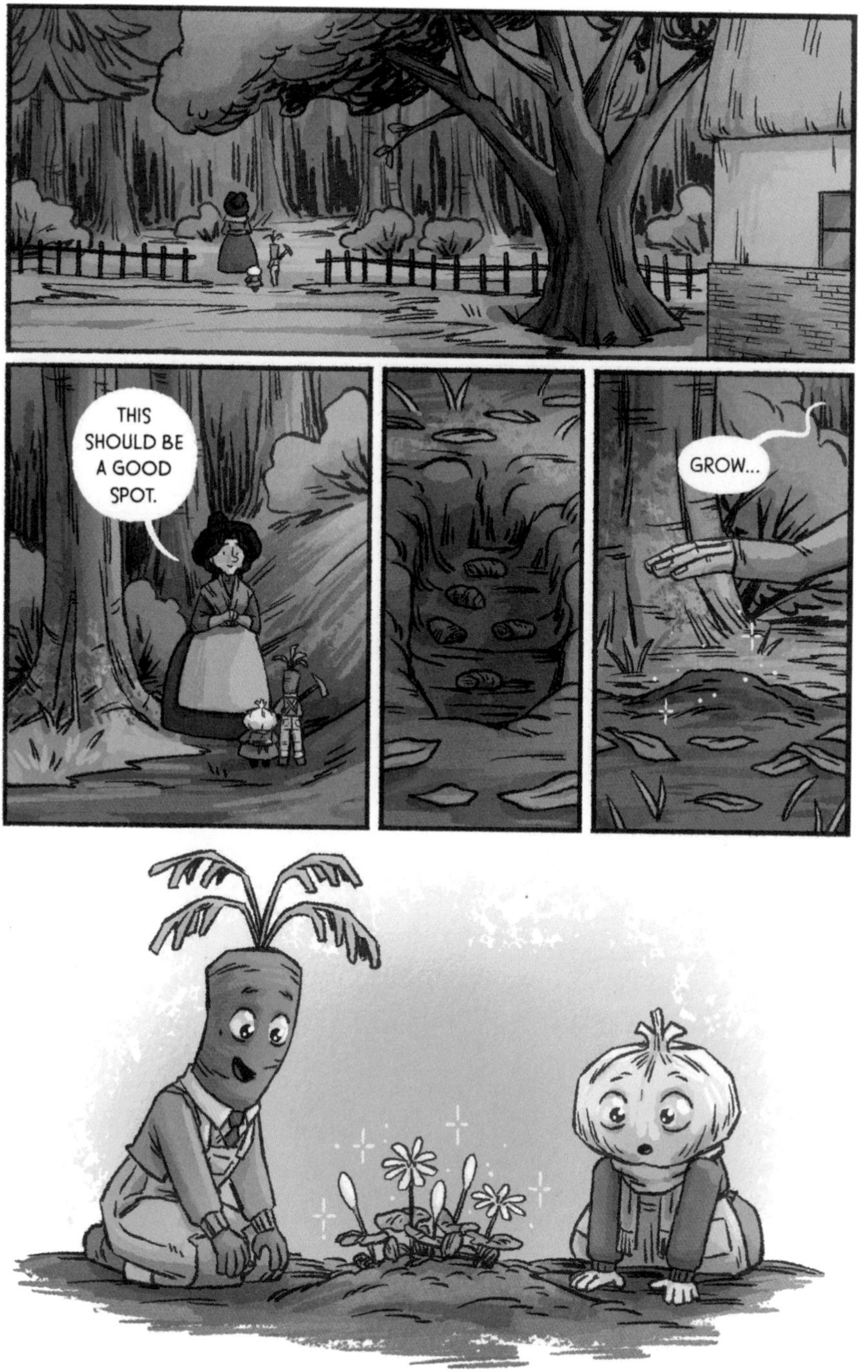
THIS SHOULD BE A GOOD SPOT.
GROW...

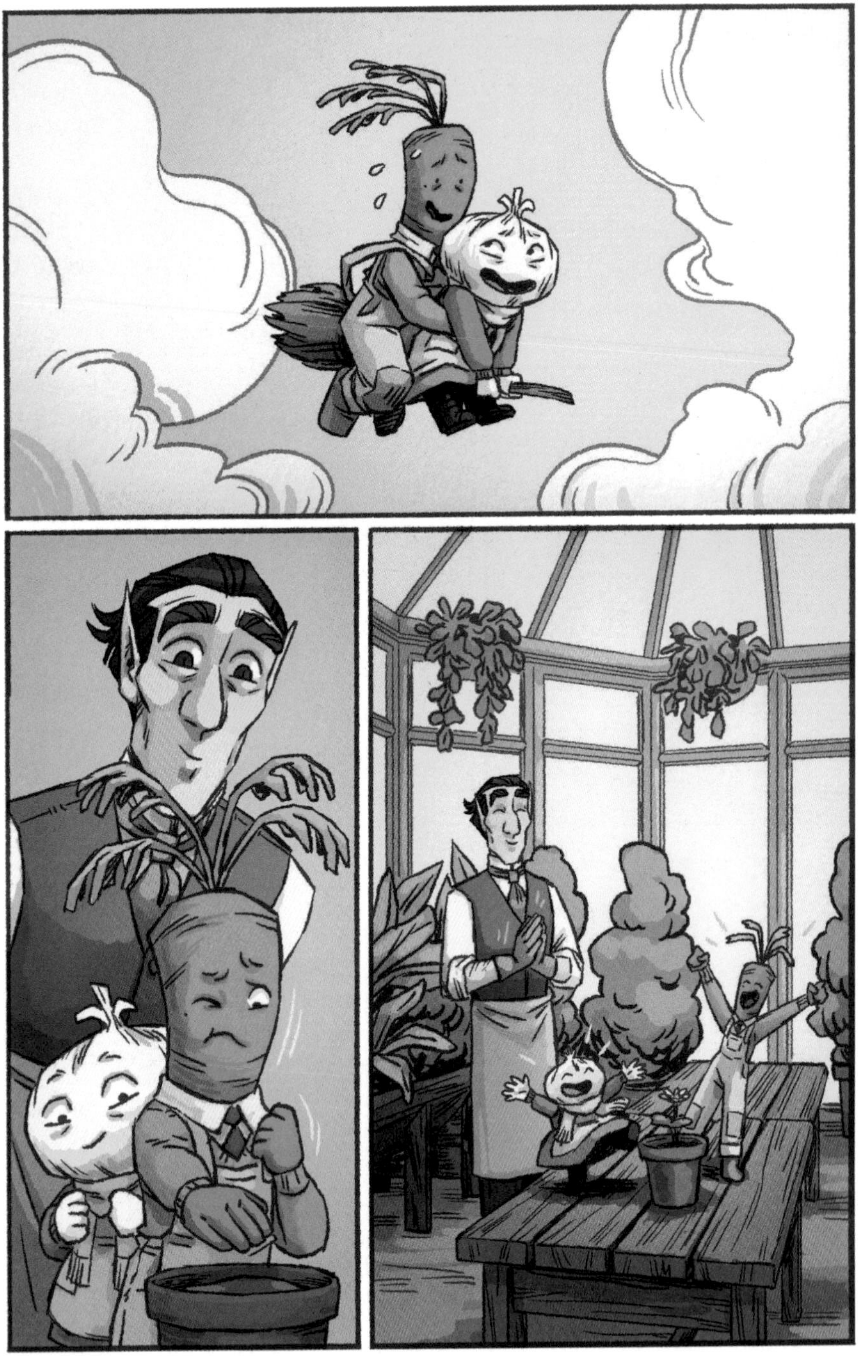

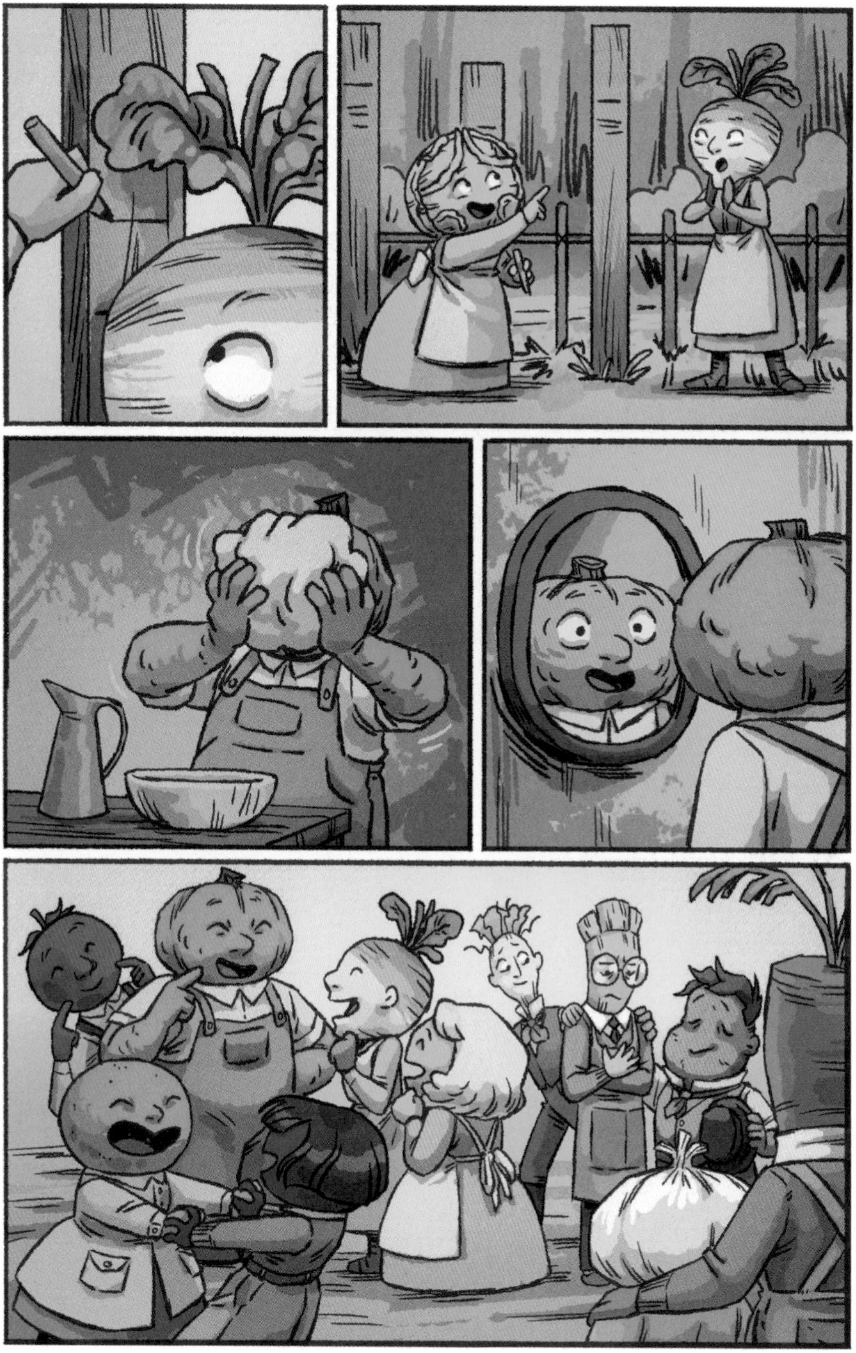

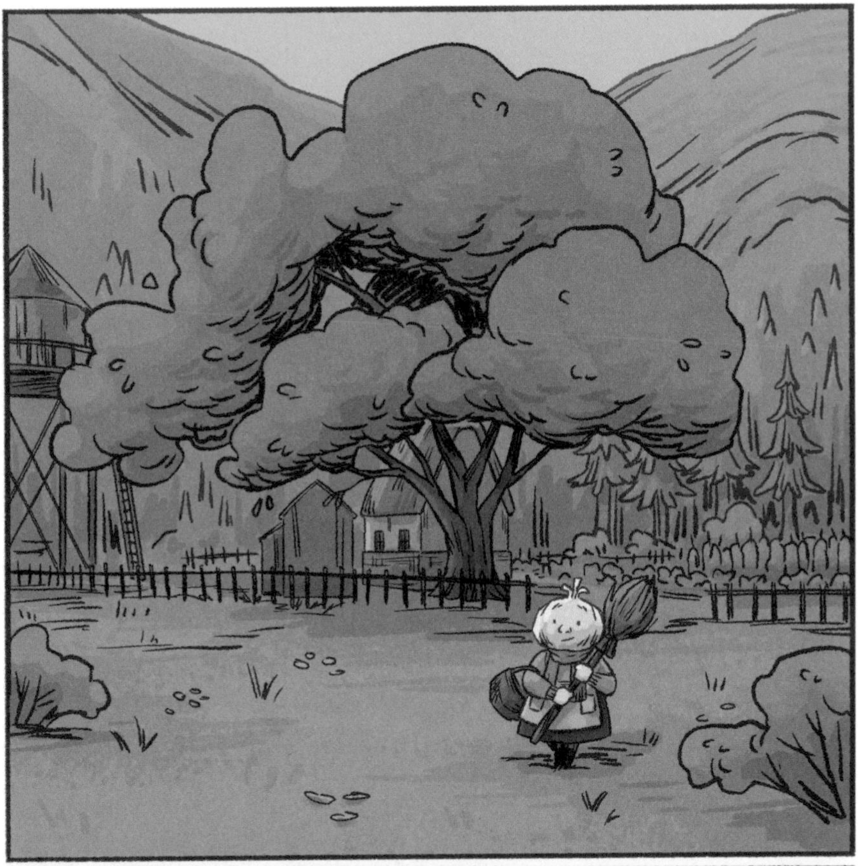

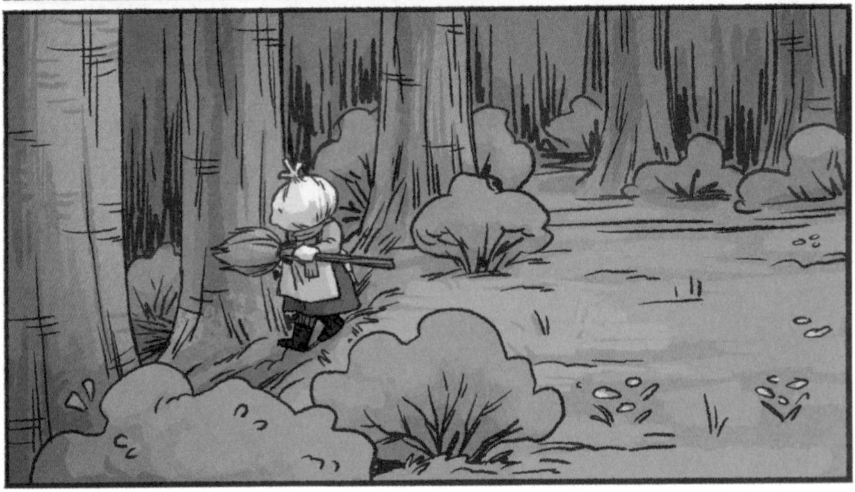

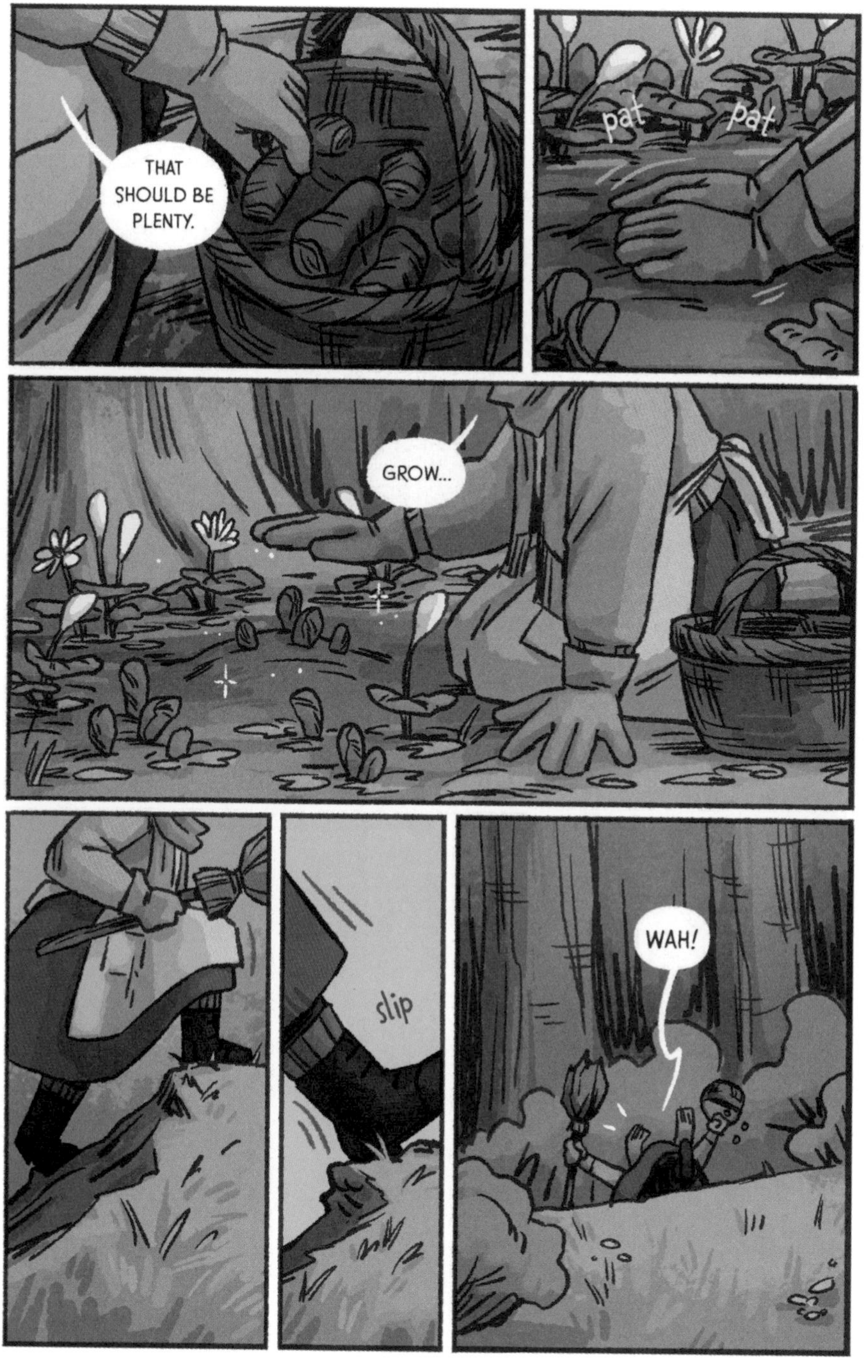
THAT SHOULD BE PLENTY.
pat
pat
GROW...
slip
WAH!

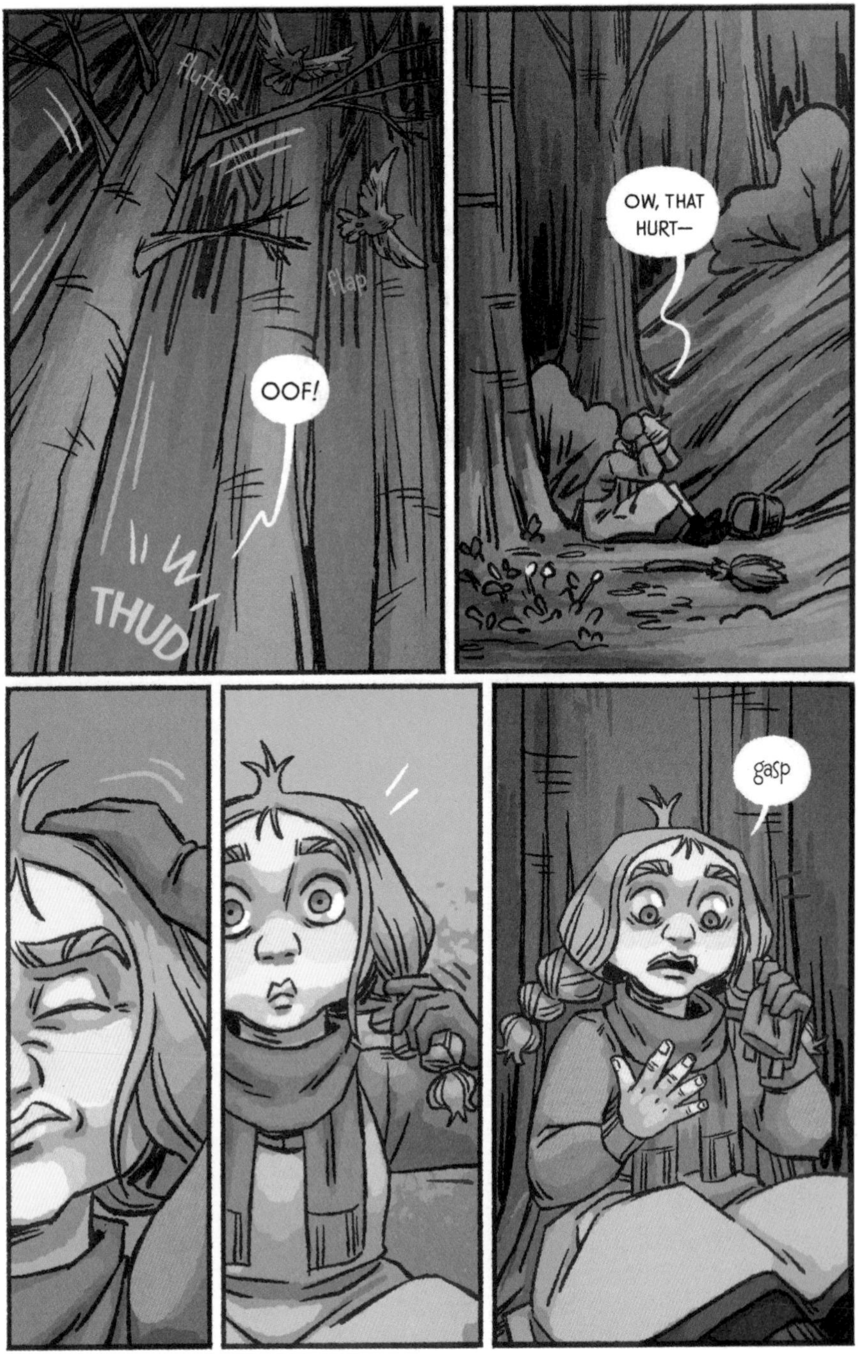
flutter
flap
OOF!
THUD
OW, THAT HURT—
gasp

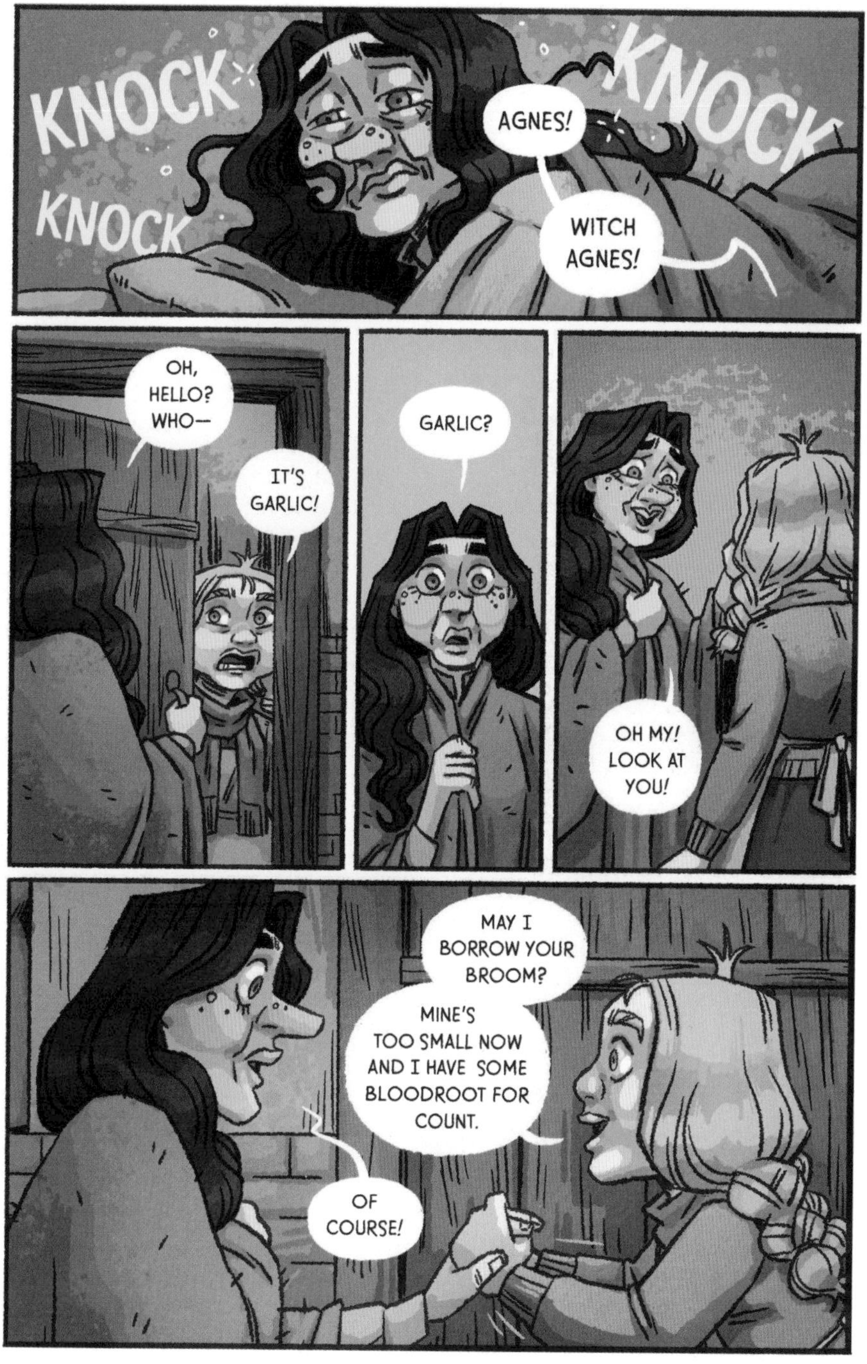
KNOCK
KNOCK
KNOCK
AGNES!
WITCH AGNES!
OH, HELLO? WHO—
IT'S GARLIC!
GARLIC?
OH MY! LOOK AT YOU!
MAY I BORROW YOUR BROOM?
MINE'S TOO SMALL NOW AND I HAVE SOME BLOODROOT FOR COUNT.
OF COURSE!

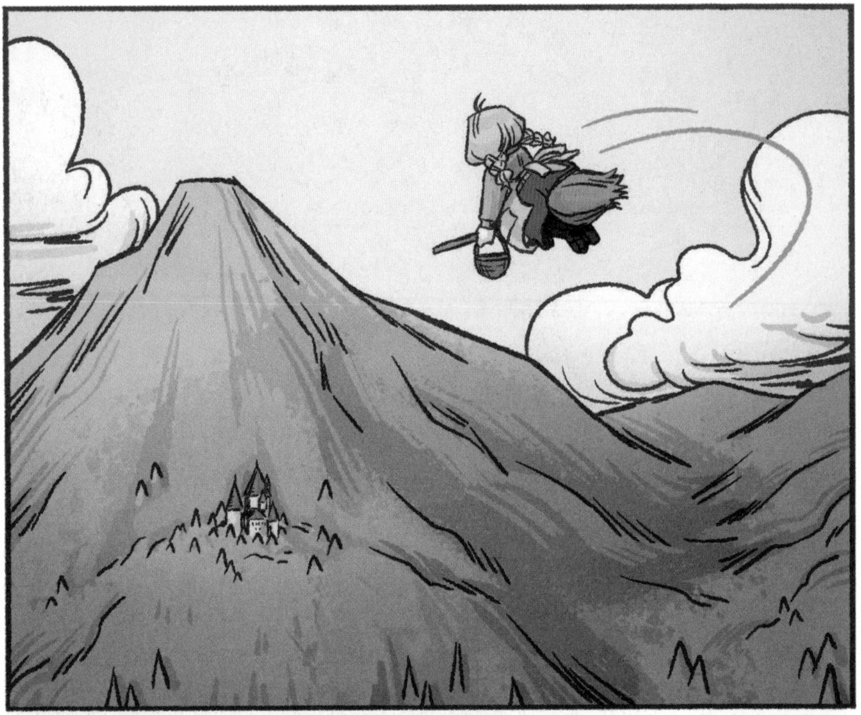

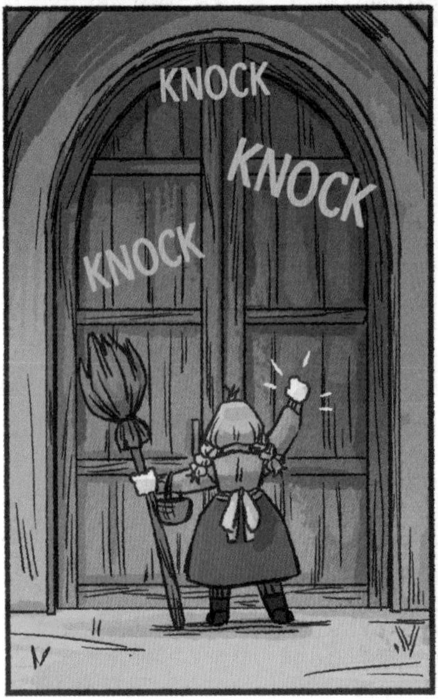
KNOCK
KNOCK
KNOCK

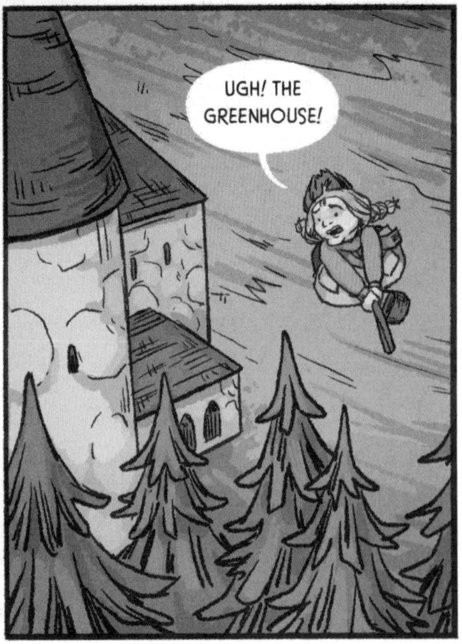
UGH! THE GREENHOUSE!

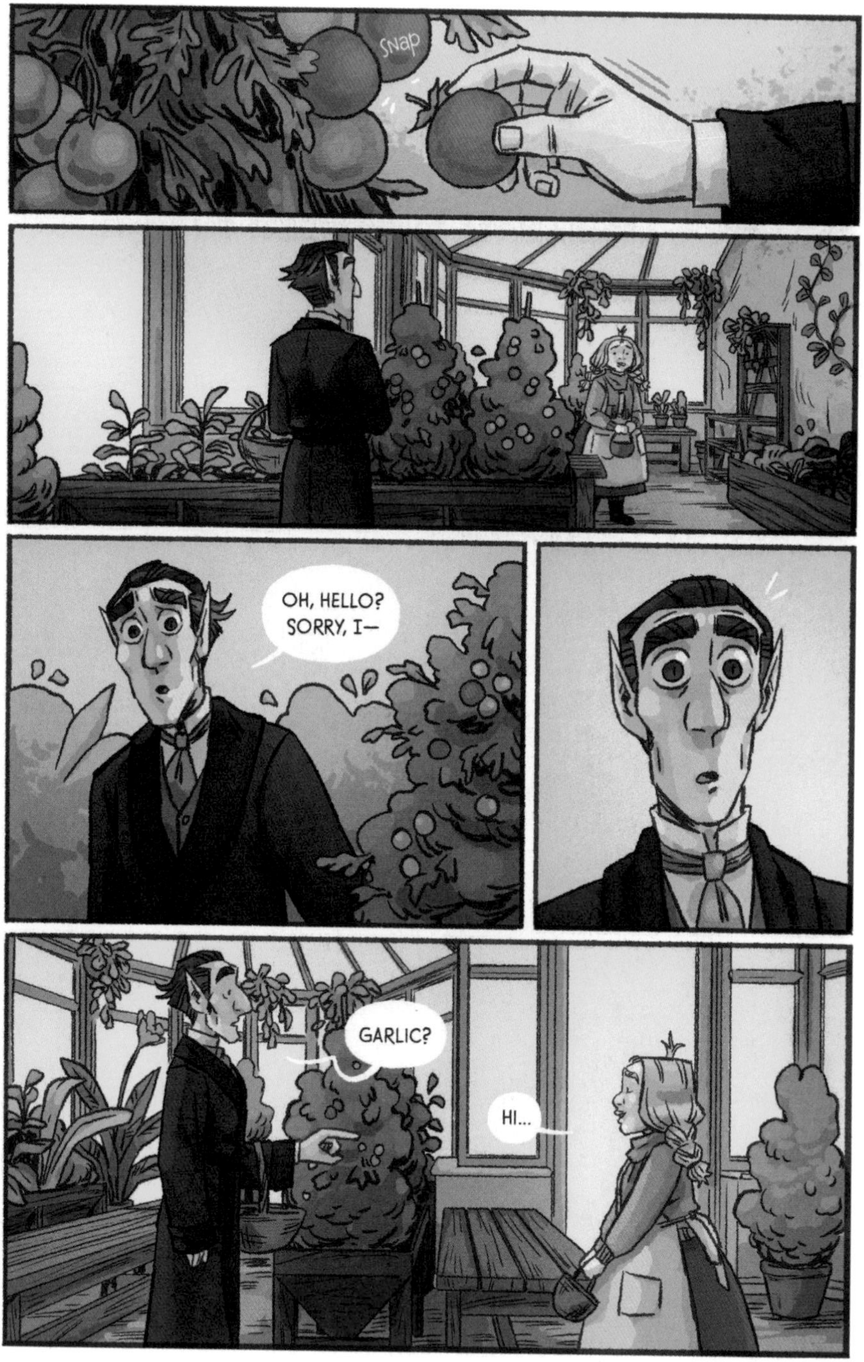
SNAP
OH, HELLO? SORRY, I—
GARLIC?
HI...

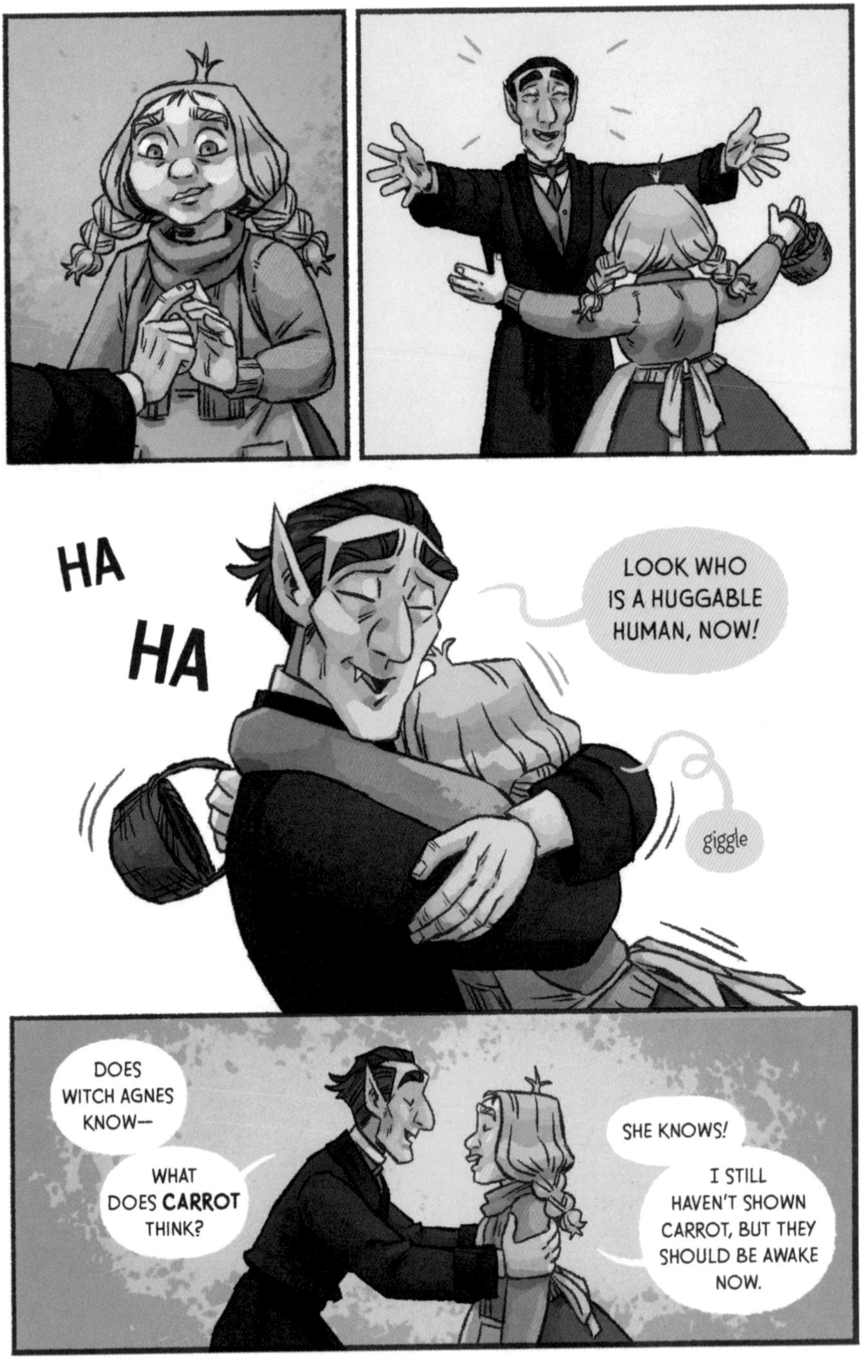
HA
HA
LOOK WHO IS A HUGGABLE HUMAN, NOW!
giggle
DOES WITCH AGNES KNOW—
WHAT DOES **CARROT** THINK?
SHE KNOWS!
I STILL HAVEN'T SHOWN CARROT, BUT THEY SHOULD BE AWAKE NOW.

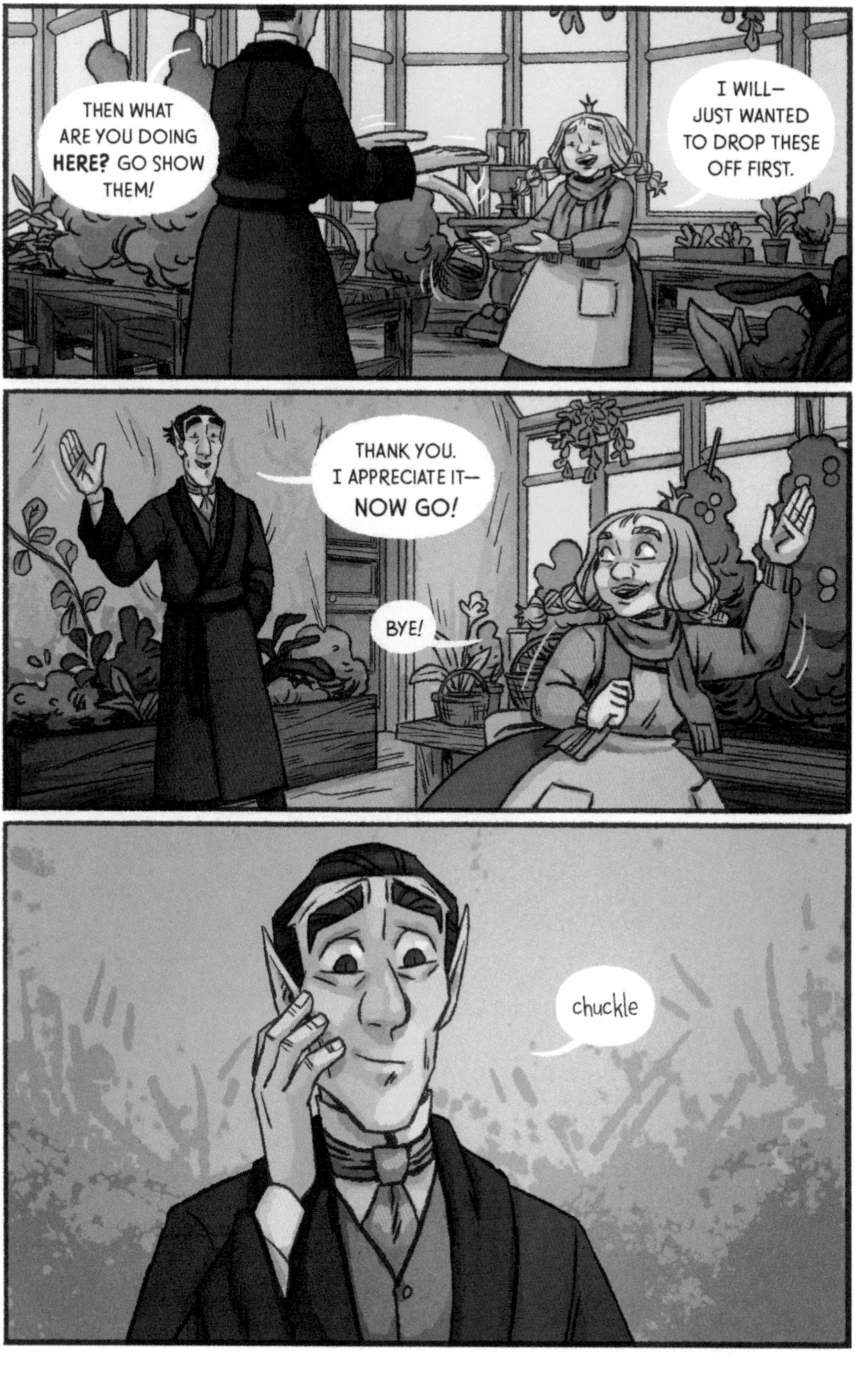
THEN WHAT ARE YOU DOING **HERE?** GO SHOW THEM!
I WILL— JUST WANTED TO DROP THESE OFF FIRST.
THANK YOU. I APPRECIATE IT— NOW GO!
BYE!
chuckle

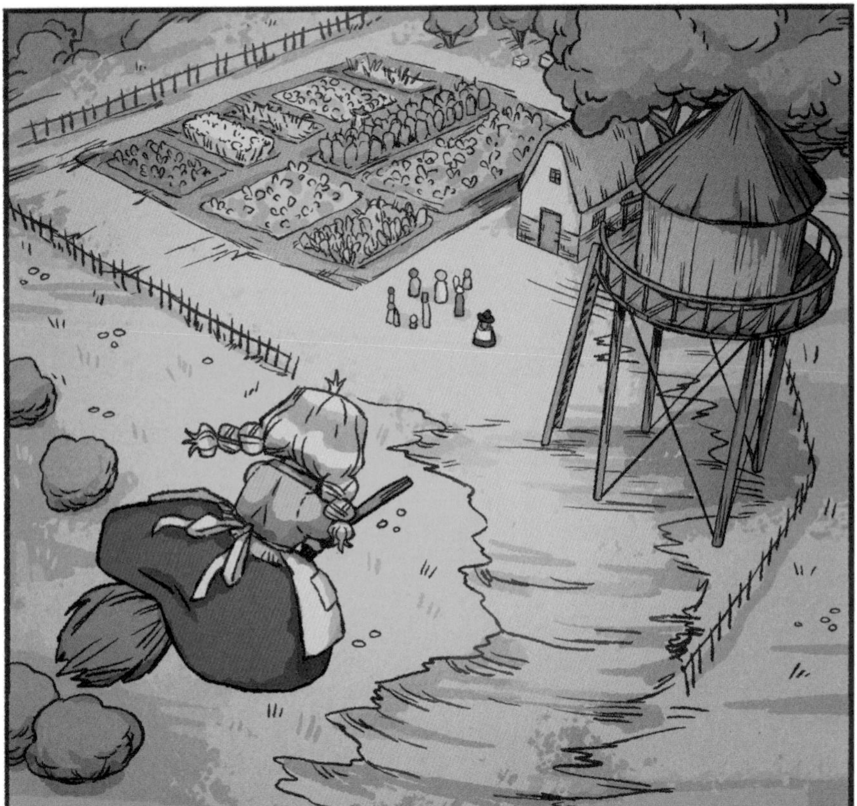

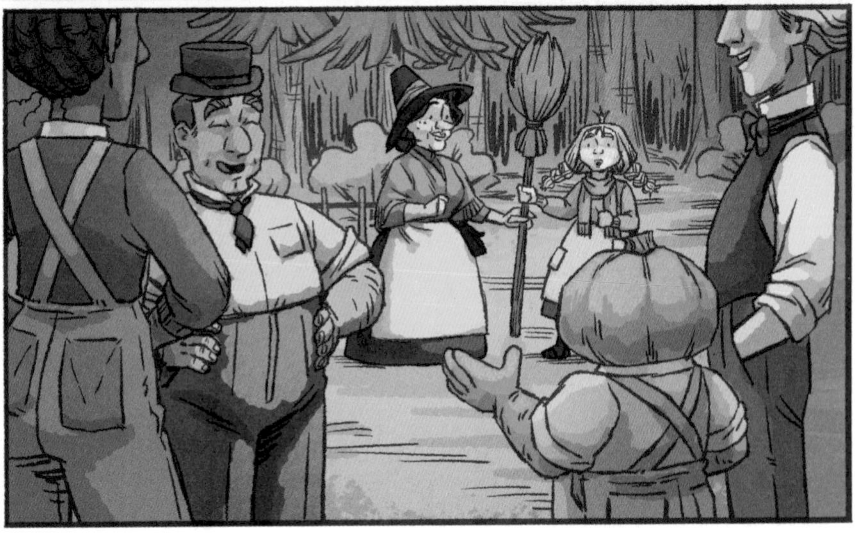

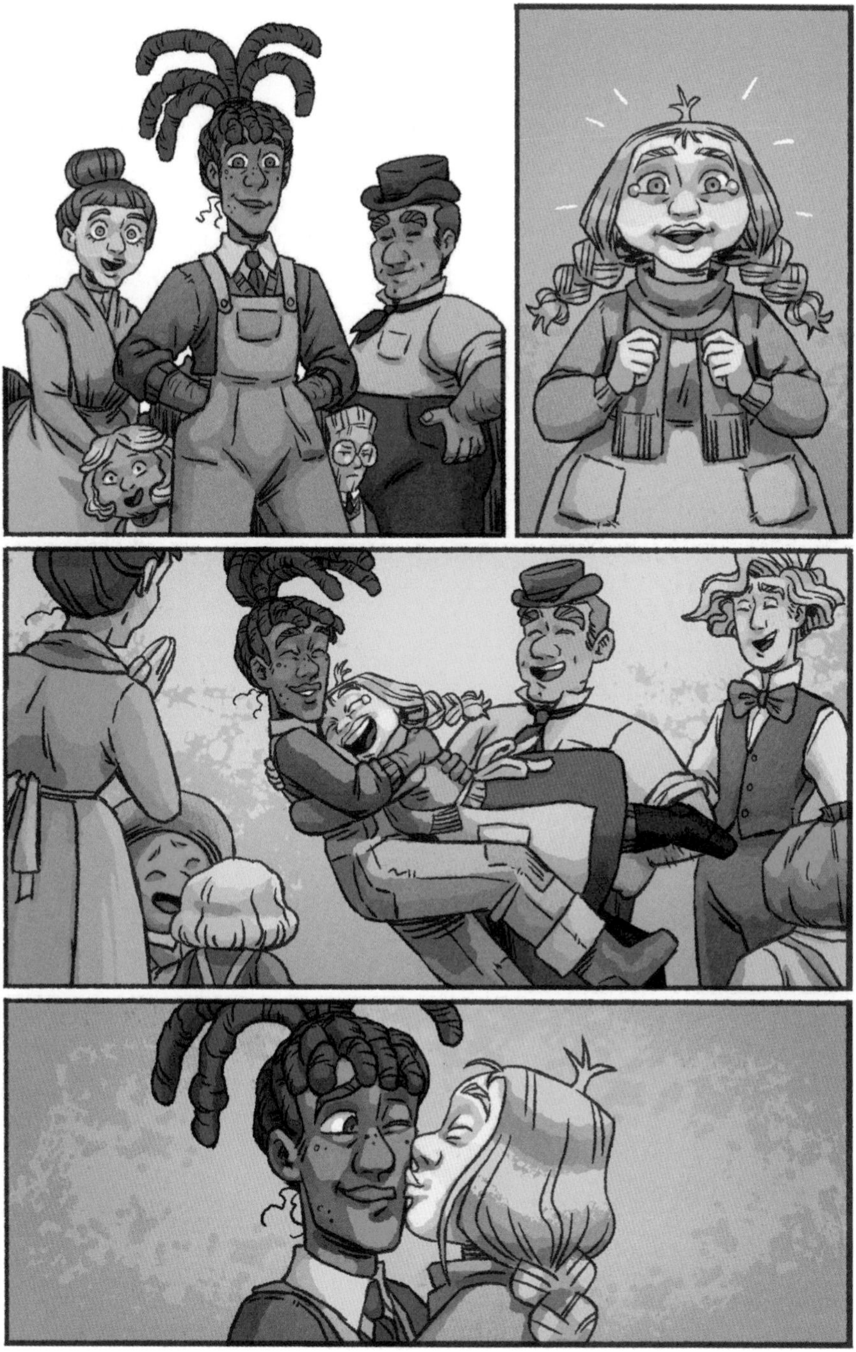

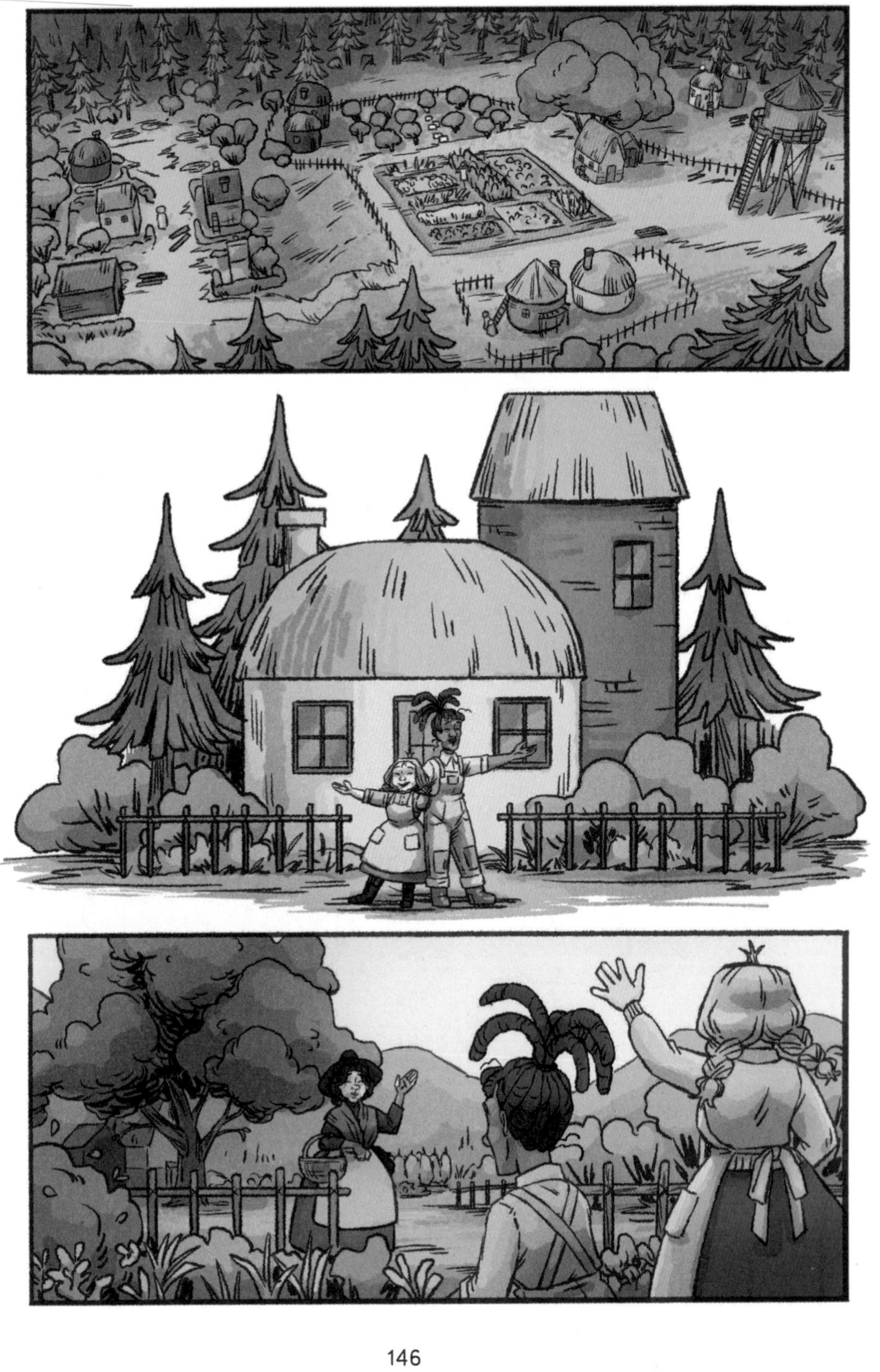

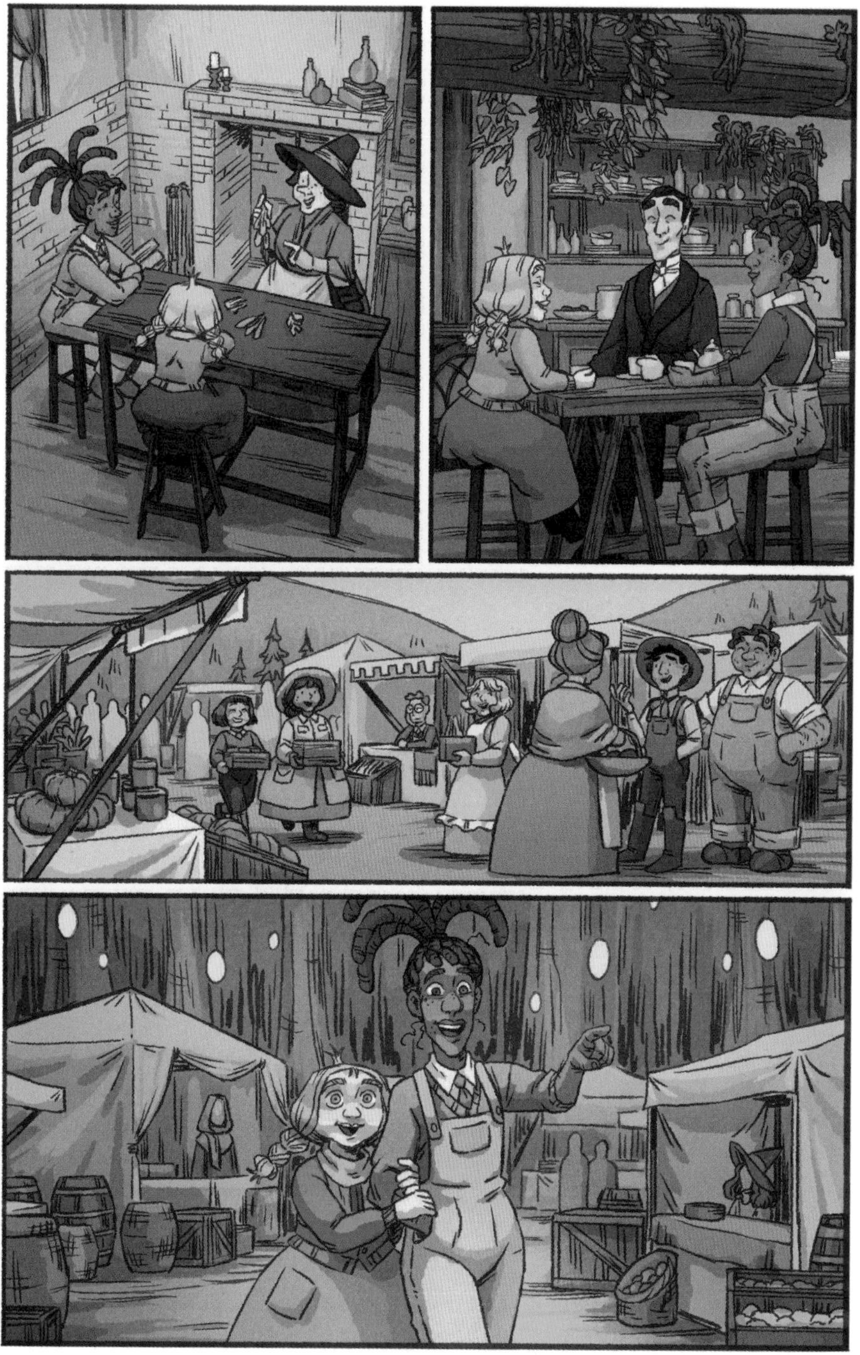

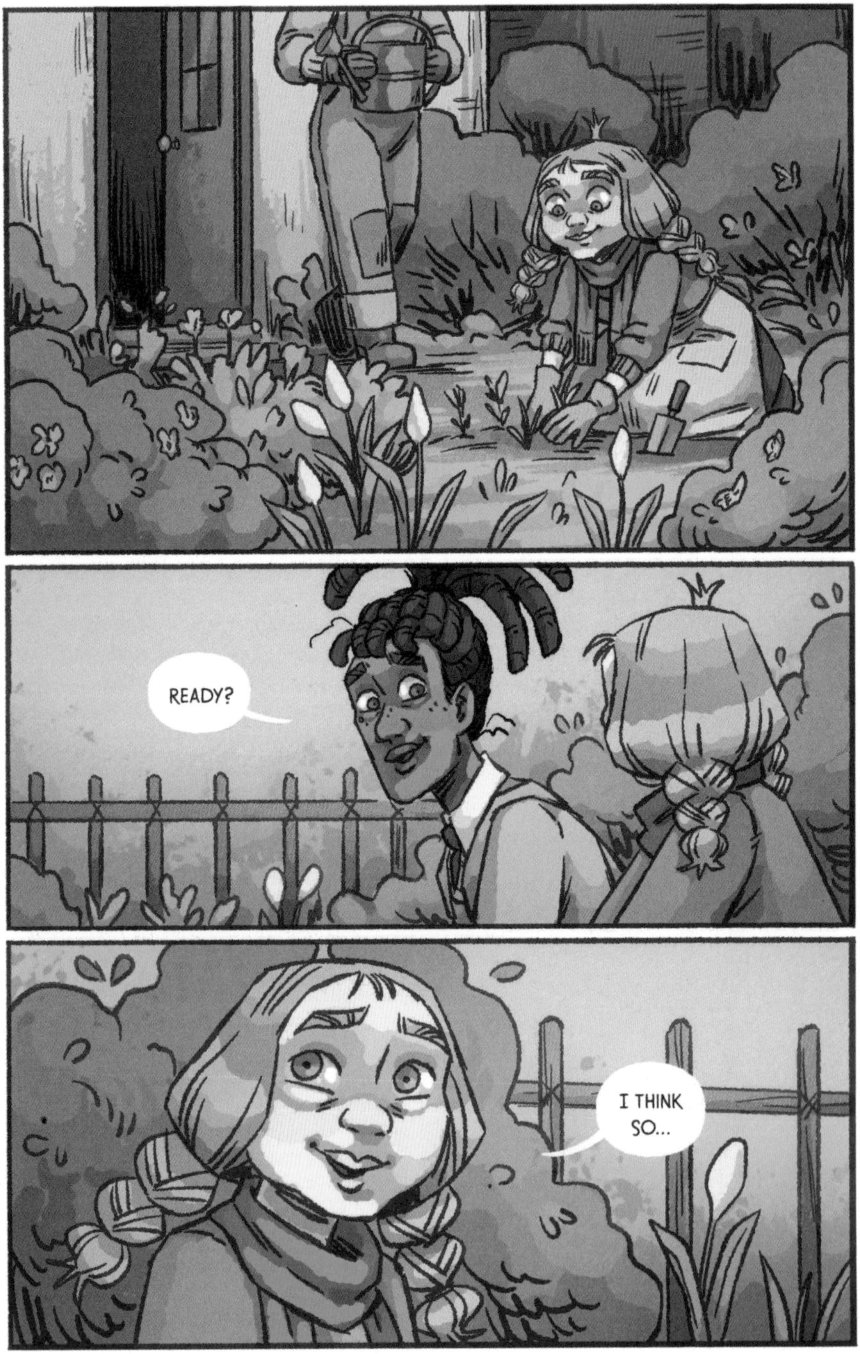
READY?
I THINK SO...

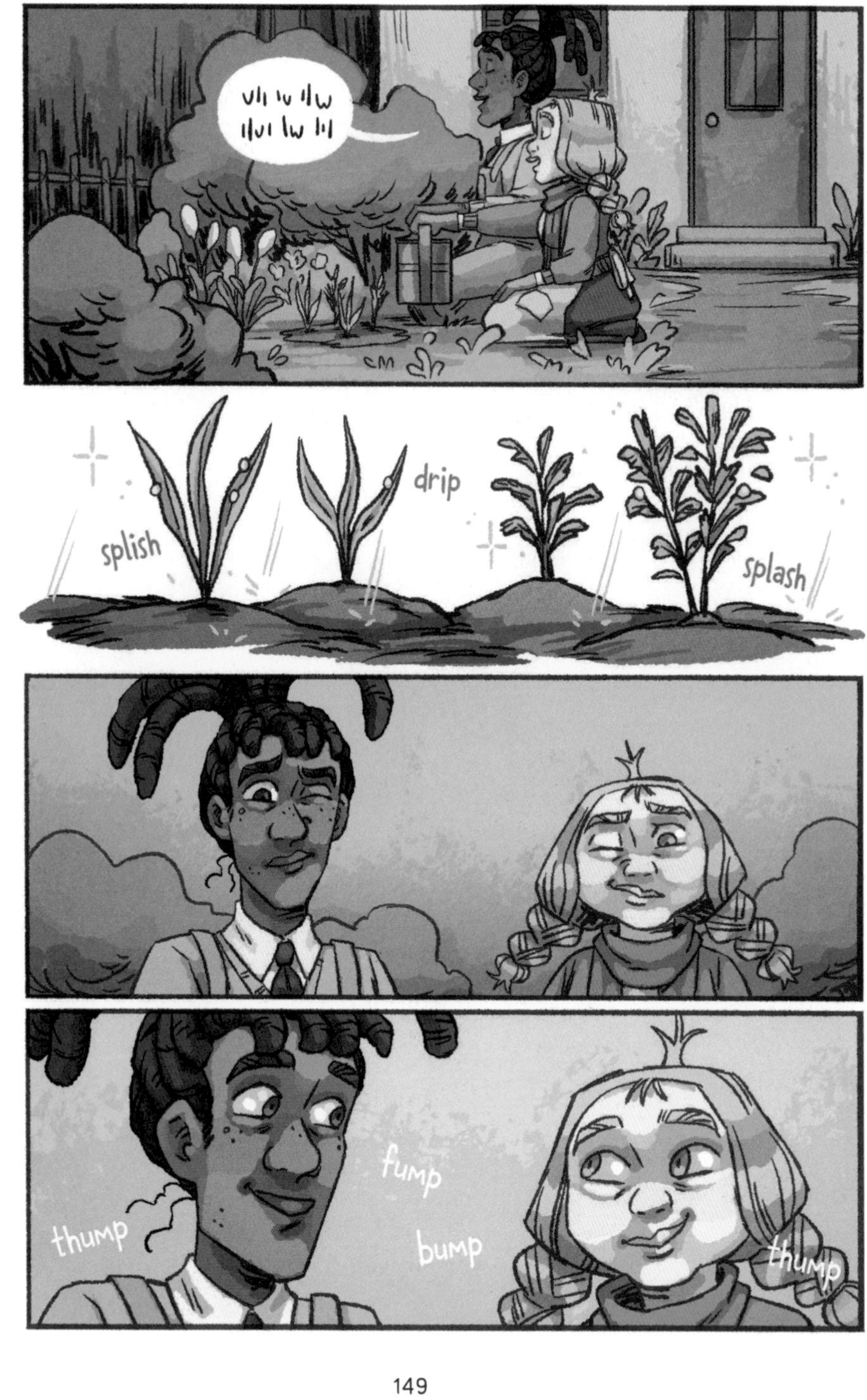
splish
drip
splash
thump
fump
bump
thump

the end

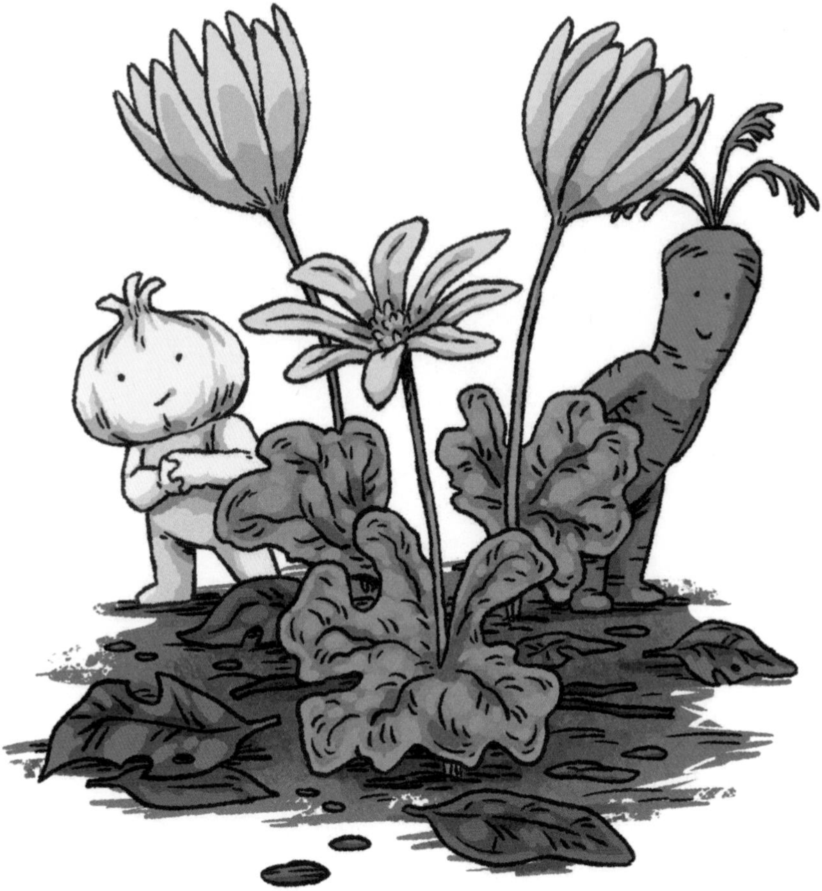